SPINNING AT THE EDGES

ALSO BY ELIZABETH POLINER

As Close to Us as Breathing
What You Know in Your Hands
Mutual Life & Casualty

SPINNING AT THE EDGES

A NOVEL

ELIZABETH POLINER

HARPER
An Imprint of HarperCollins*Publishers*

This is a work of fiction. Any references to real people, events, establishments, organizations, or locales are intended only to give the fiction a sense of reality and authenticity and are used fictitiously. All other names, characters, and places, and all dialogue and incidents portrayed in this book are the product of the author's imagination.

HarperCollins books may be purchased for educational, business, or sales promotional use. For information, please email the Special Markets Department at SPsales@harpercollins.com.

hc.com

FIRST EDITION

Designed by Bonni Leon-Berman

Library of Congress Cataloging-in-Publication Data has been applied for.

ISBN 978-0-06-343453-0

Printed in the United States of America

26 27 28 29 30 LBC 5 4 3 2 1

For Edward

The night before last I dreamed I was skating
right here in our living-room.

—*Anne Frank,* The Diary of a Young Girl, *March 8, 1944*

But is this law?

—*William Shakespeare,* Hamlet, *Act 5, Scene 1*

PART ONE

1

Netherlands, January 5, 1941, by Order of the Dutch Cinema Association (under pressure from the occupying Nazi regime): Jews are banned from all but two cinemas.

January 8, 1941: Jews are banned from the remaining two cinemas.

THE LAST TIME RUTTIE AND Sophia Jacobsen ice-skated at the Apollohal they bought licorice at a candy shop afterward. Ruttie didn't even know that Sophia had the coins for it. While they'd skated on the indoor rink, outside the sun had set, and they reentered the streets of Amsterdam in the dark. They were tired; the skating lesson—Sophia's to Ruttie, sixteen-year-old to fourteen-year-old—was rigorous, its focus the impossible one-foot spin.

Outside the Apollohal the late November air was cold, hinting of the frigid winter to come, 1941 into 1942, and the sisters, instantly recharged, rushed from the rink to a nearby tram where a couple in the seat ahead argued about dinner—meatballs and potatoes, but boiled or baked? With the start of some rationing, food was dull, the wife complained to her husband with an accusing edge, as if he could change that fact, and as the tram traveled forth, moving directly eastward, the couple went round and round—"Can't you cook something else?" "Can't *you*?"—stuck in a circle of blaming. The couple wasn't having fun, but the conversation was indeed funny, the sisters agreed once they hopped off, Sophia tugging at Ruttie's arm as they did, and then holding her elbow, asking, "Boiled or baked?" For a moment they laughed, the mimicry spot-on. They were giddy by then, the work of skating—a different kind of going round and round—having set off pinwheels in their minds. The city's streetlamps glowed appealingly. The chill in the air felt less harsh. Home was east of the Amstel River, which they'd just crossed, but now Sophia motioned to Ruttie that they needed to take yet another tram north. Ruttie didn't know why Sophia wanted to go that way, but she followed her older sister's lead, just as she had earlier when they'd sneaked out to go to their beloved Apollohal. They hadn't been there yet that season. Too risky, their parents had said. Still, the thought that they would never return to skate there again was inconceivable, or so Ruttie had said when Sophia, just moments ago, had wondered out loud about just that.

The candy shop, on Sarphatistraat, was tiny, with chocolates and fruit jellies displayed in its narrow storefront window. As they stepped inside a bell tinkled. They browsed for a moment, staring into a glass case filled with pans of chocolates and toffee; bowls of wrapped peppermints sat atop the case. Like flowers, each candy when leaned toward emanated its own gentle scent. The girls took their time, looking, sniffing. Finally, they bought licorice drops, and a moment later, standing just outside the doorway, they indulged in one delicious piece each.

"We'll save the rest," Sophia told Ruttie, shutting the bag. They were about to start off again when voices rose from next door. Dr. Cohen and his wife were there, standing outside a restaurant. Dr. Cohen had just been to the sisters' home a month ago, when their father's coughing wouldn't cease. The problem was most likely a simple cold and not a diamond polisher's dust lung, Dr. Cohen had concluded after listening to one cough after the next. "They sing different songs, those ailments," he had explained, and told their father to rest for a spell. "Diamonds don't melt," he'd said. Reluctantly, their father had nodded.

Now, upon recognizing Dr. Cohen, Ruttie stepped forward, eager to report the good news—Papa was well again—but she stopped when the maître d' of the restaurant rushed out, frowned at Dr. and Mrs. Cohen, then turned his back to them and pointed to the sign in the restaurant's window, lit from within. "Can't you read?" he said, not harshly, but more as a warning.

Ruttie, who'd been struck by the elegance of the couple's attire—a silk scarf over Mrs. Cohen's head, a bow tie at the doctor's neck—turned from them to the restaurant window. Dr. Cohen was revered.

At that last visit he'd charged them, as he did everyone—the entire Jewish community living around Oosterpark—almost nothing. Before the recent rationing their mother would have baked for him, given him cinnamon cookies or even a cake to take home for his family.

The maître d' still pointed at the sign. It read, simply, *Voor Joden verboden.* Forbidden for Jews.

"But you know us," Dr. Cohen answered. He spoke just above a whisper. "Until recently we've come here nearly every month, and every year for our anniversary. Our twenty-first today. Twenty-one years is a long time." He paused, then added, "Willem, it's *me.*"

Ruttie stepped back, bumping into Sophia, who grabbed her by the shoulders. Similarly, Dr. Cohen held Mrs. Cohen's shoulders, pulling her close.

The maître d' spoke more gently. "But it's the law," he said, shrugging. He crossed his arms and shivered. When a look of bewilderment crossed his face he shivered more, as if to shake himself free from the discomfort. "Yes, law." A moment later he disappeared inside.

With the maître d' gone, Mrs. Cohen stepped forward, shading her eyes despite the darkness, as she leaned in to examine the sign.

"Twenty-one years," Dr. Cohen repeated, his tone now angry but his voice still hushed. Then he kissed the top of his wife's head. When her scarf slipped, Ruttie could see that her hair had been done up beautifully, as it always was with Mrs. Cohen.

The couple began to walk away. Their direction was the same as the one Sophia and Ruttie were to take, but with Sophia gripping her shoulders Ruttie knew not to move. As the Cohens proceeded, the doctor kept his arm around his wife's waist, supporting her. Still, she stumbled once.

Ruttie and Sophia continued staring long after the couple had disappeared, and as they did the Cohens' presence, brief though it had been, became a palpable absence there on the sidewalk of Sarphatistraat. Ruttie could even still smell Mrs. Cohen's perfume, though she didn't know how that could be so. Yet indeed it lingered. Finally, the sisters set off, careful to step far from the restaurant entranceway.

Voor Joden verboden. Ruttie had seen the words before, on signs posted just that fall, a burgeoning wave of them throughout Amsterdam. Even earlier that day, as she and Sophia made their way to the Apollohal, they'd passed at least one at a restaurant near Sarphatipark, but they were so focused then on the skating to come ("Keep your frame straight, Ruttie, your shoulders back," Sophia had counseled, to which Ruttie had replied, "But I do! I do!"), that the sign registered only at the edges of Ruttie's vision. Likewise, if there had been a sign at the Apollohal, she hadn't seen it. But now, Ruttie saw plainly the three additional signs they passed as they walked: in the window of a café near Alexanderplein, at the entrance to a restaurant on Linnaeusstraat, and, finally, a new sign nailed to a tree just past the entrance to Oosterpark. Almost home, they began to enter the park to take a familiar shortcut, but the new sign stopped them. They approached it silently, warily, just as Mrs. Cohen had approached the sign in the restaurant window. They'd walked through Oosterpark at least once every week of their lives. "Every week," Ruttie told the tree, just as Dr. Cohen had told the maître d' *twenty-one years.* Furthermore, Ruttie argued to herself, had they not hidden behind every tree in Oosterpark as they played their childhood games? Had they not sat on every bench, reading and talking? Walked every path? Skated on the park's pond to no end?

"But you know us," she finally blurted out.

Sophia said something else: "Who cares?" And then she kicked the tree.

For the first time in as long as Ruttie could recall, they took the long way home, around rather than through Oosterpark. At one point Sophia held the bag of licorice out to Ruttie, but she shook her head no. "Me either," Sophia said, closing the bag again.

For several days they didn't speak of Oosterpark. Finally, four days later, it was Sophia who mentioned it. They were in their shared bedroom, on opposite beds. Dinner would be soon; the smell of simmering pea soup wafted through their third-floor apartment. "I won't miss Oosterpark. Who wants to skate there, anyway?" Sophia said, speaking of her very favorite activity there. "Such an ugly, lopsided pond," she continued, lying. Though small on one side and large on another, the pond was anything but ugly. Throughout their years they'd practiced a world of messy spins on its lovely, frozen surface. Still, Sophia repeated, "Oosterpark, Oosterpark, your ugly, lopsided pond." She would repeat the words, too, to Aaron Taube, her boyfriend, when he stopped by briefly after dinner. Later that night, as Sophia bent over the kitchen sink while their mother lifted a pot of warm water and rinsed her hair clean—such long, dark, remarkable hair—Ruttie, standing in the kitchen doorway, listened as her sister chanted the words again.

It was six days before they remembered the licorice. Sophia had put the bag in a drawer that first night, keeping it just for herself and Ruttie. Now, dinner just finished—more bland pea soup and boiled beans—she pulled the bag out and handed Ruttie another licorice drop. But despite the unsatisfying meal Ruttie took her piece with reluctance. She sat on her bed, put the small candy in her mouth, and glanced outside, where snowflakes scattered, windblown, directionless. "Was the sign there too, at the Apollohal?" she soon whispered to Sophia, who, lying on her back, nodded without looking Ruttie's way.

"OOSTERPARK, OOSTERPARK, YOUR UGLY, LOPSIDED POND," WAS THE mysterious song that Stephanie Pearl's mother—as a girl called Ruttie, as an adult called Ruth—chanted whenever she washed Stephanie's long, difficult hair. "Mamma, why do you say that?" Stephanie asked for the first time when she was four. Abruptly her mother stopped chanting. For a long time, she said and did nothing. When she resumed washing Stephanie's hair, she barely touched her scalp, a sudden faintness that scared Stephanie, as if her mother were barely there. Stephanie was six when she asked again about the words, still sung every so often, but again her mother wouldn't say. This time she continued to rub Stephanie's scalp, but the sudden and sustained absence of her mother's voice created such a gaping void that it felt to Stephanie as if she were free-falling into it. Terrified of the abandonment,

Stephanie never again asked about the odd song. A year later she began to wash her own hair, but by then her mother had stopped chanting it anyway.

Stephanie was an adult, already thirty-nine, when her mother, quite suddenly, uttered the haunting words again. Even more surprisingly, her mother had begun to speak, finally, of her past. At Ruth's request, Stephanie had come up to Connecticut from Washington, D.C. At first Stephanie ascribed her mother's will to talk to the brush with mortality she'd had the day before. Her mother had felt faint. The problem was dehydration, but at the time her mother had feared it was a stroke—the recent stroke of her neighbor's father, a man close to her age, coming to mind just as soon as the wobbles overcame her, or so she'd told Stephanie. Ruth had called Stephanie, who told her to dial 911. The medical incident, a true scare, seemed to affect her mother even more than the news of Stephanie's surprising recent trip to Amsterdam, which she'd told her mother about after she'd recovered. But hours later, her mother's story unfolding, Stephanie sensed that the talkativeness, an opening, had mostly to do with the boy, Ian Lima, whom her mother had pulled from icy Lake Topaqua—saving his life—some three months back. Their growing friendship since then had been working a more gradual but sure change on her mother's spirits than anything recent and sudden.

It was early evening, the first Wednesday in May, and Stephanie and her mother, rested from her medical ordeal, were sitting side by side, staring out the kitchen windows at Lake Topaqua. Her mother still lived in Wells, Connecticut, in the same lakeside bungalow in which Stephanie had grown up. The day's light was fading. An early spring wind that had whipped all day had, come evening, calmed. Stephanie, tired from her travels and from worry, had finally calmed too. The lake water lay flat, stilled. In time her mother mentioned that Ian, who had attempted suicide at the lake, was coming along. Stephanie then spoke of her recent trip to Amsterdam. She was cautious and brief, fearing her mother would shut down. But instead, as the darkness came, her mother told Stephanie about the sign in Oosterpark, and then about the sign on Sarphatistraat, and then about Dr. and Mrs. Cohen. "Her lovely hair," Stephanie's mother said, before putting a hand to her mouth, as if Mrs. Cohen were standing before her. *Whose hair?* Stephanie almost asked, wanting to know for sure if her mother had meant the doctor's wife or, perhaps, the beloved lost sister, Sophia.

Her mother continued talking. "You can't imagine, Stephanie, the kind of life we had until 1940. We knew nearly everyone on our street. In our building our friendly neighbors, the Naftaniels, were opposite us on the third floor, and the Eikens, a family of five children, *five*, were below us. But they were quiet. Never fought, never raised their voices. We were the loudmouths, Sophia and me. And I had such a good friend, Henny Ganz. She lived in a first-floor apartment, identical to ours." This woman now of many words was not the mother Stephanie had always known. Without pause Ruth continued, "We were born the same week, Henny and me. I was welcomed at Henny's home anytime, as if the proximity of our births gave me an ever-open door. Henny was small, with crooked teeth and thin hair. 'Homely,' Sophia once said, 'but like a little sun.' Unlike Sophia, I never felt bad for Henny. The way she would smile, just at my presence in the doorway! She *was* a little sun. I adored her, though not in the same way that I did Sophia. I *worshipped* Sophia. Henny Ganz I merely loved." Stephanie took a quick breath. Her mother never spoke of love. "And that's why we planned our lives so that we could stay close: we'd marry two boys already friends, and live right there, by Oosterpark. We envisioned only the obvious: our future married lives, which were always happy, naturally. Easy dreams. Because why not? What else did we know? Stephie, you could never have imagined how things would change. *Voor Joden verboden. Dat was nog maar het begin, al wisten we dat toen nog niet.*"

This was the first Dutch her mother had uttered in Stephanie's presence. She continued in English. "You could never have imagined . . ."

BY THIS TIME, MAY OF 2001, Stephanie did know a thing or two about sudden, unwanted change. In just the last year she'd had breakups with both her boyfriend, Freddy Taylor, and her best friend, Rona Adler, the two people who for so long had been closest to her heart. At thirty-nine she was single, childless, lonely. Without seeing it coming she'd turned into the kind of professional woman she spotted sometimes in D.C., good with a career but bad at life. Until realizing she was one, she'd pitied women like that.

She'd been in D.C. for eighteen years, arriving in 1983 after college to begin fundraising for One Earth, a nonprofit committed to raising awareness of environmental harm from acid rain, hazardous waste, and the greenhouse effect, a problem almost unheard of then. But the crisis was coming, Stephanie learned, and the possibility that she could have a hand, however small, in saving the planet matched her compulsion—a drive she'd always felt—to do just that. But after she had been at One Earth for nine years the organization split in two: the activists at odds with those inclined toward incremental change. And that's when Stephanie moved on to the Girls to Women Education Fund—"GTW"—which had, flatteringly enough, recruited her. There she soon learned that helping a girl who otherwise couldn't afford college was its own force for good. GTW offered scholarships and a college prep program. Stephanie liked their homey suite of offices, located south of Dupont Circle on 19th Street, almost as much as she liked her much-needed pay raise.

Almost immediately at GTW Stephanie befriended Rona Adler, the only other child of a Holocaust survivor she'd ever met. Back in Connecticut, save for her immediate family, Stephanie had grown up isolated from Jews, her mother's nonreligious background and fear of being recognizably Jewish dominating her parents' choice not to join a synagogue. In little Wells they were the only Jewish family, and during college, at Bowdoin in Maine, Stephanie's unfamiliarity with Jewish traditions, and with Jews themselves, didn't matter—the smallness of the Jewish population there, as she perceived it, felt perfectly normal. Once in D.C. she never considered going to a synagogue. Her knowledge of the Holocaust, then, had come mainly from books, not from talks with other Jewish people. But one afternoon at GTW, still new there, she passed by Rona Adler's office, its door open, a small group inside. Stephanie would have walked past but Rona rushed out.

"Come join us," she said. Then she added, urgently, "*Cake*. Leftover. My oldest turned four."

Stephanie grinned, the tone relative to the subject matter absurd. "I shouldn't," she said, though she loved eating cake of any kind. They all did, her mother and grandmother too.

"Please." Rona was small and plump. "I can't stand it when people like you don't eat." She eyed Stephanie, who was thin and rangy. "Just eat, okay? Please eat."

Stephanie worried that she'd already insulted Rona. But Rona simply pulled Stephanie into her office. "Make way," Rona called, "and give the new kid a slice."

Over the next weeks Stephanie often visited Rona as she passed by and found the door open. Rona seemed pleased. She made conversation easily, describing the chatter between her two young children or retelling news stories from *The Washington Post*, unfailingly closing with the phrase, "Can you believe it?" They often couldn't. Former tennis star Arthur Ashe announcing he had AIDS, downtown Chicago closing from freak flooding, Vice President Dan Quayle misspelling *potato* while visiting a sixth-grade spelling bee. "P-O-T-A-T-O-E!" Rona exclaimed about that one, but none of the news really fazed her. She just liked to chat, and Stephanie felt welcome.

They talked shop, too, about fundraising, and then, while sipping tea in the office kitchen, they spoke about ice skating, which they both liked to do, a happy coincidence. They talked about their hometowns, colleges—the common background stories—and, eventually, three months or so into getting to know each other, about their mothers: one Dutch, the other Polish; one quiet, the other talkative. One a refugee, having escaped from Europe—but Stephanie could not yet say how—the other having come to America after the war as a displaced person, a camp survivor, and Rona knew exactly how. "She sang beautifully, as well as played viola, and once she'd been deported, imprisoned at Auschwitz-Birkenau, she found her way into an orchestra there. An ensemble of captives. My mother's God-given musicality saved her life. When the group dissolved, she survived a move to Bergen-Belsen. That's my mother, Stephanie." Rona paused and then added, quietly this time, "Can you believe it?"

This, then, this history, unfailingly incomprehensible, is what she and Rona had between them, and Stephanie felt something in Rona's presence, a kind of mutual understanding—a recognition, even—that she hadn't known with any friend before. The bond felt warm, comfortable, even comforting, though until Stephanie felt that sympathy she didn't even sense she needed it.

In the spring of 1993, a year into knowing each other, Rona invited Stephanie to her home for Passover. The occasion felt important—Stephanie had been to only one seder before, a surprising invitation during her last year at Bowdoin—and on the day of Rona's seder, a Friday, she went to Woodward & Lothrop department store during her lunch break to find a new dress. That evening, the dress she'd purchased a perfect fit, she fussed with her makeup and hair and arrived at Rona's home, just outside D.C. in Bethesda, Maryland, fifteen minutes late.

"So sorry," she said to Rona, whose blouse was nearly the same blue as Stephanie's dress. They laughed to see that.

"Don't be. It's going to be a long night," Rona said.

From the foyer Stephanie heard Rona's two girls, who were in the living room, on the carpet, playing with dolls. The girls wore matching red dresses and white tights. The dolls, via the girls, were talking, though in a language all their own. The babble didn't surprise Stephanie. Rona had said a lot about the children already, including how Hannah, the oldest, was dear to her younger sibling, Beth, but tough on Rona. "She thinks she's the mother," Rona often noted. Then she'd sigh and shrug.

A house tour followed. Beyond the living room was a study, "for Daniel," Rona said, referring to her husband, an attorney. "He brings work home, but I can't." She pointed at her girls and a familiar shrug followed. In the other direction was the dining room, its long table covered in yellow linen and set formally with the seder plate at the center. Next they toured the kitchen, large enough for both a cooking area and an eating nook, and off the kitchen the laundry room, piles of play clothes atop the dryer. Stephanie, who stashed quarters for the machines in her building's basement-level laundry, stared longingly.

"Here's the best spot," Rona then said, opening a door off the kitchen to a screened porch. Though Rona didn't take Stephanie upstairs she was told about its four bedrooms and two bathrooms. "It's a house," Rona concluded, her tone matter of fact. But to Stephanie, who since moving to D.C. had lived in a one-bedroom apartment on Connecticut Avenue, Rona's home seemed a near palace. Even Stephanie's childhood home, the lakeside bungalow, seemed drab and minuscule compared to this.

The girls, aged five and three, were allowed to bring their dolls to the seder, and when it began the dolls, leaning against water glasses, seemed as attentive to the ritual as everyone else. Daniel's brother and sister-in-law were there, as was Rona's widowed mother, Lena, who lived just a mile away. Upon meeting Stephanie, Lena said, "I'm Bubbe. That's babysitter in English." She smiled at her joke. Stephanie hadn't expected merriment. She knew little else about Lena besides the list of who she'd lost to the camps: her father, mother, three sisters, and countless uncles, aunts, and cousins. "No one was left," was how Rona had once put it. Lena was small, like Rona, and had the same curly hair. Her earrings contained garnets, which were as deep a maroon as the wine Daniel poured. Lena was surprised by Stephanie's height, a full five eight to Lena's five feet even. "Tall and pretty," she remarked of Stephanie, emphasizing the second word as if the first were strange. Stephanie explained that it was the Dutch in her—by way of her grandfather's mother—that gave her that height. Rona sat her mother by her, and Stephanie was across from the woman. Though Daniel led the service, he deferred to Lena for any singing, and soon the pureness of her soprano voice as she led "Dayenu" surprised Stephanie even though Rona had described her mother's life-saving musicality more than once. As the seder progressed Stephanie noticed Rona often touching her mother's sleeve, and they leaned near when they spoke, which was also often.

As Rona had foretold, it was a long evening. Finally, they ate: matzah ball soup, brisket, potato kugel, green beans, and for dessert meringue cookies. After the girls excitedly found the *afikomen*, the hidden matzah, they were taken to bed—kissing even Stephanie before they rushed upstairs. Rona then disappeared into motherhood for most of the post-meal service, returning just in time for several closing songs. As the family around her sang, Stephanie tried to follow but soon stopped, yielding to the power of Lena's voice.

When Stephanie arrived home near midnight her belly was still full. Of everything that had happened at the seder, what stayed with her the most was the soft touch of the children's lips on her cheek as they said goodnight. That and the sight of the many pats on the arm that Rona gave her mother. Stephanie flicked on her bedroom lights and within minutes readied herself for sleep, hastily turning the lights off. She didn't want to see it, her apartment's smallness, its paltry furnishings—the sense she had when she walked in that it was austere, barren, sad. During the last decade in D.C. she had dated two men, for over a year each, but neither had compelled her to the point that she'd fallen deeply in love. The breakups came as inevitably as seasons, and she'd moved on. Had she made a mistake? She briefly wondered, her eyes blinking open. But it seemed impossible just then to know. For now, she figured wearily, she'd buy flowers the next day, brighten the place up, which is what she did.

On Saturday afternoon she also called her mother, telling her, "The seder was interesting. Judaism is, well, detailed."

"I wouldn't know," her mother said.

Because her mother's tone was defensive Stephanie knew not to press on. She talked instead about the flowers and then Rona's girls. Her mother listened, told Stephanie upon being asked that she was fine, then mentioned the weather and how the cloudiness over the lake made for "a somber beauty," the kind she liked. They hung up soon enough.

Stephanie then drifted to her kitchen, made tea, and sipped it while sitting on a stool by the stove. She didn't think so much as float away in her mind. Without actually seeing it, she stared and stared at the kitchen floor. When she finally looked up, something inside her returning, she saw that almost two hours had passed, in silence, while she sat on the stool, and she quickly gathered herself to go for a walk.

From a shop on Connecticut Avenue, she bought a second bouquet of flowers.

SHE MET FREDDY SOON AFTER that. Late the next Wednesday, Stephanie dashed out of the office to buy Rona flowers too, a belated thank-you gift, and as she approached Rona's office with the bouquet she heard Rona talking with someone. From the doorway Stephanie saw Rona and a man leaning over paperwork. The man, about their age, had a pencil in his mouth. When Rona introduced him to Stephanie, he didn't remove the pencil at first, then plucked it out, as if just realizing it was there. "Freddy Taylor," he said.

Freddy, who grew up in Mahone Bay, Nova Scotia, was the second of five boys in his family, the "rotten lot of them" (as Freddy would eventually put it to Stephanie) raised by their mother, his father gone from cancer just a year after his youngest brother's birth. Witnessing his mother's hardship—she cleaned homes for money—was the reason Freddy was so keen to help women, as much as he could in his professional life. He was an economist, teaching at the Massachusetts Avenue–based Johns Hopkins School of Advanced International Studies. He researched micro-investments in poorer nations, investments that often supported women. His education was a marvel, he would later tell Stephanie, given that his mother's ended at ninth grade. But he'd gone all the way, on scholarships, to McGill and then to Harvard. "And here I am," he said.

That conversation came several months after Stephanie first saw Freddy at GTW. It turned out he came by twice monthly or so to help Rona prepare grants; Stephanie just hadn't run into him yet. "He's my secret sauce," Rona explained the day after Stephanie first met him. "A once-over from Freddy and a grant's chance of success goes way up." Rona had met Freddy, she explained, two years back, at a dinner party. "He already knew about GTW. He asked me if he could help, not the other way around. I couldn't believe it."

Stephanie saw him again three weeks later. She was leaving work and rushing past Rona's office, an umbrella and raincoat in her arms, the heavy rain of the morning just as steady at the day's end. "Still here?" she called, surprised to see lights on. With kids at home, Rona rarely stayed late.

But it was Freddy sitting at Rona's desk. "Just me," he said, looking up. A banker's lamp with a green shade was the only light on. A pencil lay on top of some pages. The simplicity of the scene—the lamp, the pages, the pencil—appealed to Stephanie. She could see several handwritten comments on the top page.

"Didn't mean to interrupt," she said, almost embarrassed. "Thought you were Rona."

"Everyone says that," Freddy said, smiling.

They spoke again a month later. That night Stephanie was en route to a figure-drawing session at the Washington Studio School, and as she left work she carried a bulky sketch pad. Passing by Rona's office she again saw the light on and mistakenly assumed it meant Rona was still there. This time Freddy stood when she walked in. They exchanged hellos, and when he asked about the drawing pad she mentioned the session. "You mind?" he said, asking to see a sketch.

Though hesitant, she nevertheless opened the pad, randomly, to a scene in Amsterdam, from a postcard her grandmother once gave her. "I forget the name of that bridge," she said. "Blauwbrug," he replied, surprising her. He turned the page to the next sketch, of a nude, an older gentleman, then turned back to the Amsterdam scene. "Snow and water. Reminds me of home. Have you been to Amsterdam?"

"No. My mother lived there until they couldn't. 1942." Freddy began to nod as the implications hit him. She then told him what she knew—just that the family had fled during a particularly cold winter. He nodded again.

The next time they saw each other, six weeks later, they went out together. "I'm crazy hungry," Freddy said, upon knocking on Stephanie's office door. "Care for dinner?"

They settled in at a French bistro in nearby Dupont Circle, and it was there that Freddy told her about his life in Nova Scotia. His surprising trajectory from such a humble beginning sometimes left him feeling lost, he claimed. "I get that," Stephanie said, and then she told him about Wells, its smallness, the very few in her high school class who went to college, the nothing going on day in and day out. "If it weren't for the lake—Lake Topaqua—it wouldn't offer much," she said, then described the three churches, the equal number of package stores, and an everyday sense of a heyday gone by. "There used to be several bell factories—bells, of all things—but by the time we moved there the factories were closed and the town was lacking. The lake's now the town's jewel, its only one." She added, "People don't think of Connecticut that way—towny, impoverished—but this isn't a New York suburb. Central Connecticut is its own world."

"Sounds like mine," Freddy said, amused.

They didn't see each other for another month despite Stephanie lingering at work, especially on Wednesdays, Freddy's most likely time to show up. He finally phoned her some five weeks later, before work, asking her to dinner again. Over those weeks she'd told herself that his silence and absence were no big deal, but at the prospect of dinner with him that night she happily wriggled into the blue dress she hadn't worn since the seder.

Freddy explained at dinner that he had just returned from a trip home, his mother having fallen ill. It was early September, the evening air warm despite a steady drizzle that day and into the night. They were at the same bistro in Dupont Circle. With the rain outside and candles glowing inside, the place felt especially cozy. He talked of his mother's recovery from pneumonia and of a younger brother, John, living close by in Halifax but with chronic depression, unable to help.

"I got the education. But everyone should have gotten it, especially John." Freddy described his brother, a book always in hand. "Not sure how I turned out to be the lucky one. Really, I was just the good one. Did every homework assignment, that kind of thing."

She'd been like that herself, Stephanie said, then wanted to say more about how being responsible, never a problem, seemed the best way to cope with what was missing in her mother. But she didn't know how to put all that.

"Here's to good," she said instead, and they clinked glasses. She told him then of her own visit north to see her mother two weeks back. "The lake was lovely," she said.

Later, readying to leave, she glanced his way and felt she already knew him. She was thirty-two and longing for the right person. Since Rona's seder nearly a half year ago this was especially so. In fact, she'd been longing to meet someone even before then, and such yearnings, she sensed, could lead to unreliable, all-too-quick assessments about men. So she checked that sense of closeness, and when she and Freddy stepped outside and Freddy merely shook her hand, she was glad she had. To hide her feelings, she looked less at him than at the evening traffic going around Dupont Circle.

But when he called out, "Stephanie?" she quickly turned back.

"I'm here," she said.

IN AUGUST OF 1996 RONA became pregnant again and soon left GTW for full-time mothering. Stephanie and Freddy, by then a couple for over three years, attended the baby's bris the next spring. Stephanie briefly held the baby while the mohel organized his tools. During the ceremony Rona and her mother clutched hands and then they hugged, fiercely, once the circumcision was done. Freddy seemed to have stopped breathing, and Stephanie held his arm to steady him.

That day, as always, Rona's life seemed fuller than Stephanie's, with the big house, the growing children, the affectionate mother, and the devoted husband. But after the bris, sipping tea, Stephanie realized her sense of things had shifted. She felt touched to be chosen to hold the baby, happy to share an experience once again with a family she'd come to know, warmed to exchange giggles with Hannah, Rona's challenging oldest, and especially glad to be there with Freddy. She was in love, finally, the sureness of it settling something in her. She felt her age, thirty-five, without simultaneously feeling a sense of lack. She and Freddy had no plans to marry yet but recently they'd discussed it, gladly, in general terms. As Stephanie saw it their marriage was inevitable; they were happy, good. The other evening she'd sketched his face from memory, and realizing how well she knew it had reminded her of how glad she'd felt when she first met him alone in Rona's office, the banker's lamp casting a warm glow, the pages before him marked with pencil.

The next fall Rona suggested skating each Wednesday evening at a public rink in Wheaton, just north of Bethesda. Stephanie and Rona had occasionally skated there before but suddenly Rona *needed* to skate. And it was there, on the ice going around the rink, that Rona began to complain about her husband, Daniel, and then about her eldest, Hannah, and then about the next child, Beth, and even baby Joey. On the first of their outings she complained while they skated five laps around the rink. The next time she complained for ten laps, and the time after that she ranted for what seemed like all the laps.

"I'm drowning, Stephanie." This was their fourth trip to the rink, an early November evening.

Stephanie slowed. It took Rona almost two strides to keep up with Stephanie's one, so Stephanie always held back, but this time she nearly stopped.

"Depression? Postpartum?" She dared to broach the subject at last.

Rona was quiet while a group of teenagers zipped past. Then she shook her head. "Just too much to do, and most of it involves crap. One kid's or the other's. Hannah rules the roost. Daniel does nothing, spoils them, gives them cookies whenever they ask—which is all the time, cookies and *cookies*." She nearly yelled the last word.

But soon Rona had gotten her frustrations out, and she pulled Stephanie off to the side for a pause. When they pushed off again, Rona asked, "How's Freddy?" to which Stephanie answered, simply, "Fine."

The friends stopped skating that spring and summer, then resumed when Rona's older children returned to school in the fall, just when the chilled air inspired thoughts of skating again. Their conversations on the ice were as they had been before: Rona venting, Stephanie listening. But by winter Rona was even more agitated. One December evening when Stephanie picked her up, Rona raced from her house to Stephanie's car, calling out as she got in, "Let's go! Fast! Fast!" Later, on the ice, Rona was, as always, going round with it. "On top of everything else—toilet-training Joey, driving the girls to school and playdates and soccer games and why did I ever get my driver's license? And what was college for?" Besides that, Daniel was up for partner at his firm and insisted he be left alone in the evenings in his study. "He's in there sulking. I know it," Rona said.

They skated in silence until Rona spoke again, this time of a dream she'd had the night before, a recurring one, in which she wore a forest-green velvet dress. "I'm in my best shoes too, rushing in them and carrying a viola case. As always, I'm late for my viola lesson. I just know this is so. And then I see the street—the church and bakery and tailor's shop and the cathedral in the distance—and realize it's my mother's street on the outskirts of Kraków, that it's in fact no street I've ever seen. And it's my mother's dress and my mother's shoes, and even the music, by Mozart and Brahms, are my mother's sonatas to practice, not mine. And then I'm relieved because I don't know anything about playing viola. But then, waking, I'm devastated, because like my mother I feel adrift, like I'm floating through time . . ." Rona looked sadly at Stephanie, who sensed that Rona really did feel that way, often, even right then. Rona continued, "And what I miss most is that velvet dress, which I never saw, yet which my grandmother seemed to have sewn for both my mother and me."

While Rona spoke the two continued to glide side by side. The power of the dream all but silenced the sound of pop music, endlessly blaring. Later, after Stephanie drove Rona home, wishing her well and feeling that night only a touch of envy at the sight of Rona's house, Stephanie called her mother. While skating Stephanie had longed to answer Rona's dream of her mother with one of her own. She longed to be close enough to her mother to have such a dream, even with its sad content.

"How are you?" Stephanie asked her mother.

"Fine. As always," her mother said.

After a pause—the inevitable pause—Stephanie said, "I should move back. Be closer."

"But what would you do here?" Her mother often spoke of the smallness of Wells.

"I don't know." Stephanie paused. "Or you could move down here?"

"Stephie, I need my lake view," her mother said, this time without pause, the words a near rebuke.

She did need it, Stephanie knew. The view was her mother's greatest comfort.

Her mother continued, "It's not like we could afford to live fancy-fancy on the banks of the Potomac."

While thinking of what else to say, Stephanie reminded herself that she loved her job, and she loved Rona and Freddy. She couldn't just up and move anyway. She closed with, "Goodnight, Mamma."

"Of course. Goodnight."

◊

WHEN STEPHANIE TRAVELED SOLO TO AMSTERDAM IN APRIL 2001—a month before her mother would finally tell her about her past—she went first to see the park of her mother's odd chant, Oosterpark. It was a sunny day, and people were out in droves. Children played and ran about, which made it easy for Stephanie to envision an earlier time when her mother and aunt—Ruttie and Sophia—likely did the same. She could also see her grandmother, Tessa, sitting on a bench, no doubt embroidering. Throughout the afternoon Stephanie moved from bench to bench, as if to experience the park from all its angles. The last bench she sat on faced the pond, the lopsided one of the chant. Nearby, daffodils bloomed. A water fountain in the distance created a vertical tower from which elegant arcs cascaded. Everything seemed beautiful: the pond, the flowers, the children, the fountain. That there was danger there once, that Oosterpark was closed to Jews, seemed impossible. As impossible to Stephanie, finally rising from her bench, as losing your two dearest friends in the very same year.

◊

THE BREAKUP WITH FREDDY CAME FIRST, DURING THE FIRST WEEK OF March 2000, a Tuesday evening. He'd come by after work with a bag of takeout Chinese food. He'd brought a big bouquet of flowers too, which was unusual. When he told Stephanie to sit as he handed her the flowers she got flustered, thinking he was about to propose to her. But then he began, strangely, to cry.

He was turning a page, he managed to say.

"A what?" Stephanie asked. A page, he said again. He was turning a page.

She still didn't understand.

"I'm breaking up with you. But it's not that I don't love you. I do."

They stared at each other, stunned, for some time. She said, finally, "What is this?"

"A change," he said, looking down. "A change. Stephanie, I need it."

"I'll change too," she said quietly, after a time.

"Not that kind of change," Freddy gently told her. She, too, was crying by then.

They went back and forth with it, Stephanie asking him what he was saying and Freddy telling her again and again the same thing.

"There's some kind of heaviness," he said next, which was a new message.

She was baffled. *Her* heaviness? She wanted to ask but didn't dare.

Finally, he rose to go, the food uneaten, the flowers still wrapped and on the table. Alone again, Stephanie sat for some time then rose, carefully cut the stems of the flowers, placed them in a vase, moved the cartons of takeout into her refrigerator, wrote a check to the electricity company, and dropped the bill in the hallway mail slot. Then, for the next three days, she took to her bed.

After the breakup the conversations between Stephanie and Rona at the skating rink changed, with Stephanie's woes equal to or dominating Rona's. Fall of 2000 and now it was Stephanie going round and round with it: how Freddy had led her on, how she was the most vulnerable insofar as her biological clock was beyond ticking, it was clanging. She was thirty-nine! She'd put her already fragile fertility further at risk, sure he was the one, happy to wait. She'd thought he was as certain as she was. Rona, for her part, took her turn with her chronic gripes: Daniel's permissiveness, and Hannah, twelve by then, manipulating them both into giving in to her demands—staying up late, attending endless sleepovers—and the next one, Beth, learning the same tricks, and fast. "A manipulator is always showing the next one what to do," Rona once grumbled.

The night of the friends' split, the last Wednesday in October, seven months after Stephanie's breakup with Freddy, they'd done the usual talking at the skating rink, but this time Rona said something new. "Stephanie, there are other men, you know. I mean, you're just going on about Freddy." The song "Y.M.C.A." played in the background. A moment before, they'd raised their arms to form the letters, like most everyone else on the ice. The silliness, as always, was contagious. But upon hearing Rona's criticism Stephanie dropped her arms and took off, moving too fast for Rona. For the last two-plus years Stephanie could have said the same thing to Rona about going on and on, but she hadn't. She had an urge to remind Rona of that. But when she lapped Rona and slowed, she said instead, "Not ready for that yet."

"Clearly," Rona answered.

A silence then fell between them, and they skated once more around the rink. They were still not talking as they left, rushing to Stephanie's car as if to flee the slight chill in the fall air. Their next talk, when Stephanie dropped Rona off, was one that Stephanie would return to again and again once she realized in the weeks following that it had most likely been their last.

"Don't you dare envy me," Rona said, catching Stephanie staring at her house. "You, who get to go home to privacy and quiet and no one else's messes and complaints. You always do this, and it needs to stop. Don't you envy *me*."

But Stephanie's apartment was small and austerely furnished, a reflection, or that's how she saw it lately, of a life that never really got going. Moreover, since she'd lost Freddy, hers had become a life that was lonely beyond measure, and surely Rona knew that. Stephanie would have loved a child's mess. Nearing forty, she'd already begun grieving the possibility that she'd missed out on motherhood.

She was about to say that, but different words came out, swift as a slap: "I can't stand it. Don't you dare envy *me*."

The two looked at each other, astonished. "By the way," Stephanie added, "I wouldn't mind your problems. In fact, I'd *love* your endless, endless problems."

"You're cruel," Rona said, quickly opening the car door.

"So are you," Stephanie retorted, though Rona was already rushing to her front door.

IN THE WAKE OF HER argument with Rona, Stephanie traveled more frequently to Connecticut to see her mother. The week after the fight, Stephanie flew north on Friday, taking the workday off. From Bradley Airport she rented a car, and upon arriving in Wells she saw her mother standing in the bungalow's front doorway, which was unusual. It was only one p.m., and Stephanie had thought her mother would still be at work. Her mother was assistant to Wilson Keller, a lawyer with a general practice in Middletown, two towns over.

"Read this," her mother said, failing to say hello first.

Stephanie leaned forward to kiss her mother's cheek, then took a note she held out. Their neighbor, Bill Cousins, who for the last fifteen years had lived with his family in the bungalow next door, was planning to build an addition, the note said. *Knocked but no answer,* it began, in an obviously rushed scrawl, then continued, *Need more space. Parents coming aboard. But don't worry. We'll build down the bank, close to the lake's edge. Will hardly change your view at all.*

"My view," her mother said. "They're going to block my view."

"It says 'hardly at all,'" Stephanie replied. She stepped inside.

"Which means he's blocking something. That's what he's saying."

Stephanie read the note again. "I'll speak to him," she finally said.

Her mother sat down in the living room, dropping onto a wingback chair as if exhausted. She was thin and of average height; her hair, mostly gray, was rolled into a bun. She wore earrings, small gold loops, and over her eyes she'd brushed pale green shadow, as always. She was dressed for work: a skirt, sweater, shoes with small heels. Clearly, she'd gone in that morning but had left early, which was not her way. She liked her job and refused, even at seventy-two, to retire. She'd long ago moved past her original tasks of typing and answering calls to searching titles and even, with Wilson Keller's permission, to finding case law, researching the law reporters meticulously in a way he'd lost the patience for. As far as Stephanie knew, her mother never missed work, except for occasional planned holidays.

"What will you say?" Her mother kicked off her shoes, almost violently.

Stephanie had no idea what she'd say but she walked next door anyway. Bill Cousins and his family—his wife and three young children—weren't there. The house was dark, its doorbell unanswered. It was the same the next day. They must have left for the weekend, Stephanie reported to her mother both times she checked.

"I'll ask Wilson if there's a law," her mother said the next night, Saturday. They were downstairs at the kitchen table, which allowed them to have a good view of Lake Topaqua through the sliding glass doors. Their bungalow was built into a bank that sloped down to the lake's shore. The living room and two bedrooms were upstairs at street level. The kitchen and dining area were downstairs and had a broad lake view, which was why they'd settled there despite the bungalow's snugness. Bill Cousins had somehow packed his family of five into the same amount of space that Stephanie's smaller family had. She'd always thought the space was cramped, certainly when they were a family of three, her father still there, but even after he left, when Stephanie was twelve and the bungalow belonged to just her and her mother. But to ease the tightness inside there was always the outside, and through the kitchen's sliding doors they could step onto an expansive wooden deck, or they could follow a path downhill to the lake where, at its shore, an old wooden dock was anchored. As her mother voiced the idea of Wilson Keller checking to see if a law protected them from an obstruction of their lake view, Stephanie, despite the darkness settling in, thought she saw the dock bob, moving with the motion of tiny waves beneath it.

"A law?" Stephanie asked, almost mindlessly.

"I'm thinking there's probably a law banning Bill Cousins from stealing my view."

"You own it? Is that what you're saying?"

"I don't own the land he plans to build on. But maybe I nevertheless own the view. I feel I own it. Stephie, I feel"—after the inevitable pause came a surprising word—"*violated*. And I wouldn't feel that way if I didn't own *something*." Her mother nodded, convincing herself. She rose and then began to clear their dishes, working silently, hastily, just as she'd done all day, anxiously cleaning an already clean house. For dinner they'd eaten cod, salad, and rye bread toast. Her mother liked toast for both breakfast and dinner. But the familiar meal had only momentarily calmed her.

The next week, on Tuesday evening, when Stephanie was back in D.C., her mother phoned to report that she didn't own her view; in fact, she had no legal right to it. Wilson had looked up the matter and found that there was no ordinance in Wells that prevented a person, building on his own land, from obstructing another's lake view. She had checked his research just in case. It was true.

"There's no law." Her mother's wobbly voice evoked a vision of their wooden dock, old and fragile. "Stephie, it's happening again," she then said.

"What do you mean?" On Connecticut Avenue cars began honking.

"It's happening again. They're taking things from us. It's within the law, Wilson said. He said, 'He can do this by law.' It's happening again, Stephie. See?"

Stephanie knew her mother was speaking of her childhood, of Amsterdam. "No, no. It's not the same thing. This is America, Mamma. Nothing like that can happen here."

"You don't think so?" The subtle tremble in her mother's voice continued.

"I know so. This is America." Stephanie stood up from her couch. "Things like that aren't possible here. It's not happening again. Besides, it's a home addition, a private matter, no government involved. It's not the beginning of the end." As she spoke, Stephanie looked out her window to Connecticut Avenue below, where the usual traffic passed, one vehicle after the next. When she turned back, the frugality of her furnishings, not so different from the look of her mother's home, saddened her. "No, no. It's not happening again. Go to bed, Mamma," she said. "You'll feel so much better in the morning."

* * *

ON ELECTION NIGHT OF 2000, Stephanie went to a party, and it was there, as the November evening rolled on and on—Florida's count for the president too close to call—that she learned from an acquaintance that Freddy had already married the woman he'd apparently dropped Stephanie for, another economist. She learned, too, that he'd been dating her for some weeks, maybe a few months, before he'd broken up with Stephanie. At the election night party, dizzy with the news, Stephanie dropped onto a couch where she sat alone, stunned. She gripped a gin and tonic she forgot to sip for some time until she abruptly downed it all. "Rough night," someone said, a man she didn't know, and he joined her, equally stunned, but not for the same reason. "Might as well call it a night," the man eventually decided, rising to go. "Maybe we'll have it all figured out by morning." Stephanie nodded but didn't go. By the time she left, after one a.m., only a few stragglers remained, staring at the TV, intent on knowing the election results but tired, too, their heads drooped like hers.

She wept for the first time about the double losses—Freddy's marriage and his betrayal—the next day at work, inside a restroom stall, a spill of tears that left her neck and face blotchy. Upon her return her coworkers thought she was having an allergy attack, and Thea Basa, the new hire who'd recently replaced Rona, whipped out Benadryl tablets from her purse. "Thanks, no," Stephanie said, as she so often did to Thea, who, young and anxious to please, had offered Stephanie several unnecessary gifts lately: a scented candle, some lilies, a chocolate bar. "Thanks, no," she repeated, this time her voice audible, normal. Later that day Stephanie wept again as she rode the subway's steep escalator up to Connecticut Avenue at the Van Ness cross-street stop. A young woman, passing Stephanie, stared at her briefly and then pushed on. Another, though, asked if she was okay. "Just a bad day. The worst." "Election got to you?" "Yes, what a shock." "Bad days a-comin'," the woman said, and she stayed by Stephanie for the rest of the escalator ride.

Stephanie went to Wells again that weekend, and once at the bungalow she sat for hours on the dock, despite the November cold. She arrived on Friday, before her mother had come home from work. The familiarity of the lake view consoled her like nothing in D.C. had. Saturday morning, settled again on the dock, she stopped tearing up and simply looked. Their bungalow sat on the bank of a small offshoot of the lake, cove-like. In the distance the lake opened wide, and she spotted the familiar sight of two small islands at the center of that expansive sphere. Closer by, the trees lining the banks were mainly oaks and maples, their leaves mostly fallen, which caused the shore to feel exposed. Mallards swam about, but she didn't call out to them as she usually did, a habit from girlhood. Eventually, sore from sitting, Stephanie brought down a pillow and a blanket to wrap herself in. She also carried a thermos of tea, and as the hours passed she unwound from the blanket several times to rush inside for the bathroom. Each time, she passed her mother, who was at the kitchen table, sipping tea and staring at the view despite the newspaper before her. Her mother, apparently, didn't think anything of Stephanie's need to look and look, probably since she herself had been doing the same for decades. As Stephanie rushed inside, then, no explanations for her behavior were necessary, and for the first time the silence between her and her mother, that ancient chasm, felt like a blessing.

TWO WEEKS LATER HER MOTHER flew to D.C. for her annual Thanksgiving visit, staying a week. In recent years, with Freddy there, her mother's holiday visit had passed if not quickly then at least without incident. Freddy, the Canadian, had prepared the turkey, entertaining them as it cooked with stories of Nova Scotia, its old families and the bitter work there of coal mining and fishing. Her mother had listened, lulled—as Stephanie often was—by the warm inflections of Freddy's speech. But those holiday visits had in fact been hard, an endurance of her mother's stolid solitude, and at the week's end, her mother dropped at the airport, the two would return to Stephanie's apartment and dive into bed, their lovemaking especially passionate, a necessity suddenly, like air.

This year, without Freddy, Stephanie did what she could: made a Moroccan tagine instead of roast turkey for the holiday meal, and early in the week, holiday-sale coupon in hand, took her mother to Lord & Taylor for something special—a new dress, or a pair of winter boots—but "No, I'm good," her mother said with each suggestion. On

Wednesday she brought her mother downtown to skate on the rink by the National Gallery's Sculpture Garden, but the rink was overwhelmed by the holiday crowd, and they could barely move. When several children tripped and then screeched in pain, her mother decided she'd had enough. She and Stephanie returned uptown to recover in the Bishop's Garden behind the National Cathedral. There, at least, was some quiet. Upon entering the garden, they walked toward some rose bushes which, though barren, their stalks cut back, nevertheless beckoned. Her mother leaned toward the stunted stems, then straightened with an air of satisfaction as if she'd indeed breathed in life from the scraggly plants. The following day, after their holiday meal, the tagine merely okay, they returned to the garden, settling this time on a bench in its open space, a broad field. From there, Stephanie looked skyward at the cathedral's spires, and she stared ahead at a stunning old pine, and glanced, too, at the few people passing them, walking a dog or pushing a baby carriage despite the late-November chill. She assumed that her mother, quiet, watched too. When a toddler ran across the open grass, her glee adorable, her parents forgotten, both Stephanie and her mother, almost in unison, laughed.

But the moment passed, the quiet between them returned, and the truth of Freddy was what Stephanie so wanted to tell her mother, there in the Bishop's Garden, the toddler and her parents gone, the garden once again empty. She wanted to lean over and sob into her mother's chest, but even as a girl she'd never shed tears in front of her mother. For it had always seemed implicit that nothing that happened to Stephanie would ever compare to the tragedy of her mother, torn from Amsterdam as a young teen, her parents with her but her beloved sister, Sophia, left behind, dead. Even that much of the story, a bare outline, told to Stephanie secondhand by her father, was enough to stop Stephanie's complaints. Freddy Taylor versus the Holocaust. Let's not be ridiculous, she could almost hear her mother say. Which is just what her mother said when Stephanie, talking at last, explained instead about the latest on the election battle still ongoing in Florida, a quagmire of punch card ballots with hanging, dimpled, or even pregnant chads.

* * *

THE SATURDAY AFTER THANKSGIVING STEPHANIE took her mother to the airport, walked her in, and watched as her mother strode toward her gate.

Home again, Stephanie felt the absence of her mother acutely. She paged through the newspaper, then began to tidy up, remaking her bed, washing dishes, folding laundry, all the while seeing her mother on the plane, stiff in an aisle seat, unopened magazine in her lap, alert to any announcements. An hour passed, then another and another. Finally, her mother phoned.

"Glad you made it. Uneventful trip?" Stephanie asked.

"Yes."

"Well, good. Good. So nice to have you here."

"Nice to have visited."

"Wish I could have gotten you something at Lord & Taylor. I really do."

"I have enough."

"Just thought it would be nice."

After a pause her mother said, "It's still here."

"What's that?"

"My lake view. He hasn't taken it yet. I worried all week that when I got back it'd be gone."

"Why didn't you say something?"

"What can we say? There's no law."

"Maybe we can still say something. I'll talk to Bill. Sorry I haven't yet. Rest now, Mamma."

"Hard to rest."

"Try, Mamma."

"I'll try." Then her mother added, looping back, "But what can we say?"

◊

"YES, STEPHANIE, BEFORE THE NAZIS INVADED, AMSTERDAM WAS FINE, was *Mokum*," her mother said that evening the following May when they finally talked of her past. It was three months after she'd helped pull suicidal Ian Lima from Lake Topaqua. It had been midwinter then. Just before the rescue she'd been about to go skating. She was looking down at her laces but then looked up, hearing something. On the ice a boy was running.

"*Mokum*. Yiddish, for place. The Place. Safe Place. *Mokum*, Amsterdam. The place for Jews to flee *to*, not from. First there, Jews fleeing the Portuguese Inquisition. The Sephardic Jews. Around 1600. Then, not long after, Jews fleeing pogroms, arriving from central and eastern Europe. Ashkenazi Jews, our kind. And poorer than poor for so long. Papa's work, diamonds, helped change that." Her mother paused. "And before the war," she finally continued, "so many Jews arriving from Germany. So many, including Aaron Taube's family. Aaron, whom Sophia loved."

By the time Ruth reached the boy, who had run right into an ice fisherman's hole, Judge Arthur Cantrell was there too, pulling and pulling. Where he came from, Ruth didn't know. But she did know, even as it happened, that without the judge there she wouldn't have been able to lift the boy herself.

"But let's go back to Oosterpark, Stephanie, before the war, before we ever saw that sign on the tree. That's where Sophia and I played as children. Where all the children played. My mother, of course, embroidered, and in the warmer months she stitched in the park as we played, which gave us lots of time, as Mamma got lost in the stories of her embroidery. We'd wander from her, Sophia and I, all the way across the park, or across the pond. Maybe that's why we never felt as scared as we should have when the dark days came—we were still eager to wander off, as we did to go skating that day at the Apollohal. We'd been stretching beyond Mamma's grasp for some time, really. But when we were young, in Oosterpark, all Mamma had to do was look up and she could find us, waving."

Ruth and the judge dragged the boy to her bungalow, and together they stayed with him until the judge, who said he had an appointment, told her that if anything looked questionable about the boy she should call an ambulance. But nothing looked strange. Just a boy, shivering, crying.

"Yes," her mother continued. "We seemed to know just when Mamma would look up. A connection, almost like magic. We'd race back, she'd look up and smile, and then we'd race off again. That was our game, to and from Mamma, tirelessly. Until we got older, of course, and wanted our independence. But I'm describing now when we were girls, Stephie. Two little girls. Sisters."

Ruth drew a bath for the boy and told him to get into that warm tub, pronto. The judge gone, the boy soaking, she knocked on the bathroom door and pleaded, "Please, please, don't try that again." The boy answered, quick enough, "I wouldn't try it twice."

A half hour passed before her mother finally said more—Stephanie didn't dare move, then, for fear of breaking whatever spell caused the talking. "On Sundays Mamma always baked a cake—apple or lemon, many kinds really—and we had cake and coffee on Sunday afternoons in our apartment. No matter the weather. Even on the nicest days we waited inside, quite calmly, for cake and coffee. For Sophia and me the coffee was just a drop that Mamma then drowned in milk, then in time it was less milk and more coffee, until it was finally coffee with a little milk, just like Mamma and Papa had. I often invited Henny Ganz to visit for cake and coffee. She giggled at every sip because it was just so daring, truly, to have coffee when you're still a child."

When Ian Lima came downstairs to the kitchen, he was wearing one of Ruth's bathrobes, which fit him fine. Ruth poured him tea, but he wanted coffee. It took another few minutes for her to make some. He was young, maybe fifteen, but took it black, which she found strange. At the kitchen table, staring at the lake, he held the steaming cup in both his hands. His wet hair, combed slick, came halfway down his neck. His earlobes were red. No, she thought, she would not have been able to drag him out without the help of Judge Cantrell.

◊

Months before, just home from her Thanksgiving trip to D.C., her call to Stephanie completed, Ruth Pearl unpacked, then readied herself for bed. But she was more restless than tired. Glancing out her bedroom window she saw that snow had begun falling, but only the lightest scattering of flakes. Still, the weather woke her further. Instead of going to bed, then, she went to her bedroom closet, where she pulled from a shelf an expandable file folder she'd labeled years earlier with the word *Good.* Contained within the file were photocopies of legal cases she'd collected since she began to research for Wilson, and she pulled one out at random: the Connecticut Supreme Court decision *Horton v. Meskill,* where she read again that the right to an education in Connecticut was so fundamental that any intrusion on it must be subject to the court's strict scrutiny. As she read, the snow outside fell softly, then waned, and glancing out she thought that even those lovely flakes deserved the protection of strict scrutiny, as did every moment in life, really. Strict scrutiny: the idea, as she neared sleep, seemed beautiful, even holy. Before nodding off, then, she forced herself to rise from bed and stare at the falling snow until it filled her with a sense of lonely, spectral wonder. When she fell asleep a minute later it was as if to a silent spell. Perhaps the hushed snowfall had cast it, she mused the next morning. Or the soundless pages of the protective legal decision, still there, right beside her.

2

> Netherlands, February 11, 1941, by Decree of the Secretary-General of the Department of Education, Science, and the Protection of Culture: Jewish students seeking to enroll for the academic year 1941–42 can do so only with the express approval of the Secretary-General.

IN THE FALL OF 2000, Wells, Connecticut, was, as ever, a small place, with just three primary roads—Route 66, Lake Road, and Main Street—from which all other roads branched forth, and over the past two decades it had become a sorry place, too. Missy Lima, Ian's mother, thought this almost daily as she drove around Wells, the downtown businesses barely hanging in there: Ebbitt's Grocery, Franklin's Gifts & Jewelry, and two package stores, their inventory largely six-packs of Schlitz and various cheap wines. Only the newest of the businesses, the Moretti School of Dance, housed above Franklin's, was doing well. The cluster of downtown buildings—also including a bank, a post office, a town hall, and a small public library—encircled a roundabout, and nearby were two churches, Congregationalist and Catholic. A half mile away, on Route 66, stood a third church, Lutheran, and a third package store, Henry's. Wells's only other enterprises were a pharmacy, a gas station, the lakeside Topaqua Grill, where Missy Lima was the head lunch chef, and another small restaurant on Route 66, Mitchell's Dairy, where Missy used to waitress. Everything else was two towns away in larger Middletown: clothing stores, movie theaters, Kmart, better restaurants, a distinguished university—Wesleyan—and a YMCA. In Middletown Missy bought her son Ian's clothes at Bob's Surplus, known for its rock-bottom prices, and more and more she got her own clothes there too: overalls, painter's pants, T-shirts, hoodies.

In fact, these days she and Ian dressed almost identically, and with Ian now sixteen and rapidly gaining height and her still a redhead at forty, barely any gray, they could both pass for university students—a notion that either amused Missy or made her cry, depending on her mood. Truth was, back when she was Missy Mulligan—before Frank Lima ruined her—she would have liked to go to Wesleyan, but such a plan was unthinkable, too good for her, and too expensive. Instead, she'd gone to the University of Connecticut, simply determined to, despite her father's insistence that his college fund was only for her brother—"He'll be providing for a family someday. You won't," went her father's thinking. She consequently earned that tuition money on her own, waitressing at Mitchell's Dairy nearly every day after school. Stephanie Pearl, her high school best friend, worried Missy would exhaust herself before she even left home. But Missy told Stephanie not to worry, adding, "I'm going to *college*, period." They were on Stephanie's dock that day, where they always did their best talking, their bare feet dangling in the cool lake water. This was fall of 1978. The next year Missy did go to college, studying late into the nights, taking an interest in biology, and getting mostly A's. But the next spring she met Frank Lima and her plans shifted. Life was nothing without love, she suddenly knew, writing as much to Stephanie. And she threw herself at it, trailing Frank Lima around campus, stripping down to nothing in his locked dorm room and watching him, unbelievably, in his beautiful nakedness, walk toward her. How easy it was to give up molecular biology and Greek mythology and modern philosophy and the value of all her hard-earned savings because Frank Lima loved her and that's what truly mattered. Soon her grades slipped, reflecting her shift in priorities. When she was finally summoned by the registrar and learned that her financial aid was in danger of being revoked, it didn't matter because she was already engaged to Frank. So she dropped out of college early in her junior year, with no regrets until later. Because in the end Frank loved her only for a while, and when Ian was just two and a half Frank left, never to be heard from again. Before then they had moved back to Wells, and there she and Frank began their marriage typically enough, starting a family, fitting right in, Frank—until his baffling departure—an assistant engineer at the Pratt & Whitney plant in East Hartford, she a waitress again, and at Mitchell's Dairy no less, but she took the job gladly knowing her tenure there would be short. But after Frank left, and without his income, she'd kept the job for an entire decade, which embarrassed her, stuck as she obviously was. Finally, in 1997, she landed her better and current job at the Topaqua Grill. Though she worked even harder there, she at least wasn't as ashamed anymore of what she did. Moreover, being a chef was physical in a way she truly liked, especially since she'd started taking dance lessons, which gave her "body awareness," or so Angelina Moretti, her dance instructor, said. So these days she worked and took a dance class when she could and managed all the while to be the single mother of a growing boy, just turned sixteen, who seemed of late more or less happy. Which meant that when you added it all up, she had in fact survived losing Frank Lima.

The last Tuesday in November—the presidential election still undecided but Thanksgiving and the first hints of snow marking the month over and done with—Missy, passing through the downtown, pausing at a stop sign, tooted her horn at Angelina Moretti, who was just then unlocking the door to head up to her dance studio. Angelina was also a single mother, of a seventeen-year-old named Jase, a friend of Ian's and his fellow dancer. For some time now Angelina had been a friend of Missy's too. Indeed, years ago she'd saved Missy with her dance lessons, or so it seemed in hindsight. The downtown that morning was forlorn as always, but Angelina Moretti wasn't. She turned, smiled, waved, and Missy Lima, hitting the gas, waved back.

A HALF HOUR LATER, AT the Topaqua Grill, Missy made onion soup, a restaurant staple, shredding onions in the food processor while the beef broth simmered. Then she prepared her sandwich board, loading it with sliced turkey, pastrami, roast beef, and various cheeses. She arranged her breads, then rinsed lettuce to be used for salad. Quickly, she mixed tuna and egg salads. Finally, with only an hour before customers would arrive, she made something new: a variation on Waldorf salad using pecans instead of walnuts, yogurt mixed with the mayonnaise, and cranberries along with the usual chopped celery and apples. She added lemon, salt, and honey. Calvin, the head chef, tasted it and nodded, and she listed the dish with the day's specials. Pecan Waldorf, she called it. By one thirty p.m. they'd nearly sold out, which was a triumph. For a moment she let herself feel it, how she was in fact pretty good at being a lunch chef even if all she made were pots of soups, everyday sandwiches, and simple salads. It wasn't like she'd gone to chef school or anything. "I'm a mother," Missy had said years back when applying for the job. "I've made my kid maybe four thousand lunches, maybe more." Those reported lunches for Ian, plus a lucky test run with the onion soup, had been enough to get her the job, and upon being hired she'd driven to see Roy Kirk, her longtime friend with benefits, knocking on his door despite it being midday Wednesday and not early Friday, their agreed biweekly time. He'd been kind, holding her while she cried, the tears of relief unstoppable.

This day, Tuesday, Angelina Moretti was the last person to order Missy's new dish. Seeing her friend come in, Missy took a break and joined her, a cup of black coffee in hand. Angelina was in the habit, once weekly or so, of lunching there, on the late side, when Missy could leave the kitchen for a few minutes.

Missy watched as Angelina loaded her fork. She wore her hair in a ponytail, and a turtleneck, as black as her hair, covered her thin upper body. In Angelina's presence Missy always felt huge, though her dance classes at the Moretti School had long ago helped her lose the extra weight she'd gained after Frank left her.

"I was feeling creative." Missy pointed at her dish then rolled her eyes. Creative, she knew, was too good a word for anything she made.

But Angelina wasn't as skeptical. "Yummy," she said. Then, "Coming to dance tonight?"

Missy, tired from standing all morning, wasn't sure. They sat in silence for a while. Their table was by a window and outside, across the road, the lake spread forth for as far as Missy could see, the day's wind creating visible ripples on it. Clouds had gathered and it looked as if snow might fall again. Missy, mentioning that, watched as Angelina turned to study the sky.

"If only it would start now so I could cancel tonight. Tired, like you . . ."

Missy nodded. Their relentless fatigue—the single-working-mother kind—had long been their deepest bond. Angelina lived in Portland, the town between Wells and Middletown, and even the short drive from Wells to her home often seemed too much at the day's end.

They didn't speak more while Angelina finished eating. Missy sipped the remains of her coffee, which quickly became lukewarm. Outside, a speck of sunlight broke through, landing nearby.

Missy pointed at it, adding, almost triumphantly, "Maybe I will dance tonight."

Angelina looked up then out. "Ah, damn. Was all set to cancel."

EVEN BY THE TIME IAN was four Missy had already made him hundreds of lunches, but hundreds weren't enough. No, it was never enough with a small boy and a missing husband and a life down the tubes, which was why she started drinking at night—the sweetest wine she could find or sometimes Kalua with milk—as she endlessly watched TV. And she made fudge, an easy recipe combining melted marshmallow fluff with chocolate chips and condensed milk, then watched TV while the fudge cooled, then stuffed it down, sometimes eating an entire batch save the few pieces she gave Ian, the TV droning on and on, her little boy right beside her for all those hours, watching, nibbling, until he fell asleep.

It was a Thursday, January of 1989, Ian just turned five, the night another frozen one, when she got the wakeup call: time to be a better mother. Typically enough, she'd dozed off on the couch with the TV on. Earlier, on her way home from Mitchell's Dairy, she'd stopped at Litten's, one of the downtown package stores, and arriving home she'd downed a bottle of wine in less than an hour. That day, Ian had gone from kindergarten to his after-school play group, and upon being dropped off at home had leapt at her on the couch, and, in her arms, exhausted from his day, had fallen asleep almost as soundly as she did in her inebriation. Soon she dreamt that a bird was tweeting, a delightful, tropical bird. That a tropical bird could survive such a cold New England night was not confusing in the dream—it was just the reality. As the bird continued its song—at first in intermittent bursts and then in a stream of birdcall—Missy was tempted to join in. *Frank, Frank, Frank,* she longed to say, and finally was saying, the single word a relief to speak and speak again, but the respite ended abruptly. Something jolted her awake. And then someone was yelling at her, and Ian was there too, holding a spatula smeared with eggs, and bawling.

"Did you not hear the smoke alarm?" Her neighbor and landlord, Mrs. Cousins, was speaking, scolding. The woman dropped the door key still in her hand into her apron pocket. "And what's your little boy doing, cooking by himself?"

Ian bawled again, louder. Fran Cousins kneeled and told him to blow his nose into her hanky. "Good boy," she said, stuffing the hanky into another apron pocket. The Cousinses lived on the first floor of a large Barton Hill home they owned, a Victorian. Missy had taken the second-story rental apartment eight months after Frank left, selling their little house close to the lake, the mortgage and upkeep of which had already become too much. Mrs. Cousins, as Missy called her, was happy enough to babysit from time to time. Thus, the woman knew where to find Ian's pajamas, toothbrush, and school clothes for the next day. "He's staying with me tonight," she said, holding his things. "Sober up. You need coffee," she added, before leaving with Ian.

Missy rose, made coffee, and drank it black, not heavily sweetened and milked as she usually had it. But the bitterness was what she deserved, she felt, drinking the coffee, hating the taste, but nevertheless pouring herself more. She'd drink it that way from then on, she decided—a reminder to wake up and to stay awake. Indeed, she remained awake that whole night, crying, pacing, grabbing from her bottom dresser drawer the one remaining photo of Frank, grinning at her from the banks of Lake Topaqua on the day he proposed marriage. She ripped it to shreds.

In the morning, she knocked gingerly on the Cousinses' door.

"I took him to school already," Mrs. Cousins said. She looked fed up with Missy.

"I'm so sorry."

"I bet." Mrs. Cousins stood in the doorway, her bulk almost filling it, her expression indifferent. She wore the same apron, trimmed in red, as the night before. Behind her, Mr. Cousins stood silently. Missy smelled bacon. With her, breakfast was Fruit Loops, and that would change too.

"It won't happen again," Missy said.

"No, it won't," Mrs. Cousins told her, her voice rising. "I saw you another time on your way up here, gone to the moon, remember?"

"No."

"Of course you don't."

The next day, shortly after Ian caught his bus to school, a social worker showed up at Missy's door. Missy had just washed her hair and was running her blow dryer, which meant she didn't hear the knocks at first. A complaint had been issued, the social worker told her, alleging child neglect. Missy knew it had to be from Mrs. Cousins, and she was surprised. Despite Missy's indulgences with wine Ian had never tried to cook before, nor had the smoke alarm ever blasted. But from the grim look on the face at the door, the delayed time Missy had taken to answer it seemed to prove the point of the complaint. The social worker, reading from a notepad, told Missy that with the possibility of imminent risk of physical harm to Ian—an unsupervised five-year-old cooking a meal for himself and causing the smoke alarm to go off, a sleeping, drunk parent, et cetera—she felt the need to come quickly. Missy nodded. The social worker then explained that if she notified the state's Department of Children and Families there'd be an inquiry and maybe a hearing.

"A what?" Missy said, stunned. "But it's never happened before. Never."

"Law's the law," the social worker said, and then repeated the phrase "imminent risk of physical harm to the child." She seemed but a child herself, younger than Missy, her skirt short and tight. Her voice was girlish too, but her face was serious. She reminded Missy about the tragedy of a month ago, a four-year-old girl in nearby East Haddam who, in a context of parental neglect, had died of poisoning after drinking liquid cleanser. "We can't be too careful," the social worker said, and Missy nodded. For a week the previous month the local news had been filled with details of the child's death in East Haddam, including that the Department of Children and Families had been late, after many complaints, to investigate.

The possibility of a hearing—as well as the grim tone of the social worker and the fact that, since the East Haddam incident, social workers were, as this one noted, "not taking chances"—prompted Missy to make an appointment with Gene D'Orrino, legal partner to Wilson Keller, in Middletown the next week. It was there, waiting to be seen, Ian with her, that she ran into Ruth Pearl, Stephanie's mother, whom she hadn't seen for so long she'd forgotten that Mrs. Pearl worked there. College had at first tied Missy and Stephanie more tightly together. They wrote letters, phoned occasionally, got together during breaks. But then Missy had dropped out, gotten quickly married, then pregnant, then abandoned, and Stephanie had not, and with each step the two friends had grown more distant. By the time Missy was single again Stephanie had settled in Washington, D.C., where she had, Missy assumed, a great career. In her shame, Missy never tried to revive the friendship.

In the waiting room Mrs. Pearl took Missy's hand momentarily, a gentle touch, and then motioned for her and Ian to sit. "I'll get you some water," she said. They sat at opposite sides of a small table covered with stacks of *National Geographic*, *Forbes*, and *Time* magazines. If Mrs. Pearl was surprised to see Missy she didn't show it, which was a kindness, Missy thought, her knee jiggling from nerves. When Missy returned from speaking with the attorney, her forehead perspiring, his words helpful ("It doesn't sound urgent yet. But look, the East Haddam incident has put them on edge. So now would be the time for any improvements"), Mrs. Pearl was sitting in the chair that Missy had taken. The chair was now beside Ian's, and Mrs. Pearl had made him cocoa. As he drank she called him "Mr. Hot Chocolate," which made Ian kick his legs in delight and giggle. Then Mrs. Pearl laughed, which was odd, Missy thought, as she knew from the hours she'd spent at Stephanie's house that her mother rarely smiled.

◊

THE DAY RUTH PEARL PULLED IAN LIMA FROM THE LAKE—TWELVE YEARS after Missy's law office visit—she didn't learn his name until he was sitting at her kitchen table, wearing her robe, drinking her coffee. Then she remembered. His face had matured and yet he looked in many ways the same. "We met a long time ago." The boy's confused expression told her that he didn't recall that time. She shook her head as if to tell him it didn't matter what she'd just said. But she could see him, so little then, sitting in the waiting room chair at the law office, his feet—in rubber boots—not able yet to touch the floor. He was as vulnerable then as he was now, she observed, staring at both the child of her memory and the living presence before her, two boys who held their drinking cups identically, gripped tight with both hands.

◊

TWO WEEKS AFTER MISSY MET WITH ATTORNEY D'ORRINO, SHE WAS BACK at Bob's Surplus, rummaging through a bin of wool sweaters, on sale. Ever since the social worker's visit she'd been shivering, though the days hadn't gotten colder. She chose a sweater in a maroon color, size extra large. She was thirty pounds heavier than when Frank had left. Her sweaters at home were all size medium, and tight on her frame.

Tacked to a wall near the doorway hung a bulletin board for community announcements, and as she passed it on her way out, a pale blue flyer caught her attention. It advertised a class at the new dance school in downtown Wells. She had noticed the place when it opened but was never curious to know more about it. But just then, as she paused by the door to Bob's Surplus, the description of the dance class compelled her. "Musical Movement," it was called. "No experience needed." "For adults." "Simple Steps." At the bottom it read, "Change it up!" The cost for seven weeks came to thirty-five dollars. The next night, Tuesday, was the first class. Missy ripped a pull tab from the flyer and pocketed it. On the drive home she tried to imagine herself in such a class, moving musically—whatever that meant.

She was wary of asking Mrs. Cousins to watch Ian again, but Mrs. Cousins didn't seem to mind once Missy explained that she was cleaning up her act and that the new class, which would help with her fitness, was part of that. "I'm changing it up." "Sounds about right," Mrs. Cousins said skeptically.

But in class that night Missy felt like a fool. The music was classical, which she didn't know anything about, and she felt out of place, even stupid. Moreover, she'd worn sneakers, not knowing that ballet slippers were expected. And her sweatpants bagged; the others, five women, all wore black tights. *But how did they know*, Missy wondered. Angelina Moretti explained that she was classically trained, and that they would start with ballet basics then move on to modern dance. But Angelina would always keep it simple, she said, adding, "Promise." At that Missy kicked off her clunky Nikes and socks and went forward, as Angelina suggested, in bare feet. Her thick toes embarrassed her. The students stood at a barre with a mirror behind it, which meant she could see herself, which was hard to take. Her hair needed a trim. Her stomach pouched. Even her hands, trembling slightly, were ugly. The movement began: "Point the left foot forward, point to the side, point to the back," Angelina called, demonstrating as she did. Again and again they followed the pattern—which was indeed a series of simple steps, Missy soon realized with relief. But after a few minutes she began to tire. The music was by Tchaikovsky, Angelina noted. "Just listen," she said suddenly, stopping all motion, which gave Missy a needed rest. The music was complicated, new, but Missy finally warmed to it. Briefly, she thought she might be okay. But then Angelina's tone changed. "Tummies tight, heads high, shoulders back," she intoned, stopping in front of Missy. Angelina looked, waited, while Missy clenched everything in her body that she could, feeling as she did so a familiar sense of failure, as if by her very awkwardness Angelina could tell that Missy, a college dropout, still worked at Mitchell's Dairy and had lost her husband and was maybe, if she wasn't careful, about to lose her son. Indeed, all her secrets seemed exposed: how much fudge she'd eaten that month, how much wine she'd drunk, and the recent knock at the door of the social worker while the blow dryer wailed on. She clenched tighter. She refused to glance at the mirror or the teacher. Unwittingly, she caught sight of a framed poster featuring a ballerina sailing through the air, legs and arms gracefully outstretched, and she turned from that too.

She didn't go back the next week or the week following.

Three weeks later she ran into Angelina Moretti at the Stop & Shop in Middletown. Angelina's boy, Jase, pushed their shopping cart. He looked about Ian's age, a pale boy, yet with hair as black and straight as his mother's.

"Where'd you go?" Angelina asked Missy.

"Still here. Just hurt my ankle." She glanced at her left foot then at her right. She wasn't sure which foot to suddenly avoid putting weight on.

"It looks fine now. Time to come back?" Angelina's voice wasn't as stern as Missy remembered it. She signaled to Jase to push the cart forward and then, with a nod to Missy, she walked off. But the next minute she returned. She held out some money. "Look, you only came to one class. Here's a refund."

"Thank you." Missy took the money, which came to thirty dollars. Angelina stood for a moment, not speaking. She wore lipstick but otherwise no makeup. Under an old ski jacket, ripped in front and patched, she wore the same brand of cheap sweater from Bob's Surplus that Missy had recently purchased. There couldn't have been money to spare, Missy realized.

If she can give me my thirty dollars back maybe she can teach me something, Missy told herself in the next days, thinking about that refund, surprised by it each time it came to mind, and she returned to the dance studio the next Tuesday evening. It was now the fifth class. At the start Angelina had everyone still at the barre, but by this time the movements involved legs lifts and squatting. Arm gestures accompanied each movement. The music playing was by Debussy, Angelina explained, and the piece—all piano—was quiet, tender, and utterly beautiful. Missy had never heard anything like it. She felt herself falling away as she moved in time with the sound and in coordination, easily, with the others. She even had the right clothes this time: black tights and soft slippers she'd bought over the weekend at Kmart in Middletown. The refund had covered it.

When she got home, she collapsed in a chair at the kitchen table, rubbing her calves. "I made it," she grumbled to Ian, who then brought her the ice she requested, wrapped in a towel. As she iced her legs and feet, Ian watched.

After the next class she returned home just as sore. This time she grabbed the ice and simply sat for a while. Ian, who'd eaten already, joined her at the table, quietly waiting, though for nothing in particular. Just some talk, she knew. So she hummed what she could of the Debussy, then told him the music was better than that, but it was the best she could do. "Nice?" He nodded.

She felt almost good after the next and last class, the seventh, and after picking up Ian at Mrs. Cousins's she danced around the kitchen for a minute, humming as she did.

"Can I dance too?" Ian asked as she swooped past him.

"You?" She stopped.

He nodded. "Can I go to class too?"

She looked at him, surprised. "I'll have to ask the teacher. Honestly, Ian, you sure? You're a little kid, I mean. It's a bunch of old ladies there, like me." She was twenty-eight. For some time she'd felt ancient but suddenly she didn't. Debussy's dreamy music still swirled in her mind. Maybe her life really wasn't over, she mused. Ian now twirled from corner to corner, just as she had. Then he pranced around their kitchen table. She wondered if she'd ever seen him this happy, then wondered if he'd ever seen her this happy.

"Well, okay," she said as Ian waltzed toward her. She held her arms out, then pulled him close. They stayed that way for more than a moment. They were good, very good. She would make a note of that in the file she now kept—just in case—labeled "Info: Attorney D'Orrino."

◊

That Ian Lima's fallback emotional state was a kind of gloom was something he would realize only in the weeks after he jumped, impulsively, into Lake Topaqua. Until then, he didn't question that he woke each morning to an invariable "sinking feeling," as he'd long ago come to call it, an emotional ache at his core as if overnight he'd plunged into a pool of anguish from which he had to emerge each morning. The feeling began early in his life, probably after his father had walked out, he'd always assumed, though he stopped connecting it to that old time, which he couldn't even remember well. These days the pain of waking up was just what was. He used a routine to shake himself out of it: upon rising from bed, a few hops in the morning cold followed by a cool shower. It was his body's shivering, he thought, that did the trick.

The last Tuesday in November, just two weeks after his sixteenth birthday, he'd done just that: woken up, shivered, gotten going, and now he was at his best friend Maddie Brent's for the afternoon. He spent the other weekday afternoons dancing at the Moretti studio, where he and Jase, the teacher's son, were the only two male dancers to stick with ballet into their teen years. It was a faggy thing to do, Ian knew from hearing others sometimes say as much. The first time he'd heard the word, at ten years old, though he didn't understand its meaning he distinctly felt its hate, and he quit the Moretti School for the next three months, throwing himself into the baseball season. But he returned, finally, craving the music as much as the movement. The bit of ridicule he risked mattered less than his feelings for dance, even then growing deep within him. Indeed, the art and craft of it was like an ever-enlarging box, he explained to Maddie, meaning that no matter how much he developed, the box would never fill. This endlessness was dancing's best part, even better than performing. "It's freedom," he told Maddie, who nodded, her eyes fixed more on him than on the wet clay in her hands—she was throwing a pot. When she smiled, he considered telling her another of his private truths. Jase, he wanted to say but still didn't dare—I can't stop thinking about Jase Moretti.

Ian and Maddie were inside Maddie's house, in the upstairs bathroom her mother had recently turned into a pottery studio, which was strange and interesting to Ian, much like the location of Maddie's home, in the village of Middle Haddam, bordering Wells. Because the only public school in Middle Haddam ended at sixth grade, the kids there got bussed into Wells for their remaining school years, and that was how Ian had met Maddie some years back—she was a new and particularly bright presence in his seventh grade class. Middle Haddam—with just an Episcopalian church, a tiny library, and an equally small post office its only public spaces—was perched between the Connecticut River on one side and the outskirts of Wells on the other. Yet despite its proximity to Wells, Ian understood Middle Haddam to be a world away. He could say things there, like what he'd just told Maddie about the ever-enlarging box and all, that he knew just wouldn't make sense inside Wells.

Even the interior of Maddie's house—its many books, antiques, and works of art—was a world away from the plain, all-things-functional apartment Ian lived in, and Maddie's parents (her father a history professor at Wesleyan University, her mother a professional potter) were completely unlike Ian's mother, who'd been born and raised in Wells and was a waitress-turned-short-order-chef. Middle Haddam had class, Ian gradually concluded, which was just what Wells was lacking. That fact accounted for the dinginess of what should have been Wells's quaint downtown. And it was class, or classiness—something less to do with money than with taste, as Ian meant it—that accounted for the charm of Middle Haddam's old New England homes overlooking the Connecticut River, which, flowing forth, seemed to carry a more sophisticated beauty than even Lake Topaqua, Wells's best feature by far.

The renovated bathroom-turned-studio at Maddie's house still contained a working toilet and sink. But Maddie's mother had covered the bathtub with a wooden plank upon which she dried her newly thrown pots. Beside the tub was a pottery wheel, a folding chair, and a small table for wedging the clay, necessary to clear it of air bubbles. Maddie had demonstrated wedging upon Ian's first visit there, four months back, when Maddie, fresh from getting her driver's license, brought him over. Maddie's mother had long been a member of Wesleyan Potters, a craft cooperative in nearby Middletown. But the home studio was new. "What I didn't expect," Maddie told Ian, "is that when she pots at night the turning wheel helps me sleep. I hear it and it knocks me out."

"I'm bad at sleeping too," Ian replied, meaning, really, that he struggled with waking up. But he left it at that because the nighttime sinking and morning pain were still nothing to talk about.

As Maddie potted, Ian lounged in the dry bathtub beside the wheel, the wooden plank over the tub removed, the few drying pots that had been on it carefully relocated beside the toilet. While the two talked, lazed, and potted—the bathroom door closed, the window over the wheel opened a few inches, the late afternoon sunlight streaming their way—they were also smoking a joint that Maddie had rolled, far more expertly than she shaped clay. Her dinner plate, or whatever she was making, tilted unintentionally. If she let go, its outer edges would likely collapse. Maddie's parents were away, Ian knew, or he and Maddie wouldn't have been smoking. With the window opened they were a bit chilly, they'd just noted, then laughed about it, then couldn't stop. When they quieted again, Ian scrunched down further into the tub as if the act, a literal sinking, could warm him.

"You were a kick today," Maddie said next.

Ian knew that she was referring to their geometry class, where he had imitated Mr. Hanley, their math teacher, racing out of the classroom for more chalk. Before that, Mr. Hanley had broken each chalk stick he'd used while working a proof on the blackboard. With the teacher gone, Ian approached the blackboard, mimicking the man leaning too hard as he scribbled, sneezing each time the imagined stick broke, and broke again. The class cracked up, especially at the sneezes, which were embellishments. And they laughed harder when Mr. Hanley returned, resumed his writing, and finally turned and bowed, amazed to have made the group so crazy-happy. For a thousand reasons, including the weirdness of teachers like Mr. Hanley, Maddie's parents didn't think Wells High was good enough for her, she told Ian.

"And there are no AP courses, which really bugs them," she added, noting that her parents were pressuring her to attend a private school.

Her father, the professor, had created a list: Choate Rosemary Hall, Loomis Chaffee, Cheshire Academy. "And Miss Porter's School," Maddie said, "where Jackie Kennedy went. But who wants to be like Jackie Kennedy? So skinny! So tragic!"

Maddie was skinny too, and had the same deep brunette hair as Jacqueline Kennedy, at least in any photo of her Ian had ever seen. And Maddie's smile was just as bright.

"What's AP?" he asked, only to be quickly sorry he had. Maddie's swift glance embarrassed him. But I'm from Wells, he almost said, justifying his ignorance.

"Advanced Placement. For college prep. The courses can count toward college credit if you do well. Better schools have them, and I'm disadvantaging myself by staying in Wells, my parents say. Wesleyan students typically come with AP courses under their belts. But in Wells who even goes to college? We don't do AP. We do remedial, right?"

As Maddie resumed potting, Ian considered how much he liked his teachers. Even weird Mr. Hanley was bright enough for him, which meant something given that he, along with Maddie and Phil Tuttle, were the best in their class at math. Maddie was tops in everything. "Hanley's always one step ahead of us," he said, defending the man he'd so easily mocked hours before.

Maddie agreed, then added, "Besides, without AP courses our homework is light, so I can read what I want." She was just then halfway through Gandhi's autobiography, a book she'd pulled from her dad's home library, and before that she'd gone for the collected poems of Wallace Stevens, a Connecticut man, by day a Hartford insurance guy. "I don't get them, really, but I like them still," she'd said as she passed the poems on to Ian. He read just a few before giving up. Like his father, an engineer—or so the myth of the disappeared man went—Ian was better at math than reading.

"Going to a crappy high school has its benefits," Maddie continued. "Truly, I like the freedom. AP courses would interfere with my education. I said that to my dad who told me he just might handcuff me and lock me in at Choate. I told him, Choke? Did you say Choke?"

They were quiet for a time while Maddie continued to fuss with her platter. She stopped to snuff out their joint, half smoked. "Ian, you should join the theater group," she soon suggested.

"No time."

"But you're a ham. A natural. Look what you did today."

Ian knew what she meant, but he didn't ham it up for attention. The moments just came to him as if from habit. He performed—was always, in a sense, performing. For instance, no one, not even Maddie, knew he liked boys. He could hide this side of himself, bury it underneath the more acceptable parts of his identity, like being an ace at baseball, currently the town's best catcher, and being funny enough—a ham, as Maddie had just put it. And his being a math nerd was another oddity of his character, but not an ostracizing one. Indeed, his human composition contained the same quirky panoply of thises and thats as everyone else's in Wells. And since it was such a small place, with the same kids in his class year after year, everyone knew all the parts of him, except the one he used all his other parts to hide. The one he feared would become his only identity marker once known. He'd be just a faggy dancer then, or worse, just a fag.

"I'm not a ham when I dance." By that he meant he was his fullest self then, or trying to be, which was more serious than people knew.

Just then they heard a car pull up and Maddie instantly squashed her plate, lifted the wet clay, and dropped it into a canister beside the wedging table. Without missing a beat—they'd done this twice before—Ian rose from the tub, re-covered it with the wooden plank, and without speaking the two moved Maddie's mother's drying pots (a bowl and two mugs) back onto it. Maddie wiped the wheel clean before she washed her hands. They were about to leave when Maddie opened a cabinet, grabbed a can of Lysol, and began spraying the room. "I think my mother knows what we do. I think so, but maybe not." She left the window open a crack.

"Let me spray you too," she told Ian, who spun full circle as she did.

On two earlier occasions when he'd returned home from Maddie's reeking of pot and Lysol his mother had believed him when he told her the smell was wet clay. "It's pottery," he said then, months ago, his wackadoodle-clean mother instantly alert to anything malodorous, including him. Now, to Maddie, he said, with as much shame as regret, "My mother doesn't have a clue."

WHEN IAN ARRIVED HOME ABOUT an hour later the expansiveness he'd felt while in Middle Haddam instantly shrank. It had been there, a fullness he felt in his gut, even as Maddie had driven him home, talking the whole time about Gandhi. It was there, too, when Maddie stopped the car beside his home, her hands still gripping the steering wheel exactly as she'd recently been taught, her commentary—she was already as much the professor as her dad—over for now. They had waited before leaving her home, chomping Fritos while coming down from their mild high. But Ian knew as they approached the center of Wells that his stomach was filled less with chips than with hope. Maybe he really could tell Maddie about Jase, he thought as he said a warm goodbye.

But once he was inside, the noise of TV hitting him even before he saw his mother sitting on the couch, absorbed by *Jeopardy!*, the friendly signals from his gut receded and his spine straightened, his body's alert system kicking in. Home was a place to be loved but also to be careful, his body knew. On the coffee table before his mother were two sandwiches from the Topaqua Grill; those, along with a house salad, would be their dinner. His mother had stopped cooking when she became a lunch chef, complaining—reasonably, it always seemed—that even the thought of preparing food after a day at the Grill was too much. On *Jeopardy!* a woman with hair the same rusty red as his mother's bet on the game's Daily Double. His mother told the woman, "Go big. Go big." For a few seconds the sound of the TV blared until, like magic, his ears adjusted, and it sounded normal.

His mother's engagement with the show allowed him to call hello and then dart into the bathroom for a shower, where he scrubbed off any of the wrong smells he'd carried in. He knew that messes, even funny smells, could get his mother going like nothing else. Years ago, about the same time that his mother had taken up dancing, she'd also taken up cleaning, and she could get aggressive in her insistence on order. "You never know when a social worker might knock on the door," she said sometimes by way of explanation, referencing an old scare. But that incident had come to nothing, Ian had been told, except for her relentless vacuuming, dusting, mopping, and polishing. His role was to lay low and keep anything important—the one remaining photo he had of his father, for example—hidden in the farthest corner of his bedroom closet, a place even she would never go. For all the technical challenges ballet presented, the greatest dance in Ian's life was in fact the daily one with his mother, and for every step she took toward him he had learned how to take one, gracefully, away. When he joined her some minutes after he'd showered, reeking only of Ivory soap, he, too, urged the redheaded contestant to "go for it" in Final Jeopardy. His mother nodded. When the woman lost, they groaned in unison. "I was so hoping," his mother said, then added, "Reuben night," as she pointed at the still-wrapped sandwiches. "Good choice," he told her, though in fact she'd brought home Reubens the night before and two nights last week.

After they'd eaten and cleaned up, they regrouped on the couch. He didn't have homework. Maddie was right; the load at school was light. Like Maddie, he could read a book of his choice. Or he could go to bed, start in early on his nightly dive under the four blankets he used in winter, where these days each time he thought about Jase Moretti he'd overheat in an instant. He could do that but chose instead to stay with his mother, who began to switch channels. "Feel like a movie?" she asked.

"You decide," he said, glad when she threw her arm around him. He felt good then. Safe. And satiated by the Reuben, which turned out to be a fine dinner. For a moment his mind looped back to his last thought before leaving Maddie, of telling her about Jase, about himself, and he wondered, glancing at his mother, if the loose thread had finally found its needle. He leaned closer. Got something to tell you, he almost said. She settled on an old western that didn't interest him, but he stayed anyway. Finally, realizing he wouldn't say what he longed to—that doing so was risky, foolhardy, and, in so many ways, *messy*—he instead said goodnight.

"Everything okay?" she asked, surprised when he abruptly rose. She stood too and put a hand to his forehead, soon declaring, her voice alarmed, "You're a touch off."

He nodded, looking at her face—the roundness of it, the funny feather earrings she often wore, an everyday familiarity that reminded him of the fact that they knew each other if not perfectly then well enough. Probably as well as anyone knew another person, he figured. Despite her concern she smiled warmly, which meant as much as anything that she loved him, still loved him. She didn't mind that he was a fag. She didn't mind, he silently reasoned, because she didn't know.

He was a touch off, Ian wanted to tell her but didn't. So many touches off.

THE NEXT MORNING, AFTER RIDDING himself of the sinking feeling, he ate a quick breakfast and set off for school. The day passed uneventfully except that he was quieter than usual. He didn't make jokes. He stopped taking notes halfway through history class. At lunch, sitting with Maddie and Phil Tuttle, Ian barely touched his sandwich as Maddie and Phil chatted, though Ian never grasped about what.

That afternoon, in the technique class he shared with Jase, he was likewise quiet. Over the last year Ian had often performed card tricks for Jase—a way to draw him close. Ian would practice ahead of time for hours to be sure he could pull them off and mostly he did, to Jase's consistent amazement. ("How'd you do that?" "If I tell you, it wouldn't be magic.") But this day, when Jase said, "Anything new? Any cards?" Ian simply shook his head.

Jase walked to the barre then and Ian followed. In silence the two worked through a series of exercises, slow tendu, fast tendu, et cetera. Angelina was in her office. Later, she joined them, selecting a Mozart concerto to work to, and she asked them to begin with turns across the room. Next she called for leaps, jetés, one foot to the next, then for more jumps, from two feet onto one foot, from one foot onto two feet. In the background, Mozart's flute concerto seemed too balanced, and it annoyed Ian. But when Angelina switched to Mozart's 40th, its anxious undercurrent settled him. During the break, the music off, the silence was momentarily strange, then calming, then awkward as it lingered, even after Angelina broke it by asking how Ian's day had gone. He shrugged. "Cat got your tongue?" Angelina finally asked.

Jase repeated the phrase. "Seriously," he added after another silent moment. He was striking, with eyes as dark as his hair and a searing look when he threw himself into leaps as he'd just done. Ian got a little crazed seeing that. The cat *had* got his tongue. But it hadn't always been this way. His first years at the Moretti School he'd enjoyed a simple comradery with Jase. Older by a year, Jase was the big brother Ian had always wanted. That was the case still when he was thirteen. But at fourteen Ian began to feel a charge around Jase, an energy he didn't understand except to know that he particularly craved Jase's closeness. That's when Ian took up card tricks, devoting entire weekends to perfecting them, insisting his mother be a stand-in audience as he rehearsed again and again. Earlier this year the energy took on definition, sexuality, Ian's body under his winter blankets making its longings clear.

Ian finally said, "Who's 'the cat'? 'The cat got your tongue.' Where'd that even come from?"

Jase smirked. Angelina laughed. "Welcome back," she said. "Where you been, hon?"

He shrugged. The rest of the class was more of the same, with different moves and finally stretching. Upon finishing, they threw on warmer clothes and got ready to leave, Angelina flicking off the studio's lights even before they were set to go. Outside it was dark, the downtown's few streetlights barely illuminating the scene. In the dim studio Ian stood briefly at a window, staring as cars slowly circled the roundabout before heading on.

Soon Jase joined Ian at the window. He looked out, saying nothing, the seriousness of his profile indicating boredom, perhaps, or maybe fatigue—a familiar inscrutability that reminded Ian that his failure to grasp a thing about Jase's feelings for him, even after so many classes and so many card tricks wooing him close, closer ("Pick a card, Jase, any card"), was just the truth of things. Jase was equally unreadable in partnering class with the ballerinas. Watching him hold the hand of one of the Moretti School's many ballerinas, Ian would wonder what Jase was feeling. Did he like the girl? Did he like girls? Or did he like boys? Did he like Ian?

(Pick me, pick me, pick me.)

AFTER SEEING ANGELINA AND JASE head off to Portland, Ian decided that rather than walk home, just minutes away, he'd go instead in the opposite direction, to Lake Topaqua. Once there, he bent low to feel the water, which was icing over in parts. He dangled his hand until it ached from the cold. Night had fully fallen. Cloud cover obstructed both starlight and moonlight and he found himself gazing out, but at nothing, really. The sound of waves lapping at the shore anchored him. In the darkness he sought that perennial sound, heeding it hungrily as he would the voice of a friend.

In the last two days he'd wanted to but hadn't told Maddie. And he likewise hadn't told his mother. And then he hadn't told Jase as they stood beside each other in the darkness at the studio window, which could have been a perfect time to ask, finally, "Do you know?" He could try again tomorrow with Maddie, he figured, but he soon sensed he was just going round and round with it.

He gathered some stones and flung them lakeward, uncertain in the darkness where they'd landed. "Son of a bitch!" he suddenly called, surprising himself, unsure to whom the words were directed. Then he resumed throwing rocks, this time in quicker succession, until, exhausted, he trudged home.

The next morning when he woke with the sinking feeling—which despite its predictability shocked him with a new, striking sense that in all ways he was entirely alone—he did the usual: rose, hopped, shivered, got going. But for the first time the heaviness didn't lift. After a brief return to bed, the weight of his four blankets a comfort, he dragged himself to school, arriving some forty minutes late, grateful that his first period class, which he'd all but missed, was only a study hall.

Maddie was there and glanced up as he dropped in the seat beside her.

"Hey," he said glumly.

"Hey," she answered, surprising him some, for her tone, strangely, was as grim as his.

FRIDAY, A FULL WEEK PAST THANKSGIVING OF 2000, JUDGE ARTHUR Cantrell—some three months before he would help Ruth Pearl rescue Ian Lima from Lake Topaqua—began his day, as he sometimes did, with an early morning walk. He lived on the outskirts of Middletown, in a section known as Wesleyan Hills. The housing developments there included an abundance of walking paths, trails he knew well from mornings like this, when he woke agitated and needed to relax. The day was bright and cool. He walked down a hill, under the branches of a pine, by any number of tall oaks and some marvelous weeping willows, and then into a clearing, the path now a straightaway that went past a lineup of houses. With each step, though, he grew not calmer but more apprehensive. He dreaded the meeting he'd soon attend featuring the newly divorced Jack and Stacy Byrnes, co-owners of a horse farm in nearby Moodus, a couple who, unable to manage the farm post-divorce as planned, were now suing each other anew over that. In that context they'd sought mediation, and Arthur, enrolled in Connecticut's Judicial ADR, an alternative dispute resolution program, took it on—but given his long friendship with Attorney Wilson Keller, counsel to Stacy Byrnes, he did so only after both parties had been informed of the relationship and given their permission. A first meeting, some weeks back, was a disaster, the dispute less about the farm than about the pair's lingering hate, with Stacy Byrnes calling Jack Byrnes "a selfish shit," "a disgusting pig," and "a cold-hearted monster," and Jack retorting, finally, "you always were a crafty bitch." Their lawyers couldn't contain them, nor could Arthur, who just minutes into the meeting wouldn't have been surprised if one stood up and shot the other dead. In the end he told them to leave his chambers and that if they were to meet again—he'd give them another chance to reach a settlement—he'd duct tape their mouths shut if he had to. "Or do you want to go to trial and waste even more time and money?" His question had quieted the former couple at last.

As Arthur walked on, his ears growing colder, his thoughts turned to Willa Fletcher, who of late also made him anxious. He'd begun dating Willa earlier that fall even though he'd told himself seven years ago, when he was thirty-eight, that he wouldn't date again. Willa—an attorney he'd met that past August at a meet and greet of the Middlesex County bar, a small woman standing near a doorway, endlessly scanning the room as if waiting for a specific person—had ultimately seemed as alone as he was. On their first date he'd taken her to Fiore, an Italian restaurant on Main Street in Middletown, and because she talked readily about her previous law practices, in Hartford and before that in Windsor Locks, the evening passed enjoyably enough. She had an eye for detail: the hilarity of a certain judge's nose twitching right before he'd blow his stack, the poignancy of a senior partner's hair falling out as his wife grappled with cancer. Her habit of laughing at herself amused him too. "Oops," she said several times, chuckling, as she heated up when describing the manic Hartford traffic and then the exhaustion of her recent move to Middletown. For their second date they went to Luigi's, another Italian restaurant on Main Street. Middletown, heavily Italian-American, was as dense with Italian food as it was with Catholic churches. Discussing this, Arthur mentioned that his family was also Catholic, although from France: his father—as a young man, before Arthur was born—had come to America after he'd bankrupted the family business, a small hotel they'd owned in Bordeaux for four generations. "The family treasure," Arthur said. Willa's American lineage went back to the *Mayflower*. "Fact is, I'm a card-carrying member of The Mayflower Society," she said, and then explained how the group preserved the Pilgrims' history, tracked descendants, "and whatnot." When he thought about their dinner later that evening, the memory of her attentiveness, a kind of eagerness, as well as her proclivity for saying "and whatnot," made him smile. He didn't mind, then, that soon she began to phone him, and frequently. The calls could have seemed like too much, but in fact the near-daily chat was a balm to a loneliness he hadn't dared in the longest time allow himself to feel.

The fall passed, then, with near-weekly meals out and then with meals in, and even before Thanksgiving of 2000 (which he celebrated with a law school pal in Boston) he knew Willa was ready for the next step of spending nights together. Just before the holiday, in the dimness of the evening lighting at Luigi's, she'd even suggested as much, but then threw in a quick, "Oops. No pressure." She followed that with her light laugh, a form of self-rebuke he'd come to know. But he did feel pressured, and on his walk that morning, almost home, his dismay about her comment mixed with his dread of facing the acrimonious Jack and Stacy Byrnes. His gut sank, a familiar plunge that had started in his childhood when he would witness his father's all-too-common tirades and his mother's subsequent silent retreats. *What's the point, anyway?* he'd finally asked himself about romantic relationships. For the last seven years he'd let that question be a kind of answer. When he arrived home that day, he whipped open his front door and then slammed it, hard, behind him.

BY NINE THAT MORNING HE was in his chambers. He was dressed carefully, as always: a pressed shirt, shoes swiped clean. Even a bad mood wouldn't keep him from his meticulous habits. *You never know* was the motto he lived by. You never know when someone might not take you seriously because you have a spot on your shirt or mud on your shoe. You never know when someone could turn on you, on a dime, as his father had done so often. You never know what could trigger someone's rage, but you could try to anticipate as best you could and be careful about absolutely everything.

Another habit: starting each workday by reviewing his calendar while sitting at his conference table, which was round and oak. It was a simple furnishing, and he'd had an immediate affinity for it when he found it years ago at a junk shop he sometimes visited off Route

66 in nearby Wells. There, inside an old barn, he occasionally liked to hunt for something to fix up and use, and one Saturday he'd spotted the table in an unlit back corner. It had a cracked and uneven leg, and most of its top was covered with stacks of musty sheet music, the rest with dust. The table seemed forgotten there, useless, even lonely, and Arthur had felt drawn to it. Once he'd climbed over the boxes to inspect it further, he saw a handwritten sign taped to its edge: *damaged goods; free for the taking.*

He had it delivered to his home and put it first in his kitchen beside another wreck of a table he'd refurbished some years back, its pine planks skillfully sanded and stained. He dusted the new table, then took measurements to make a new leg. His workshop was in his garage, but for now, he figured, he'd leave the new, forlorn table in the kitchen where it could find fellowship with the rehabilitated pine table. Objects, he sometimes thought, had lives too—beating hearts and complex souls. In the last few years this feel for nursing broken things had given him a satisfaction almost equal to that of practicing law. He'd gone to Yale, graduating fifth in his class, and while his knack for legal reasoning had served him well enough, with time he'd come to sense that there was a need in life to get your hands dirty too. Once Arthur had fixed the junk shop's table, he moved it to his judicial chambers, where its modest and still-fragile presence reminded him of the professional principles that he aspired to keep: that everyone was equal under the law, that the loudest voice didn't win the argument, that the little guy—with a broken leg, say, and a dust-covered past—deserved to be heard. If every day the world offered its familiar stories of justice denied or justice delayed, at least in his own courtroom and chambers he could try to do better.

There at the table—a kind of sanctum—he arrived at a sense of calm, the very serenity that his morning's walk never achieved. But at nine-thirty, when Jack and Stacy Byrnes arrived, with their lawyers, the peacefulness dissipated. "Let's get to it," Arthur said, sighing, without hope.

But they did get to it, agreeing after some forty minutes of debate between the attorneys, in which each party refused to buy out the other, that they'd keep the horse farm. Its value was good. And time would see it improve further. Wilson Keller clinched the deal by characterizing the farm as a veritable gold mine. "A solid investment," he then said, reviewing the valuation figures again. But to jointly run it—which had become impossible post-divorce, with bills unpaid and their trusted veterinarian therefore quitting—the couple had to cooperate or get out of each other's way. "Can't really get along," Stacy Byrnes said, in a tone just snarly enough to inspire another argument. But before Jack Byrnes could reply Arthur leapt in, lauding Stacy's realism. "These things take time," Arthur said, speaking of the inevitable aftermath of a divorce, and everyone nodded. A schedule was then set up for caretaking—to be sure the two never physically overlapped at the farm—and for making payments to a general fund. A manager would handle bills and serve as a go-between. Leaning across the table, the deal set for drafting an agreement, Stacy and Jack shook hands.

"But isn't this stupid?" Stacy suddenly said, holding her former husband's hand a moment before letting it go.

No one replied. Arthur grew tense, uncertain if she would continue.

"It just seems sad," Stacy finally added. She stood up to go but not before she'd grown teary. "Our marriage was once a solid investment. A gold mine. And now look at us."

She sat again. She wiped her eyes. "Are we done?" When Arthur told her yes, she said to her former husband, sorrowfully, "Well, then, that's it. Have a good life"—a comment to which Jack Byrnes, whose head was hanging low, could only nod in response.

The meeting, then, wasn't bitter but tender, and as Arthur held the door to his chambers open while everyone filed out, he gently patted the shoulders of Jack and Stacy Byrnes who, in their sudden grief, needed comfort.

"Judge Cantrell," Stacy said. "Everyone told us if you couldn't help us then no one could."

"Not sure I did anything," Arthur replied.

"Two meetings. Above and beyond. And a good scolding." Stacy paused. "You must think we're idiots."

He'd certainly thought that, but not any longer. "Best wishes," he said, shaking her hand, to which she replied, simply, "Bye now."

Once they'd left, he sat again at the conference table. Satisfied, he patted the tabletop as if it, too, had helped to resolve the conflict. He felt a small tug then to call Willa Fletcher, who'd left four phone messages about a week ago. He'd left one in return, promising to call soon but, undecided about what to say, he hadn't yet. *What's the point?* he asked himself next, stifling the impulse to reach out to her. He picked up the moist tissue Stacy Byrnes had used and threw it out. Then he went to his desk, opened the next file, and got to work.

THAT EVENING HE PLAYED BASKETBALL at the YMCA with Wilson Keller, and because it was a professional matter between them, they didn't talk about the small miracle, as Arthur saw it, of the horse farm settlement, except when Wilson remarked, "That farm is their baby. Joint custody. Makes sense how it turned out." Wilson, as always, played basketball aggressively, and Arthur defensively in the face of that, but he was good at defensive play. That was the game of his life. That he was two inches taller than Wilson helped. So far that night he'd won four consecutive rebounds as the ball ricocheted from the rim after a missed shot.

They stopped for a moment and Wilson said he thought the Byrneses' divorce settlement—not the farm but everything else—hadn't resulted in an equitable split of their assets.

Arthur looked down and saw drops of his own sweat on the basketball court floor. He dribbled the ball a bit. Wilson's comments were making him uneasy. "Not possible. Can't talk about it." He was speaking about judicial ethics, the rule that he could talk about a matter before him only with both parties present, never just one.

"But the divorce is over, and that part of it wasn't your matter," Wilson said. "Not asking for anything. Just on my mind."

"Nope, nope. Not possible. And you never know what's going to happen with them next. For all we know today's agreement won't work and they'll be back."

Wilson nodded, then affectionately slapped Arthur's back. "Good man," he said.

Arthur passed the ball Wilson's way, giving him the next shot, which Wilson took quickly, a long one that swooshed nicely as it went through the net. They both enjoyed the success of it, whooping in unison. Then it was Arthur's turn. He shot the ball and it teetered on the rim after circling it in its entirety. Finally it dropped outside the rim.

"Was sure you had it," Wilson said.

"You never know," Arthur replied.

HOME AGAIN THAT EVENING, ARTHUR heated soup, sliced a block of cheese, and ate at the kitchen table unaccompanied by the radio, which was not how he usually had his meal. Nor did he pick up the newspaper. Rather, he sat in silence, which highlighted his solitude. It felt neither good nor bad but was just what it was: a reality. A grand quietness. When the dishes were done, he pulled out his trombone, began to assemble it and, in doing so, realized for the first time that in his entire adult life no one else had ever heard him play.

The trombone held so many secrets, Arthur thought as he attached the slide to the bell. That it was particularly suited to the sad songs of life, the ones Arthur was often moved to play in the evenings, was a thing unknown—perhaps *the* thing unknown—about the awkward hunk of brass. He had been gifted it after surviving a bout of rheumatic fever that had him bedridden for a year when he was eight. Upon his recovery, his father had thought the trombone to be appropriately celebratory. Boom, boom, oom-pah-pah. Et cetera. Looking back, it seemed ridiculous to expect his father, that failed hotelier, to see anything beyond the obvious. Still, it was the only useful thing his father had ever given him.

If I loved you, Arthur began, hearing the lyrics to the song as clearly as if the trombone were speaking. The words expressed a longing to talk freely to a beloved. He played the song through and as he did various people came to mind—his father, and the two women Arthur had dated before he'd decided to stop all that: Beth Tierns, quiet and thoughtful, someone he really could love, he'd thought, even as he parted ways with her, and Rachel Abbott, a Boston attorney he'd met at a conference, someone skilled and dedicated, and she'd thought the same about him. And now there was Willa Fletcher, eager for the next step in their fledgling relationship, despite having told him, "Oops. No pressure." *If I loved you. If.* A simple word that reminded him that the hardest thing about love was that you had to dare to love back. And he hadn't. Couldn't. He'd spared them, is what he'd reasoned each time he'd said goodbye to the women of his past, no matter their tears, no matter that in choosing not to love them he'd obviously hurt them. The song was different as applied to his father. *If I loved you,* he sometimes imagined his father, dead now some fourteen years, singing to him. But he never imagined singing the same words back. In a hallway closet Arthur had stashed an unopened box marked "To Arthur, with love." His mother, just before her death two years ago, had given him the box, claiming his father had written the words on it and had filled it with tokens of his affection, but Arthur knew from his mother's handwriting that that couldn't have been the case.

At ten o'clock he readied himself for bed. His routine was rote. First, he spread a towel over the bed's fitted sheet. Then, before changing into pajamas, he discarded his cotton shorts for a pair of disposable underwear designed for those with urinary incontinence. Diapers for grown-ups. It didn't happen often, his pissing in his sleep, but it happened enough to make the precautions worthwhile. *Let's face it, waking up to a wet puddle was the deepest humiliation of all,* he'd thought many times in the last dozen years since the problem—psychological, he'd discovered after seeing several urologists—had mysteriously re-emerged. It was a problem of his youth too, another reason, then, for his father to rage. As an adult, after the doctors found nothing physically wrong, Arthur began talk therapy, but it didn't stop the problem. So he'd hidden it. None of his lovers knew. He'd kept the women at bay, making love during the daytime only, never risking staying a full night. And then he'd just stopped the whole ordeal of dating. In doing so he packed away his desire, as if leaving it in storage for another time. As with the other women, he couldn't bring himself to tell Willa Fletcher, now that the time for that had arrived. Throughout the Thanksgiving holiday, and in the week since, he'd tried to find the trust. Willa was small and wiry and even her smile, always tentative, spoke to a vulnerability within her.

Seeing that, Arthur had been thinking these last weeks that perhaps now was the time to make a different choice—to be honest.

The funny thing was that the people who showed up in his courtroom or chambers generally thought he was something. Stacy Byrnes's comment as she left was one he'd heard before. He was respected, he knew, but only because he was, in some basic way, unknown.

If I loved you, he still hummed quietly as he tossed in bed, tugging at his awkward underwear, then finally settling down before he reached over to click off the lamp.

A YEAR AND A HALF AFTER SOPHIA JACOBSEN HAD BEGUN, SO VERY EASILY, to fall in love with Aaron Taube, he suddenly disappeared from Amsterdam. By then—December of 1941—Sophia knew others who had also disappeared. Some months before, one of her schoolteachers, Mr. Flora, was fired, along with the other Jewish teachers, and in this way Isaac Flora was gone from her life. And then Dr. Cohen, whom her mother had spent a full week frantically trying to reach when their father began another bout of fierce coughing, was suddenly gone. This was a month after Sophia and Ruttie had seen the doctor and his wife on Sarphatistraat, trying to enter their favorite restaurant. But absences like these, jolting as they were, didn't stop Sophia from believing in a world that would someday, when the darkness lifted, brighten again. Patience was the key to everything good, she so often told Aaron, determined to remain hopeful. But then she lost him, without warning, and—just as Aaron had often said—nothing made sense anymore.

They had met in late January of 1940, though living just around the corner from each other in the streets near Oosterpark they might have met sooner. Aaron's family had come to Amsterdam in 1936, leaving Germany after the enactment of the alarming Nuremberg Race Laws, which excluded Jews from German citizenship. In Amsterdam, despite the proximity of their homes, Sophia and Aaron didn't cross paths until winter four years later, and this was in the midafternoon, a Sunday, in Oosterpark. In four months the Germans would invade the Netherlands, but the winter of 1940 was still what was considered in hindsight "normal time." The two were in separate schools then, enrolled in the same year, though Aaron was older than Sophia by ten months. Their different schools explained why they hadn't met sooner, or so they concluded when they finally did become friends. In Oosterpark that day Sophia was walking with Ruttie. In the cold, they were rushing along, but they nevertheless stopped, briefly, to observe the pond, Sophia stepping onto the ice, testing its firmness despite the fact that others were on it. Just as she did Aaron walked past and called to her, oddly, to watch out. But she knew she was safe: many people were on the ice. As she turned his way, wondering why he'd called out, two small girls skated into her, crashing. The children fell, and Sophia nearly did too.

"I can manage," she told Aaron, who, along with Ruttie, had rushed over to help. Her balance recovered, Sophia smoothed her coat where the girls had run into her. Meanwhile the boy, Aaron, who had reached for her, stepped quickly back. She looked at him, but he looked at the ground as if embarrassed. The children who'd fallen had risen and dashed off. For a moment Sophia, Aaron, and Ruttie stood watching them.

Sophia turned to Aaron to thank him, which seemed to embarrass him more. He wore glasses and held a book in the gloved hand that had not reached for her. They introduced themselves. "Aaron Taube," she said, repeating his name. She was almost fifteen and popular with the boys at school, though uninterested in any she knew. But this boy, so very shy, already seemed different, his concern for her clearly an act of generosity rather than a game played for attention. Stepping toward him she noticed that his book was about the galaxies in the night sky. A good topic, she thought, but, as she'd tell Ruttie when they watched Aaron go, "a little serious."

It turned out that Aaron Taube was known for his knack for the sciences. It was Ruttie's friend Henny Ganz who reported the news two weeks later. The girls were huddled outside their apartment building,

Ruttie and Henny playing a quick game of hopscotch before they got too cold, the squares scratched into the packed snow, while Sophia watched. Ruttie told Henny about the boy who'd tried to warn Sophia at the pond in Oosterpark. "But he just confused me," Sophia added, "and I never saw what was coming." She and Ruttie laughed. When Ruttie told Henny the boy's name, Henny said, "Aaron's brilliant at biology and chemistry. My mother knows his mother. Everyone thinks he's going to be a doctor. His mother says it's his destiny." Henny giggled upon saying *destiny*, which was too momentous an idea for someone so young, Sophia concluded.

But it was indeed destiny, Sophia decided some three weeks later, that brought her and Aaron together again. It was a Tuesday evening and she'd gone to the Apollohal, where she was practicing her technique in between the skating lessons she had there: the one on Monday focusing on back crossovers, the one coming up on Thursday focusing on spins. Her father had been willing to pay for the lessons, though money was tight. "I'll sell an extra stone or two," he'd told her mother, who had questioned the expense. But it was the Jacobsens' way that the parents wanted what, within reason, their girls wanted, and Sophia had gotten her cherished lessons. She had promised that Ruttie would learn everything she learned, making the expenditure—for a total of ten lessons—even more worthwhile. And so Ruttie was there too, trailing Sophia, often mirroring her.

Aaron Taube was simply skating, going round and round by himself, his head turned down as if he were reading something printed on the ice. Sophia, recognizing him, and curious now about him, deliberately bumped into his side. Instantly they were holding each other up, grasping each other's arms. Aaron quickly apologized as if the accident were his doing. Shaking her head, she told him her name again. "I remember. Sophia," he said, which quietly delighted her. She pulled away and spun as fast as she could manage, flirting by way of performing, something she already knew that Aaron, as unpretentious as his wooden runners, would never do. She felt stupid about it even before she intentionally slowed. When it was over, she almost fell from dizziness but didn't. She merely wobbled, feebly. All the while Aaron simply stood there, watching, his expression the same concerned one she'd seen the day they met.

"I'm practicing," she told him, and he nodded.

She left him for a time and rejoined Ruttie, near the rink's center. But after a time Sophia again sidled up to Aaron, who was circling the rink. It took a moment for him to glance at her but when he did she was glad to see him gently smile. "Done practicing?" he asked, and she nodded.

Aaron had come that night with a friend, but he'd left sooner than Aaron, who stayed on once Sophia appeared again. With Ruttie in tow, they traveled home that evening together, and that's how they realized how near they lived to each other. "I could have known you sooner," Sophia lamented to Aaron as they parted.

"That makes no sense," he answered, laughing, and walked off.

"I could have known you sooner!" she called more loudly, into the darkness, and he called back, "But that makes no sense, Sophia. No sense at all."

In the next weeks, Aaron began visiting Sophia at home—to help her with homework, he'd say, though her family knew otherwise, taking in the muffled giggles that transpired as the two sat on the sofa, looking more at each other than at whatever books lay open on their laps. Before that winter passed, they'd skated at the Apollohal rink again, gliding side by side, and once they skated on the pond in Oosterpark in the same way, just inches from each other. When spring arrived, they bicycled in the streets of Amsterdam, sometimes well into the evening, the daylight holding as it did. Aaron was a coffee drinker and sometimes they stopped at a café, lingering there, which was a new activity for Sophia—excitingly grown up. Weeks later, when the Germans invaded in early May, they did what everyone did—kept inside, kept quiet—and for over a month, despite living so near, they didn't see each other. But the world hadn't come to an end with the new occupation, and in the summer they felt the return of enough normalcy to bicycle outside the city, eventually resting in a nearby field. For hours they would lie side by side, though still not touching. It was on one of these trips, in early July, that Sophia wondered if the contentment she felt in Aaron's presence, a joyful calm, was what people meant when they spoke of love. She didn't ask Aaron, though. Instead, she initiated that old game with the clouds—seeing images, comparing them—talking about nothing until Aaron, sitting upright again, reported that his mother had recovered since attempting to end her life upon the German takeover those weeks back. Recently his mother had begun to leave her bed and to manage the household again. Neither Aaron, an only child, nor his father blamed the woman for despairing, Aaron told Sophia, who already knew about the suicide attempt but not about the recovery. Sophia sat up too, listening as Aaron explained how so many in their Jewish world had reacted to the invasion by attempting suicide or succeeding at it. "Nothing makes sense," Aaron concluded, and Sophia answered by taking his hand.

In the next months Sophia became a consoling presence to Aaron's mother, sitting near her while they both knitted socks and mittens, sometimes brushing and braiding the woman's hair, which in her recovery was still often in tangles. Sometimes Sophia prepared the evening meal while Mrs. Taube, often tired, sat nearby, at the kitchen table, offering directions and sipping tea. Aaron caught up on his studies then, and Sophia was glad to see that. What Henny Ganz had once reported about Aaron—his knack for the sciences—was unquestionable. By early 1941 Sophia had begun to think of the Taube home as hers, its oddities familiar at last: the blaring chimes of the grandfather clock, the piercing screech of the teakettle, the narrowness of the four rooms, the hand-knit wrist cuffs Mrs. Taube wore, hiding her scars.

That spring when Sophia and Aaron resumed bicycling, they again rode outside the city. As the weeks passed and summer set in, they stayed away for longer stretches, passing time by resting in the haven of a grassy field, far from the city's rising tensions. Sometimes they talked, sometimes they didn't. Sometimes as they nibbled a picnic of bread and cheese, the nourishment simple but satisfying, it could feel to Sophia like any old day. When they traveled Aaron always had a book with him, and she brought knitting along or sometimes a sketch pad. But just breathing air, she came to see, was its own worthwhile pursuit. "Take a deep breath," she once told Aaron on an August afternoon, bright and cloudless. He'd just dropped the book he was reading to tell her that his mother was once again on edge. "Take another," Sophia said, and soon they reclined, stared at the endless blue above, and Aaron took to counting their deliberate breaths. They'd gotten as far as fifty-two when he stopped, going silent. "You there?" he asked after a time. "Eighty-seven," Sophia answered, which struck them both as hilarious. For a minute they lost their breath, laughing.

In the fall of 1941—Sophia now sixteen—she and Aaron were suddenly in school together after a new law mandated that Jewish students be schooled separately from non-Jews. Sophia and Aaron were already stunned to find themselves banned that fall from going to concerts, restaurants, and even libraries when they were barred from going to their schools too. By necessity, then, they'd parted ways with their classmates and teachers and found solace in walking to and from the new Jewish lyceum together, often touching elbows. Then, finally, Aaron kissed her. This was after school, a Wednesday in mid-October, while they sat on a bench just outside of Oosterpark. She'd waited so long for his physical affection, though she knew that he loved her—didn't need the kisses to know. But when they arrived, in such a fury of passion, she knew even more. They then sat for a time, leaning shoulder to shoulder, and she wondered if he felt as dazed as she did. The kissing did that, spun the world that much faster. When it was time to go, she stood then quickly sat again. "Everything's different now," she said, and Aaron, apparently thinking she meant something else, replied, "It'll come back to us, this world. I know it will."

The world's goodness may have been dissolving, bit by bit, but Sophia and Aaron grew closer, the door to physical passion now opened, their bodies ever more charged. Over the next month they took to finding private spaces in their neighborhood to touch, kiss, and finally—venturing to South Amsterdam, a neighborhood now filled with German Jews, above the pharmacy that Aaron's father ran—to lie down atop their coats in an empty storage closet. Their first time there Sophia began to disrobe but Aaron rebuttoned her blouse. "Not yet," he said protectively. Then he sneezed, an awkwardness that made them laugh almost too loudly. Even in the dimness of where they lay, she could see how beautiful he looked, his glasses off, his hair askew, his eyes momentarily closed.

Sophia wanted to tell Ruttie about what was happening—that open door and the new reality beyond it—but Ruttie was only fourteen, and the world between fourteen and sixteen, Sophia knew, was as wide a distance as that between sun and moon. That fall, then, Sophia often stood mute in front of Ruttie and would simply shake her sister by the shoulders and laugh into Ruttie's lovely but stupefied face. Sophia understood the confusion. Even she was baffled by the arrival of so much joy, and just when the worry all around was exploding. But external circumstances didn't have to limit her desire for Aaron, she came to believe. "They can't ban us from falling in love," is how she put her argument to Ruttie.

Aaron, too, clutched at optimism. He would still go to the university, he told Sophia one evening in early November, his head on her belly, his eyes gazing at the cracked ceiling of the storage closet they took to frequenting after his father's pharmacy had closed for the day. By then they did this routinely, on Friday evenings, pretending they were going to shul to welcome in Shabbos. They'd suddenly become, to their families' surprise, just a touch religious. He'd go to the university, if not next year then soon, and he would in fact study to become a doctor, just as planned. Nothing was going to change that. He wanted to be everyone's doctor, a general practitioner, for he longed to cure it all, he insisted, to heal the city's abundant maladies. "It's a sick place," Aaron insisted, not for the first time. And that's how they acknowledged what was happening beyond the bubble of their love. "Sick, yes," Sophia agreed. "But we're well, Aaron. We're even better than well," she told him, leaning over to brush her nose against his forehead.

In December Sophia had to deliver an oral report at school, and she chose to talk about the Dutch athlete Rie Mastenbroek, a queen of the 1936 Olympics, who swam her way to an astonishing three gold medals and one silver. A week before the report was due Aaron helped Sophia prepare, listening as she practiced delivering it. Rie Mastenbroek was poor, Sophia explained. The year after her great wins she'd had to earn money and did so by becoming a swim instructor, which meant she couldn't compete again as this changed her status from amateur athlete to professional. "See? There's a thousand ways in which life isn't fair," Sophia concluded, and Aaron, moved, said, "Yes, a thousand ways."

Wednesday, the third week in December, the day the report was due, Sophia woke early. She'd washed her hair the night before and in the morning chose to wear it down rather than twisted on her head. The new hairstyle matched her sense of being already grown up. She may have been only sixteen, but she felt married, at least in the way that mattered most. In the confines of the storage closet at the pharmacy she and Aaron had pledged themselves to each other for all time. And because of that love she knew with surety who she was from head to toe. She waited for Aaron that morning inside the entrance of her apartment building, but when he didn't arrive she assumed he had a cold or fever, and she rushed out on her own. At school her report went well; everyone, it seemed, felt for the plight of Rie Mastenbroek. After school, Sophia stopped by Aaron's home, and when no one answered the door she still wasn't concerned. His mother might be napping; she'd seen that many times. And Aaron could get lost in his reading or perhaps was out just then. She spent that afternoon with Ruttie, daringly sipping several cups of tea and baking sugar cookies—despite the rationing of tea, flour, and sugar. Though they made but a tiny batch Sophia urged Ruttie to eat as much as she wanted. "Forget the world!" Sophia joyfully shouted. The day, then, was in fact a good one, even celebratory. But Sophia's anxiety set in the next day, Thursday, when once again Aaron didn't show up for school. She waited for him as always at her apartment building, then decided to stop by his building. There, she rang and rang to no avail. She began to feel it then, a sickness in her stomach, a tightening in her throat. "Hello!" she called, peering into his family's first-floor window, only to see darkened rooms. She rushed off then, convincing herself she'd find him at school, sitting as always at a desk two rows behind hers. But like the day before his desk was vacant.

All day she stared at that desk. Turned from it. Stared again. Once she thought she saw him at it, working equations, his brow familiarly furrowed. But the vision was a memory. Soon, the empty desk, a physical reality, came back into focus.

School over, she returned to his apartment, staring again into the street-side windows. The grandfather clock in the living room ticked loudly, as always, and finally chimed on the hour. Aside from that, though, she heard only silence. No lights were on, nor did anyone move about. She didn't bother to knock or call hello; the emptiness within was a certainty.

That night her father explained that several weeks back non-Dutch Jews—who were mainly Jewish refugees from Germany, like the Taubes—had been ordered to register for what the Germans called "voluntary emigration." Sophia nodded; she'd heard about that at school. The Taubes might have complied, her father guessed. What he knew with more certainty was the order's effect: panic and more suicides within the Jewish community generally as people sensed they could be "asked" to leave next. "*Voluntary*," her father said contemptuously. "But maybe Aaron's father thought it was a way out. A chance. I met the man not long ago. He could see the writing on the wall, he said. Just like when they knew they had to leave Germany."

She could see the writing on the wall too. *Sophia and Aaron*, the words said.

"But why didn't Aaron tell me?" Sophia asked her father.

"It's risky for others to know. Perhaps he didn't even know until his father told him."

"But if they left, where did they go?" Sophia pressed her head against her father's chest.

"A refugee camp, perhaps," her father answered, holding her. He was thinking of Westerbork, a camp built a few years ago to house German-Jewish refugees, but quickly realized that now, with the country under German rule, it was likely no place to go. He paused, then said, "Or maybe freedom. Maybe they found their way out of the Netherlands, out of Europe." Her father shook his head before adding, "I'm sure they're fine, Sophia, fine." But because of the way he held her, more firmly, she knew that wherever Aaron and his family had gone they were not fine. She knew that her father, too, saw the writing on the wall.

JUST ONCE AFTER AARON'S DISAPPEARANCE did Sophia return to their nook in Aaron's father's pharmacy. This was two weeks later, a Friday afternoon, a day she'd spent at home in bed, nursed by her mother, rather than at school. There, yet another student that week had failed to show up. Sophia had begged her mother for a reprieve from seeing the two vacant desks and her mother had nodded, then had brought her tea as she lay in bed. But late in the day Sophia felt compelled to journey out, to sneak her way up the staircase in the pharmacy—now run by a stranger—and sit in the empty closet, door shut, where she and Aaron used to hold each other. She spoke to Aaron, deliberately rattling on, telling him that they were not caged by circumstances nor were they actually apart. She sensed that indeed her words were reaching him, wherever he was. Still, she wept and wept.

ON FRIDAY, WHICH WAS THE EIGHTH OF DECEMBER, 2000, RUTH PEARL was home, inside her lakeside bungalow, drinking a calming chamomile tea and reading the latest decision on the still-undecided Florida presidential vote, *Albert Gore, Jr. v. Katherine Harris*. The decision, she hoped, would distract her from her dismay about the construction next door. Earlier that week a foundation had been laid and the first wall had started to go up. Even on this day, Friday, when she'd arrived home from work, Bill Cousins had been at it, hammering away, which added to her exhaustion from not having slept through a single night that week.

But when the hammering finally stopped, she ate her evening toast and some yogurt and then sat in the wingback chair in her upstairs living room, the light from the lamp beside the chair aimed at the pages of the decision, which she'd printed before leaving work. Her feet ached from the pacing she'd done the hour before, frantically walking from room to room while the hammering banged, and now she rested both feet on a small footstool covered with an embroidery of her mother's—a simplified map of Amsterdam, the Amstel River a central feature in a deep, pretty blue. As always, the stool made her feet feel better, as if they were actually dangling in the river's cool waters. Ruth felt even more soothed upon reading the Florida Supreme Court's decision that votes in various Florida counties must be recounted. It was the principle of the ruling that so consoled her. She even called Stephanie to read to her from the majority opinion: "The right to vote is the right to participate; it is also the right to speak, but more importantly the right to be heard." Before heading to bed Ruth read the passage again, then placed the opinion in her expandable file marked *Good*. But the opinion, in the end, was little comfort. That night, like the ones before, she couldn't sleep.

The next day, despite being Saturday, was quiet, no hammering, and yet she paced as if Bill Cousins was at it nevertheless. That night her dreams—where she ran senselessly from path to path in Oosterpark, not seen since childhood—had her waking more than once in a fit of terror.

Because of that dread, which carried into her waking hours, it was almost predictable to Ruth when she read the next day that the U.S. Supreme Court had stopped the recount—and then, three days later, Tuesday night, when she heard that the Court had reversed the Florida opinion. Such a downturn seemed foretold by her dreams. The recount in Florida was over; the voices of any remaining voters still needing to be heard had been hushed. "But the right to vote is the right to participate," Ruth said aloud, startling herself. She read *Bush v. Gore* throughout the next afternoon even though she was at work. They were all reading it—Wilson Keller, Gene D'Orrino, and her.

When she arrived home, just after dusk, the hammering next door was ongoing, and she went downstairs to her kitchen to watch her neighbor, Bill Cousins, helped by his son, make headway on the renovation there was no local law to stop. For now, Ruth's view of the lake remained intact, but something inside her nevertheless unraveled.

"Stephie," she said when she called her an hour later. "It's happening again. This time it really is." She described the hammering, the sleepless nights, the bad dreams, and even the legal opinion, which foreclosed the possibility of recounting the votes. As she did, she stared at her neighbor, Bill Cousins, building his wall.

"Mamma, this is America," Stephanie answered, firmly, as she'd done before. "You have to believe me, nothing like that can happen here."

Meanwhile, the hammering next door continued.

3

Netherlands, January 27, 1941, Regulation on the Procedures Involving the Registration of Jews: Jews = J. Bastard Jews = B. Bastards are subdivided into B1 (two Jewish grandparents) and B2 (one Jewish grandparent).

ON WEDNESDAY MORNING STEPHANIE PEARL heard commotion in the hallway of the Girls to Women Education Fund. The night before, the Supreme Court had decided *Bush v. Gore*, and quickly all the talk in the office turned to that. Everyone there, a group of ten, commented even as they stood spellbound before the little TV in the office kitchen, crowding around it, eager to hear one pundit's thoughts after the next. All day the TV droned. Yet Stephanie found herself staying away from the matter as best she could. In the late morning, she grabbed some coffee and then quickly fled the scene. Later, she chose to eat her lunch outside, sitting on a bench in the park at Dupont Circle. It was almost too cold for that, but she sat there anyway, nibbling an apple and watching people walk past. All the while she was fighting an urge she'd had all day to talk to her ex, Freddy Taylor, and the intensity of the desire, combined with the energy it took to resist it, had her keeping to herself. Already that morning she'd picked up the phone twice but had not followed through. A third time she'd actually dialed Freddy's home number, assuming it hadn't changed, but just then Thea Basa knocked on her door. She'd come with another small gift, a cotton scarf, and though Stephanie shook her head at the offer, she was nevertheless appreciative of the timeliness of the interruption. Mistake aborted. "It's just a little something," Thea said, handing it to her. "Thea, you mustn't," Stephanie said, as she had of the other gifts Thea had most recently offered: gourmet coffee and a box of note cards. "I'm just grateful," Thea replied. Stephanie wanted to tell Thea that she could relax, was doing great, that the gifts were lovely but not called for, but she instead said nothing. She simply looked at the scarf, a lush jade green, and fought a new urge—to drop her face into the soft fabric. By the time she looked up Thea had gone.

It was confusing, this sudden, gnawing desire to hear Freddy's voice. But Stephanie hadn't been the same person since learning on election night that Freddy had already married someone else—just eight months after their nearly eight years together, during every one of which she believed he loved her as much as she did him. Even their breakup hadn't convinced her that Freddy was truly gone from her life. Despite what she'd said to Rona she'd remained secretly hopeful for his return. But the news of his marriage made their parting a permanent reality. After that, her grief, now fully felt, had intensified almost daily, as if it were a snowball rolling down a steep wintery incline, taking on unstoppable momentum and heft. Rather than recovering from the shock, she was suffering all the more from it, and on this day, even as she finished her small lunch and gathered herself up, rising from the bench in the park at Dupont Circle, another round of anguished desire to hear Freddy ensnared her. For a moment, looking northward, she thought she saw him just entering the park, an average-sized man in a dark coat and sunglasses, walking fast, angling toward Massachusetts Avenue, and she cleared her throat as if they would of course begin a long talk. But as the man neared, she saw that he was no one she knew. She left the park then, hustling away from downtown, up Connecticut Avenue, after some minutes reaching Kalorama, where she crossed a lengthy bridge into the neighborhood of Woodley Park. She continued up Connecticut Avenue to the next neighborhood, Cleveland Park, then, some minutes later, crossed the intersection of Van Ness Street, and finally arrived at her apartment building at Connecticut and Albemarle. The walk was long and steadily uphill, and once inside her apartment she kicked off her shoes, called in sick, and went to bed. That evening, when her mother phoned, anxious about both the Supreme Court decision and the construction next door, Stephanie was still in her bed, not trusting herself to do anything all day beyond lying there, staring at the walls and ceiling. She was clearly not well, and it had taken some gumption—she realized when the phone call with her mother ended—to find the words to reassure her that everything would be okay.

The next day at work Stephanie focused on catching up, and the busyness deflected the still-pressing impulse to call Freddy. After work she chose to walk home again, the physicality of the long walk the day before having done her good. This walk, too, had its benefits. As she crossed the bridge between Kalorama and Woodley Park, a stretch that soared high above the land below, the height was intoxicating and she momentarily forgot she'd lost everything. But the rest of the walk was just time passing. A body moving. Storefronts and apartment buildings to glance at in passing. Something to do that was not staring at a phone.

On Friday morning she did call Freddy. He'd be at work, she figured. All she wanted was the sound of his voice on his answering machine, not actual conversation. But Freddy in fact picked up and she instantly disconnected. For some time after, pacing in her office, the word *stupid* rolled in her mind.

She was still at it—*stupid, stupid*—when Thea came by again, this time with an idea to pitch. GTW, she began, could start an internship program for their scholarship students. The internships, which she hoped to land at the National Museum of Women in the Arts, would be educational and practical, helping with job placement. Thea, sitting across from Stephanie, recalled her internship with GTW the summer before she attended Georgetown. "And voila," she said, "here I am."

Stephanie sighed tiredly, which had nothing to do with what Thea had just said.

But Thea didn't know that. "Stupid?" she asked.

"Don't say that," Stephanie answered, though *stupid* was still what she was telling herself. She tapped a pen on her desktop. "It's a good idea," she finally told Thea, who broke into a huge smile. But then Thea yawned, deeply, in a way that Stephanie had seen before. "We're not working you too hard, are we?"

"I love this job." Thea's tone was both earnest and anxious. She walked to the door, then turned back to Stephanie. "I'm trying to be like you."

Stephanie glanced at her silent phone. Clearly, she needed to tape a note on it reading, *Stop. Just stop.* She shook her head.

Then she yawned, which caused Thea to reactively yawn again, which had them staring at each other and, momentarily, laughing.

LATER THAT AFTERNOON STEPHANIE, IGNORING her own warning, dialed Freddy again, this time getting his machine. "Fred here. Or not here, actually . . ." Hearing that brief greeting was supposed to satiate her craving for his voice, but it only made her hungrier. She dialed again, listened, hung up, then did that three times more.

On Saturday Stephanie drove to Freddy's neighborhood and looked for him. He lived in an old and beautifully renovated apartment building on the corner of Wisconsin and Massachusetts Avenues. His apartment was at the back of the building, which made it a quiet place despite the outside traffic. She'd always liked it there for that reason. Often on Saturday nights they would cook and then watch a movie. The day would have been spent slowly dreaming up dinner, buying the ingredients, napping, making love, then finally cooking. She could see herself there as she sat in her car, parked on Garfield Street, which ran along one side of Freddy's building. She'd parked there a thousand times before. She kept the heat on and waited, hoping to catch a glance of Freddy—as he took a morning walk, perhaps. After a time, she moved her car to 38th Street, behind the building. She knew how unlikely it would be for him to pass by, yet she remained there until, bored, she got out and walked around the block, then around again. Finally, she drove off, a mindlessness seizing her. On Wisconsin Avenue, she unwittingly passed the turn onto Albemarle Street to go home, then she passed Military Road, an alternative route. Soon she was beyond the District line and into Bethesda, where she finally turned onto Walsh Street, then traveled a few blocks until the sight of Rona's familiar house awakened her from her dream state. A child's bicycle was parked outside near the front door and inside a kitchen light shone. How she'd arrived at Rona's she couldn't say, though she'd had moments like that before, when, driving in a trance, she'd simply arrived—and always, strangely enough, safely. She had things to tell Rona, she realized, staring at her house, like how sorry she was about their stupid argument, not to mention how crazy she'd been since hearing on election night about Freddy's betrayal and marriage, and then there was the election mess itself. Stephanie could almost hear Rona say, "Hanging chads? Can you believe it?"

But Rona was sick of hearing about Freddy, Stephanie knew, and to say even more would likely provoke a sad look of pity or perhaps another reminder that there were other men out there. "But something's broken," Stephanie almost said out loud in her own defense. Just then the light in Rona's kitchen went off. The front door opened. Rona's husband and oldest child, Hannah, walked toward the sedan parked in the driveway. As Stephanie started her ignition again and pulled out, she watched Hannah gently pat the seat of her bicycle as she passed it.

IT WAS ALREADY PAST ONE in the afternoon when Stephanie arrived back at her apartment. She threw off her coat and shoes and dropped onto her bed. For a time, she sobbed. Upon rising to use the bathroom she couldn't help but see herself in the mirror over the sink, and the sight of her own wretchedness shocked her. It struck her then to cover the mirror. She grabbed a cotton scarf and masking tape to do so, then grabbed several more scarves, including the jade green one Thea had just given her, and covered the full-length mirror in her bedroom. She then lay on her bed, feeling more protected than she had in weeks. Being unable to see herself was freeing too: in the next moment she went at it—wailing into a stack of pillows—more wildly than before.

Several rounds of crying later, she recalled Rona describing the Jewish custom of covering mirrors following a loved one's death, and Stephanie wondered if the first people to ever cover a mirror knew what she now knew, that grief could feel just this bottomless. Before bed, brushing her teeth in front of a scarf-covered mirror, Stephanie considered that. And how kind the custom seemed. Because no one needed to see themselves like this, shattered yet shattering again.

HOW DO YOU FALL OUT of love? Stephanie asked herself this the next morning as she sat in her car in the Safeway parking lot, unable for a time to open the car door and get to it. She asked the question many times that week, showing up at work promptly at nine, leaving at seven, but what she did in the hours in between she couldn't be sure of except for persistently wondering, *How? How do I do it?* She stared at a lot of paper. She fiddled with her phone cord. She attended several meetings—including one where Thea successfully presented her internship idea—at each gathering maintaining her composure only to lose it afterward behind her closed office door. She sat in the GTW kitchen once, sipping tea, Thea across from her silently radiating an empathy that Stephanie breathed in, like much-needed oxygen. "Whatever it is," Thea said after a time, rising to leave, "it's going to get better." Stephanie nodded and stayed in the kitchen for some time alone until their office administrator, Aileen, walked in for her daily dose of *All My Children*. "You mind?" Aileen asked, and Stephanie shook her head. Numbly she watched the show, grasping none of it, then stayed until the program's end even though Aileen had long ago left to resume her work.

How do you fall out of love? she asked the old pine tree at the Bishop's Garden behind the National Cathedral. She'd gone there on Saturday morning. Only days before Christmas, but not so cold outside, she sat on a bench and simply stared. No more, she eventually told herself. No more would she duck from the truth that Freddy was gone. That she'd been a fool about that was as clear, suddenly, as the cloudless sky.

She drove home from the Cathedral slowly, down Massachusetts Avenue, then turning at the corner of 34th Street. Heading north, she glanced mindlessly at the familiar sites, the St. Albans tennis courts and a row of attractive houses. Once home, she went to bed. She thought of calling her mother but then thought better of it. She wouldn't find the comfort she longed for, that was a certainty. But maybe she could find it, just as her mother had for so long, by staring at something naturally beautiful, like Lake Topaqua. It made sense suddenly, the solace, for one's very survival, of a good view.

"Is the wall any taller?" she asked her mother moments later.

"A little." Her mother's voice was flat but not neutral. "Already it blocks the view. But only some for now, and just from downstairs in the kitchen."

"Did you ever talk to Bill Cousins?"

"But there's no law."

"I know, Mamma, but you can still talk to him."

"But why would he listen to me?"

"I should have said something. I'm sorry. I've been"—Stephanie sat upright—"distracted. I'll come next week."

"But you need the force of law, Stephie."

"Not always. I'll try. Worth a try, right?"

"If you say so," her mother said in that same flat voice.

"Mamma, could you go out and have a look for me?"

"A look? I'm looking right now."

"What do you see?"

"I see the lake. Ice and banks of trees, and those two islands. Several ice fishermen."

"That's good to hear." Stephanie adjusted her pillows. Her world wasn't ending, she knew, but her mother's might as well be. "I'll talk to Bill Cousins when I come up next, Mamma," she said.

◊

Four months later, in April 2001, Stephanie spent her third day in Amsterdam "finding the Holocaust," as she put it, which turned out to be easy to spot. First she visited the Anne Frank House, waiting in the ticket line for just over an hour to get in, and then she went to the Jewish Historical Museum, and then, not far from there, in a park, to a memorial for victims of Auschwitz, where so many Dutch Jews were murdered. The monument looked like a large, shattered mirror inlaid in the ground of the park, which bordered the city's old Jewish section. Staring at the brokenness, Stephanie considered that her mother and grandparents might very well have perished at Auschwitz if they hadn't fled in the nick of time. The very wonder of her birth hit her next. The day was a comfortable temperature, the sun in and out, and once she'd examined the memorial she sat for a long time near it. Earlier, at the Anne Frank House, the ordinariness of the girl's diary, covered in a common plaid, had pierced her heart, but not as much as the well of silence—holy silence, she'd felt—within the hidden annex despite how many tourists wandered the cramped rooms with her. On a bench by the Auschwitz memorial she took that in.

Later, on her way to her hotel, she stopped at a market and bought a bundle of pink tulips to liven up her hotel room. She bought a vase too, but upon returning to her room she saw she'd bought more than she realized, some forty odd flowers, more than the vase could hold. She made more vases by cutting off the tops of several plastic water bottles. Soon tulips were everywhere: beside her bed, on the room's desktop, even in the bathroom on the sink's ledge.

The flowers comforted her as she continued absorbing her day. As the evening came on, a racket outside kicked up; to drown it out she turned on the TV but soon tired of news from the BBC, the only program in English she found. She ate her dinner then, salad and cheese, while watching the sunset, far later than she'd ever experienced. The noise outside finally quieted. In the dark, the mass of tulips beside her bed took on a strange, even ominous shape, and she moved them away. For a moment everything scared her: the memories of the day's sights, the new darkness, even the deep quiet of her hotel room, despite having longed for just that all evening. In the morning, her heart heavy, she placed a group of tulips in the shower. She'd never done that before—bathed with flowers—and the sight of them lifted her spirits. Soon she felt ready for the day, another spent walking on haunted streets. But she could do that, she figured, and she could buy another batch of forty tulips too, if necessary, at the day's end, because if she'd learned anything the night before it was that if she were going to do what she was here to do she needed her room to be a sanctuary, her own *Mokum*, and it turned out that filling it with far too many tulips did the trick.

◊

THE NIGHT OF THE SUPREME COURT RULING BILL COUSINS GOT READY for bed before the news was reported. But earlier some smaller news had reached him by way of two phone calls. The first was from Missy Lima, who rented from his parents; she was phoning about a clogged bathtub drain. He told her that he'd get to it in the morning, but once he hung up he realized that adding Missy to his list of appointments—he was a plumber—meant rising that much earlier. He then apologized to his wife, Ellen, for setting the morning alarm for an even earlier hour. But he didn't want to leave people in the lurch with the holiday coming. He was almost asleep when the second call came—his father complaining of an upset stomach. Supper had been another of his mother's recent bizarre concoctions: sautéed liver with beets and mustard. Bill advised his father to chew an antacid tablet or two. "Maybe three," he added, sighing. Two nights earlier his mother had served cottage cheese slathered with sardines. The truth was his mother was losing her marbles, feeding her family nonsense. And Bill knew his father could never say no to his mother—about a meal she'd made or anything else. By building the extra room for his parents Bill hoped to put an end to the late-night phone calls and the stomachaches. Even Ellen agreed that, given the number of oddities of late, the renovation made sense.

The next morning Bill rose before sunrise. He showered, made enough coffee for himself and Ellen, and entered his workday routine: spreading peanut butter and jelly onto bread for the kids' school lunches, then peeking in on them, calling gently to the three to get up. His twin girls, eleven years old, didn't budge in their bunk beds until he called again, louder. Nancy, on the top bunk, finally told him to "please shut up, *please*," which was how he knew he'd gotten through.

He brought Ellen coffee to sip in bed. He was about to wake his boy, Rich, thirteen years old and the deepest sleeper of them all, but Rich was already stretching, surprisingly awake. "Going to your shitty job, Dad?" he asked, loudly so they'd all hear. The girls cracked up. They loved that joke. Sometimes Bill grabbed a plunger and stood before his children, which made the joke even better. This morning, rushed, he did not. Now that the sun had risen, he could see that the day was gray, the lake and sky a monochrome. He made himself a stack of bologna sandwiches, poured a thermos of coffee, and hit the road. It was only then, turning from Lake Road toward Wells's downtown, the gray cloud cover growing denser, that he felt the dread that hit him lately whenever he neared his parents' home.

Minutes later he parked just past his parents' house on Barton Hill. He grabbed his equipment and went inside where, ever since the house had been turned into two apartments, a closed-off foyer served as the entrance to both homes. A stairway ahead led to Missy Lima's place, and his parents' front door was to his right. He stopped and breathed deeply, preparing to see them, not sure what he'd find. A week ago, his mother, who'd been ironing, had nearly burned through a tablecloth when she'd left the iron face down on it while she'd gone to the bathroom. Three weeks back, his father had handed him a book to return to the town library, five years overdue. "Finally done," his father had said, which was not what he'd said of the unsightly stack of newspapers piled in a corner of the living room. The home of Bill's youth—the foyer open, the upstairs housing their bedrooms—had been orderly and clean. His mother, who had run that home, did so impeccably, with a competence that in more contemporary times would have taken her far in a career. Bill had told her that once, when she was fifty-three and he was eighteen. "But you're my career," she'd said firmly. "And, by the way, I like my career," she'd added, turning her back to him. He never said such a stupid thing to her again. Last week, after he and his mother had taken care of the burned tablecloth, throwing it in the sink, he'd sat with her for a long time, both of them silent, the late afternoon light dimming all the while, until they had found themselves in the dark.

Now, he balked at entering his parents' world. Instead, he headed upstairs; Missy Lima, in a bulky bathrobe, let him in. Her boy, Ian, was eating at the kitchen table and nodded at Bill. "What's up, pal?" Bill called. Missy then thanked him before he'd even done anything. "Let's get to it," Bill said.

"Can't thank you enough," Missy said yet again when he finished, the tub's drain cleared. She offered coffee but he declined.

"Seen my parents lately?" he asked her.

"I see that they're home. But I haven't seen them personally in a bit. Everything okay?"

Bill nodded. He had reached the door when Missy said, "Your mother did me such a favor all those years ago. You've no idea. She really did."

He assumed she meant his mother having rented Missy the apartment, which she'd stayed in all these years. Bill looked around. He and his brother used to play tag in the area that served as Missy's living room. In the summer, they used to climb through their bedroom window onto the roof at night and either howl like coyotes or hoot like owls. Their mother was the stricter parent, but even she made room for the rooftop jaunts.

"Glad to hear my mother helped."

"Sure did. She's a straight shooter. I like that," Missy said.

DOWNSTAIRS, BILL STOOD ONCE AGAIN in front of his parents' door but, as before, he didn't knock. Instead, he rushed to his van, got the heat going inside it, then simply sat there, much as he had with his mother the week before, in silence, doing nothing. After a time, he lifted a sandwich and then put it down. He looked from his parents' house to the road, then back to the house. Some fifteen minutes passed before he reluctantly left the van again. During the short walk to the house the day seemed to be getting colder. In the foyer, chilled, he knocked, despite the key in his pocket, so as not to startle them.

Inside, the TV was on, but it was silent. His father, wearing underwear and a cardigan sweater, sat reading the *Hartford Courant* rather than watching the screen. His mother, who'd let Bill in, wore a robe and slippers. Her thin hair was askew. On the stove something bubbled over, and Bill ran to it, turning the heat down on a pot of oatmeal. "I know," his mother said when he looked at her, concerned. "I would have turned it down already, but you showed up. Nothing's burned. See?" He'd indeed overreacted. He apologized.

It was nearing eight in the morning. There was no need for his parents to be dressed for the day this early, but he wished it were so. Seeing his father in his underwear particularly disturbed him. "What is this?" he asked the man, who said, "Retirement, son. This is retirement, full steam."

But he didn't find the sight of his father, gangly legs exposed, and his mother, shuffling in her big slippers, funny. "Come on, now. You two get dressed and we'll have breakfast together." Bill stirred the oatmeal as his parents left agreeably, even obediently, for their bedroom. Their compliance rattled him. They'd once had all the authority in the world over his life and he missed it suddenly, the fullness of their being. His father had been the fun one, a juggler, easily swayed to perform for his young sons. In his work life he was a gifted carpenter and had built much of their home furniture, including the table Bill now sat at, waiting for his parents' return. A few minutes later they emerged, dressed in pants and sweaters. His mother's hair was combed, his father's face shaved. His mother had even put on lipstick, and Bill smiled to see that.

As his parents settled themselves at the table Bill turned the TV off, then reached for the newspaper, its headlines noting the election results. He glanced at a photo of Bush, a man not that much older than Bill, soon to take on the troubles of the entire world. "Godspeed," he muttered, thinking it was nuts to want a job like that. He folded the paper and then flicked on the kitchen radio. Music of yesteryear wafted forth—a big band, clarinets and trombones. Played quietly, the music soothed, and he kept it on. While his parents had dressed, he'd made coffee and set the table. They now thanked him for the pleasant surprise of his visit. They loved the oatmeal he'd made, his mother said.

"But you made it," he corrected.

"Whatever." She smiled at him. "You always ate two bowls, which is why I made so much."

The comment didn't make sense—she had no idea he'd show up—but Bill didn't mind. They ate contentedly, not talking, the food as comforting as the big band sounds. Perhaps in the time remaining before they moved in with him he'd do this more often, he thought, helping himself to more oatmeal, which he liked as much as his mother had claimed. He would come by, make them breakfast, eat with the bands of yesteryear going in the background, get them off to a good start. Bill was glad to hear his father hum along to "Begin the Beguine" and then, more heartily, to "Stardust," crooned by Nat King Cole. His father then showed Bill a drawing of shelving he would make, starting that afternoon. Bill poured his parents cups of coffee and then sat back, relaxing finally. Perhaps the push to get them into his house, that tiny bungalow, didn't need to be so pressing, he reflected, feeling his own fatigue at the extra effort of late. Besides, in the cold weather, progress on the addition was nearly impossible anyway.

As he took his first sips of coffee, envisioning them enjoying more breakfasts, his mother pulled the sugar bowl near and began to add to her small cup one then two then three then four then five teaspoons of sugar. At six, Bill reached for her spoon, pulled it from her fingers and spilled sugar on the table as he did. Then he grabbed her cup and threw the over-sweetened coffee down the sink drain. After pouring her a fresh cup, he added one teaspoon of sugar and a drop of milk, the way he knew she liked it. He removed the sugar bowl from the table and then swept up the spilled crystals. All the while his parents sat still, watching him. When the table was clean again, they resumed eating. But his father no longer sang. And his mother sipped her coffee without comment. When her upper lip quivered, Bill grabbed her hand. "It's all right," he said. "Everyone likes sugar." He checked his watch then and was glad to see he had to go.

◊

THAT NIGHT WILLA FLETCHER ATTENDED HER THIRD POTTERY CLASS AT the Wesleyan Potters studio in Middletown. Earlier that fall she'd discovered the place, a plain brick building, by driving past it on her way to and from work. She'd finally asked someone about it and had learned that it was a craft cooperative for making pottery, but also for making silver jewelry and for weaving. Upon stopping by she'd been taken with the earthy scent of wet clay and had signed up for a class. That was in late October, when she'd still been hopeful—her relationship with Arthur Cantrell going well, a slow but steady progression, and her recent move from Hartford to Middletown seemingly a sound one. Some years back, by moving from Windsor Locks to Hartford, she'd put Husband Number One, as she'd quickly renamed him, behind her, and by moving from Hartford to Middletown she'd done the same with Husband Number Two. But now that Arthur was clearly dumping her—by way of blowing her off, not returning her calls—she doubted that her moves marked any progress.

She took that sense of self-defeat to the pottery class. Even before that night she'd learned that she wasn't good at making pottery, a confusing discovery given how simple it appeared to be: slapping a blob of clay on a wheel, wetting your fingers before you pressed in, specifically with your thumbs, and then pulling up the clay surrounding the indentation. But she pulled too determinedly, she was told. That night, her teacher, Kate Brent, watched Willa's attempt to shape the simplest of objects, a small bowl. "You don't have to do it all," Kate said after a time. "With just a little nudge the clay will help you. Willa, you're holding on too tight. You're getting in the way." Those last words, which echoed those of Husband Number One when he was packing to leave, unnerved Willa. She didn't get them then, or now. But she nodded anyway. Then she squished the nascent bowl back into nothing. It was hopeless, she figured, so she'd start again.

Later, on her fifth attempt at the same bowl, she stopped and looked up. All evening she'd barely noticed the others around her. Her pottery wheel was in a cluster of wheels on one side of the studio. The students were all women. Several were talking, their wheels stopped, and as Willa tuned in, she heard, "Doesn't matter how I look. How bad I dress. My boss needs a touch at least once weekly. I try to avoid him, but I can't." The speaker sat two wheels away.

Another woman, behind Willa, then said, "Following long weekends my supervisor—sixty years old, paunchy, long-married—comes into my office, no knocking, to ask if I've gotten lucky over the weekend. Meaning, did I have sex. 'Ha, ha, ha,' he then laughs. To which I want to say, *So lucky I didn't see you*. But what I do say is, 'Ha, ha, ha,' until he leaves."

The group then laughed in the reflexive way the woman did to get rid of the man.

"If you don't laugh, they say, 'There's a gal who needs to get laid.' And *that* comes with a laugh." Kate Brent, their teacher, said that, surprising Willa. Until then she'd talked only of pottery.

The group agreed that no one wanted to be known as the one who needed to get laid. The key was not to draw attention to yourself, and *ha ha ha* did the trick. As if born with it, they all knew that quick fix. The stories continued. One woman had been asked out by her supervisor, declined, asked out again, declined, asked out yet again, then lost the better work assignments. "That was it. I just quit," she said. "I was a librarian. And I liked my job. I had to change fields when I couldn't find another job as a librarian."

"That's called harassment." Willa's voice surprised even her. "That shouldn't have happened to you. And you and you," she said, pointing.

She rose, washed her hands, then raced to fetch her business cards. "Sexual harassment in the workplace is a legal matter," she said, moving from wheel to wheel. "If you need help just call."

The women thanked her, and one by one they got back to their pottery making. The wheels, again, were spinning. The various bowls took shape. Even Willa's. Without even trying, it seemed, and just like she'd been told, the clay, more than Willa, had done its thing.

HAVING FINALLY MADE A BOWL, and even some possible business connections, Willa left the class a little lighter than when she'd arrived.

Perhaps it didn't matter, then, she decided as she drove home, that just a month ago, still so very confident about Arthur, she'd thrown out the old love letters from both her ex-husbands, letters she'd kept in a shoebox upon which she'd written *Proof: Of Love.* In the last year she'd opened the shoebox only occasionally anyway, she'd figured, unfolding random letters when her doubts resurfaced and she needed evidence to remember she'd truly been loved, if only for a time. But when Arthur began to date her over the summer, spending long evenings with her at local restaurants and then at her home dinner table, talking, just talking, and then, eventually, kissing her briefly goodbye, it seemed to Willa that her need for such proof was finally a thing of the past. The way she and Arthur moved ever so cautiously forward was the gradual, steady courtship she'd always longed for. "Call you soon," Arthur would invariably say as he left her, and though she was the one more likely to phone he was consistently happy to hear from her. All fall the constancy of their courtship was a balm, calming Willa's jittery soul. After just six weeks of dating Willa felt like herself suddenly: competent at law, good with her clients, solving their legal problems, even winning a small civil trial—a contracts matter—and with that, beginning to make a name for herself within the Middlesex County bar. In October, when the elderly widow who lived in the townhouse next to Willa's, Mrs. Rizzo, whose eyes were weakening with macular degeneration, mentioned that she could no longer read newspaper print, Willa, feeling generous, told her, "Let me read to you. Sundays, after church?" "You're better than God," Mrs. Rizzo said, clasping Willa's hand.

Willa and Arthur lived on opposite sides of Middletown, and throughout that fall they'd sometimes meet on Main Street for a meal out. He liked Italian, though his family was French, his parents having immigrated hastily, he had told her, running from money problems. She liked anything. Whatever he liked. Her family had arrived here by way of the *Mayflower,* umpteen generations ago. She couldn't even count that high, she had quipped early on to Arthur. They were two months along when she told him that the reason she ate so little was simply habit. Her parents, and probably their parents, were drinkers, and food wasn't their focus. "Functioning alcoholics," she'd said, as she explained to Arthur the cause for her steadfast sobriety. "Well educated, well employed—both lawyers—the kind of people you'd never suspect, or maybe you would." She explained that her mother had died of pneumonia when Willa was twenty-four. She barely knew her stepmother, whom her father wed just ten months later. When Arthur told her, sympathetically, that she'd been dealt a difficult hand, she nodded, relaxed some. "I'm not like my parents," she insisted, except in that she, too, cared little for food, only ate to stay alive. In fact, some of her worst moments were connected to eating—her parents at each end of the dinner table, there but not there, her mother's eyes glazed, her father silent. But after telling Arthur that she ate only to stay alive, she'd said, "Just kidding," to assuage his startled look. They were at his kitchen table halfway through a meal. It was late October then. Earlier that evening, on a walk, Arthur had told her about a matter he had agreed to mediate—a dispute over a horse farm—but the hostility between the owners, recently divorced, kept getting in the way. He didn't talk about the legalities but about the couple, their insults, their lack of self-control. "The meeting was a shitstorm," he said, his laughter, as Willa experienced it, appealingly sad. He then spoke of his friend Wilson Keller, counsel for one of the parties, noting Wilson's goodness and how far back the two went—all the way to law school—an attachment that signaled something hopeful to Willa. She could trust Arthur, she sensed. They had walked before sunset, on various paths that ran through his neighborhood. Inside again, Arthur had made beef stew. After her awkward comment—that she ate only to stay alive—she lifted her fork, took a bite, and forced herself to chew slowly, actually tasting the meat. "Yum," she said, which was a new word for her. She smiled then, genuinely. By November she'd developed a passion for Mrs. Rizzo's ravioli with marinara sauce, something the woman offered her two Sundays in a row after the newspaper was read. By mid-month Willa craved pistachio ice cream too. Always a touch underweight, she could eat what she wanted and, feeling loved, she in fact wanted to eat. The week before Thanksgiving she stopped twice at Dunkin

Donuts on Washington Street, both times on her way back from her pottery class. She'd never thought of doing that before, but just seeing the place gave her hunger pangs. "I want a glazed one. *Really* want it!" she said to the boy behind the counter that second visit. That was the night, sugary donut in hand, when she'd thrown out the old shoebox containing the former husbands' letters, proof of love no longer a necessity. Though she'd been living in Middletown for only eight months, she'd finally landed in the right place, she'd thought then.

BUT ARRIVING HOME AFTER THE pottery class and seeing, yet again, no messages on her answering machine, she wanted the letters—the proof. In fact, she craved them. To distract herself, she knocked on Mrs. Rizzo's door, the afternoon paper, *The Middletown Press*, in hand. Whether Mrs. Rizzo's welcoming smile was for Willa or for the news was not clear, but it relieved Willa to see it. The two settled in matching armchairs, as was their custom. Mrs. Rizzo wore a familiar checked dress, and her gray curls were freshly combed. A bowl of peppermints sat on a table between them, and as Willa read to Mrs. Rizzo she popped mint after mint into her mouth. The advice column that day focused on how to say no, politely, to a wedding invitation. "Small potatoes," Mrs. Rizzo concluded about that. So Willa turned to bigger matters on the paper's front page, reading to her about the presidential election and the legal theories that put the matter, finally, to rest. Bush was now the winner. He'd lost the nation's popular vote but with Florida's vote decided in his favor he'd nevertheless won the electoral college.

Mrs. Rizzo asked Willa about the Court's decision, and Willa, reading to herself for a time, eventually said, "It wasn't unanimous. The majority thought that since Florida counties used different ways to count the votes the recount ordered the other day by Florida's Supreme Court violated the Constitution's Equal Protection Clause. So the Supreme Court stopped the recount." Willa then explained that the recount was exclusive to undervotes, 61,000, missed by machines.

Mrs. Rizzo frowned, thinking, then said, "Doesn't that make *all* the counting in Florida invalid? Wouldn't there have been differences between counties' voting practices this whole while?"

"Mrs. Rizzo, you're thinking like a Supreme Court justice," Willa said, looking up from the paper. "Or maybe better than one . . ." Reading on, Willa finally said, "I can't tell yet about your theory. I need the decision itself. But you're right, voting methods often vary from county to county, and in many states, not just Florida. And another oddity here is that disputes about elections, which are ruled by state law, are almost always left to state courts to decide. The majority's justices, especially, typically rule against stepping into state matters. Nor are those justices leaders in the world of equal protection claims. Justice Ruth Ginsburg, the one who is, and Justice Stevens, say this is baloney."

A minute later Willa reported that the four dissenters either disagreed that there was an equal protection problem or—in the case of two of them but not Justice Ginsburg—agreed that there was a problem with how the undervotes were being counted, but they also proposed a remedy: developing a statewide standard for tallying those votes and then adhering to it in a recount. "By proposing a remedy, the dissenters are at least willing to put their money where their mouths are," Willa concluded.

Mrs. Rizzo leaned forward. "You mean the other justices aren't sincere?"

"They're flipping on their judicial principles. So maybe they're not sincere. It's easy to say you stand for a new principle when you simultaneously shut down any chance to put it into action. If I'm reading this correctly, due to a timing issue the majority, while finding a problem, also found no time to remedy it. Which means they didn't have to walk the walk on their equal protection argument. But the two dissenters who agreed there was a problem, finding both a remedy *and* time to implement it, were willing to walk the walk *and* talk the talk. Their sincerity is more obvious, no?"

"But if the justices can make an insincere argument to get a result," Mrs. Rizzo said, still frowning, "then what is law?"

"All too often, I'm so sorry to say, it's people being people. That's what law is. Trust me."

Mrs. Rizzo grabbed more mints. "But integrity is everything."

Willa agreed. She promised to read the opinion and tell Mrs. Rizzo when she visited next where they got it right and where wrong. "But, goodness, we've had quite a talk. You ever think of law school, Mrs. Rizzo?" Willa's question was part tease, part compliment.

"Oh, for Christ's sake, in my day we thought of nothing, nothing. I'm a woman, Willa. A woman of a certain age." Mrs. Rizzo shook her head. Then she laughed to herself, and though Willa would have liked to ask her what was so funny, the moment was clearly a private one.

After that Mrs. Rizzo insisted that Willa have some minestrone soup, and Willa nodded, eager to stay distracted, away from her home phone. Mrs. Rizzo's small kitchen table abutted a wall, and for the next minutes the two sat—Mrs. Rizzo facing the wall, Willa at the table's end—sipping soup while Willa told Mrs. Rizzo about the stories of the women in her pottery class. "This is pretty depressing, this line of stories," Willa noted after a time. By then Mrs. Rizzo had stopped eating as she'd become more involved in Willa's news than anything the newspaper had offered, even about the election. "Surprising?" Willa finally said.

Mrs. Rizzo glanced at Willa then stared ahead, as if through the kitchen wall she faced. "No, Willa. Sadly, not surprising. Not at all."

They sat in silence for a moment. Mrs. Rizzo finally offered Willa more soup, which she took. She didn't realize that as she'd talked she'd also been eating steadily as she hadn't in weeks, the soup and its chef proof enough, as it turned out, of the existence, still, of some kind of love. At least that's how she saw it in the time after she arrived home, the women's stories still weighing on her but not as much as before, her phone still painfully silent but the urgency that it ring, right then, less pressing. Soon enough, she got to sleep.

WEEKS LATER, ON THE FIRST TUESDAY OF JANUARY 2001, IAN LIMA finished his morning routine of waking, hopping, shivering, and showering. The election news of late hadn't registered a lick for him—his political awakening wouldn't begin until he learned, much later, that weapons of mass destruction in Iraq didn't exist—and his routine, as usual, assuaged the sinking feeling. He then crawled into his bedroom closet, sat on the floor against its back wall, and pulled from an empty box of Fruit Loops the one photo he still had of his father. He'd last sought out the photo a year ago, after he and his mother had squabbled over his having stayed out too late at a New Year's party. There, he'd smoked his first joint, and though he hadn't felt high or even loopy he'd felt more adult. The next day, after his mother's tirade, he'd told her that she was going to have to get used to things being different. "I'm growing up," he'd said. But in the wake of what followed, a momentary estrangement from her—she'd finally walked off—he'd crawled into the closet, searching for his father. Just looking at the man in the photo, an old habit, was soothing.

Now, a year later, nothing besides the usual morning routine had yet happened to draw him toward the photo. But a New Year's resolution to finally tell Jase his feelings made him uneasy, especially since he'd be seeing Jase that afternoon, the first time since their holiday break. In the photo his father wore glasses and read the *Hartford Courant*. His hair was buzzed short. His T-shirt was tight and his chest and arms, though thin, looked firm. Settled into a kitchen chair, the newspaper spread before him on the table, he appeared content. Why he'd packed up to leave them not long after that very morning was anyone's guess. Had Ian cried too much as a baby? Did he wake them at night? Did his father want a girl and not a boy? Every time he'd asked, his mother had said no, no, and no. Ian liked to believe when he stared at the photo that his father had a snapshot of him, too, which he pulled out every so often. He liked to believe that his father still cared about him and would someday return. His father would do this after the understandably overwhelming event that had pulled him away had finally been resolved. Everything would make sense then. Even that morning Ian still thought this way, and he subsequently felt no anger toward his father, just mild confusion. "Do you still love me?" Ian asked the man in the photo. "Because I've always loved you."

Later that day, at the first rehearsal of the new year, Angelina

Moretti chose Ian over Jase to dance the central piece—a duet—of the spring performance, scheduled in mid-March. Ian thought she'd made a mistake. Jase was the better dancer and had landed the part last year, along with the same ballerina, Sarah Toms, who'd been assigned the female role again this year. They'd dance to Debussy's "Clair de lune," which, though only four and a half minutes long, was plenty to do. Angelina had choreographed the work, and the story the dancers would tell, as Angelina put it, was of young, blossoming love. The lovers knew next to nothing. That's when she'd looked at Ian and said, as if seeing him all too clearly, "You. You this year."

Even beyond the three lifts Angelina included, the male part was challenging, and that rehearsal and the next—no more classes until post-performance—it took Jase demonstrating the movements over and over for Ian to catch on. Perhaps it was jealousy on Jase's part that caused him to pace the perimeter of the dance studio, his eyes critically glued to Ian, while Ian and Sarah pretended to yearn for each other from afar and then finally join as partners. Whatever caused Jase's rapt attention, Ian was glad for it. It buoyed his hope that he could follow through on his plan, and he hoped, too, that once he told Jase his feelings they'd be returned. Ian knew he was at least well liked. He moved, then, with believable passion in those early rehearsals, willingly looking Sarah in the eye as he circled her, revved up by Jase, there in his peripheral vision.

Sarah, in turn, stared back, but with her mouth routinely upturned she often seemed ready to laugh. Ian didn't mind her cheer, but mid-rehearsal on Thursday, Angelina did. "Imagine he's the love of your life," she pleaded to Sarah, "not your favorite cousin!"

Repeatedly Ian and Sarah approached each other and finally touched, Ian taking Sarah's hand, holding the small of her back, lifting then spinning her, and, before they each dashed away, briefly embracing her. Sarah's lithe body was muscle-bound. Even after hours of rehearsal she never went to bed without doing one hundred sit-ups, fifty push-ups, and ten minutes of standing on her head. "For circulation," she told Ian that day, explaining the protracted headstands. They were on their first break. Sarah's mother had multiple sclerosis and walked with a cane, she told him next, then added of her own nightly routine, "It's preventative. Illness often gets passed down." Sarah's potentially doomed biological inheritance moved Ian. It wasn't attraction, but for the rest of the rehearsal when he felt her tight muscles something inside him warmed.

That afternoon Jase continued to scrutinize Ian, and he criticized too—"What are you thinking?" or "Stop thinking, too much thinking"—which Ian decided was okay. It meant Jase cared, at least about something. Still, it wasn't until the next rehearsal, on Tuesday of the following week, when the two finally caught each other's eye. Jase smiled then rather than frowned. He looked like the person Ian had tried umpteen card tricks on. But in the next moment Jase's face relaxed into its usual inscrutable expression.

Still, the smile was enough for Ian to decide that the bit of hope he still carried wasn't entirely nuts. "Like this?" he called to Jase a minute later, just as he deliberately flubbed up.

Jase was soon adjusting Ian's posture.

After that, Ian purposely stumbled. He let his back go slack. Once he almost dropped Sarah. But then he quickly caught her. Her potentially doomed inheritance. His reckless efforts. Jase wasn't even looking. "Sorry," he said, relieved when Sarah told him she was fine.

THE NEXT DAY HE HAD no rehearsal. At lunch he told Maddie he was free that afternoon and she promptly asked him over, looking up from Dostoevsky's *The Idiot* to do so. Over the holiday she'd chopped off her braid, cut her hair into a rough pixie, and dyed it bright blue. Her nails were painted black. Self-destruction, she had decided, made for good "nonviolent resistance" against her parents' ongoing pressure about her attending a private school. "Gandhi had it right. Do I look awful?"

They were in her living room by then. She looked weird, but not bad. "Super different," Ian said.

"But I'm shooting for awful," Maddie complained.

Maddie's mother was home, upstairs potting, so they settled downstairs. In the living room two couches faced each other and Maddie took one while Ian relaxed on the other. Maddie had brought *The Idiot,* and when Ian said, "I'm happy to hang," Maddie dove in. As before, being at Maddie's had a good effect on him. From upstairs, the pottery wheel hummed soothingly. Maddie had made tea, and its cinnamon smell, wafting from his cup, was equally pleasing. Ian stretched and sighed—apparently too loudly.

"My father's study is there," Maddie said in response, which is how he realized he'd been noisier than intended. She glanced toward the study. "Tons of books in there. Take what you want."

Entering the study, Ian flicked on its overhead light, then flicked it off, the brightness too much. He'd not been there before. He walked to a corner and turned on a standing lamp behind a leather reading chair, bathing the room in a contained, warm glow. Then, perusing the bookshelves—which were floor to ceiling on two sides of the room, with an attached ladder to reach the higher ones—Ian imagined what it must be like to have taken in this much of the world by way of reading. Most books were about some aspect of history, many on the Renaissance, the professor's specialty, yet there were novels and poetry collections too, and books on other subjects, like biographies. Ian even spotted Gandhi's autobiography, returned from Maddie. He pulled it out but soon another caught his eye, one about baseball, the summer of 1949 in particular, when the great batter Joe DiMaggio, a Yankee, met his match with an up-and-coming Red Sox player, Ted Williams. Intrigued, Ian took the book to the leather chair, lit by the lamp behind it. He began to read, slowly, then skipped forward until he hit a section of photographs. The gentle humming from the wheel upstairs continued. Just beyond the door to the study he could see Maddie, sprawled on her couch, occasionally turning a page. The day's light outside was fading, Ian noticed, which increased the cozy feeling he had there in the study, the lamp behind him an even more delicate glow, the leather chair that he sat in, cross-legged, worn and comfortable. The room was decidedly masculine, he noted, observing the dark tone of its wooden shelves, paneling, and desk, and the leather chair that he sat in that must have been a uniform mushroom tone at one point but was now variegated tones of brown, black, and gray. The messy spread of books and papers on the desktop was masculine too, Ian thought, at least compared to his mother's compulsive neatness. After a few minutes Ian stretched his legs out on an equally worn leather ottoman. He turned another page of the book and found a photo of DiMaggio gliding past home plate; he yawned, and soon he couldn't help but close his eyes. Just before he fell asleep, he sank deeper into the chair, resting his arms on each of its thick arms. *Dad?* he almost said out loud, the question seemingly invoked by the feel of the leather chair surrounding him, almost embracing him, and of the room itself.

Sometime later—he had no idea how long he'd slept—he rushed back to Maddie, who was still reading. A moment earlier he'd woken with the sinking feeling—for the first time experienced in the late afternoon. Before he sat again, he took a moment to hop and shake while Maddie watched, amused.

"Reading about me?" he asked, pointing to *The Idiot.*

She motioned to her chopped, blue hair. "No, about me," she answered sadly.

THE NEXT DAY AT REHEARSAL Angelina wanted to focus solely on Sarah's part, and together Angelina and Sarah took to the floor. The boys, Angelina said, should rest.

Jase, already resting, sat on the floor, his back against a mirrored wall, knees pulled to his chest. His expression was typical, sullen. Carefully, Ian sat beside him and pulled his knees up, mirroring Jase's posture. The two looked ahead until Ian, nervous, began scanning the room. Nothing about the two walls covered with mirrors, the barres, or the floor's openness was unusual. Still, he stared and stared.

Gradually, he straightened his legs, pretended to stretch, then wriggled closer to Jase. Quickly, he resumed the former posture: knees bent, head raised, eyes fixed ahead. Some quiet talk between Angelina and Sarah ensued, words he couldn't hear yet pretended to. He thought Jase did the same. Angelina was now taking Ian's part, leading Sarah through several pirouettes. She'd never spun so well. When she finished Ian whooped, and Jase joined him. When Ian turned Jase's way, Jase had already turned toward him. For a moment their eyes met, even lingered. When they turned away again, Ian slid another inch closer. The two were touching elbows then, slightly. Sarah continued to pirouette, her outstretched leg propelling her nicely, her newfound gracefulness reason enough for Ian to look ahead, feigning interest when the physical closeness with Jase was the thing consuming him. He didn't care if Jase didn't look his way this time, as long as he didn't move away. When Ian whooped again Jase lightly punched his shoulder.

"She's good," Jase said.

"She is."

Which wasn't much of a conversation. Nor was Jase's quick touch much of a gesture. Still, on the elusive yardstick of hope Ian allowed himself another inch.

ON THE FOLLOWING TUESDAY IAN would see Jase again, and he woke early, free for once of the sinking feeling. He was still hopeful and, momentarily, his head resting on his pillow, he allowed that hope to stretch endlessly, beyond an inch, beyond a yard, beyond two. Hope, if you could believe it, all the way to the moon. The sun hadn't yet risen, and his mother was still asleep. Before she woke, he dressed and left, rushing down Barton Hill, through an empty downtown and toward the lake. Once there, he stepped onto the ice, testing it. He stepped a bit farther then stopped when a sharp sound, like the crack of thunder, surprised him. The ice was breaking somewhere, he knew, but the sound was from far away. He moved tentatively forward, toward the lake's middle, and soon pushed off, as if skating. He glided farther out but stopped as he envisioned himself there with Jase. Circling the lake, they circled each other, a game. "Do you love me? Because I've always loved you," he said to Jase in his dream. He was about to repeat the words when another pop—the ice cracking yet again—jolted him from his fantasy. He slipped then, crashing on his tailbone.

He was sore as hell, he realized a moment later, hobbling toward home.

Six years later, in his senior year at UConn, he'd be hobbling just like that after getting jerked around by brutes one night after a rehearsal. He and another dancer had been taunted outside the theater—*hey queers*—and Ian had sprinted off, running for his life. Just yards from his dorm he tripped and fell. By then, though, no one was following him, and he rose slowly. He felt entirely alone. His dancing colleague, who was straight, had run too, but in a different direction. Inside his dorm room Ian sat at his desk. On it was an unopened letter from his father, which in time he picked up, staring at it as intensely as he'd just stared, in a stupefied daze, at the wall ahead of him. Starting in his junior year of college his father had been writing to him every so often. Ian never responded, a fury within him—something he didn't feel until the first letter arrived—blocking any impulse to write back. Still, on this night he longed to reach out, to say something to his father, though the man had written, as he typically did, just a few, trite words of hello. It was only in the first letter that he'd let Ian know that it was his "feelings for men" that had driven him so far from home. He'd been afraid to return, his father had said—afraid even of himself for a time, but he wasn't any longer. Times were changing and so was he. *Dear Dad,* Ian began. Then he crumpled the paper. *Dear Frank,* he tried next. Then, *Dear Mr. Lima,* and finally, *Dear Son of a Bitch.* That one felt good, and before he trashed it, giving up, he'd written, *I'm often afraid too.*

THAT DAY OF HIS FALL on the lake was a day of watching. At school Ian followed the slowly spiraling hands of various clocks. Twice he observed Maddie yawning, and once, clearly dying of boredom, she bit off her entire pencil eraser without knowing it. Seeing that, Ian began to think her father could be right about a different school. Later, at rehearsal, Ian did nothing but watch others; his tailbone was too sore for him to dance.

He sat against a wall, just as he and Jase had done the other day. Without moving he felt chilled, but he didn't want to get his jacket as he didn't want to disrupt the something—he didn't know how to put it—that was happening between Jase and Sarah. She seemed electrified by Jase's poise. Dancing in the strength of Jase's surety Sarah became sure too.

Seeing that, Ian ached worse than before. Soon he lay on his belly and stared at the floor, its thin coat of dust only noticeable with his face pressed this close. He turned toward the mirror next, only to see in it his odd face, round like his mother's, but with a more defined chin than hers, something he'd been told was like his father's, though in his one photo Ian didn't catch the resemblance.

By the time he turned again Sarah and Jase had stopped dancing. Angelina was talking to them, her arm falling across Jase's shoulders. She was probably giving the part, finally, to Jase. Sarah spoke to Jase too. His face was unusually easy to read. He was happy. Glad to be her partner. He squeezed her hand, smiled, and she smiled more.

Ian rose in pain. He wanted to hoof it home, but Angelina called his name, asking where he was going.

"Quick walk," he lied.

"Not yet. This is still rehearsal. A *still* rehearsal." She smiled, pleased with her cleverness.

Later, when Angelina and Jase drove him home, insisting he take the front seat, Ian resumed the watching he'd been at all day, seeing as they passed through the downtown that Ebbitt's Grocery needed a paint job, as did the decrepit package store. Angelina needed to get to the pharmacy before it closed, which took them up Main Street where they passed large houses that once might have been grand but tonight, at least, looked out of place and old. Wells was depressing, and he couldn't remember why he'd ever loved it. Jase didn't speak the whole drive, even when they waited while Angelina dashed into the drugstore. When Ian looked back, Jase continued to stare out a side window.

Finally, they dropped Ian off. Getting out, he groaned in pain, more emotional than physical. Another car, coming in the opposite direction, was just then passing, but still he stepped forward, something deep within him daring him on. He thought he heard a shriek as the passing car swerved around him. He hadn't jumped out of the way but had stood still, waiting.

Angelina was the one shrieking.

"I'm good," he called. Angelina, her car door open, was about to rush to him. He apologized and waved fervently until she retreated.

As he opened his front door, he prepared himself for another night of takeout and *Jeopardy! ("The ugliest town in Connecticut." "What is Wells, Alex?")*

But inside he found his mother absent—*errands in Middletown,* her note read—and without her company he never turned on the TV. Nor did he bother eating. He kept the lights off. For a long time he simply sat in the dark. He recalled, vaguely, the car that had nearly hit him and the ice that morning that had sounded like a shattering. He recalled that he'd walked toward the shattering rather than away from it, just as he'd walked onto Barton Hill, dimly aware that he and the oncoming car could very well collide. Jase might notice him then, he must have thought. He felt numb, remembering, as if those moments had happened years ago already, or as if he really had fallen through the ice that morning and was still frozen, though not in a way anyone could see. At eight or so he crawled into bed. He covered his entire body then, even his head, with his four heavy blankets. He sought sleep knowing that sometimes, like just that morning on the ice, dreams would give him what real life could not. But though he sought the dreams, his mind homed in on familiar ground: *Alex, I'll take Connecticut lakes for one thousand dollars. Alex, when is loving like death?*

In late December of 1941, three weeks after Aaron Taube had disappeared, Sophia Jacobsen began to show signs of despair. Ruttie could hear her sister at night, tossing in her bed, weeping. In the days that followed Sophia began to unravel some knitting: first a wool scarf she'd made the winter before, then a whole blanket her mother had only recently finished. In silence, Sophia would spend hours slowly pulling free one stitch and then the next, leaving the yarn that accumulated beside her in a tangled pile. When the blanket was finally reduced to just loose string, Sophia began to unravel her body by way of starving herself. Her parents had to insist, "A bite, Sophia. A bite." Finally, their mother took to holding a fork to Sophia's lips, feeding her as she had in infancy. Luckily, in this way, Sophia stopped resisting. As the fork approached, she dutifully opened her mouth, closed it, and chewed her food. Ruttie watched her sister stare blankly ahead as she waited for the next bite. Even when Sophia resumed feeding herself the next week, she remained stone-faced as she did.

But then, a month after Aaron's disappearance, Sophia suddenly took up skating again, which Ruttie, accompanying Sophia to the ice, mistook as a return of her sister. This was now the second week of January 1942, a Thursday evening, the cold weather as bitter as any they'd known. But whatever discomfort might come from going outside was outweighed by the joy of Sophia wanting to do something, with Ruttie no less, and Ruttie agreed readily to accompany her to the ice at Oosterpark. As they had before, Ruttie figured, they'd practice their spins, getting loopy doing so. Maybe they'd buy licorice again, a way to celebrate Sophia's choice of movement over collapse.

When they left their home Sophia assured their parents they'd be right back, were only going around the corner. Henny Ganz from downstairs, Sophia said, would be coming too—on a brisk walk—but Ruttie knew that Henny wasn't joining them. She and Sophia flew past Henny's door and once outside grabbed the skates they'd hidden earlier, in a closed basket just beside the steps to their building's entranceway—grabbed them and ran. Then walked. Then ran again.

In Oosterpark, even though night had already fallen, the sign they'd seen months before was still visible—*Voor Joden verboden.* But this time it didn't stop them. This time they rushed past it. This time the cold was unbearable, yet still they sat on a bench and methodically secured their skates. Besides them, no one was there. Too cold, Ruttie figured, taking in the quiet.

"No Jews," Sophia whispered, finally rising. Then she spit, as if at that sign they'd passed. "Hurry," she said, and Ruttie obeyed as if taking another lesson from Sophia. Before them the pond was empty, as were the paths in the park and the few streets they'd just traversed. It was dinnertime. No Jews allowed in the park or almost anywhere in Amsterdam—no Jews in theaters, hotels, sports arenas, art exhibitions, concerts, restaurants, libraries, museums, even zoos.

"No, Sophia, no," Ruttie whispered, afraid suddenly of the risk.

But Sophia gave Ruttie a stern look that silenced her. Sophia then rose, her arm reaching for Ruttie's hand.

They skated onto the ice together, silently going around the pond once, then again and again, Ruttie clutching Sophia's hand the whole time. But Sophia soon split off, setting her own pace, too fast for Ruttie. Sophia leaned into a series of back crossovers, then front crossovers, moves Ruttie still had to perfect. Close to the low branches of a willow Sophia practiced a spin, holding her arms out and then slowly pulling them in across her chest, which caused her to rotate faster and faster. There was moonlight but few stars. The only sound was their skates scraping the ice—not much noise, but enough to cause Ruttie, circling the pond at her own pace, to almost vomit with dread.

Ruttie was the first to see them, two older boys at the pond's edge, barely visible but for the light glimmering from the park's lamps in the distance. She could just make out that they wore the green uniform of the Nazi police. Whether they carried guns or clubs Ruttie couldn't be sure, but even through the darkness she could see that they carried weapons. Ruttie froze for a moment, shut her eyes, wished for an impossible invisibility, and then, after a quick breath, she sprinted toward the bench where they'd left their boots. Frantically, she freed herself of her skates. She sat there then, waiting for Sophia, shivering as she never had before. Even her head shook, even the littlest of her toes.

The policemen looked young, though in the dark it was hard to tell. They moved to a bench across the pond, and once they were seated Ruttie saw the small flame of a match appear, then she saw the tiny glow of a cigarette move back and forth as they passed it between them.

Sophia skated on—back crossovers, front crossovers, then another spin. As she slid across the pond there were times when she skated close to the policemen's bench, as if she didn't see them or didn't care even if she did. Ruttie couldn't tell if Sophia, engrossed as she surely was in the rapture of her skating, had actually seen them. But she suspected Sophia had. And suspected, too, with horror, that this performance—clearly one of madness—was in fact for them.

Come to me, Ruttie called to her sister without words, her heart screaming in a silent language she hoped Sophia could hear. *Sophia, come to me,* she begged, sure that if Sophia didn't turn her way this very instant and race to the shore, this moment was the last she'd share in Sophia's presence—that Sophia would be as swiftly disappeared as Aaron Taube.

The boys on the bench lit another cigarette. One of them rose, knocked a heel to the ice, and then stepped onto the pond. Sophia skated on, close to him then far from him. He stared as she passed, and continued to stare, even as he returned to his bench a moment later.

Sophia moved to the pond's center, stopped, caught her breath. The moon was like a spotlight, trained just on her. Gently, she pushed off on her left foot, raising her right leg behind her, gliding in a circle, the first of a figure eight. The circle completed, she shifted her weight onto the other leg and spiraled in the opposite direction. She moved slowly, her skates quiet, her balance a perfection above the blades she so carefully controlled through her knowledge of their edges.

There she is, circling under the moon, one leg outstretched behind her, her posture upright, and so many times Ruth Pearl, staring at Lake Topaqua as she was just then—the second week of January, the same date as all those years back—remembered this moment, remembered the yellow star on Sophia's coat, like a real star, remembered it though it couldn't have been like that, the mandate to wear the yellow stars not yet in place. That law would come in the spring and by then they'd be gone. But in Ruth's vision there Sophia was, wearing the star. Once in a dream the moon, too, became a yellow star, and Sophia skated on the pond at Oosterpark under its light—light which that night seemed like an invincible force, the very thing that protected her, that had made it so that the young Nazis, once Sophia skated toward Ruttie and sat beside her on the bench, merely got up, clapped, then turned, walking into the darkness.

But, of course, there was no protective light. That night the moon was just its ordinary, celestial self, and nearly full, all too bright. The glowing ash of the boys' cigarettes, sinister. Sophia out on the ice, reckless. *Come to me,* Ruttie silently called and called again. But for so long Sophia didn't come to her. And it was during those minutes of wild abandonment, as Sophia spiraled, as the boys with their uniforms and weapons looked on, that Ruttie knew what it would be like to lose Sophia for all time, knew how utterly dark a world it would be however much the moon was glowing.

"Come, Ruttie," Sophia said, simply enough, after the boys had clapped and gone, after her boots were pulled up. "Mamma and Papa will worry."

And they rushed home, walking some, running some, carrying their skates and then hiding them in the basket outside, then opening their apartment door, calling *hello! hello!* to those two in their old sweaters, sitting close and sharing the light of a lamp, then looking up from their reading as Sophia and Ruttie rushed toward them, Ruttie bounding onto her father's lap and clutching him as she hadn't since she was small, Sophia's voice particularly merry and girlish, as if it were any old night, with Aaron Taube where he belonged, right around the corner, and as if their lives by way of all those terrible new laws hadn't already been shattered and forever changed.

4

Netherlands, April 15, 1941, by Order of the Commissioner-General for Security: Jews must forfeit their radios.

THE NIGHT IAN LIMA ASKED, *When is loving like death?* Bill Cousins was wondering much the same thing. Earlier that evening his father had had a stroke. His mother, in her confusion, didn't call Bill right away after his father had fallen to the floor, nor did she dial 911 until some minutes had passed. Nevertheless, his father survived. The stroke, by all appearances, was mild, its damage blessedly minimal, limiting for the time being his father's abilities to swallow and speak. The next day, Wednesday, he was bedridden and silent in a hospital room in Middletown. All Bill wanted to do, sitting by his father's bed, was talk to the man who couldn't talk back. The room had one window, looking out over a parking lot. Whenever Bill glanced out the window he took to counting the cars below. Something to do. A way to pass another fraught moment. The night before he'd taken to counting stars, as hopeless as that endeavor was. Even with streetlights brightening the night sky he saw too many to count. He would get to fifty, give up, and simply stare. Then he'd return—not at all fortified—to his father's bed.

While Bill was at the hospital, his wife, Ellen, was with his mother, having brought the woman to their bungalow, bumping their son, Rich, to the living room couch for sleeping. To care for the woman in the days ahead Ellen arranged for time off from her accounting job, which, she told Bill, would be a bit of a rest—watching soap operas and afternoon talk shows with his mother. The stroke wasn't her fault, Ellen had told Bill's once-stalwart mother many times that day. "You sure?" Ellen reported his mother meekly asking. Ellen and

Bill were talking on the phone. "Tell her that of course, *of course*, you're sure," Bill had counseled Ellen, though he thought it best that his mother be kept away from his father just then to avoid another unintended mishap. The additional room he was building was far from finished, the cold outside difficult to work in, yet he knew with even more clarity that he should get them moved in there soon. As he had with his father's sudden incapacitation, he took the now-urgent problem of the renovation to the hospital window where, by way of his thoughts—including the unsightly memory of his father lounging in his underwear—he threw the matter out to the universe, what little he could see of it from that lone hospital window. "Help me," Bill said, his voice carrying an ambivalence he was ashamed of anyone hearing.

The afternoon light was still strong when Stephanie Pearl called him on his cell phone, a call that surprised him. The phone was new, for emergencies only, and he hadn't shared the number. But Stephanie explained that Ellen had, when Stephanie called their home moments before. Bill didn't mind, as he had been thinking of giving the number to Mrs. Pearl anyway in case she needed his help. She'd been receiving it over the years whether she knew it or not. Without her asking, he'd shoveled snow from her walkway and also from the ice on the lake so she'd be sure to have a clear spot for skating. In return, he'd enjoyed the sight of her out there, often at dusk. Though Mrs. Pearl was remarkably private, on the ice she had a grace she couldn't help but share.

What Bill said to Stephanie was, "Glad you got the number. Give it to your mother, too." He sat at his father's bedside, his hand over his father's limp one. He added, "Good of you to call. Really kind, Stephanie." Then he told her about his father's condition, ending with, "I've never seen my pop so sick." He paused and Stephanie didn't speak. "Your mother need something?"

"No, no. Was going to ask you something, but it can wait." Stephanie's voice was noticeably anxious. "She's fine, by the way. My mother's fine."

"She's a healthy woman," Bill said. Stephanie's obvious worry was a kindness too, he figured, a concern for his father. He added, "I mean, she skates like a dream."

"She learned early. If there's anything we can do, let us know."

"Nothing to do," he said.

A moment later, at the window, he stared at the hospital's parking lot. Its ugliness only made him hurt more.

◊

THAT SAME TUESDAY EVENING OF BILL'S FATHER'S STROKE, WILLA FLETCHER unexpectedly ran into Arthur Cantrell playing basketball at the YMCA. By then, she'd thought she'd come to terms with the fact that their relationship, however promising it had seemed, had dwindled to an unexpected nothing. And she'd thought she was moving forward from all that. In the last month she'd taken on two new clients, both contract disputes, her reputation growing. At the pottery studio she was making her first set of coffee mugs. At night, in bed, she still dwelled on Arthur's abandoning her, but only for a few minutes, when she couldn't help herself from trying to grasp the precise moment when she'd blown it. The possibilities were endless: she talked too much, ate too little and then too much, laughed loudly, revealed too quickly the news of her parents' troubles. But no amount of taking stock solved anything. Inevitably, she fell to sleep in a stupor of helplessness—an old feeling, experienced since childhood like a gust that gained force, eventually knocking her over. Her mother, for example, arriving home from work each evening happy enough to see her, but over time growing detached, then taciturn, then angry, finally snapping at her family, sometimes even Willa. But what had she done? She couldn't tell then, either. *Think*, she'd always told herself. *Think*.

Just last week she'd tried to cure her self-doubt in a new way, by meditating, not thinking, not even trying to know, but that had only made matters worse. The prescribed stillness was too much like the impotency of her younger self—unable to understand addiction, overwhelmed, it always seemed, by capriciousness itself. Instead of inner peace, the meditating induced rage, another old feeling that, while better than helplessness, got her heart so heavily pounding and her body so charged that she had to rush outside to quickly burn it off by running. Day after day this was so—meditation, rage, running—until she'd finally turned to the noisy ebullience of a Jazzercise class at the Y, a happier and more communal way to recover, which was why she was there that Tuesday night when she ran into Arthur, playing basketball with several attorneys she recognized, including Wilson Keller and Gene D'Orrino.

She'd gone there only to take the exercise class and then she'd planned to go home, maybe stopping just before to say a quick hello to Mrs. Rizzo, who never failed to offer her a little talk and food.

But after the class, on her way to the women's locker room, she passed a basketball court and popped her head in, curious to see whatever game was on. The Jazzercise had revved her endorphins, and in the giddy haze of that she considered grabbing a ball, taking a shot. But to her surprise there was Arthur, dribbling as he dashed around Gene D'Orrino and then Wilson Keller. The fourth player was someone she didn't know. The others looked sluggish, but Arthur ran energetically. She stood in the doorway to the court, watching him receive a pass and then rush forward for a layup, which he missed. As he turned from the hoop he saw her and, pretending not to be surprised, and as if all between them were normal, he walked over, leaned her way, and kissed her on the lips. It was quick, but still it shocked her. She barely heard him as he said, "Meant to call again. Had to catch up after the holiday and things got away from me. I'm awfully sorry."

"Yes. I can see. Very busy," Willa answered, gesturing toward the basketball court. She closed her lips, pressing them, confused by his kiss, and then, a second later, infuriated by it. They were both drenched in sweat. She crossed her arms over her chest, aware of how revealing her skin-tight exercise attire was. Briefly, she regretted having stopped by, but then she decided that he might as well see her body. In fact, it was about time. "Oh, you're going to be very sorry," she added, dropping her arms, hiding nothing. Her body was suddenly pulsing, just as it did in meditation when she tipped from helplessness into rage.

"What does that mean?" A moment earlier Arthur had placed his hand, gently, on her arm, but now he quickly lifted it. He stepped back. His face was reddening. "I should have called," he said. "Entirely my fault."

"I'll quote you on that. Entirely your fault."

"Willa, what are you talking about?"

"You'll see," she said as she turned from him, not knowing in the least what she was talking about. She was just spewing forth in a way she couldn't stop. Experience had taught her that the best thing to do with her rage, however induced, was to run, and she quickly spun to go. But before she did, she turned back. "Do I look like a toy? Do I?" He was halfway across the basketball court. He turned when she called, throwing his arms out, a gesture of surrender, which infuriated her further. Just before calling it quits Husband Number One had made the same gesture. As did Husband Number Two.

A minute later, in the women's locker room, she glanced in the mirror. She was tiny and, dressed in a leotard, leggings, and sneakers, didn't look like a toy but rather a child. However eager she'd been to dress for the class, she now detested her appearance.

Once outside, she stood for a moment, cooling off before getting into her car. In the dark she could see only the Y and its parking lot, which were awful places, she told herself, though she'd loved the recent Jazzercise classes there. Soon enough, she decided she hated the entirety of Middletown, even her new home with her first bag of marshmallows she had bought that fall still on the kitchen counter, even Wesleyan Potters, where sitting at a whirling wheel was becoming comfortable, even the Connecticut River that flowed beside the city. *Yes,* she told the river, driving along its bank before exiting off Route 9, turning away from it, *you're nothing too.*

◊

Three days later, the third Friday in January, eight fifteen in the morning, Missy Lima eased herself onto the several down pillows Roy Kirk had stacked just for her in his bed. They were done with lovemaking, if that's what you called such a thing between two people who determinedly called themselves friends. Twice monthly for six years the friends had done this, the one friend smiling when the other friend showed up exactly on time, then kissing her warmly on the forehead, then taking her hand, leading her to his bedroom, where, with little fuss or talking, they'd simply begin. It was only after the act—of sex, of physical intimacy, of the flying-over-the-moon feel of it that never failed to take the edge off, as Missy experienced her time with Roy—that they slowed down, talked more. Somehow the friendship—sexual from its start, a fling—had stretched across time. But the years hadn't changed how Missy thought of it, as a convenient liaison soon to run its course, and she'd never told anyone about it. Not even Ian, though Roy Kirk, who covered local sports for *The Middletown Press*, knew of Ian and even admired his skills as a catcher for his baseball team. In the kitchen Roy made coffee, as he always did once they'd finished, and he brought a mug to Missy. She sipped it and gladly sighed. Between the familiar sex, the fluffy pillows, the light blanket resting on her body, and the freshly brewed coffee prepared the way she truly liked it, with milk and sugar and not black, she felt better than she had all week. About her stubborn sweet tooth, something she just couldn't shake, Roy had once said, "Life is short, Miss. Go big." Two times monthly, then, she had it her way. Two times monthly, she figured, wasn't too often to give herself this little gift.

Roy's dog, a beagle named Sam, joined them on the bed. Roy scratched Sam's head before settling himself on his stack of pillows, not as high as hers.

"Can make you some oatmeal," Roy said.

"No need. I'll eat later, at work."

"Can get you a sweater."

She'd pulled her T-shirt back on, but she wasn't cold, especially with all the blankets he had.

"Tell me something then?" he said.

"Tell you what?"

He looked at her. "Tell me something that happened this week that made you laugh."

But had she laughed? Ian had fallen that week on the ice, which had gotten her worried. He was in pain. She told Roy about Ian's needing to sit out rehearsals for now.

"What ice?"

"Lake ice."

"What was he doing on the lake?"

"Not sure. Taking a walk. Being a kid."

"Kids shouldn't be on the ice. I should know. I was a kid who was always on the ice."

She thought of telling Roy, a nonparent, that mothering, especially of a teenager, meant giving your kid some space. That was the art of it—knowing when to back off. And clearly the lake ice was solid, the fishermen scattered about, and skaters, proof of it. "Fishing?" she asked instead.

"Fishing, yes. Sundays, when the ice was good."

"And here you are now. Plenty fine." She took another sip of coffee.

"Plenty fine," he agreed, then he grabbed her into a bear hug. She almost spilled her drink. "Hey, careful," she said, laughing.

He flipped on the TV. She loved the luxury of that, a TV in the bedroom. *Girlfriends* was on, a repeat. "Oh, goodie," she said. This was another indulgence, a girls' show, enjoyed only at Roy's.

"Christ, Miss," he said, but he watched it through to the end with her, snuggling with her for a time and then bringing her another cup of perfectly sweetened coffee. At one point the dog moved between them, then onto them, then jumped to the floor, where he stayed, as if he were glued to the show, which today was about the charming lead actress, one of four young adult girlfriends, giving up on love.

"Don't give up!" Missy called out, mid-program. When Roy turned to her, surprised, she wished she hadn't spoken. It wasn't love, what she and Roy had; love was for fools, a lesson she'd learned when she'd given it all up for Frank Lima. Roy, too, had gotten burned in an early marriage. "Young and dumb," is what he said of that.

She sipped the last of the coffee. The show closed with no love in sight except between girlfriends, group-hugging the pain away. Roy rose to let the dog out. Missy zipped into the shower then dressed. In the doorway, he kissed her goodbye, taking time to do so. Then he told her to keep that kid of hers on dry land. She smiled and said, "Hey, no worries. I got this." And that's how she felt just then, stepping outside, the morning crisp and sunny. The responsibilities of work and mothering and everything else were in the future, which seemed, momentarily, ages from just then. Feeling carefree, almost loopy—he'd kissed her for so long she'd nearly lost her breath—she took a second to look up to the sun, surprised by its common enough radiance.

No, it wasn't love there at Roy's, but just twice monthly in the early mornings gave her something she considered possible still: friendship, with certain benefits. Which was plenty good enough. Nearly fulfilling. That she missed him, sometimes terribly, in the time in between their meetings was something that just was. By now she barely noticed the quiet ache. She started her car, pulled out. The dog, Sam, still in the yard, yapped and yapped, as he always did to see her go.

◊

LATER THAT FRIDAY, JUDGE ARTHUR CANTRELL ATE A LATE LUNCH WITH Wilson Keller at Luigi's. Arthur ordered eggplant parmesan and Wilson ordered baked cod. The day was clear, the restaurant uncrowded in mid-afternoon, and the men sat looking out at Middletown's Main Street. The cars passing by, as always, streamed steadily. For a time, as they ate, they discussed Willa Fletcher's cryptic words at the Y the other night, "You're going to be very sorry," figuring, finally, that they were words of anger, the precise meaning of which didn't matter. Arthur had thought as much already. He was sorry to see her so hurt by his failure to act. He'd been on the fence, he'd wanted to explain, not about her but about himself. But Willa, fuming, clearly had already drawn her own conclusions.

Soon they moved on to discussing the legal topic of the day,

Bush v. Gore, Wilson concluding that because the situation was unprecedented—"Election workers holding ballot cards up to ceiling lights? Really?"—the Court was willing to end the matter as it had. And the Florida election had to be settled to meet deadlines for other key events—the certification of electors and the inauguration—by then in just a matter of days. "In the interest of national order, they did what they did," Wilson said. "That's how I read it. Though maybe the logic of the opinion was a bit off."

"A bit?" Arthur lowered his fork. "They decide Florida voters are being harmed by their votes being subject to variable counting standards, which they claim violates the Equal Protection Clause. And then, bingo, they block any recount, a move that harms those very voters even more."

Though Wilson nodded, he wasn't as perplexed as Arthur, who, seeing that, pressed further. "And, apparently, there really was an equal protection problem in Florida, involving race. *Race.* A primary concern under the Equal Protection Clause. There were wild irregularities at voting precincts—dropped registrations and the like—in several predominantly Black counties. Any number of people who showed up to vote never got to, and those votes would likely have been for Gore. Members of the Congressional Black Caucus spoke out about this on January 6th, but without support from a single senator the congressmen couldn't formally object to the certification of the electors. Gore himself gaveled the speakers into silence. Talk about ironies." Arthur lifted his fork like it was the very gavel Gore had used. "Talk about human *restraint.*"

Arthur, now angry, took a deep breath. In so doing he remembered he was talking to his friend and not to his mother, who was never willing to challenge his father, and not to his father, who always won his often-senseless arguments by the sheer force of his rage. "All I'm saying is that the justices should have drawn their conclusions in the interest of fairness. Count the votes. That was settled law, there was still time. At least the Florida Supreme Court might have found that if given the chance. And that would have been fair even if the result remained the same."

Arthur paused while Wilson stared, waiting for more. "You're not crazy if you find all this a little fishy," Arthur continued. "Five hundred fifty-four law professors say the same thing." Arthur was referring to the recent full-page ad in *The New York Times* signed by that many law professors, Republicans and Democrats, claiming that the ruling was obviously political. By stopping an ongoing recount, they stated, the majority effectively suppressed the vote, suppressed the facts, and acted in service of Bush—not Florida voters. Arthur reported all that.

"I believe you," Wilson finally said, words that swiftly returned Arthur to himself. He exhaled. Sat up. Ate more. Wilson continued, "But it was so chaotic. A once-ever kind of crazy. Let's give the justices the benefit of the doubt. Maybe it was hard to see the road in the blizzard."

When Arthur raised his eyebrows, skeptically—silently questioning whether it was a blizzard the justices faced or an opportunity—Wilson smiled. "What you consistently fail to see, my friend, is that everyone's not as good as you," he said.

IN FACT, IT WAS THE unfair process that bothered Arthur more than the election's result. Its consequences were matters of policy, important certainly, but not a crisis. A Republican, a Democrat—they'd lived through it all before. He told Wilson as much. "But that Reform Party . . ." The third-party nominee was conservative commentator Pat Buchanan, who'd had to duke it out, messily, with physicist and transcendental meditation practitioner John Hagelin. Before that, businessman Donald Trump had briefly run for the nomination.

Wilson raised his eyebrows, then glanced at his watch. "Didn't realize the time. Have a meeting," he told Arthur, who shooed him along.

Once outside, Wilson waved at Arthur sitting at the window. Arthur, in response, held up his water glass. When their waitress, Clarice, soon asked about dessert, Arthur explained that Wilson had already left.

"Anything for you, Judge? We've got something yummy today. Pineapple upside down cake, with a scoop of vanilla. Or tiramisu. You often get that." Clarice nodded encouragingly.

Arthur put a hand to his belly. He shook his head.

"Come on, Judge. A little sweetness won't hurt you." Then, to Arthur's surprise, she sat down in Wilson's empty seat. He shook his head again.

"Can I ask you something then?" Clarice had worked at Luigi's for several years. She'd waited on him and Wilson often and had urged many unnecessary desserts upon them. But from the way she held herself, fully upright, Arthur suspected her question wouldn't be about food but rather about a legal matter. That he shouldn't get involved was his usual reply in such moments.

But her question wasn't what he expected. "You dating?" she whispered.

Arthur sat as straight as she was.

"Don't mean to pry, Judge, but if you're single then I think I know someone for you." Clarice blinked rapidly and her cheeks pinkened. "I'm prying." She stood up. "Sorry, Judge. Just thought you might like, you know, a fix-up."

On Main Street an elderly woman carrying a large basket passed by Luigi's. Clarice waved and the woman waved back. "That's my friend Gloria's mom," she said. "Gloria's single."

"I see." Arthur sipped water. "I'm dating," he finally said. "An attorney. Willa's her name." He said this for the sake of convenience, but it felt good to say, too, which surprised him.

"You're taken," Clarice said. "In that case it's settled. Too bad for Gloria."

"And me," Arthur heard. Another waitress, Gina, had spoken. She was behind them, wiping a table. "I'd date you, Judge Cantrell. But I never dared ask." She laughed, as did Clarice. "You know, we can say this now. A handsome bachelor your age. And a judge, no less. That's a wonderful position. Given all that, we wondered."

"Yes?"

"Which way you turned," Gina said. She added, to clarify, "What side you sleep on, Judge."

"Ah . . ." Arthur, understanding, distractedly scratched his forehead.

The women laughed again. Clarice offered him dessert on the house. "Because we've been so nosy," she said.

Arthur raised his hands, motioning no. "This is all very flattering, ladies. Surprising and flattering. I didn't know I had so many admirers at Luigi's."

"Here and elsewhere." Clarice's smile, combined with a slow shake of her head, suggested that she found his cluelessness to be charmingly incorrigible. Then she snapped up his credit card and went off. Gina resumed wiping the table.

He sat for a while before paying, staring out at Main Street, waving when the elderly woman with the basket trundled past again. Turning to settle the bill, he tripled the tip.

As he approached his chambers, his mind stunned by the overtures of the waitresses, he felt both happy and sluggish. He thought he'd quickly nap, then finally call Willa. He didn't need to be so afraid, he figured, the compliments from the waitresses as much as the food he'd just eaten settling him nicely. The comfort of snuggling in bed with the one you loved and doing so all night came to mind too, as he hadn't allowed it to in ages. Inside his office again his attention was drawn to his conference table, on top of which lay a large manila envelope. As he sat down, he patted the tabletop as if it was a friend to greet, and then he lifted the envelope. *Hand delivery*, it read.

Inside was a complaint, marked "draft," directed to the Connecticut Judicial Review Council, and written by Willa. She claimed that he'd engaged in partiality regarding the Byrnes matter. Quoting him, she described his having spoken to her while they were having dinner one evening that fall and disclosing details about the case, then ongoing, that revealed his bias toward the desired result of his longtime friend, Attorney Wilson Keller, representing one of the parties. Moreover, she stated, she'd witnessed Judge Cantrell engaged with Attorney Keller at the basketball court at the Middletown YMCA and knew of Judge Cantrell's pattern of meeting with Attorney Keller there, including while the Byrnes matter was ongoing. She provided dates and times of each occurrence she discussed. She closed with citations to the state's rules of judicial conduct. *Canon 1: A judge shall avoid . . . impropriety and the appearance of impropriety. Canon 2: A judge shall perform the duties of judicial office impartially, competently, and diligently.* Here she quoted specific rules, against bias and ex parte communications and on when to recuse. She made particular note of Rule 2.4: *A judge shall not permit family, social, political, or other interests or relationships to influence the judge's judicial conduct or judgment.*

He read the complaint, then read it again. Finished, he threw it down, hard, on the conference table, then picked it up and threw it down again. The table, though he was sure he'd fixed it securely all those years ago, quivered.

THAT SAME AFTERNOON, WHILE ARTHUR CANTRELL READ AND THEN reread the draft complaint, and while Willa Fletcher paced inside her office rather than read the cases on her desk, and while Bill Cousins sat worriedly at his father's hospital bed, and while Ian Lima watched Jase Moretti and Sarah Toms dance to near perfection yet again, Ruth Pearl was at work at the law firm of D'Orrino & Keller, where her employers were celebrating her twenty-fifth anniversary there. It wasn't a surprise party. Wilson had told Ruth about it a month ago and she'd been looking forward to it. When the day finally came, she dressed in a skirt and matching blazer, onto the sturdy lapel of which she'd stuck a pin of her mother's, a bronze rose—which, along with her mother's wedding ring, had miraculously survived their journey out of the Netherlands and to America. Her mother had sewn both the pin and the ring into the lining of her winter coat, just the way she'd sewn into various coat linings the diamonds that had been crucial to their successful escape. Ruth thought of her mother, Tessa, as she straightened the pin. "I still have it," she told the deceased woman. In the States, her mother's pastime of embroidering had become a lifeline, a way to grieve and, beyond that, to lull a tenacious anxiety, even after she'd moved to West Hartford. Just a year after Ruth's parents came to live in Connecticut, the Wadsworth Atheneum Museum of Art in Hartford showed several of her mother's works—scenes of prewar Amsterdam—along with the work of other "local artisans," and Tessa's embroidery, so familiar to Ruth, looked different, important, framed by the Wadsworth's staff and hanging on the museum's walls. At the time Ruth was newly married to Felix Pearl, who had told the curator about her mother. After viewing the show, the family ate at a Greek restaurant in West Hartford, a treat from Felix. That night, wine glasses raised, Felix was the one to say it: "We've made it." He spoke the words with both sincerity and seriousness as if he, too, had fled a deadly Europe, though in fact he hadn't. Ruth took his "we" as a testament to his deepening connection to her and her parents. Still newlyweds, they were off to a promising start, his sympathy a good sign. "Oh, Mamma," Ruth said following Felix's remark. "I'm so proud of you." The morning of Ruth's twenty-fifth year celebration at work—twenty-seven years after Felix left her for another woman—she said the words again after giving her hair a final pat, straightening the pin once more, and locking the bungalow's front door. She was in her car but had yet to start the engine. Though she shivered, the silence inside the car felt serene. "I know it wasn't easy," she told her dead mother, breathing the words into the chilled air. "Not easy at all."

The office party was simple enough: a sheet cake from Stop & Shop and freshly brewed coffee. Wilson gave her a bouquet of twenty-five roses, which felt ludicrously extravagant to Ruth, who delighted in it nonetheless. She breathed in the roses' scent, and something went off in her mind, a ringing, like joyful bells. "Beautiful," she whispered, then inhaled again. "What would we do without you?" Wilson said. The other secretary, Connie Flanders, who so very often turned off the classical music station Ruth preferred, declaring it "too European for me," handed Ruth a box of chocolates. "For a sweet lady," she said, then kissed Ruth's cheek. Even Gene D'Orrino had a gift: stationery, cards decorated with windmills. "For our gal from Holland," his own note read.

They ate cake, drank coffee, and got back to work. In the remaining two hours of the workday Connie never mentioned the classical music that Ruth had going a touch louder than usual, an accommodation, Ruth knew, to the afternoon's orientation toward her. When a Rachmaninoff piano concerto began, Ruth hummed along without concern. She was retyping a brief for Wilson, due in court the next day. Connie was answering calls but otherwise just twiddling a pencil. She'd been at the firm eight years to Ruth's twenty-five. For just a second Connie, too, hummed to the Rachmaninoff. Then she laughed, catching herself. "You're changing me," she told Ruth from across the room they shared. "And who knows, probably for the better."

The afternoon was peaceful enough, and with the roses and the slight acknowledgment from Connie, it generated more delight than Ruth had expected. Decades ago, after reading a biography of Abraham Lincoln to improve her English, Ruth had taped a small picture of him to the wall beside her desk, a reminder when she glanced at it that despite loss—Lincoln had lost a cherished son to illness—life went on. *See?* she longed to tell the man, thinking momentarily of Sophia, and then of Felix. *I went on.* At five o'clock Connie gathered her coat and purse to go to a happy hour. Wilson had a late meeting, scheduled just that afternoon, with Judge Arthur Cantrell, who walked in looking haggard. When Wilson came to greet the judge, he turned to Ruth to ask, "Mind staying a bit?" She didn't. "Have you met Ruth?" Wilson then asked the judge, and they shook hands.

After his meeting Wilson had to rush home; he left it to Ruth to lock up. Rising to go, she covered her new Dell computer. It had taken her a full year, countless lessons from Connie, and weekly stomachaches to transition from her typewriter, an IBM Selectric, to the Dell. But once she caught on, Wilson had gifted her the Selectric, which she'd gladly brought home and used whenever possible, even for her weekly grocery lists. Only this past year, after the Y2K hoopla had turned out to be nothing, had she bought her first home computer. The World Wide Web was baffling, until it wasn't. "Holocaust Survivors in Connecticut," she'd once researched—her first attempt—then she narrowed the search to "Holocaust Survivors in West Hartford, Connecticut." Soon she looked only for local Dutch Holocaust survivors. Quickly she'd found an article about her mother's Wadsworth Atheneum show and printed it. For safekeeping, she put the article with the legal cases in her file marked *Good.*

"Okay, Mamma, here we go," she said once she was in her car, resuming the conversation she'd begun that morning. Then, as if the woman were really there, she began to tell her that her own life, too, wasn't easy: the marriage, the divorce, the working life that she'd never asked for but had nonetheless sustained for twenty-five years. "Isn't that something?" she asked out loud. But by then she'd arrived home in Wells and her mother's presence had waned.

HER STORY, THE ONE SHE didn't tell her mother, began with her meeting Felix Pearl. He'd come into Welty's, the children's shoe store on the Upper West Side of Manhattan, where Ruth was then working. This was July of 1957, and Ruth had been a saleswoman there for close to ten years. At twenty-nine years old she knew she already qualified as a spinster, but she didn't care. After all, what right did she have to marry, to be loved, when Sophia's life had been cut so short? And how could she be even one bit happier than her ever-grieving parents?

Felix came to Welty's seeking shoes for a niece, he told her, having approached her deliberately. Ruth noticed that he'd been staring at her in the minutes before as she'd fitted a two-year-old with a pair of saddle shoes. Having tied the child's shoes, Ruth then lifted her, twirling her before placing her down so she could walk in the new shoes. The child's parents, and Ruth, had clapped at the toddling, which delighted the child—who then ran straight into Ruth's arms. When the sale was completed, Felix stepped forward, his hand extended. He sought shoes for his five-year-old niece, he explained. Ruth began pulling boxes, girls, size six. While selecting the shoes, Felix mentioned that he was an insurance man, from Hartford, a vice president at his company, but he came to New York sometimes on weekends. He mentioned museums, restaurants, a shop he frequented for his suits. Once he'd chosen which shoes to buy, he nervously asked Ruth to dinner that evening, surprising her, and it was there, in a quiet corner of the restaurant he'd chosen, that he eventually mentioned he'd lost his mother when he was two years old. Dinner was simple: chicken and baked potatoes. He and Ruth barely looked at each other while they ate. She assumed, based on their shared reserve, that they wouldn't eat another meal like this. But then he mentioned losing his mother. "I was just the age of that child you fitted. What a lovely sight," he said, which made her smile. She did like the children who came into Welty's. "But not so much the parents," she said, rolling her eyes. The next week he sought her out again. He couldn't stop envisioning her and that child in the saddle shoes. He added, "It's something you don't ever get over, losing your mother at a young age." "Yes, yes, I understand," Ruth said, thinking of Sophia.

Felix returned to Manhattan the next weekend and the next. On their fourth date he told Ruth that though he was thirty-four he'd not married yet, as the right woman simply hadn't appeared. "I never thought to look in a children's shoe store," he said, startling her. The thought of marrying him hadn't occurred to Ruth, though she was grateful for the attention and the dinners out, away from her parents, with whom she still shared a small apartment. Felix's sudden presence in her life made the place feel roomier. Two weeks later he returned to the city again. They strolled through Central Park, then sat, watching people pass. Later, at dinner at an elegant midtown steakhouse, Felix began the evening by ordering an expensive wine. "You're that special," he told her after she protested. As she cautiously sipped, she pondered telling him she wasn't the marrying kind. But before she spoke, he did, his face warmed by a kind smile. "I really don't know a thing about wines. Just trying to make you happy," he said, to which she answered, "I am happy. It worked." Later, he told her, as he had once before, that he couldn't forget the sight of her with that girl at the shoe store. "The way she ran to you, like you were her mother. My mother died when I was just two, so I don't have a true memory, just a sense that I once ran like that, into her arms." He looked at Ruth expectantly then, as if, like the child at the store and the child in the recesses of his memory, he wanted to rush to her for whatever maternal solace she could offer.

If the subtext of Felix Pearl's life was loss, then the subtext of Ruth Jacobsen's was both loss and guilt, a pervasive, unhealable survivor's guilt. She said no the first time Felix proposed, only six weeks later. ("But, Ruth, you're everything I've ever sought," he said.) She said no again to the second proposal, at four months. ("But you make me so happy, so whole.") Still, they kept dating. He drove into Manhattan each weekend and took her for more long walks in Central Park. Often, he bought her ice cream after their stroll. "You're so thin," he remarked once, not unkindly, urging her to have a sundae, not just a single scoop. She ate the sundae at once, then apologized for downing it so quickly. But Felix only laughed. He, too, was thin, and balding. When he smiled, which was not often, he looked years younger, and he was smiling just then. They'd known each other seven months when he brought her to Connecticut, and there they'd gone to the Hartford Symphony, a Sunday matinee performance. She'd almost cried at the beauty of the music—Brahms, Beethoven. The concert over, she linked her arm in his as they left the music hall, which was the first time she'd initiated contact between them, and she kept her arm linked in his as they walked to a nearby restaurant. She said yes, then, over dinner. "Okay," she said, still teary, the music having nudged forth feelings she didn't even know she had. "If we can hear the symphony regularly. Season's tickets." She laughed suddenly, though shyly. "I mean, yes, of course. I'll marry you. I will."

They moved to a four-bedroom house in West Hartford, enough room for her parents too, but Felix insisted he and Ruth have their own place. "For our children," he said, which triggered her old guilt. *But I have no right to bear a child, not when . . .* She couldn't bring the thought fully to consciousness, but it was lodged there nonetheless, controlling her choices, including the decision to feign headaches each month midway through her cycle. A year went by. Then Felix used his savings to buy an apartment nearby for her parents, which created a new form of guilt. Ruth was indebted to Felix Pearl. Her parents felt so much safer in West Hartford than they had in New York, intimidated there by the city's massiveness. Moreover, in New York her father had had to take janitorial work before finding his way back to the diamond trade, but in West Hartford he'd promptly found work in diamonds. A local jeweler, Herb Grober, hired him and soon, with her father's thorough training behind him, he was the diamond expert at Grober's Fine Jewelry. They had him buying and polishing and even talking about cuts to customers. Most remarkably, it didn't matter to Herb Grober or his staff when her father so very often failed to know the exact English word.

Ruth gave in then, and within a year bore Stephanie, whom they named for both Sophia, the deceased sister, and Estelle, Felix's long-dead mother. Ruth worried that the family ancestry embodied in the name, fraught with tragedy, would burden the child. But Felix so wanted his firstborn, a girl, named after his mother. And her parents so wanted the child to be named after their lost one. And who was Ruth to deny them? She was the one, then, to come up with the compromise name, a blend of sounds. "Stephanie," she told them, stating it firmly. "Stephanie. That's my girl."

ON THE DAY OF RUTH'S twenty-fifth work anniversary, upon arriving home she began to rearrange a dozen of the roses she'd brought with her. She then heated water for tea but removed the kettle before the water boiled. She wandered to her kitchen window and glanced over her neighbor's wall at what she could see of the lake beyond it. The ice, she knew, was thick, and the moonlight bright. She grabbed her skates and trekked down to her dock, where she laced up.

She glided forth into a large space shoveled free of snow. She knew Bill Cousins shoveled a space for his children to play on, but luckily for her the children never skated at night when she did. Even on weekends, when she wasn't working, she preferred this time of day—dusk, the sun low but not gone, the moon out but becoming on a clear night ever more visible. Something in her came alive at this hour. She leaned into a spiral, raised a leg, and turned in a perfect circle.

She could almost see her suddenly—Sophia, skating next to her. She was still sixteen and still skating too fast for Ruth to keep up. "Sophia, come to me," Ruth called, which was as strange and untamed a sound as an owl's. That she'd stepped out into the dark to allow herself to make that very call, as necessary as any animal's attempting to survive the night, was not lost on her. She'd done it before, many times. And, like before, a feeling released within her. She skated more, reached out, felt an answer in the form of a pure and simple joy filling her body. It took skating at dusk, a form of magic, to generate that wholeness.

Some minutes later, after she'd stepped indoors, the phone rang, and it was Stephanie. "Mamma, can you bring Bill Cousins and his family some flowers? His father is very ill."

Whatever positive spirit had imbued Ruth instantly left her. "But the wall, Stephie."

"Forget the wall. Send the flowers."

"But he's blocked my view, Stephie."

"Just send the flowers, Mamma. Get them tomorrow morning. Drop them off yourself."

"But I don't want to give him a gift right now."

"I think it's right," Stephanie said. "He's in pain, Mamma. Won't you do it?"

Ruth paused. She eventually nodded. Into the phone she said, "I'm not buying him roses."

"I didn't say roses. Mamma, please, any flowers will do."

DURING HER MARRIAGE TO FELIX Pearl the headaches were at first feigned—to avoid sex, avoid pregnancy—but in the year after Stephanie's birth actual headaches began to seize her, pain that felt like nails being driven into her skull, and she needed to retreat to her bedroom more and more. She needed the lights out, pure quiet. The child's cries, though rare, were unbearable to endure. Felix hired a part-time nanny. "Until you feel better," he said, to which she answered, many times, "I'm so sorry. I don't know what's come over me."

Luckily, even as a toddler Stephanie was a good girl, a mostly calm girl, attuned, it seemed, to Ruth's ups and downs. By the age of four she had learned to tiptoe into Ruth's darkened daytime bedroom, bringing aspirin and water, and promising when Ruth asked not to tell her father. "Say that we played checkers all afternoon," Ruth said, "until Mamma napped." Or, "Tell him we went for a very long walk that tired Mamma." Stephanie always agreed to tell Felix just what

Ruth requested, but whether she in fact told him the lies Ruth, bedridden, door closed, never knew.

She suspected otherwise, though, insofar as Felix increasingly seemed to take her debilitation personally. He tried to help at first, cooking simple dinners, reading to Stephanie and then putting her to bed, but with time seeing Ruth bedridden so often touched off an old anxiety within him. That she was supposed to redeem his past rather than remind him of its worst trauma was something she understood. She lied even more in efforts to cover it up. "Tell him we made paintings today, Stephie." "Tell him we baked cookies, but they burned, and we threw them out."

Felix took to sleeping in a separate bedroom those nights when she had a headache. Then he took to staying late at the insurance firm. Stephanie was in kindergarten by then, and coming home she had an almost miraculous capacity when Ruth was laid up in bed for occupying herself with coloring books or dolls. On those bad days when Stephanie more or less cared for herself she would always begin the afternoon by stopping in Ruth's room, whispering to her sympathetically, checking to see if she needed anything. Sometimes, though more rarely, Stephanie lay beside her. Once—Stephanie was in first grade by then—she claimed that she, too, had a headache. "I'm just like you," she said.

Ruth got up after that, headache or not, but Felix, still wary of her, continued to stay at work late. He continued to sleep in the guest bedroom, regardless of Ruth's health. And time passed. They lived quietly, tensely, with no more children as once planned. The highlight of Ruth's life was visiting her parents every other day, sitting with her mother while she embroidered, watching her father take Stephanie in his lap and listening as he told his granddaughter a story. Always the stories were set in Amsterdam. Always they had a false, happy ending. "Children need not know," he once said to Ruth, who in her childhood had found out by running smack into the signs, the literal signs—*Voor Joden verboden*. "I think children know," she replied. "They can't help it. They're alive."

Stephanie was eight when Felix moved them to Wells, into a little bungalow he'd bought by the lake there. "We need to be closer," he explained as they prepared to leave West Hartford. "Too many rooms here. Too many ways to not talk." Ruth was anxious about leaving her parents in West Hartford, but glad too. Something had to change, and Felix was determined enough for that to happen, to give a new way and a new place a try. And, for a while, the change worked. They moved in the fall, just before Stephanie began third grade. That first winter, after the ice froze, Ruth skated out on Lake Topaqua, surprising Felix, who didn't know she could do that. Early afternoon, the sun still high, he stood at the kitchen window as Ruth glided past with Stephanie trailing her, wobbling. That night Felix made love to Ruth with a passion she thought they'd forever lost. "You're beautiful," he told her again and again. The next day she was back at it on the ice, spinning and gliding to keep her marriage alive. Stephanie was beside her again, eager to learn from her. She gave her daughter a few of Sophia's basic tips. "Head up. Back straight." Simple instructions, but Stephanie couldn't get enough of them. "What next, Mamma?" she asked gleefully, following Ruth around and around. "What do I do next?"

IRONICALLY, "WHAT DO I DO next?" was the question Ruth put to Stephanie when Felix left them four years into "the experiment," as he called it, of living in Wells. He'd been unhappy for a long time, he said. Moreover, he was in love again, with Alice Crane, his secretary of sixteen years. Ruth blinked, taking the news in. They were sitting side by side on their bed. The door was closed. Only the bathroom light was on. He had asked to speak with her privately, something he never did. It would have been a cliché, his falling for his secretary, if it weren't for Alice Crane being some years older than he was and plain. Moreover, she wasn't Jewish, and he was a committed Jew, a man who, especially given Ruth's family's travails, gave generously to the Anti-Defamation League. Ruth had an urge to tell him these things but instead she begged him to stay.

"I've packed the car already," he finally told her. "All set."

"Too sudden," she managed to utter, then she ran to the bathroom, fearing she might heave. But when she got there, she simply stood, gazing at him from the doorway.

"I can imagine," he whispered. "But not sudden, not for me."

"Can't you give us a little time to get used to the idea?"

"I'll drive my things over and then come back tonight. Sudden, yes. Of course. I didn't mean to make it so sudden for you."

"What do you want for dinner?" He was about to leave. They stood at the front door to the bungalow. Stephanie was there too, staring at them in silence.

"Nothing special," he said. "I'll come for dinner and then go."

"I'll make your favorite."

"And what's that?"

She fell into a chair, held her head in her hands. The door was shutting. "I know I should know," she said.

THAT WAS THE END, THE ribeye steak she broiled that night doing nothing to redeem the situation. By eight o'clock that evening he was gone. The next day she sat at the kitchen table, staring at the lake. Stephanie left for school and then returned. When the sky darkened, Ruth rose and made them toast with peanut butter for dinner. The next day was the same but for the fact of her spreading jam on the evening toast. Felix would gladly provide for them, he'd said. But how, she wondered, would she raise the child alone?

A week into the new life she removed herself from the kitchen table and took to lying for long hours in her bed. Near dinnertime Stephanie came in, lay beside her, took her hand. "We'll find a way, Mamma," Stephanie said, as if she knew, exactly, Ruth's doubts.

Stephanie was twelve by then but seemed older, wiser. Her words were comforting, much like the meal she prepared for them, heating up a can of chicken noodle soup and serving it with crackers and slices of an orange. She had brought the food to Ruth on a tray so she could eat in bed. When she told Ruth that they would find a way, Ruth stopped eating and looked at her girl.

"You sure?"

Stephanie nodded.

It didn't happen the next day, or the next week, or even by the end of that year. But finally, midway into the next year, Ruth did find her way, answering the phone at D'Orrino & Keller, then taking dictation, then researching titles, and finally finding case law, which opened horizons for her that she'd never imagined, even leading to her suggesting to Wilson an argument or two based on the precedents, as she knew by then to properly call them. "What would we do without you?" Wilson had said to her earlier that anniversary day, and then he'd pointed at the box containing twenty-five roses. "Beautiful," she'd said upon opening the box, as surprised by the bounty within it as she was by the length of time that had passed, and by the growth of her capacities over that time. "Just beautiful." Which is what Felix had said, staring at her, when he returned to Wells some seven years back, tired, apparently, of Alice Crane, and hoping for a reconciliation. But Ruth was long past such dreams and simply shook her head. And it's what Stephanie had said—"Just beautiful!"—even more years back when, upon Ruth receiving her first paycheck from D'Orrino & Keller, she'd walked into the bungalow carrying two pairs of brand-new skates.

◊

Several years into her father's second marriage, Stephanie saw him once with members of his new family: his wife, Alice Crane, and two of her grandchildren. Alice had been married before, with two daughters, who in turn had kids. Stephanie knew of the extended family, but they'd never met. Her father was fifty-eight then, and in the new life, which apparently came with more food, he'd developed a belly. The whole family, Stephanie noted right away, the adults and two children—about five and seven, it seemed—had a roundness to them, a softness. Stephanie was twenty-one then and home on a break from college. Looking for something to do, she'd driven to Hartford to attend an orchestra performance at the Bushnell, her mother's suggestion. By chance her father and his family were at a park across the way. Mid-October, and her father wore a sweatshirt and sneakers, like he'd never done when she was a kid. But as *their* grandfather—the two children he gently chased—he not only dressed differently but also *was* different: jovial, engaged. She thought of saying hello, but a sense of being outside her father's new life kept her at bay. In all the years since he'd left, he'd called her once weekly, on Sundays, save for the one Sunday a month when he drove to town and took her out to lunch, most often at the Topaqua Grill.

Finally, she did go over, calling out before approaching. For a moment her father seemed not to know her but then he threw his arms wide, and she rushed forward, glad to be held. Gladder than she knew. Soon she was crying and embarrassed to be doing so. She didn't even know why.

"What's wrong?" her father asked. Alice Crane took the grandchildren's hands and walked them away from Stephanie and her father.

"Nothing. Just didn't expect to see you."

He offered her his handkerchief. After she'd wiped her face, she explained she was there for the concert, which would soon start.

"I'll call you. We'll have lunch," her father said as she started to turn from him.

The Hartford Symphony performed a special all-Beethoven program, which was why her mother had suggested it. But the music sounded off, inaccessible, even a bit out of tune. Beethoven was complicated, Stephanie complained to herself at the concert's close, as she struggled to exit the auditorium, wriggling her way through a dense, talkative crowd. On the way home, she stopped at the public park at Lake Topaqua—a parking lot, swing sets, and a rocky shore, which she traversed, collecting stones. She hurled the stones, sometimes two at a time, into the lake water, and when her first pile was gone she grabbed more. Then she searched for larger stones, small boulders, to roll and lift. There was a legend about the lake. The Princess of Lake Topaqua, a member of the Wangunk tribe, had jumped into the lake to her death, a willing human sacrifice to the gods for the sake of her people. Misfortune had befallen them—some unusual drownings, a plague. She had jumped from right there, the tale went, where a rocky spit jutted out into the lake. The next week, back at Bowdoin, Stephanie would learn in a class on New England folklore that Wells's special legend was just the same tale told in any number of New England towns. But now Stephanie perched herself just where the princess had and heaved several of the boulders from that spot. "Hello, Princess!" she called, releasing a particularly heavy one. She only stopped when a car passed through the parking lot, honking, its riders calling, "What's up with you?" *My father plays with someone else's kids like he never did with me*, she wanted to call back. *We were abandoned*, she then longed to scream. Instead, she dropped the boulder she held, which landed just a half inch from where it would have crushed her foot.

Once home, she tiptoed inside, thinking her mother was asleep. It was still early evening but the darkness of the autumn night suggested otherwise. To her surprise, her mother was up, in the kitchen, brewing tea. As she poured a cup for Stephanie, she asked about the concert.

"It was good. But maybe too loud. Weird acoustics." Stephanie glanced out at the lake, its surface serene, unperturbed by the violence she'd just enacted upon it. The memory of what she'd only just done felt distant, impersonal, as if that person on the other shore wasn't really her but rather the princess of the legend. She'd been outside of her body, that much she knew. And that separation from her own being rose in her as a great sadness.

"Long trip," she told her mother. In fact, by way of running into her father she'd traveled all the way back to her childhood, taking the longest, and loneliest, trip ever.

Her mother seemed to be in her own world. Still, she nodded. "Long trip, yes," she said.

◊

THAT NIGHT OF HER TWENTY-FIFTH WORK ANNIVERSARY RUTH SAT AT HER home computer, where she searched, as she still did sometimes, "Dutch Holocaust Survivors in Connecticut." Along with the sites she'd seen before, there was a new find, a recent obituary in the *Hartford Courant*.

The woman who'd died, Betti Leib, was eighty-two, had married twice, was a mother of three, and had lived in West Hartford not far from where Ruth and Felix had once lived. Born in Utrecht, Betti had moved to Amsterdam by the time of the German occupation of 1940. She'd left promptly after that, fleeing to Switzerland by way of southern France. Getting out relatively early was the key to her successful survival, she was reported to have said. She'd waited out the war in Switzerland, tutoring orphaned children. When the war ended only a brother—one of three—had survived. Eventually she came to America, a "displaced person." That's how she always felt, the obituary noted: "displaced." Nevertheless, she had become a leader at her synagogue, a chairwoman for the sisterhood there, as well as for the local Hadassah group.

Ruth read the obituary three times, reaching out, finally, to touch the words on the screen. "Betti Leib," she said out loud, wishing she'd met her back in those days in West Hartford, but always Ruth had refused to join a synagogue, telling Felix repeatedly that it wasn't safe to congregate that way.

Maybe she'd been wrong.

She rose, walked down to the kitchen, and stared out the window. Over what she could see of the lake the moon had moved, which meant the world was indeed spinning. She could feel that grand spin and steadied herself by sitting down. She dropped her head into her hands. She was remembering, suddenly, and feeling heavy as she did.

Toward the end, before she and her parents had fled Amsterdam, she'd gone out once, by herself, to find Sophia. As on the night when she and Sophia had skated at Oosterpark, Sophia was once again taking off, waving goodbye, telling them all she'd just be a minute, no worries. But they did worry, each minute of the increasingly long periods that Sophia dared to be away.

Toward the end, the fear for Sophia had spread to fear for herself and everyone she knew. The police, be they German or Dutch, were more present on the streets, and increasingly merciless. Cruelty, she'd come to see firsthand, was contagious. There were raids, brutal with beatings. And the anti-Jewish laws were like blows of a hammer, incrementally clubbing them down and down. They couldn't leave Amsterdam . . . They couldn't possess a radio . . . They couldn't drive a car . . .

Toward the end, her friend Henny Ganz was too afraid to open her first-floor apartment door when Ruttie knocked and knocked. "But it's me," she called.

"Go home," Henny whispered. "We're never to open the door anymore. Papa said so."

"He said never?"

"Never."

"Will you no longer come to school?"

"He said better to learn at home."

"But how will I see you? I have to see you."

"Ruttie, as soon as it's over," Henny said, "I'll be right here."

PART TWO

5

Netherlands, September 1, 1941, by Edict of the Secretary-General of the Department of Education, Science, and the Protection of Culture: Jewish children are to attend separate schools called "unsubsidized institutions of special education."

THAT DURING THE HARD TIMES in Amsterdam Sophia and Ruttie's father, Jozef Jacobsen, had found help in, of all people, Ollie van der Waal, a person so very difficult for Jozef to come to like much less trust and love, was a fact that Jozef would ponder again and again as death approached him. Jozef lived then in the one-bedroom apartment in West Hartford, Connecticut, that Felix Pearl had purchased for him and Tessa nearly twenty years before, though Jozef had quickly assumed the mortgage. Jozef's employer, Grober's Jewelers, was just off Main Street on Farmington Avenue, and from his apartment Jozef could walk there, stopping along the way to buy a sandwich he'd eat for lunch later in the day. At five-thirty he'd trundle home and there would be Tessa, sitting by the window as she embroidered onto square linen panels the stories of the past, before it all turned bad. Recently, in early spring of 1976, as his final illness progressed, Jozef came to see that despite their having fled from everything and everyone they knew, because Tessa had been with him he'd never felt completely lost. Death was fast approaching and he suddenly grasped that. Knew, too, that he loved his friend, Ollie van der Waal, not seen in thirty-four years, almost as dearly as he loved Tessa. Though Jozef's voice in the last month had diminished to but a crackly whisper, there was so much to say before he went, so much to tell Tessa about his understanding, however modest and still unfolding, of love.

* * *

HE'D LEARNED ABOUT LOVE, FIRST and foremost, from his mother, Margreet Annevelink, the daughter of Dutch Calvinists, an only child who had fallen in love and defiantly married his Jewish father, Simon Jacobsen. The year they met was 1900 and Simon, like many within his world, had gone into the diamond trade—historically ungoverned by the Dutch guild laws and therefore, unlike most occupations that excluded Jews, long open to them. By then the diamond work was factory based, with polishing wheels powered by steam. And the factories were hiring. As a diamond polisher, even one still learning the art and craft of it, Simon knew he could earn a worker's wage. He knew too that he and his family would no longer be, like his neighbors and like most Ashkenazi Jews, the poorest among Amsterdam's poor. If he worked hard enough, he could leave that crowded slum of a neighborhood behind. In the months following his two-year apprenticeship, a true polisher at last, he moved his brother and parents from Rapenburgerstraat, a poor Jewish neighborhood, to Nieuwe Kerkstraat, a less poor Jewish neighborhood. Simon's family now had a separate dining room and kitchen. His younger brother still slept in the kitchen, by the stove, but Simon slept upstairs, smothered in blankets in his own room. At the time, because the Sephardic Jewish community from Portugal had arrived in Amsterdam earlier and integrated deeper, they were often wealthier than the average Ashkenazi Jew. Simon, of course, knew that. And so when he came to work for the Boas brothers—Ashkenazi, like him—his pride was as outsized as the Boas diamond factory on Nieuwe Uilenburgerstraat. Israel and Marcus Boas, and their late brother Hartog, were the kings of that enterprise, but at night, within the walls of his snug but private bedroom, Simon felt himself as self-made as each of them. Hartog Boas had succumbed to the dust lung that took so many diamond workers, but Simon accepted the risks. How else to move up?

Come the new year he decided to buy himself a new winter coat. His current coat was in tatters, and he could use the extra funds he had to finally replace it. The tailor he decided upon worked across the Amstel, in a shop off Dam Square. He'd never been to that shop, owned by a family he knew wasn't Jewish. But a coworker at the diamond factory had told him that the coats produced there were sewn to last, a wise investment. When Simon arrived at the tailor's shop near closing time one snowy February evening it was the remarkable warmth there, from a wood stove, that convinced him he'd come to the right place for the task at hand. His shivering had been irrepressible as he'd crossed over the Amstel, his nearly useless old coat flapping about his frame as the winter winds whipped past. But merely entering the shop calmed his rattling, convincing him further that a coat from here would do that too. From the doorway he saw a few finished coats, enticingly long and thick, hanging on hooks along one wall. Three sewing machines lined the opposite wall. In the room's middle stood a large table strewn with bolts of wool, piles of buttons, and spools of thread.

Margreet approached him. Her father, the tailor, was sick, she said, and then, "No need to worry!" as Simon stepped back from her, turning to leave. He couldn't imagine getting fitted by a woman. Her presence disoriented him. A woman in a shop? But then she moved away and a male tailor, her father's assistant, emerged, tape measure in hand. As Simon—his old coat hanging on a hook and his arms akimbo—stood before the assistant tailor, Margreet took notes about Simon's preferences for his new coat: belted or not, this kind of collar or that . . . She understood the helplessness, as she put it, of a relentless chill. He nodded. Helpless. Yes. That was exactly the pain of it. He studied her face. She had blue eyes and tawny hair that she wore pinned up in the back. She was serious, but she was smiling too, a look he considered, for some reason, quiet.

Simon saw Margreet again three weeks later when he returned for a fitting, and he saw her again the following week when he returned for the finished coat. He stood in the shop's fitting room with the coat on, buttoned to his neck. The assistant tailor tugged at the sleeves, just to be sure. But it was a perfect fit, just as Simon had been told by his coworker to expect. During this time Margreet, as she'd done before, had taken a step back, sensing his discomfort around her. But he was no longer wary. "Yes?" he asked her. "Oh, yes," she said, nodding happily. How was her father, Simon then asked, but he was soon sorry to have done so. The young woman's face—he still didn't know her name—crumpled into sadness. "Don't know," she said.

Two weeks passed, during which time the new coat, thick with its double lining, relieved Simon from the cold in a way he'd never felt before. He arrived at the Boas factory each day with renewed spirit and even took to praying with coworkers in the little shul within the factory. His life was improving just as the late February days were—still dark but lightening with steady incremental movement. Amsterdam was, more and more to him, his *Mokum*. Though he knew it would take years more to perfect his knowledge of diamond polishing he also sensed how he improved day by day. Every rock had its flaw, and the art of polishing diamonds—beyond the complicated craft of technique—was knowing what to do with the flaw. Yes, you could remove it, but sometimes it worked best to shape the stone around it.

He returned to the tailor's shop with the thought of purchasing coats for his parents. He didn't know it yet, but a part of him went to see Margreet. A month had passed since he'd walked out with his new coat, but when he returned Margreet smiled as soon as she saw him wiping his feet in the cramped entranceway. To his surprise she even clapped. "Spin," she suggested, and soon he was turning in his coat. "Is there a problem?" she asked, suddenly worried.

When he told her that he would purchase two more coats, she said, her eyes big, "You sure?" He could afford it, he told her. Then her face flushed red as if something intimate had passed between them. And maybe something had. He was barely working class—how could she not know? But he went on determinedly with the sizable order. One coat for his mother, who was about Margreet's height and shape. She could do the fittings. The other for his father, who was the approximate size of the assistant tailor. These were to be gifts. Surprises. He would pay the coats off in installments over the next year if they allowed it. He was a *diment-shlayfer,* he finally explained, using his father's Yiddish. He quickly corrected himself. A diamond polisher. They could trust him for the money. Amsterdam was awash with the gems. His job, he said, was to shape them and make them sparkle as brilliantly as a snowflake. Her cheeks flushed again.

Over the course of the several fittings for the two additional coats, something between them came alive. Each month when he returned to the shop to pay the next installment he spent more time with Margreet. The first month she made him a cup of tea and then another. The second month, April, she offered him tea and slices of an apple. In May, the daylight already lasting well into the evenings, he suggested they go for a walk, and she agreed to. They crossed the Amstel, ambled south, then crossed the river again, this time stopping on the bridge to watch the swift flow of the waters below. They lingered, watching and watching. In June she held his elbow as they walked, then held it again when he returned a week later—for the first time not to make a payment but simply to see her. From then on theirs was a secret courtship—the only child of a sickly Protestant tailor waiting eagerly for each visit from the eldest son of a poor Jew. By September he had joined—despite the Boas management's antagonism toward it—the General Union of Dutch Diamond Workers. Economic progress was now his hope of the future, and everything seemed possible. In November Simon asked Margreet to marry him. They had yet to talk to her parents. Oh, yes, she said anyway. Yes.

MARGREET WAS A WOMAN WITH delicate features and a round sweetness to her face—by any standard a picture of loveliness—and Jozef Jacobsen recalled his mother as a person fierce in her attachments and her loyalties. She would not pull herself from the orbit of those she cared for most deeply, be it her sickly father—who died the second summer of her marriage to Simon—or Simon himself, despite the fact that marrying him had put a wedge between Margreet and more than a few members of her Protestant world. But Margreet was firm, and that's where Sophia had gotten her capacity for love, Jozef realized, seeing more and more as the years passed, as the memory of Sophia loomed in his mind larger and larger, that his elder daughter's will to love—that quality that brought her so swiftly to ruin—was an inheritance, something she could no more shake herself free from than her beautiful face and hair. It didn't matter that Sophia had never met Margreet, who died when Jozef was eleven years old—gone even more suddenly, his father explained, than Margreet's father was those years before. No, Sophia hadn't known her grandmother, but something had been passed down nonetheless, seemingly through the very core of Jozef's being. After his mother's death, Jozef's father, Simon, had not recovered easily from the grief. So maybe, Jozef reasoned, Sophia had inherited something from that line too.

AS FOR OLLIE VAN DER WAAL—the man who would become Jozef's greatest friend, who would take Jozef's family in to protect them and who, in the end, would bury their beloved Sophia—there was simply no love at first but rather an antipathy on Jozef's part that kept him as far from Ollie as possible. They met through the chess club that Jozef had joined some years back. The other club members, seven men, were diamond workers like him at the Asscher factory. All were Jewish. But when one died—another man taken by lung disease—Ollie van der Waal, a friend of a friend and owner of his own small diamond enterprise, was invited in. But he didn't belong with them, or so Jozef thought right away, and this was not because Ollie was Christian—Jozef's mother, Margreet, was too—but because of the way Ollie couldn't stop talking throughout the chess games.

The club met twice monthly, on Wednesday evenings in an empty backroom of a warehouse just beyond the flea market in Waterlooplein. One of the men, Franz Hoffman, had access to the space, and over time the tables they used were set up permanently, with chessboards placed upon them and crates at each end for sitting. The walls were bare but for a single photograph, of Dr. Max Euwe, the famous Dutchman who in 1935, the year before Ollie's arrival, had won the world championship in chess and sent the country into a craze for the game. Under the exacting eye of Dr. Euwe, then, the men played and smoked and talked little. The quiet and focus relaxed Jozef—the world fell away those few hours every other Wednesday—and he assumed the others felt that too. They'd been a club for four years before Ollie joined them.

At Ollie's first meeting with them, a rainy evening in late October 1936, he'd shaken the hands of each of them, pressing and pressing, and saying *misjpoge*, Dutch-Yiddish for "family," again and again, which was not how they greeted one another. Ollie was tall, lean, his chin sharp, his hair overgrown and curly. He wore three sweaters, the top two of which he tore off once the games got going, as if playing chess were a physical exertion. He arrived with a thermos of coffee, which he drank in tiny sips throughout the hours. He smoked a pipe rather than a cigarette, and his tobacco smelled of the woods. It wasn't a bad scent, just out of place, and engulfing. Twice Jozef stepped outside for what he called "simpler air." Throughout his game Ollie spoke of the weather, of his family—in Amsterdam just him and his wife—and of the last time he'd played chess, several years ago already. He didn't know where the time had gone. Business was hard, he said, but wasn't it everywhere? He spoke and spoke and none of it mattered. "Good one," he exclaimed every so often that first night, even over the mere loss of a pawn or bishop. "Good one!" he cried louder when it was finally checkmate and he lost to Eli Winnick, the second weakest player in the club.

The other men didn't find Ollie troublesome, but Jozef avoided him, sitting at each gathering, if possible, at the opposite end of the warehouse room. Somehow a year passed and Jozef played directly against Ollie van der Waal only once. Another year passed and another, and still no friendship grew. Though Jozef adjusted to the tobacco smell, the constant sipping of coffee, and by then a variety of odd greetings, he nevertheless remained incurious about the man who would one day aid his family in their terrible need. The phrase "good one" particularly grated on Jozef, and in the winter of 1939, when he unwittingly voiced the words himself one evening while helping Ruttie with math equations, he rushed to the kitchen to gulp water as if to rinse his vocal cords clean. Returning, he told Ruttie, "I only meant you're doing nicely. Very nice."

It was a Wednesday in April of 1939 when Ollie didn't show up for chess. That meant one man had to sit out from playing, and Jozef didn't mind being that man. He simply sat, watching the others, enjoying the renewed peace. When the next Wednesday came round and Ollie still didn't show, it was Franz Hoffman who reported that Ollie's wife had died. Though the news was sad, Jozef felt some relief too. Without Ollie they'd have another calm session. Jozef won that night, his concentration perfect. Two weeks later—the third club meeting without Ollie—Franz Hoffman had more news: Ollie wasn't doing well since his wife had passed. A visit might help. Even a note.

Jozef wasn't one of the several men from the chess club to visit or write, but one evening, mid-June, making his way home from work, Jozef saw Ollie as he emerged from a grocery store. Walking only steps ahead of Jozef, Ollie moved slowly, holding grocery bags in both his hands. Despite the warmer weather he was wearing a typical layering of sweaters and his hair was wild. To avoid a run-in Jozef slackened his pace, almost stopping, and then he did stop, because that's what Ollie did. Ollie put down his bags on the sidewalk beside him. A minute passed, during which Ollie simply stood, staring ahead—and then he began walking again, though without his bags of groceries.

Jozef sprinted forward to retrieve the forgotten bags, and as he reached them so did a clerk from the grocery store.

"These are his," he explained to her, pointing ahead toward Ollie.

"I know. He does this sometimes," she replied. "Probably won't remember to cook food tonight anyway." The woman told Jozef she would take the groceries to him. "You know, he lost his wife," she said and then walked forward, arms full, toward Ollie.

A week later Jozef did visit Ollie, whose apartment, not far from the grocery, smelled familiar to Jozef—it was the same woodsy tobacco scent with which Ollie had infused the chess club. Jozef gave Ollie a gift of cookies and Ollie nodded, taking them. Then, in silence, he brewed tea. A few minutes later they sat sipping their drinks at Ollie's kitchen table, which wobbled a bit and caused the tea in one of the cups to nearly spill. "Careful," Ollie said. This was his first spoken word. Jozef nodded and moved his chair closer in. Outside, through a window by the table, Jozef could see that children were playing below, throwing a ball. Jozef went back and forth watching the children and watching Ollie. On a scrap of paper near Ollie's cup Jozef read some scribbled words: *A free man thinks of death least of all things; and his wisdom is a meditation not on death but on life.* "The philosopher Spinoza," Ollie said, catching Jozef reading the note. "I thought it would help, but I'm not a free man. Not at all." Jozef continued to ponder the words, then to watch the children again. He was about to tell Ollie how sorry he was for his loss when Ollie, his voice cracking, said, "I didn't love her as much as I should have." But it wasn't so, Jozef could see, and he told Ollie as much. The silence continued. The children below went inside. Some minutes later Ollie rose to wash the tears from his face. Jozef rose too, stepped into the living room, and was surprised to see, as he hadn't before, so many books strewn about. Ollie was a reader, though from his mindless prattle at the chess club he seemed anything but. Jozef read too, at night when he wasn't too tired. Though philosophy was his passion he hadn't gotten to Spinoza yet.

The next time Jozef visited, some weeks later, he brought Ollie a book, Dr. Max Euwe's *Strategy & Tactics in Chess.* "It's not Spinoza but thought you might like it," Jozef said. Ollie put the book on top of one of his many piles. He again brewed tea. He didn't weep this time, but over the hour of the visit he said two times more, "I didn't love her as much as I should have."

"Of course you did," Jozef answered both times. But he knew his reassurances wouldn't help. For it was his own father, crippled by loss after his mother died, who said the very same thing again and again.

JOZEF BEGAN TO VISIT OLLIE regularly after that, bringing him the gift of a new chess set at one point, and the two began to play regularly at the rickety kitchen table. Ollie no longer engaged in shallow prattle. The loss had deepened something in Ollie, it seemed, or silenced something. Either way, Jozef began to enjoy the time there, by the window, which Ollie kept open as the summer advanced and moved into fall. By then Ollie had rejoined the chess club, though the two men continued to play on their own, too, as the weather turned to spring. The phrase "good one" no longer grated, perhaps because Ollie now said it with the same undertone of gentleness that he said everything. A softening, the loss was, of a sort. It was early spring, 1940, before the Germans had invaded, when Ollie first broached the possibility of Jozef polishing diamonds at Ollie's workplace. No, was the swift answer from Jozef, who took pride in being at the top with the prominent Asscher company. Ollie's business was a small cutting shop, selling locally. To sustain his business during the Depression years Ollie had deftly turned to textiles—selling fabrics and carpets—for backup. Though by the time Ollie brought up the idea of Jozef's joining him the Depression had eased some, it seemed to Jozef that Ollie's business, still supplemented with carpet sales, was no place to join.

But nearly a year into the German occupation Jozef finally turned to Ollie. Abraham Asscher had just become a leader of the Jewish Council—an agency formed at the demand of the Germans, a tool for them, Jozef sensed from the start, long before the Council complied with a German order to select thousands of Jews for deportation to labor camps. Hiring anyone was absurd, Ollie knew, but hiring a Jew—even a nonreligious half Jew like Jozef—would be all but impossible to justify to his few remaining employees. The effort was especially poignant to Jozef knowing that Ollie's sister, Saskia, had recently moved from Breda back to Amsterdam following a separation from her husband. Ollie now paid for the additional rent of an apartment for Saskia and her two boys. Despite the difficulties, Ollie convinced his staff—all Protestants, like him—based on a truth he deeply believed: everyone in the diamond trade in Amsterdam knew the value of having Jozef Jacobsen to polish. He said, "I hired Mr. Jacobsen because he's the very best. A shrewd move, because once this is over"—Ollie threw his arms out as if batting an annoying something or other away—"my business, small as it is, will nevertheless be the very best too."

OLLIE HIRED JOZEF IN LATE February of 1941. The month before, the government had ordered all Jewish people, meaning people with at least one Jewish grandparent, to report in person for registration with the population administration. Identification cards resulted, stamped in large, thick type with the letter J. Under the broad sweep of the registration order—which included full Jews, half Jews, and quarter Jews—all kinds of people, even some far removed from participation in the Dutch Jewish community, were now "Jews." Of course Jozef's wife, Tessa, and their children met the definition, and Jozef did too, even though his mother wasn't Jewish and therefore the religious Jewish community wouldn't define him as such. Jewish, though he'd grown up with just a hint of his father's religion. What to do? Should they comply? This was the question Jozef brought to the man he now considered his most trusted friend. He and Ollie talked in the small office in the back of Ollie's shop. What did it mean to be registered? While the intention of the Germans couldn't be good, how they were going to use the registrations simply wasn't clear.

Moreover, it could be worse to disobey. They discussed that too.

In the end, the love of their joint life in Amsterdam, the belief that the Dutch people could be trusted, would do the right thing and weren't really under the control or spell of the Nazis, and the disbelief that a registration alone could lead to serious harm, were reasons enough for the men to agree: Jozef and his family would register. They'd follow the law.

But then came late February, a Sunday, the second of two days when the German police dragged hundreds of Jewish men into the streets. As they rounded them up, forcing them at gunpoint to their knees, then beating and kicking them before herding them onto trucks, Jozef and Ollie watched as best they could from a safe distance before they rushed away. They had come to the old Jewish neighborhood, which had been temporarily closed off but was now open again, simply to walk. Inadvertently, like others, they became witnesses, their eyes wide, their heads shaking back and forth, Ollie's body, his lanky frame covered in sweaters, trembling. Jozef gradually stiffened as if frozen. The raid, Jozef and Ollie would come to learn, was aimed at punishing a rising Jewish resistance to the increased violence of the Dutch pro-Nazi movement's assault group, which had taken to vandalizing and attacking Jewish shops and cafés. In one incident, a fight at a Jewish-owned ice cream shop between self-defending Jews and

German police who were mistaken for Dutch Nazis left several German police wounded. Revenge, apparently, was called for.

Two days after the violent raid the greater Dutch public, shocked as much as Jozef and Ollie by the brutality, went on strike, with workers from the transportation system, docks, factories, and public services all standing in solidarity with the Jewish community, and for that day and the next, while the strike ensued, Ollie told Jozef that he was reassured of the reasoning they'd come to regarding the registration the month before. There were evil forces here, Ollie said—they'd seen as much with their own eyes—but those forces could be held in check. From the strike alone they read that nine more people were dead, fifty injured, and another two hundred arrested. All true, and yet, and yet . . . civility *would* prevail. Ollie told Jozef this again and again, but in the end, Jozef knew that Ollie didn't believe his own words, spoken with the same resignation with which he'd once said, "I didn't love her as much as I should have." The tone told Jozef that Ollie couldn't shake what he'd seen: The guns. The forced submission. Men on their knees, arms raised. Over time Jozef had gotten fixated on a toppled pushcart of carrots off in the distance—simple carrots—scattered and smashed.

It was then that Jozef decided he would work for Ollie. Jozef's boss, Abraham Asscher, in his new role as a co-leader of the Amsterdam Jewish Council, following German orders and surely under threat of German retribution against the Jewish community, had helped to disarm the Jewish community that was then violated. Jozef had always admired Asscher, but now he didn't know if he could trust him.

"It might as well have been me whom they'd beaten," Ollie told Jozef that first day of Jozef's new employment, a week after the brutal raid. The two sat in Ollie's office, as they'd done many a time before, but now they closed the door. Just talking, they feared, could lead to punishment, like the beatings they'd witnessed. As they spoke, they ate freshly baked strudel that Tessa had made for all the men in the shop.

"This tastes different. Has Tessa changed her recipe?" Ollie asked.

"It's the world that's changed," Jozef said.

The men nodded, their faces serious.

"Such an odd combination," Jozef added, "good food, Ollie, and terrible dreams."

THE FRIENDS MADE THEIR WAY around the anti-Jewish laws that kept coming in the next months. In April of 1941, for example, Jews were not allowed to move from Amsterdam to other parts of the country. Also in April, the Jewish Council, under German authority, published the first issue of the *Jewish Weekly*, which soon became a prime venue for announcing many of the prohibitions against Jews that were to come. In May Jewish professionals—including lawyers, doctors, pharmacists, midwives, and translators—were barred from working with non-Jews. In June three hundred Jews were arrested and deported following a second major raid. In August Jews were ordered to transfer their assets—including cash, checks, and bank deposits—to Lippmann, Rosenthal & Co. on Sarphatistraat, which turned out to be a looting bank, a Nazi-created sham of the long-established and trusted Jewish bank of the same name on Nieuwe Spiegelstraat. In September signs appeared banning Jews from any number of public places, Jewish children could no longer attend public schools, and the Nazis even began to raid Jewish libraries, eventually including the Societas Spinoza in the Hague and the Spinoza House in Rijnsburg. In October a new decree made it easy to fire Jewish workers. In November work permits for 1,600 Jewish textile and clothing traders were withdrawn, and Jewish stamp and antique dealers were likewise shut down. Late in November all German Jews living abroad were deprived of their German nationality, and come December of 1941 non-Dutch Jews, i.e., German Jews living in the Netherlands, were forced to register for so-called voluntary emigration. But for God's sake, Jozef asked himself again and again once Aaron Taube's family had disappeared, emigrate to where?

All this time Ollie and Jozef decided it was best that Jozef stay out of sight and work only in the shop's attic. By October Ollie decided that every evening he would walk Jozef home. "We look similar enough, like brothers. You're good with me," he told Jozef, who couldn't imagine that the two looked anything alike—Ollie with his crazy hair and odd sweaters, and Jozef, close to bald and in his father's old coat. Nor could Jozef believe how the dynamic between the men had shifted; for so long, settling into his widower's life, Ollie had been the needy one, yet Jozef was now by far the more vulnerable of the two. "Thank you," he told his friend as they left work each evening in the direction of Oosterpark, Jozef a half step behind Ollie, which made Jozef feel safer. Ollie seemed to sense that and, no questions asked, led the way.

THEY TALKED ABOUT HIDING JOZEF'S family, should the worst occur. Ollie even found a place in his warehouse in the Pijp district. He'd build a fake wall in the back and the family could live there, almost comfortably, behind it. They imagined a few months of confinement, tops.

"Just until it ends. Soon," Ollie told Jozef.

"Yes, soon," Jozef responded.

There was talk, too, between Jozef and Tessa of putting the girls in hiding in a different way, sending them to live with a sympathetic Christian family, if one could be found—though not with Ollie or his sister Saskia, as that was too obvious. But the girls were already in their teens and therefore difficult to place, and it was impossible to consider such a separation. They knew, though, that other parents were discussing it: separating from their children, splitting up siblings. Inconceivable and necessary—*should the worst ensue*. That was a phrase now, common enough.

Late fall of 1941 Ollie began buying supplies: wooden boards for the wall-to-be, a mattress, then another, hot plates, two pots for their human waste. But in the end they never reached the point of hiding. Aaron Taube was gone and Sophia Jacobsen, in her way, was gone with him. Whatever had been sensible within her, whatever had been stable and grounded: gone.

Every Friday in the weeks following Aaron's disappearance, Sophia returned to Oosterpark to skate, though no longer with Ruttie, each time defying the prohibition that as a Jew she could not be in the park. She didn't tell her parents. She simply said, as she had when she and Aaron had snuck off to their nook on Friday evenings, "I have to prepare for the Sabbath." Her parents took this to mean that she left to attend a Sabbath welcoming service—no doubt at the Uilenburg Shul—in the old neighborhood. Such was the nature of Sophia and Aaron's resistance to the antisemitism surrounding them: a religious awakening.

Even without Aaron, then, Sophia would carry on going to shul, or so her parents had chosen to believe. She was adamant that she go, which gave Jozef and Tessa the idea that her grief simply required it. That's how they justified allowing her out, and they would nod, though warily, when Sophia would say, brightly enough, "Be right back!" Even if they didn't allow it they knew she'd go anyway, driven by her despair to repeat the routines she'd shared with Aaron. They lost all arguments that Shabbos was even more true when kindling the candles at home. No, no, she had to go, she insisted, and go alone. Better, they thought in the end, that she at least told them rather than feel she had to sneak off.

But sneak she did, into Oosterpark, where on the ice something else was happening, a new pattern emerging. That she'd see German police there was all but guaranteed given that they were housed in a building they'd taken over at the edge of the park. And as soon as she spotted their green uniforms she'd spin, faster and faster. Then she'd raise a leg, circling slowly on one foot. The catcalls coming from the men didn't scare her but rather enticed her to do it again, on the other foot, or so they seemed to be saying. And she would.

EARLY IN FEBRUARY 1942 MEMBERS of the green-uniformed German police, the "Green Police," showed up outside the Jacobsen home—calling "Spinning Girl, Spinning Girl, where are you?" Jozef told Ollie about the police and about Sophia, whom he assumed had been standing each preceding Friday outside a synagogue, confused, grief-stricken, and, because she was still desperately looking for Aaron, apparently turning round and round. "I know about grief," Ollie said. "Maybe I can help." He then offered to house Jozef's family with him. "Just until this attention stops. And we'll keep Sophia with us come Friday."

The guest room at Ollie's apartment had no windows and the darkness only intensified Sophia's yearning for Aaron. Confusingly, she called the room the family shared "a closet," and almost immediately she began to have nightmares, waking up screaming for Aaron. Tessa took to sleeping with Sophia, to comfort her the instant she awoke, and to smother her mouth, should the cries wake the others. And it was good for Ruttie to have Jozef to turn to at those times, for her sister's cries were devastating to experience.

Despite the tearful nights, the days that first week and the next were, to Jozef's relief, quite ordinary. The girls still went to school. Jozef and Ollie still went to work. During the day Tessa reportedly spent her time quietly embroidering. She drank coffee with Saskia, Ollie's sister. And during the evenings she began to teach the families, even Ollie and Jozef, the tricks of thread and needle—a skill that would ultimately come in handy when, months later, Jozef would apply for a visa from the American consul in Lisbon, Portugal, telling the authority, almost truthfully, that he could do the work of both a diamond polisher and a tailor.

Evenings, then, were a reprieve. The dinner table cleared of dishes and food, Tessa would then spread out her spools of colored thread, bins of needles, thimbles, scissors, embroidery hoops, and squares of linen. Saskia made tea. It was especially funny for the children to see the grown men take up sewing, and Jozef was happy enough to close the day out as a clown.

They embroidered their memories: for Sophia this was the Apollohal where she'd had her beloved skating lessons. For Jozef this was the shul at the Boas factory, which his father had once taken him to. For Tessa this was the family table, set with her best dishes and glassware. "My jewels," she sadly said, as if the scene were already part of the past.

On the third Friday at Ollie's, in late February, Sophia decided that at dusk she'd once again go to shul. "It's our duty to observe the Sabbath," she announced, her voice as commanding as the words in the sacred texts.

"Have you gone mad?" Tessa said back.

It appeared so, and if Sophia's ritual of going to shul continued, Ollie told Jozef that evening after Sophia returned, her darting eyes filled with an odd energy, they would have to leave. Should the worst happen, he argued, there was no point in hiding—Sophia would just leave as she was leaving now. By then Jozef and Tessa understood that Sophia, by way of going off alone each Friday, was determined to put herself at risk. That she was out of control. That the loss of Aaron Taube had, at least for now, ruined her. Ollie didn't need to convince them of that.

Ollie traveled then, setting off that very day for Tilburg, near Belgium, where his brother worked in textiles and where Ollie aimed to find a smuggler to take Jozef's family across the border. He returned a week later and told Jozef that his brother's colleague knew of someone who would create new Belgium I.D.s, and a different man would sneak them across the border and through Belgium. Maybe even into France, as far as Paris, but they'd need new documents to go on from there. This was on a Thursday morning, the last week in February. They talked in Ollie's kitchen, facing the window over his small table where the men had once played chess. Though Ollie's clothes were clean, he hadn't shaved in days. A new boldness in his eyes made them not larger but brighter. From his shop he had diamonds, a dozen, for them to take, and he had bills of money too, some in Belgian currency, some in French. They would leave on Saturday, he said. Between now and then—just two days—Jozef's family should return home, gather their belongings, and mark anything that needed safeguarding. Ollie would come after they left and look things over. One more Friday to endure, Ollie noted. That was it. One more.

"Tie her up," Ollie then told Jozef, who, shocked, stepped back from his friend. His daughter was not an animal. "She feels like my daughter, too. Tie her up," Ollie repeated before he pulled Jozef into an embrace, one that, upon his deathbed thirty-four years later, Jozef would remember in remarkable detail: the onion-like smell of Ollie's breath, the thickness of his sweaters, the scratch of his beard as his face brushed slightly against Jozef's face. A deepening of friendship, so many moments side by side, so many tears openly spilled, and yet they'd never embraced. But this was goodbye and, most likely, for all time. Jozef held on to Ollie as fiercely as Ollie gripped him.

"Tie her up."

"I can't."

"Tie her up."

"I will."

"I'll see you soon."

"Soon, Ollie."

They stepped back. They shook hands.

"Jozef Jacobsen."

"Ollie van der Waal."

"Soon," said one, and the other answered, "Soon."

JOZEF NEVER PLAYED CHESS AGAIN. Not after he and his family settled in Manhattan, and not after they moved to West Hartford. Jozef's chess was an act of warmth between friends. But he didn't find that kind of friendship in America.

From his first days in the new country he started writing letters to Ollie. Yet despite Jozef's persistence in contacting Ollie years went by before he heard word of him. Jozef was sixty-four already when a small package arrived at the West Hartford apartment from Ollie's sister Saskia. In it was a bundle of ten letters Saskia had written to Jozef over the years, but due to faulty addresses all had been returned to her. She'd addressed the first letter, dated 1949, simply "America. New York." The next, dated 1950, bore the same doomed non-address. Letters from 1951 and 1952 were addressed to the Jewish Museum in Manhattan, and two more, from 1954 and 1956, were addressed to Congregation Shearith Israel, New York's oldest synagogue, founded by Jews of Spanish and Portuguese descent, a place that Jozef had visited several times when he lived in Manhattan as it reminded him of Amsterdam's Portuguese Synagogue. In it, he recalled as he held one of Saskia's letters, he'd felt a little bit at home. All the rest were sent to the United Jewish Appeal in New York City and were dated from 1959 through 1964. How Saskia had finally found Jozef's West Hartford address the letters in the bundle did not say.

The letters contained the same news. Ollie had been dead since 1944, Saskia reported, telling Jozef that after he and his family had left Amsterdam at the end of February of 1942, Ollie had channeled his considerable grief over Jozef's absence into action. *He couldn't stop himself from helping another family in just the way he'd helped yours,* she wrote, her penmanship perfect, her words in a language Jozef had not read for years and years. *And in May, three months after your departure, when Jews were required to wear the yellow stars on their clothing, Ollie went about his business adorned with a yellow carnation. He'd taken to wearing a jacket over his sweaters to accommodate the carnation. During those same months Ollie made several trips to Tilburg. By summer, when the deportation of Jews set in full scale, Ollie had come close to depleting his bank account, paying off smugglers and forgers, giving his diamonds away. I didn't cry until August of that year,* Saskia continued. *My children and I lived with Ollie at this point and for lack of funds we ate but beans and potatoes. We'd become poor. Poor as Jews. But my brother was compelled to help and help again.*

This last sentence was the only one Saskia changed from letter to letter.

But my good brother was compelled to help again and again.

But my generous brother, my salvation when I was in need, was compelled to help again and again.

In the end, Saskia continued, before Ollie was arrested, his apartment raided one otherwise quiet evening in May of 1943, he'd helped three other families flee. But whether he'd saved any lives he simply didn't know. Nor did Saskia, even in the most recent letters. *Will this ever reach you?* she asked. *Are you even alive?*

And in the end, because Ollie was considered by the German authorities no different from a Jew—*and he'd have been the first to admit that,* Saskia noted—he died in Kamp Amersfoort, imprisoned there. *Just like a Jew,* each of her letters concluded. They then closed with, *My thoughts are with you, Jozef, and your family. Your eternal friend, Saskia Visser (née van der Waal).*

As Jozef read Saskia's words he realized that Saskia was not only telling him the story of Ollie, but also of herself, of her long-standing grief.

He couldn't help himself from helping. That was my brother.

Jozef knew that grief. For years already he had a ritual of looking into the night sky through a small telescope he'd managed to buy secondhand, rejoicing in the beauty of the natural world. Seeing the vastness of the universe gave him comfort, simply enough. There was always more to every situation than a person could possibly comprehend; the night sky seemed to confirm this sense and thus Jozef found a home for his chronic postwar bewilderment in that visual boundlessness. But once Saskia's letters arrived Jozef could no longer stargaze. He aimed the telescope eastward, peering instead toward what he believed was Amsterdam. "I see you," he said of Ollie, and it didn't matter that the gesture and words made no sense. For weeks, night after night, Jozef searched, until Tessa, worried he'd gone mad, finally removed the telescope from its window perch and the next day gave it to the local high school. "All we can do is remember him," Tessa said, and she insisted right then that they light two candles and chant as best they could the mourner's Kaddish, the Hebrew prayer for the dead. "There's Ollie," Tessa said, pointing to the candle on the right. "And there's Sophia," she said pointing to the other one.

But before all that there came the evening several weeks back when Saskia's letters first arrived. The deeper Jozef read into them the more he couldn't tell if Saskia was simply proud of Ollie or whether she was angry too. *Poor as Jews.* She had written that. But by 1949, the year of the first letter, the community wasn't poor anymore. Rather, the community was no more. She seemed to have forgotten that. He turned to the telescope for a minute's reflection. After the look he read Saskia's closing again, warily, describing Ollie's death. *Just like a Jew,* she said.

The day after receiving Willa Fletcher's draft complaint, Arthur Cantrell began writing down his version of the statements and events she described, to have in case she actually filed it, but he was writing in circles and soon stopped, dropping his pen and lifting his trombone instead. All morning, the third Saturday in January—the day of the presidential inauguration—Arthur had done this: write a sentence, cross it out, then play a song. Write then play, which, given his musical choices, was like writing and weeping. I'm sorry I hurt you, he wanted to tell Willa, who was hurting him, deeply, but contacting her was impossible. As Wilson Keller had noted upon learning of Willa's complaint, "You struck a live wire. I've seen this before."

Arthur had seen that kind of thing before too. So often during his childhood he'd seen his father flash-flip from rationality to irrationality, from calm to boiling anger. His truest defense to the hurt Willa obviously felt was that personal history—for surely the fear and unpredictability of those times had something to do with his problem of piss, of pissing in bed, quite possibly of being pissed off, which was why Arthur had backed away from Willa. He'd not found the courage to tell her.

But if he could, he knew, he'd begin when he was eight, when the onset of rheumatic fever gave him the best year of his childhood, even though he might have died.

He was bedridden the whole time. That first week of his illness, when he learned he'd be in bed a long time, he feared his father would call him "weak." But he didn't. Then, after three weeks, gaining weight from the inactivity, he feared he'd be called "fatty." For that sin he was sure his father would deride him, as he did them all—Arthur's mother and his older sister Amelda too. Those early sick days Arthur prepared for the worst, lying on his back, going rigid whenever his father's distinct footsteps sounded as he climbed upstairs.

But that third week, and the week after, and even the next one, when his father edged himself onto the side of Arthur's bed, he didn't say *fatty* or *weak*. And that was the miracle of that year. The whole period of bedrest, as Arthur's weight increased and his muscle tone degenerated, the man didn't say one bad word. Nor did his father, sitting close, threaten to humiliate him if he didn't eat his food faster, at the pace of the man himself, someone who wolfed it down each night. For the sin of not eating fast enough Arthur had often been chased from the dining table, his father barreling behind him, the man's fist raised as he bellowed, "You gonna eat today or tomorrow?" Arthur had run for his very life. This was so though the chase invariably ended at the bottom of the stairs. Still, when Arthur got to his bed upstairs, he'd dive under the covers, still feeling chased, and he'd stay there, unmoving, until the silence in the house seemed steady.

But the year of Arthur's illness his father only loved him. The man would, in the warm months of summer, gently lift him from his bed and carry him downstairs, then out the back door, then place him on a blanket spread on the grass and facing a vertical bedsheet pulled taut. The sheet was attached to their clothesline at the top and their lawn at the bottom. His father had made a movie screen and soon a show would begin, something funny with Charlie Chaplin or Buster Keaton, an amusement to make a sick boy feel better, his father said. And it was a miracle, too, how easy it was to see the movies there in their backyard. The only interference in watching the films was hardly a bother at all—the hiss of the film reel rolling forth. Sometimes his father lay next to him and by then, the summer of his rheumatic fever, Arthur wasn't afraid of that.

But the next year, Arthur on his feet again, the chasing resumed—not always but once in an unpredictable while—a terrifying dash from the dinner table, his father ranting, for Arthur had again committed the crime of not eating fast enough, or not answering his father's questions correctly, or some unpredictable something (for he was eating fast enough; he was stuffing his face just to be safe), his father's hand raised as Arthur dashed forth, his father's voice calling him *idiot* or *slowpoke*, or sometimes using his very name to mean those things. After moments like that Arthur began to piss his bed. He was nine. For a while the family could brush off "the accidents" as a byproduct of a boy's body not yet healed from illness. But after a year, the episodes persisting, Arthur learned to hide the peeing, which itself could spark his father's rage, which in turn generated more piss and, had Arthur not risen extra early to clean up, around and around they might have gone.

So often during those years Arthur had watched Amelda, too, run from their father. Arthur had merely watched, as he was too fearful himself to step up to protect his sister. And so was their mother, whose only safety when the bullets of his father's words spewed forth was to rush from the dining table to the kitchen where she'd simply stand, frozen, waiting for the episode to end.

Arthur had asked her once, months before her death, if she remembered those times.

"I wasn't there." Her voice was certain. "It's not possible I was there."

And that was just it, Arthur knew: right in the middle of her own kitchen, oven mitt in one hand, spatula in the other, she wasn't there.

Now that they were adults, he and Amelda weren't speaking. She'd married a weak man, Arthur had always thought. Her unsteady husband lost one job after the next, forcing her to take, finally, two jobs. As Arthur saw it, the exhaustion was killing her. Still, because Amelda could control her timid husband she was strangely content. Understandably, Arthur came to see, Amelda craved safety above all else and had found it in her compliant but deficient partner. Though Amelda lived only a half hour from Middletown, Arthur kept his distance from her, not because he and Amelda had fallen out but because Arthur hated seeing his sister living such a diminished life.

And maybe that's what Amelda saw when she observed Arthur, he figured. *Judge Cantrell.* Only she knew what a cover story that was. How he was only trying to right the wrongs of the world because he couldn't right the wrongs of his youth. How he'd stood there, in the worst of it, just like his mother, doing nothing. *Judge*: because in this harsh world, you had to protect yourself with something, anything. Amelda had a husband who would never yell or chase her. And Arthur, well, he had something better. He had the law. Which he could wield, as much as any case allowed, as a force for good, a way to protect the little guy from the madman hounding him.

But if Willa Fletcher had her way, with those powers wrecked, who would he be? The question made him shiver with fear. Who would he be without the warm blanket of law wrapped all around him?

LATER THAT MORNING HE TURNED on the TV, where coverage of the inauguration ran on every station. He watched, but not for long. The whole ordeal in Florida had the feel of his childhood—a whole lot of bullying.

He snapped off the TV and soon was in his car, aiming for the junk shop where he'd found the conference table he'd once refurbished.

The shop was in Wells, just off Route 66, down a long dirt drive that had his car rocking as he traversed it. Though Arthur hadn't been there for over a year, the elderly owner, Brooks, remembered him and offered him coffee.

"I got this new machine. Makes cappuccino. Let me try it out for you," the man said before heading toward a back room.

While Brooks was away Arthur puttered about, finally focusing on several old photograph albums. To his surprise, the first album documented a funeral, the photographs showing a mix of people uniformly adorned in black and solemnly standing outside a church. One photo even showed an open casket containing an elderly woman's body. Arthur lingered a bit, staring, the doom the photographs captured similar to his own sense that morning as he'd read, again, Willa's complaint.

The next album showed a wedding, dated 1931, beginning with a photo of the bride and groom—young, beautiful, yet bearing serious expressions in the style of the day. In the next photo the couple posed with what had to be parents, and then a larger group, the extended family, he assumed. Arthur flipped back to the first photo. "Be careful," he warned the newlyweds.

He closed the albums and continued to roam. A half hour later he thanked Brooks, who had taken all that time to brew what in the end was a lukewarm drink. During the wait Arthur had found some blue glass bottles, and as Brooks handed Arthur the tepid cappuccino Arthur handed Brooks the bottles to wrap. Arthur's mother had a collection like that on the ledge over her kitchen sink, he told Brooks. "It takes just a hint of the past to work a great change in the present," he added, uncertain if that was a good or bad thing.

AFTER LUNCH AT THE TOPAQUA Grill, he drove off, puttering along the narrow road beside the lake until he'd rounded a section of it. Soon he pulled off. Standing for a time at the frozen shore, he recalled what he'd said to Brooks, that it took only a hint of the past to influence the present. It was possible, then, that the bottles he'd just bought would brighten his home, evoking good memories. Then again, they could remind him of darker times, of his mother's kitchen, that place she retreated to, leaving her children helpless before a maniac.

Though it was growing cold, he lingered at the lake. Before him an ice fisherman came into focus, a man sitting on a crate, waiting. Behind Arthur a few cars passed, their tires crackling as they crushed bits of ice. Heavy clouds rolled in above.

Minutes later, as he drove home, snowflakes starting to fall, his mind flitted to a memory of that best year of his childhood, his sick year. The bed sheet turned movie screen . . . The backyard, quiet . . . He could dwell on that island of a memory all day. Which is what he did after he returned home, pushed away the sight of Willa's complaint on his desk, and lay down on his living room couch, pacified by the movie rolling forth in his mind. It didn't matter that he'd seen it before, a thousand times. He could see it again. Feel the relief in it, as always. Now he was that boy, safe . . . *If I loved you,* he almost sang to his father, tall and lean and right there, in the distance, manning the movie projector. Arthur rose then, opened the door to the utility closet in his hallway, stared at the unopened box marked "To Arthur, with love." He stood before it for several minutes, feeling more curious about its contents than ever before, but in the end he backed away and, as always, shut the door.

Later, he remembered the blue bottles and placed them on his kitchen window ledge above the sink. Assessing their impact, he couldn't tell if it was good or not, or even big or small. He would know, he figured, when the sun next angled toward them, illuminating them. Then, because the next days were expected to be cloudy, he realized that like the fisherman he'd seen on the ice he'd have to wait it out to really know.

6

Netherlands, September 15, 1941, by Proclamation of the Commissioner-General for Security on the Movement of Jews, Article 1: Jews are debarred from (a) public parks and zoological gardens, (b) cafés, restaurants (including station buffets), hotels, and boardinghouses, (c) wagon lifts and buffet cars, (d) theaters, cabarets, and cinemas, (e) sports grounds, bathing beaches, indoor and outdoor swimming pools, (f) art exhibitions and concerts, (g) public libraries, reading rooms, and museums.

THOUGH IAN LIMA WAS SORE from his fall on the ice, in the days after that—and after nearly being hit by a car on Barton Hill—he took to rising well before sunrise and walking in the dark to the lake. There he began to recognize the predawn sounds of the ice, its groans and crackles as it contracted or expanded, responding to variations in the temperature of the winter air. More rarely the lake ice would suddenly pop, a sound like a gunshot that echoed across and back over the lake's full expanse. Listening, Ian began to think of the ice in a way he never had, as something alive, even wild. He visited it hungrily, wanting to hear more, to know it better.

And the solitary sojourns, paradoxically, helped with his loneliness, which he felt, as usual, in the mornings upon waking but now throughout much of the day as well. He could be in any of his classes, or watching *Jeopardy!* beside his mother, or at dance rehearsal where he might have a short conversation with Jase—"What'd you do this weekend?" "Nothing." "Me too." "Nothing *to* do."—when the sadness bubbled up. His ongoing fantasies about Jase, which he let loose while on the lake, were another panacea to this new, pervasive sorrow, even though more and more the dreams were out of whack with the insignificance of any real encounter.

Ian knew that. But still, with just one step on the ice an image of himself and Jase, as if of its own accord, appeared. The dreaming had become like a medicine he required, and in higher and higher daily dosages. Invariably, in Ian's mind's eye he and Jase were there together, doing the chasing thing he'd first imagined. But soon he envisioned longer talks, and moments of affection that took place in between the two islands in the lake's middle, where no one on shore could see them. More and more he was drawn to that private enclave where, because it was sheltered from the wind, he could comfortably linger, dream on. There he felt as if he met, if not Jase himself, then his very spirit. He'd heard people describe sensing God in just this way. With a little imagination, and some concentration, Ian began to know how just about anything could seem real. In this way, his hope—"Do you love me? Because I've always loved you"—remained a thing as alive and fierce as winter ice.

Maddie had the rights to her mother's car the entire fourth week of January, which was a deal her parents had come up with to get her to grow her hair back. "See? It's working," she said, "the nonviolent resistance." Maddie's use of the concept seemed more manipulative than principled, but Ian chose his own form of nonviolent resistance in not saying that to her. She'd stopped by his apartment that first weekday, offering to drive him to school. They smoked a joint along the way. He'd risen even earlier for his walk to the lake, but the morning smoke was good too, as was Maddie's company at this time of day. Tuesday was much the same, the walk in the dark to the lake, the near-instant emergence of his fantasies, the ice gurgling, as if talking to him, coaxing him on, and then Maddie's ride, the heat blasting in the car while they rolled down the windows—front and back seats—for their smoke.

On Wednesday Ian raced from the shower to his bedroom to the kitchen for a quick bite, but Maddie had already arrived and was there, at the kitchen table, sipping coffee and talking to his mother. By the time he was ready to go, Maddie and his mother were leaning toward each other as if they'd just shared secrets. Then they hugged goodbye, something he and his mother never did when he left for school. The next day was the same, except that this time when he emerged from his bedroom his mother, sitting again at the kitchen table with Maddie, was offering her a pair of her feather earrings. Maddie put them on, gold-colored, dangly. They looked ridiculous with her clipped, blue hair, but still his mother nodded approvingly as she held up a hand mirror.

"Oh, my God," Maddie gushed. "Thank you, thank you."

On Friday, as they walked down the stairs from his apartment to the front door, he whispered to Maddie, "You don't have to do this, you know."

"Do what?"

"Talk to her." He was in fact disgusted, not with the earrings, which she wore again, but with his mother's intrusiveness into his friendship.

"But I want to talk to her," Maddie said. They were about to get into the car. Their doors were open, and they looked at each other over the car top. "She's lonely, Ian. She is." When they'd settled inside, Maddie almost scolded him. "She's not so lucky as you. Can't you tell?"

Ian stared back, incredulous, then looked away from her, out the car window. As she drove, he grew bored with the ubiquity of the icy brown snowbanks lining the sides of the roads, winter's muck. A minute later he hogged the joint. By the time they entered the school's front door he felt better, lighter, less peeved, having forgotten already what Maddie had said.

◊

Now that Stephanie Pearl had faced the permanence of her loss of Freddy Taylor—eight years down the drain, she admitted, still amazed that was so—she decided to reconcile with Rona Adler. It seemed a good move now that she wasn't driven to extremes to recover something she couldn't from Freddy. But by reconciling with Rona she hoped for other recoveries: of her closest friendship, and maybe even of her old self. Monday of that week, the last full week in January, she'd taken down the scarves from the mirrors in her apartment, and though her eyes were tired and her hair a mess, she nevertheless saw in her reflection someone she used to know.

Just aiming to reconcile with Rona did Stephanie some good. That day she got back on track at work, reviewing scholarship applications, then mentoring Thea as she developed guidelines for the new internship at the women's museum that had come through. By that evening Stephanie had an itch to go skating like she used to, talking with Rona all the while. Things had changed, she'd tell Rona, meaning the subject of her talk was no longer *Freddy, Freddy, Freddy*. Her incessant solitariness was the thing in her soul that she now went round and round with, but she wouldn't go on about that either. That would bring her and Rona right back to their central problem—the unfairness they each felt about the way they envied aspects of each other's lives seemingly without seeing the full picture, which included each other's pain.

But Stephanie did see it. She knew that since Rona had left GTW for mothering she lacked time for herself. And the dynamics of her marriage forced her to play bad cop to Daniel's good cop, which was unfair to her. And she missed her work, which she'd loved.

But when Stephanie phoned, Rona wasn't quite sure she was up for skating. Still, she told Stephanie to stop by after dinner on Wednesday to chat. And maybe to go skating. "It depends," Rona said, and Stephanie suspected that what it depended upon was the sincerity of her apology.

Upon arriving at Rona's that night, she said "I'm sorry" even before saying hello. Rona's kids were upstairs, being read to by Daniel, Rona explained. Rona ushered Stephanie to the couch in the living room. A plate of oatmeal cookies sat on the coffee table.

Rona thanked Stephanie for the apology and then pointed at the cookies. They both took one and nibbled quietly. A squeal came from upstairs and the sound of running children followed. When the noise subsided, Rona turned back to Stephanie. "One thing after the next here," Rona said, nodding as if she'd proven a point, the very one she'd tried to make the last time they'd talked. "What's new with you?" she then asked, her arms crossed, her point made.

Stephanie was unsure how to answer. Many things were new: Bill Cousins's home renovation, her mother's dismay at losing her lake view, Thea's internship idea, a new direction for GTW, a bit of a breakthrough, in fact. If she and Rona were on the ice, talking as they skated, the very process would lead to something, some new insight, that only going round and round with it would bring to light. As it was, Stephanie faltered, unsure what subject would suit Rona, who sat stiffly, waiting. Stephanie finally mentioned her mother. "They threw her a twenty-fifth anniversary party recently at work. Twenty-five years," Stephanie said. She almost added, beating Rona to it, *Can you believe it?*

"Your mother okay?" Rona remarked instead.

"Good enough," Stephanie answered, though she wasn't sure. The business with Bill Cousins was bothering her to no end. "She's okay but stressed. Calling a lot. Not sleeping so well. How's your mother?"

"Good, very good, until she isn't. Having nightmares, another round." Rona paused. Stephanie waited. "She spent the weekend here," Rona finally said. Had they been on skates they'd both have said so much more, she knew.

Something crashed upstairs and a child began to cry. She and Rona paused, waited, and the crying quickly ebbed. Rona reached for another cookie before sitting back again. "You too?" she asked. In politeness Stephanie also took one, only to place it untouched on a napkin on her lap.

Rona then told Stephanie that Daniel had taken up reading to the kids after dinner, and that little bit of open time had become quite cherished. "Of course, I threatened him with divorce to make it happen."

Stephanie smiled until she realized, from Rona's frown, no joke had been made.

Another pause followed, a silence, and Stephanie felt compelled to fill the gap. She grasped at what she could think of, which was Thea's internship program. She explained it to Rona. "Thea's a go-getter," Stephanie concluded. "Turns out she has good ideas."

The subject wasn't welcome. In mentioning work Stephanie had clearly upset Rona, who frowned and crossed her arms again. Surely, Rona signaled, they were back to competing, comparing, though in mentioning Thea Stephanie hadn't meant anything like that. Now Rona was glancing up the stairs, expectantly, though all was quiet there.

"Am I keeping you?" Stephanie felt defeated. Naïvely, she realized, she'd hoped they'd just resume their friendship.

"Not keeping me. Of course not. Have another," Rona said coolly, pointing again to the cookies, though Stephanie still hadn't touched hers.

Stephanie got ready to leave. "Well, just came by to apologize. I never meant to upset you."

"Thank you," Rona answered, her tone as detached as before. Hearing that, Stephanie thought Rona might apologize back. After all, she'd felt misunderstood too, the emotional complexity of her solitary life reduced to enviable free time. But Rona didn't apologize. "No harm done," she said instead.

The one-sidedness irked Stephanie. "Glad to see you," she said, standing, her tone businesslike too.

Rona's youngest then called for her. "Coming!" Rona answered while offering Stephanie a look of contented helplessness. She smiled and shrugged at once, still scoring points against Stephanie in the argument they'd never really finished that day, months ago. Rona obviously hadn't forgiven Stephanie for making her feel invisible. And Stephanie knew the hurt of that, could understand the lingering pain. She felt invisible all the time. "My mother doesn't know me," she suddenly longed to tell Rona—a thought that bubbled up, surprised her, as if they *were* at the rink—but glancing Rona's way she could see that her thoughts had moved away from Stephanie.

A half hour later, at the Wheaton rink, Stephanie was indifferent to the blaring pop music. She was indifferent, too, to the skaters she passed and the many more who passed her. Even when the goofy "Y.M.C.A." song came on and everyone began comically gesturing, she remained separate, her arms at her sides, her head down. Around and around she went, slowly, without momentum. The song ended. Another began. She pushed on.

THE NEXT MORNING, AFTER A near-sleepless night, Stephanie arrived at work late, only to be taken aback by the sight of a baby lying on a blanket in the reception area, playing quietly. A small stuffed elephant, sky-blue, lay by the child's side, but the girl seemed to have forgotten about the toy. Rather, her eyes were locked onto Aileen, their office administrator, who, bent over in her chair, shook a rattle in front of the child's face, humming as she did. The child was as mesmerized by the toy as Stephanie was by the child's beauty, her wisps of soft black hair, her full-moon eyes.

Aileen finished her song, which seemed to leave the baby perplexed. She murmured, as if to ask for more, but when the phone rang Aileen bolted upright. The child waited, then began to whimper. Swiftly, Stephanie lifted her, patted her back, and started singing "The Itsy Bitsy Spider."

Aileen's call finished, she then explained that the baby, named Casey, was Thea's. "I was as surprised as you are. Goodness, look at you, Stephanie. Your eyes are coming for me." Aileen reached out and Stephanie handed Casey back.

"And where's Thea?" she asked.

"At a meeting. She went back to finalize arrangements with the women's museum." Aileen lowered Casey onto her blanket, then cooed into the baby's face. When she finished, she said, "Thea's childcare fell through today. She was desperate."

"Oh?" Though the baby lay right before her Stephanie still couldn't grasp that Thea, hired straight from college, was a mother.

Aileen added, "She was worried about your reaction, but I told her you wouldn't mind. Don't look so grim, Stephanie. Thea just wants to please you. That's why she tries so hard. She admires you. She wants to *be* you. Can't you tell?" While she spoke, Aileen again lifted Casey. The child, resting her head on Aileen's chest, locked her gaze on Stephanie.

Stephanie frowned back. Since she'd left the skating rink the night before she'd been battling a sense of doom. Before bed she'd even considered re-covering her mirrors. "I'm no one to be," she told the baby, whispering the words.

Aileen laughed. "Try telling that to Thea."

Once back in her office Stephanie picked up a grant proposal she'd begun. She read the first sentence, then dropped it down. She read the sentence again and again as her mind spun with the news of Thea's baby. That Thea at twenty-two already had a child and Stephanie at thirty-nine didn't came to mind repeatedly too.

Later that morning, after an hour of getting nowhere with the grant proposal, Stephanie walked past the reception area on her way to the kitchen for coffee.

Thea had just returned from her meeting and was lifting Casey from the blanket near Aileen. The two women were cooing in equal measure. When Casey, resting on Thea's shoulder, suddenly burped, the two women laughed. Thea patted Casey's back. Stephanie watched as the mother and the child held each other quietly for some time. Stephanie then retreated.

In her office she collapsed onto her chair. After all that had happened between her and Rona, she had been sure she was done with jealousy. But at the sight of Thea and Casey there it was, the unmistakable feel of it, a small rumbling at her core, again.

ON THURSDAY OF THAT WEEK Thea again came to work with Casey. Thea promised everyone that she needed just one more day. Casey's presence wouldn't become a pattern.

By this time Stephanie had grown if not comfortable then at least used to the idea of Thea, still so young, being a mother. That morning Stephanie stopped by Thea's office twice, the first time only to find the office empty, the second time to find Casey napping on her blanket and Thea, at her desk, dropping off too. Thea's incessant yawning, along with her cautionary gifts, as Stephanie now saw them, finally made sense.

Mid-morning, Stephanie and Thea took a coffee break in Thea's office and Thea explained that she was a junior at Georgetown—thanks in part to her scholarship from GTW—when she got pregnant. When she told her mother, she'd slapped Thea across the face. When she told her mother she and the boy loved each other—a lie she felt she had to say—her mother slapped her again. "That's to wake you up," Thea's mother explained. When Thea told her mother the boy didn't want to marry her, her mother drew her close.

"But who takes care of Casey?"

"My mother. She had to cut her hours, but now I'm working so that's money for us all." Thea explained about her parents, before they had children, leaving a failed coffee farm in the Philippines. "My mother couldn't even breathe in America those first years, everything scared her so. She couldn't count the money for the buses, couldn't speak much English, couldn't understand the streets in D.C. Winter's cold shocked her too. But she finally settled in. My dad, who only knew coffee beans, became a car mechanic, and my mother still works at a dry cleaner's. But ten years after coming here my father was killed crossing our street, South Dakota Avenue. Lots of traffic. He got careless, I guess."

When some cars honking on 19th Street interrupted them it seemed Thea's father was out there, dying yet again. Once the street quieted, Thea asked, her voice low, "Are we cursed?"

"Cursed?"

"My family, I mean. We're cursed by this *thing,* following us from Batangas to here. Nothing bad was supposed to happen here because it already happened *there.* That's why they came, my parents. But then here, in America, my father dies. Cursed. And then look what I did to the family." Thea looked at Casey, just then sleeping. "Cursed again," she said even as she smiled at the girl.

"Life doesn't stop just because you've come to America," Stephanie said. "My mother could tell you all about that." She added, "Holocaust survivor. They got out."

Thea sat back, looking at Stephanie as if she'd never seen her before, which was about the same way Stephanie was looking at Thea.

Later, Stephanie was just leaving the office when Thea, carrying

Casey, came up behind her. "Can you take her a minute?" Thea handed over Casey even before Stephanie answered. The child, not yet wearing outerwear, was soft, warm, her hair smelling of the same baby shampoo that Stephanie recognized from her youth. Instantly, it transported her back. *Oosterpark*, she recalled her mother chanting during hair washings, *your ugly, lopsided pond.* At that, Stephanie pulled the child even closer, as if to protect her, as if something unknown—like a mysterious curse—was amiss.

THE NEXT DAY, FRIDAY, STEPHANIE rose early and drove to Connecticut to see her mother, an urge she'd simply awakened with. She left a message at work telling them she wouldn't be in. Driving along, she often thought of Thea, who according to Aileen wanted to be her. But I'm a basket case, Stephanie had hoped to tell Thea that week, ending the misplaced adulation, but the chance to set Thea straight never arose. Driving on, Stephanie thought, too, of Casey, recalling the softness she'd cuddled momentarily. On the endless straightaway of I-95 North Stephanie found herself moving one hand to her belly, which felt sadly barren despite her being on day three of what was still, despite her age, a healthy period.

Her thoughts continued even as she arrived in Wells, and traveling along Lake Drive, nearing her mother's bungalow, she came to, as if from a dream, at the sight of a woman walking on the road. They were going in opposite directions, and as Stephanie drew close she recognized Missy Mulligan, her childhood friend. Quite automatically, as if all the years of silence between them hadn't passed, she honked at Missy, a congenial hello. But the blast startled Missy, who leapt off the roadway in self-protection. Stephanie might have stopped then, apologized for the scare and truly said hello, but the friendly impulse passed, replaced by an unease that told her to drive on. She and Missy didn't know each other anymore. That was the truth. Indeed, Missy was no longer a Mulligan but a Lima, a long-held married name, though Stephanie knew the marriage hadn't lasted. As Stephanie glanced in the rearview mirror, she saw Missy emerge from the roadside grasses. She gave Stephanie's departing car the finger.

That night, while eating dinner with her mother, Stephanie asked for any news of Missy.

"Missy with the little boy?"

Stephanie nodded, waited. Her mother seemed to be considering something.

"Couldn't have been easy," she finally said. "Raising that boy all alone, I mean. Take it from me, not easy."

The comment upset Stephanie. Even when her father had been around, but especially after that, she'd felt more or less orphaned, raising herself, despite her mother's presence—and that sure wasn't easy. She wanted to say that, to tell her mother that she wasn't being fair, but the woman was already up from the table and what did it matter, anyway, she figured, watching her mother at the sink, delicate, pretty, meticulous with her hair and that green eyeshadow she unfailingly wore, a sense of style and propriety she'd carried over apparently from Amsterdam. What did it matter if Stephanie had raised her mother even more than her mother had raised her? That was just the way the events of history had entered and twisted their lives. As always, then, Stephanie held her tongue.

EARLY THE NEXT MORNING, BEFORE her mother was up, Stephanie skated to the secluded space between the two islands at the center of the lake. The solitude she'd find there, she knew from many past experiences, had a healing quality. Upon arriving she pushed off, glided the length of the strip, spun some, then pushed forth again. She raised her right leg and tried to skate the length of the strip holding an arabesque but couldn't quite make the distance. The next length she skated backwards. She wasn't going round and round with it but back and forth with it. *It* was that familiar loneliness she couldn't shake, and which often became heightened, as it had last night, in the presence of her mother. And yet here Stephanie had come, voluntarily home again, driving this time, driven, in a sense, to be there. *It* was also the biological clock that clanged in her belly that morning, waking her early, like an alarm clock would. As she skated on, Stephanie could almost see Thea's child a few years hence, bundled up in winter wear, learning to take tiny strides on double blades.

The vision's sweetness recalled a cherished memory, her mother on the ice singing "New York, New York," one of the few American songs she knew, as Stephanie and her pal Missy skated in the wings, each holding one of her mother's hands. Before Stephanie knew it, she'd begun to sing, just as the three had that long-ago day. And, before she knew it, she extended her right hand as if she were clinging to something, something more than air.

BUT SHE FROZE AND STOPPED singing as soon as she saw the boy, in a thick parka, coming her way. He was only yards from the strip between the islands. He smoked as he walked. Then he stopped, but not because he saw or heard her, she was relieved to realize. Rather, the boy, like her just moments before, appeared to be lost in a daydream. He extended his right hand, holding out his cigarette as if to share it with someone, though no one else was there. A moment later he began walking again toward the split in the islands.

Her solitude interrupted, Stephanie sprinted past him, leaving. "Morning," she said as she did.

The boy, clearly startled by her presence, said nothing.

She was at a safe distance when she called back to him, "Ice is for dreamers." The echo over the lake both amplified and simplified her message. *Dreamers, dreamers, dreamers,* it said.

THAT AFTERNOON, AS STEPHANIE DROVE to get groceries for her mother, she passed Missy again, in almost the same place on Lake Drive as before. This time, buoyed by the morning's old memory of "New York, New York," Stephanie slowed, unrolled her window, and called, "How's it going, stranger?"

Missy stopped, peered in, and said, "Stephanie!"

They exchanged hellos, then asked about each other's families. Everyone was good, good, they both reported. Ian was already sixteen, Missy said. "They grow so fast," she added, with the same glaring self-consciousness as Stephanie—the awkwardness of paths long-diverged, Stephanie knew, and for her of so many recent personal failures about which she felt in Missy's presence a surprising sense of shame. She had nothing to report, really. Nothing at all. They agreed to catch up soon but not just yet because Stephanie was heading back to D.C. the next morning. "Next time," Stephanie halfheartedly promised, and Missy—who looked astonishingly identical to her high school self, just as Stephanie had envisioned her that morning—replied with a lackadaisical "can't wait."

Minutes later, Stephanie was shopping for groceries. Aiming for breakfast cereal, she passed the shelves stocked with baby food. On each item the Gerber baby, open-mouthed, stared out. She stopped, reached for a jar, examined it and then another. Applesauce. Peas. Carrots. Pears. Peaches. With each one she felt less like a failure, more like a mother. She bought them all.

MONTHS LATER, WHILE WALKING ON PLANTAGE MIDDENLAAN DURING her trip to Amsterdam in April, Stephanie stopped to read a plaque on the site of the Dutch Theatre there which, prewar, had become closely associated with the Jewish community that had once populated the neighborhood. Perhaps because she bent down to better take in the words, she was asked by a man standing nearby if she could read the sign. The man then explained that the Nazis had turned the theater into a deportation center, and across the street they'd transformed a nursery into an annex of the center, confining Jewish children there. But through some clever maneuvering and doctoring of records, hundreds of children from the nursery escaped, hidden in bags or loads of laundry, or fleeing on foot when the tram came rumbling past, momentarily blocking the sight of the children from the guards across the street. The man turned to Stephanie. "Right here," he said, as if seeing the tram and the children being rushed out just then. Stephanie stared as if she could see the children too. "I'm Jewish," she then told the man, surprising herself more than she did him. He nodded and they stood, looking into the street, for some moments more.

After that she began to visit the Portuguese Synagogue daily. Though tourists came and went she never found the place to be crowded. Rather, the quiet inside felt peaceful. Always choosing to sit off to one side, she became familiar with the feel and sight of the intentionally sandy floor, the plain benches, the raised bema in the distance, the large brass chandeliers flanking it. She didn't know any prayers or even how to pray. But she wasn't there for that anyway. She came, daily, simply to sit, to breathe. As a girl her mother would never have come there, she knew. Her family was neither religious nor Sephardic. But as the days passed, Stephanie began to imagine her mother, young Ruttie, there anyway, sitting beside her, enjoying the respite that the sacred space invariably brought. One day, the sense of Ruttie beside her so real, it seemed to Stephanie that she had long ago borne the child she'd always wanted. She left the synagogue feeling full, that hollow sense at her core finally relieved. She didn't even mind that once outside again the little girl of her dreams—who'd felt safe in there, who belonged, and who, unlike Stephanie, knew Amsterdam and therefore knew where she was going—in an instant scurried away.

◊

THE LAST TUESDAY IN JANUARY MISSY LIMA WAS GLAD TO SEE ANGELINA Moretti at the Topaqua Grill, there for her once-weekly late lunch, and they sat together at a corner table. Missy wanted to talk about her run-in over the weekend with Stephanie Pearl, but Angelina quickly became absorbed in what to order, finally choosing lasagna, which was heavy for her, she claimed. But then she wolfed it down. When she was done, they ordered cappuccinos. "Let's be all-Italian," Angelina suggested. "Heck, I already am!"

Missy made some rote comments then about Ian's roots being Irish, like hers, and Portuguese, like his father's. But she quickly got to the real subject on her mind, her surprise encounter with Stephanie. "She looked so damn *good*," Missy complained. Since seeing her Missy couldn't stop thinking about Stephanie's haircut, which had layers and fell beautifully just past her shoulders. "Nobody here has a haircut like that," she told Angelina. "It's got to be a city thing."

Missy had long ago cut her hair short, a concession to being too busy to think about it. She'd first cut it after the social worker had appeared at her door, questioning her capacity to mother Ian. She'd been slow answering the door because she hadn't heard the initial knock over the sound of her blow-dryer. From then on it was all business. Along with sobering up and cleaning up, she'd shorn her hair, expediently. No blow-dryer necessary. In the same practical way, Angelina wore her hair back, always in a ponytail. The two commiserated. No time for style. No time: that's what their lives as working women and mothers was all about. A moment like this, luxuriating on a Friday afternoon with cappuccino, was stolen time. Angelina said that, and Missy nodded, realizing as she did that in fact she had some time, even beyond this moment, every other Friday morning. That morning she'd even stayed at Roy's an extra fifteen minutes. He'd said he liked her hair just fine.

"I must be nuts," she said a moment later. "To be jealous of a haircut. I'm that shallow?"

"Maybe you saw past the haircut to something else."

"I did. I saw an amazing career. Not a job; a *career*. You need one just to afford that kind of hair. And I saw dollar bills, lots. And I saw pencils and papers and computers and whatnot. All of that in a plush office. *Plush*. When have I even said that word? And I saw Stephanie wince when I told her I was the lunch chef, a short-order cook, at the Topaqua Grill."

"What's wrong with that?"

"Just about everything. Do I really have to explain? But maybe I didn't tell her. I mentioned walking to work but maybe not the work itself. I really don't remember much except the haircut, and that I felt embarrassed the whole time." Missy sipped her cappuccino before adding, "Stephanie's gone so far. I've stayed right here."

The two became quiet. The TV at the bar, perpetually on, generated the only background noise until a gust of wind outside whistled as it hit the nearest window.

"Chilly winter." Missy turned to the window.

Angelina murmured in agreement. Finishing her drink, Missy spooned out the remaining creamy foam in her cup. Once done she said, "No, I can't say I've done a whole lot with my life. But at least Ian's doing good. I did that pretty well."

"Here's to our glorious boys." Angelina raised her empty cup and Missy raised hers. They clinked then sat again in silence. Angelina seemed content, but Missy was still rattled, was still comparing herself to Stephanie and coming up short.

"It's just a haircut," Missy finally said. "The rest of it—the money, the office—I made all that up. I honestly have no idea what she does in D.C."

Angelina said, "You're a good cook, you know."

Missy shrugged. Then she jumped, shocked, when the wind rushed past, whistling again.

LATER, UPON ARRIVING HOME FROM work, Missy ran into Fran Cousins, who was outside, despite the cold, sitting on her front steps. The woman had her winter parka on, and her gloves and hat. But on her feet she wore only slippers, pink and fluffy. She seemed to be waiting for something. Missy hadn't seen her for months. Mrs. Cousins, whose presence was always marked by her height and a certain fullness of spirit, seemed to have shrunk in the cold. Moreover, she'd aged immeasurably over the season, and taking that in Missy felt a pang in her heart.

"Everything okay?" she asked. She adjusted her backpack containing the sandwiches she'd made for dinner with Ian.

Mrs. Cousins patted the space beside her, and Missy sat.

"Just out for air," the older woman said.

"Nothing quite like air." Missy sensed Mrs. Cousins shivering ever so slightly, and she inched closer. "How's your husband?" Missy knew of the stroke and had brought them some soup from the Topaqua Grill one evening and more soup and some sandwiches another time. Bill, their son, had always answered the door when she knocked.

"I haven't had any air in the longest time," Mrs. Cousins answered, as if to a different question. "This evening seemed like the night. Would you like to walk with me?"

Missy was confused. "Is Bill here?"

When Mrs. Cousins shook her head, Missy inched closer, then wrapped an arm around Mrs. Cousins. For her tough love of so many years ago she owed the woman everything. "But your shoes," Missy said. "I think you forgot them."

Fran Cousins looked down and then over at Missy. Her face registered sorrow. "Been walking in these for a long time," she said. "So long I forgot I'm in them."

"You seem cold." Missy held the woman even closer.

"That's what I hoped." Saying that, Mrs. Cousins looked lost, her eyes vacant.

"Cold? You really want that?"

"Maybe . . ."

"Mrs. Cousins? You're not well?"

"Freeze," Mrs. Cousins said, as if commanding the weather.

"Oh, no. We really have to get you inside. You're just shivering more and more."

But Fran Cousins was adamant. She shook her head.

Missy sat, perplexed, her arm around the woman. But when her shivering intensified Missy stood. She faced Mrs. Cousins and reached out to her. "Up, up," she said.

Reflexively, Fran Cousins grabbed Missy's hands. With just a tug the woman rose, easily, in defiance of her size.

"Freeze," Mrs. Cousins repeated once she stood, her hands still in Missy's.

"I think you've managed to do just that. Come on now. Let's get you warmed up."

"Freeze," the woman said yet again, though by then they'd climbed the front steps.

"Tonight's not the best night to freeze," Missy told her, opening the inside door to the woman's apartment. There she saw Mr. Cousins, in just his pajama bottoms, lying on the living room couch, a pile of newspapers by his side. He'd fallen asleep reading one. The intimacy of seeing a purple birthmark near his ribcage embarrassed Missy. She quickly looked away.

"What are we going to do?" Mrs. Cousins asked Missy.

"Well, you're not going to freeze. That's a start." Missy put the kettle on the stove. She wriggled free of her backpack. She then raced back to Mrs. Cousins, still in the doorway, and escorted her to her kitchen. Along the way Missy covered Mr. Cousins with a nearby blanket, averting her eyes as she did. At the same time, she heard a noise from upstairs. Ian walking about.

"Let me get Ian. Be right back," she said, then rushed up and brought him down. For the next two hours they sat at the kitchen table with Mrs. Cousins, who refused to remove her coat and hat but was glad to be relieved of her gloves. The third cup of tea finally warmed her.

"I didn't freeze," she said, putting her cup down.

"Good thing. I'm going to come by in the morning," Missy said before she and Ian left.

"Me too," Ian said, and Missy tussled his hair.

Upstairs, they quickly ate their sandwiches and then got ready for bed, Ian using the bathroom first. Missy took her time after him, staring at her face in the mirror as if she hadn't seen herself in a while. Yes, her hair was cut short, its style, if you could call it that, bland, its color a rusty red, as always. But the sight of it didn't bother her. In the end, what did it matter? They'd all grow old and that was the truth of it. And by "they" she meant herself and Angelina Moretti, who was still so pretty, even in middle age. And she meant Ian, who'd been eager to help that night and patient in a way she hadn't expected. He was more mature than he'd been even last week. And she meant Mr. and Mrs. Cousins, growing old then older, until one of them wanted to freeze. The meaning of what Mrs. Cousins said deepened in Missy. She splashed her face with warm water. She took a deep breath then splashed her face again.

7

Netherlands, October 22, 1941, by Decree No. 198, Article 1: The right is reserved to make the employment of Jews subject to special permits or to prohibit it altogether.

October 22, 1941, by Decree No. 199: Jews are debarred from participation in non–profit making associations and companies other than those run by Jews and for Jews.

October 22, 1941, by Decree No. 200: Non-Jews are debarred from working in Jewish households or in households where Jews continually reside for periods exceeding four weeks.

THE LAST SUNDAY IN JANUARY Willa Fletcher called a cab to take her to the Topaqua Grill in Wells to get her car, which she'd left there a week back. That night at the Grill she'd gotten drunk for the first time in her adult life, something that still shocked her, but not as much as the fact that, the day before, she'd not only written a draft ethics complaint against Arthur Cantrell but soon after had officially filed it.

She'd written the complaint, she could see in hindsight, in an altered state of thinking, not from alcohol but from her wounded ego, which, once triggered, was like a caged animal suddenly set free. Seeing Arthur at the Y, especially his attempt, via that kiss, to make it seem as if nothing had happened, to confuse her with his charm, had set her off, gotten her mind spinning and the animal growling. She was suddenly but one dimension of her full self: deeply victimized and only that. She'd shrunk, and from that diminished height what she'd subsequently written in the complaint seemed entirely justified. She was pleased, too, to have delivered it to Arthur's office, causing him, she'd hoped then, to shake in his boots while she considered whether to actually file it.

But she didn't think for long. Still aggrieved, still shrunk, she decided it was only right to mail it in.

But later that same day she became her full self again, and then the events at the Y looked entirely different. Like maybe Arthur was merely attempting to be polite that night in the face of their awkward meeting. Like maybe his presumptuousness—that kiss that had so infuriated her—was just anxiety.

The shift came late on Friday afternoon when her secretary buzzed, telling Willa someone wanted to see her. The woman she soon faced was vaguely familiar. "Eleanor," the woman said, "from the pottery class? I hope this is okay, popping in."

Escorting Eleanor to her office, Willa told her that of course she remembered her from the pottery class. Once they'd settled themselves, Eleanor told Willa, "I've been thinking about what you said and struggling with it ever since."

Eleanor reminded Willa of her troubles as a librarian, which began after she'd refused to date her supervisor. "I was the most experienced there, even more than him, but when another supervisory spot opened, he went with someone else." Eleanor had ultimately left her job, and, in need of work, had left her field of expertise. She was now a receptionist for a Hartford psychiatrist.

She then described the behavior: months of unwanted touches, often a shoulder rub or a single finger running down her entire back. Her supervisor had asked her out at least ten times before he'd finally stopped. "And every one of those times he was wearing the same brown shirt. It was as if he'd put on that shirt in the morning and think, 'How can I torment Eleanor today?' The shirt was plain. Nothing special. And yet I remember it as if he'd tried to drown me in it."

Willa asked Eleanor several questions about when all the harassment had happened and whether Eleanor had filed any kind of formal complaint, either with her employer—a small college—or with the state. Eleanor hadn't, and doing so now would exceed the state's statute of limitations for such a claim.

"I figured," Eleanor said. "But I wanted to ask you to be sure. It *is* harassment, right?"

"You bet," Willa told her, which was the same thing as telling herself that what Arthur had done, however much it disturbed her, wasn't nearly as serious as what Eleanor had endured. Moreover, Arthur wasn't a bad man, she suddenly recalled. His backing away, however cruel, was just a dating problem, not a crime requiring punishment. Yet the ethics complaint had aimed to do just that. In fact, Arthur had revealed to her only that the Byrneses, whom he didn't name at the time, were loud and crass. Also, knowing Arthur, he and Wilson had some kind of professional wall around the case, and their playing basketball was likely no big deal. And his kiss at the Y was likely not meant to manipulate her but rather to please her. She'd seen his nervous overcorrections before.

"You felt like you were drowning? Like the man was *killing* you?"

"Yes, that bad. Yet I never complained. At the time I thought I had to just take it. But why did I think that?" Eleanor stood to go. Despite her question she seemed settled, clear.

Willa answered anyway. "Woman are brought up to take it. Or maybe it's a coping method in an impossible situation. Maybe a lot of people are like that when a situation is hopeless. Just take it. Because what else can you do?" Saying this, Willa sensed her own acquiescence to a childhood home life she couldn't change. Her rage, the flip side of that very helplessness, had snowballed through her life, culminating, or so it seemed just then, in her fury-filled complaint.

She told Eleanor, almost tearing up as she did, "Glad you stopped by. I truly am."

THAT NIGHT, SOON AFTER ARRIVING home, Willa knocked on Mrs. Rizzo's door, newspaper in hand. Mrs. Rizzo, who took a minute to answer, smiled to see Willa. She hadn't yet read from the paper before she said, "Mrs. Rizzo, I'm not Catholic but I have something to confess."

And Mrs. Rizzo answered, "I'm not a priest but I've got ears. And nothing surprises me, Willa. Nothing."

But Willa in fact shocked Mrs. Rizzo.

"Dear Lord," she said after Willa told her about the encounter with Arthur at the Y, her wild anger, and the ethics complaint that followed. She simply couldn't tell the woman that every so often she did this—

fell into a psychic hole where the only business at hand was the need to punish the one who wronged her, which was just a stupid way of regaining a sense of control. She couldn't say that, though she would have been consoled to know that even Mrs. Rizzo had her moments—that she, too, could come apart at the seams, her anger ripping free of the rest of her. They were in the living room, seated in their usual chairs. Mrs. Rizzo popped a mint into her mouth. Once she swallowed, she said, "But integrity is everything, Willa. Everything."

"I know," Willa said. To which Mrs. Rizzo answered, not without sympathy, "Well, then, what are you going to do?"

WHAT SHE DID IN THE wake of that talk was spend Saturday mindlessly watching the presidential inauguration in the morning and then, still in PJs, sleeping most of the afternoon. On Sunday, she drove to Wells to poke around the junk shop she'd heard about from Arthur. It could be relaxing, she figured, and, flooring it to Wells, she knew she needed that. But once in town she couldn't find the place. Instead, she circled a lake and finally, confused, pulled into the parking lot of the Topaqua Grill, chancing upon it. Inside, she sat at the bar, almost empty then—three p.m.—except for an older woman at the bar's other end. The bartender, lanky and shaggy-haired, couldn't have been much over twenty-one. She ordered coffee and glanced at the football game on the TV looming over the bar. The Patriots were at it, huddling, scrambling, and with the young quarterback Tom Brady, even winning. What was particularly relaxing, she soon realized, sipping her coffee, watching the game and nodding hello to the woman at the bar's other end, was being lost, or at least unknown. The surety of her anonymity was freeing. Quickly, she decided to lose herself further, ordering a vodka tonic to do so. It was her first-ever alcoholic drink and she sipped it tentatively, the tonic slightly bitter but good, the vodka smooth, the squeeze of lime best of all. Two drinks later, the woman at the bar now checking her makeup, the bartender fixed on the game, and Willa was entirely lost. At one point she thought she'd sneezed but wasn't sure. "Oops," she said just in case. The football game was increasingly loony what with the tight ends, the rear ends, the end zones, and the very endlessness of it all. "Ends!" she called, first to the bartender, then to the woman, and then to no one. Somehow, a cab showed up for her. Somehow, she was in the cab. Once home she recalled of her time at the Grill only the sight of a little paper umbrella, a cocktail adornment she'd requested, daintily drifting floorward. That and a certain feeling she'd had while downing the first of what she instantly knew would be more drinks, a delicious bliss that came with forgetting herself. Momentarily, she'd even understood why her parents were seduced by the same thing.

She spent the next day in bed, her head and stomach a wreck. The rest of the week she focused on catching up at work, taking cabs to and from her office. Even sober she didn't trust herself enough to drive.

But a week later she felt ready to retrieve her car. She needed it, she figured, if only to pack up and leave Middletown. All week, in the face of her own unreliability, the old impulse to run away had returned, an internal buzz she could feel, like electricity. She couldn't read, couldn't sit still, couldn't eat except for a few bowls of cereal. She couldn't possibly face Arthur again, even to apologize. She felt too ashamed to be seen.

When the cab finally dropped her off at the Topaqua Grill, she rushed toward her Toyota, its hood covered with snow. Despite many days of sitting idle in the cold the sedan started right up. But the intense chill inside the car had Willa shaking. Moreover, the buzzing sensation in her body was back, occupying her gut, traveling even to her legs. She pulled out onto Lake Drive, and though she quickly went over the speed limit the car wouldn't move fast enough. "Come on, come on," she commanded as she drove, finally arriving at the outskirts of town where the road spread into a two-lane highway, allowing her to accelerate more. To assuage a rising panic, she flipped on the radio, then let it blare. The late afternoon glowed under a mellow sun, a placidness she found disturbing. She was midway across the Arrigoni Bridge, high above the Connecticut River, when the river itself called to her. "Come to me," she thought she heard it say, and but for the car behind her, suddenly honking, she might very well have answered the call—swerving as she did momentarily toward the bridge's side barriers, then swerving back, then swerving dangerously out again—because it was tempting to go someplace new, and to a place where, apparently, she was even wanted.

◊

NOW THAT BILL COUSINS'S FATHER WAS OUT OF THE HOSPITAL AND INTO at-home rehab, Bill found himself spending most evenings with his parents. His wife, Ellen, would typically join him, with the kids and dinner in tow. Ellen would cook at home, then pile the food and kids into the station wagon and drive into town, meeting Bill there. He'd have arrived earlier, giving himself time to pick up more of the crap that his father couldn't throw out. Newspapers and magazines mostly, stacked in piles in several corners of the living room, but sometimes there was a book stuck in a pile, from Wells's library, its return date invariably several years back. The last Thursday of January Bill wandered into the library and paid late fees totaling $214.00. "I wondered about ever seeing these again," the librarian said. His father had been reading about the American revolution and about wild mushrooms. He had borrowed three books on each subject. In November of 1997 he'd taken out a seventh book, on the role of early education in childhood development. Upon finding it that day Bill had asked his father, "Yours too?"

"It's what it all comes down to, I think," his father said, his post-stroke voice still a whisper. "Early education, of which I had none."

"No kindergarten? You think that explains things?" Bill stood beside a pile of yellowing newspapers, mostly the *Hartford Courant.* As always, clearing the pile had been slow as his father wanted to inspect each paper. In doing so he found reasons to keep them. "But this one includes the Yankees winning the series." "But it's O.J. on the sixty-mile chase." "Here comes Gingrich. And politics, my son, is never the same." Of the book on early education his father said a little more. "I'm a believer in early education. In my day, we went straight from diapers to work. A little kindergarten might have helped."

Bill smiled. His father had managed both a full sentence and a little joke, one with some truth packed into it. He was still there, despite a thousand changes, including his inability to move his own pained facial expression into a smile. Bill put the book down and hauled out another armful of the old papers. He was sad to notice that his father was too tired just then to offer the usual objections.

Bill had then gone to the library and come back, and soon, when his family arrived, they ate as usual around the old dining table, which barely fit them all. The kids were quiet in the presence of their grandfather, who dribbled or coughed upon swallowing. The man ate mostly mush but still he struggled. Bill sat close, patting his father's back when the coughing got too much. After some time, he helped the man up so he could walk to the living room couch and rest. "Supper," his father said, sinking into the cushions, "was exhausting."

Later that night, at home in the bungalow, Bill stared out the kitchen window at the lake. A crescent moon graced the night sky, but it emanated such dim light that the lake itself was almost lost to darkness. Unable to spot the Big Dipper, Bill felt momentarily lost too. But then he saw it, along with the stars that marked Orion's Belt, and he felt a moment's relief at identifying them. *There, I know something,* he told himself. But the reality was that he knew so little about things, about stars and early education and wild mushrooms and history. He knew so little about how to care for his aging parents, except to tidy up the place. Before leaving that night he'd filled the back of his van with more old newspapers that he would take to the dump in the morning.

"I'll eat dinner at my folks', you and the kids eat here," he told Ellen when he turned away from the window. "It brings the kids down to be there. They don't need to see that. Sad suppers. Not a good early education."

Ellen replied, "We'll come at least once a week. In its way it *is* good for them. They told me they like helping."

But he couldn't quite see it, what with the drooling and coughing and exhaustion.

Despite his wariness, early the next week when his family joined him at his parents', Bill let his son, Rich, walk his grandfather from the dining table to the living room couch. For a time, the two were quiet. But soon Bill heard his father say, "smart move," and he heard Rich giggling. They were playing checkers. His father was still reclined on the couch and Rich had the checkerboard on a pillow over the man's extended legs so he didn't have to raise himself or reach forward. Before his father got sleepy, the checkerboard still balanced on his body, they'd played two full games.

Meanwhile his twin daughters had pulled out a deck of cards and had a game of Go Fish going with their grandmother. He and Ellen washed the dinner dishes and then sat at the table for a time, saying nothing, watching. "Gram, you got any twos?" "Go fish," his mother said, her voice low as if to give the words extra gravity. The girls smiled at that.

"Go fish," the old man on the couch, just about nodding off, suddenly said, just loud enough for them all to hear it.

"You talking to me?" Bill's mother answered. She winked at her granddaughters. She seemed her old self, relaxed, witty.

"Been talking to you my whole life," the man said.

"Well, then, Go fish yourself," she told him teasingly. The girls cracked up at that.

On the way home, the twins with Bill in his van, it was one then the other saying *Go fish* or *Go fish yourself.* None of it made sense but the words had them laughing.

"Go fish," they told Bill just before bed instead of saying "goodnight." He paused. Outside their bedroom window he caught a glimpse of the room he was building for his parents. After a night like the one they'd just had he could finally envision all of them together, the kids helping, like Ellen had said. He'd been wrong about that. Above the wall he'd raised, in the night sky, the familiar stars dangled. A moment earlier Ellen had flitted into the bedroom, kissed each girl, then flitted past, moves that seemed starlike, quick as a falling flash of light. Quick as time.

He'd been talking to her his whole life, his father had said to his mother. The words had stopped Bill.

"Go fish yourself," he told his daughters, quietly, the phrase coming to him just then as a lament, as signaling the end of something. But the girls didn't hear it that way. They laughed again and were still tittering when he flicked off their bedroom light, said "That's enough," said "See you tomorrow," said "I *said* . . ." in just enough of a raised tone that they swiftly quieted down.

In the next moment he found Ellen, staring lakeward as she got ready for bed. He joined her there. But from their window, gazing out, he could see only the tiniest sliver of moon, hanging before them, a single thing, untethered. Looking at it, Bill recalled his father on the couch calling to his mother in a voice that could barely reach her.

He turned to Ellen.

"What is it?"

But he didn't know what he meant to say. Pulling her close, he was glad to feel her solidness. "Pretty moon," he finally noted. "What little there is of it."

"Pretty moon," she said.

◊

A long marriage wasn't an easy thing. Surely that was so for many people. Yet the courtship between young Tessa Rozman and Jozef Jacobsen began so simply that it often befuddled Tessa, during her years in America, how complicated their marriage ultimately became. But it was their old world that was complicated, Tessa finally told herself, a continent so disturbed, so awry, that nothing in their upbringing could have possibly prepared them for it.

She and Jozef had been together since they were schoolchildren, though at the time they felt so very grown up. This was April 1918, Europe broken by war, the destruction impacting even the neutral Netherlands, but she remembered herself and Jozef as happy, if not fully innocent. They were in eleventh grade, their schooling almost done. She was enrolled in a high school originally meant for boys;

that's how co-education had come about in the Netherlands, girls attending boys' schools, where the serious subjects were taught. She and Jozef had been paired in biology class for the task of dissecting a frog. Boys were partnered with girls because the year before, when dissecting was introduced, some of the girls were squeamish and nearly fainted. Or so claimed their teacher, Mr. Flora—the very man who'd be instructing their daughter Sophia when the Germans abruptly dismissed him in 1940. But back then—1918—was a different time, and the whole year, it seemed, had been leading to this very moment of slicing into a once-alive thing. The energy in the room was palpable, a little frenzied. Even Mr. Flora, young then and fit, kept swiping his brow. The dissections began, and soon enough a whole class of boys held knives while the girls gripped tongs, ready to lift the dead frogs from the smelliest of bottles. As predicted, squeals ensued from some girls, but only a few, while just as many boys yelped too. Neither Jozef nor Tessa said anything. They shared a seriousness about the task at hand. While Jozef sliced open the frog, carefully pinning bits of its skin back to better see the innards, Tessa didn't budge from her perch just to Jozef's left, peering over his shoulder, curious enough. But minutes into the dissection it became clear that their frog was special, was *pregnant*—its belly exploding with tiny, glistening eggs—and the sight of the eggs amazed and sickened Tessa at once. She reached forward, to steady herself, placing a hand on Jozef's back, which caused him to pitch forward. He squealed—frightened more of her touch, she sensed, than of their pregnant frog. Some classmates laughed at the sound, but Tessa consoled Jozef. "This will be over soon," she whispered, almost apologizing to him for the ordeal, and then she took over, scooping the frog's belly clean, placing the eggs in a small dish that Jozef promptly covered with his handkerchief. When he did, they both exhaled in relief.

Once the dissection was complete, Tessa was the one to draw the innards. Her pencil strokes were accurate, even artful. Or so Jozef said, noting that if someone had not known the image was of eggs they would have thought the work to be a still life of grapes by Jan

Davidszoon de Heem. She blushed at the mention of the renowned artist. When they were awarded a prize of colored inks for the best presentation, Jozef insisted she keep them. "We're a good team," he said. His hair was disheveled and his breath, she'd noticed earlier, just a little sour. He wasn't particularly attractive—until just then, when he became so inexplicably handsome that she had to look away. While she stared at her feet, she held the box of colored inks close to her chest. He turned from her, lifted the dish of frog's eggs, being sure to keep the handkerchief draped over the top. She was watching him again, glad to be looking. "What in the world do we do with *this*?" he said next. Not much of a comment but she thought about it in the next days again and again.

TWO YEARS LATER THEY MARRIED, and for some time their challenges were the manageable and ordinary ones of family life—what to name their firstborn, and then the second. Where to live. How to please each other and be patient with the other when they weren't at their best. Some evenings those first years, after the children were asleep, Tessa liked to draw, mostly with pencil but sometimes with the colored inks she still had from her school days. Jozef liked to read in the evening, particularly philosophy: Descartes. Grotius. Hobbes. He read slowly, determined to school himself, his formal education having been cut off finally by his apprenticeship in diamond polishing, his father's trade. *The world of diamonds will never fail you,* his father had said, many times. With a different father Jozef might have been encouraged to go on with his studies, which he had a passion for, and sensing this loss Tessa listened, deeply, when Jozef would talk about the meaning of his nightly reading. *Hell is truth seen too late,* Jozef read to her one night, quoting Hobbes. Jozef then described the philosopher's bleak vision of people as greedy, self-centered, prone to aggression and chaos. "The world of diamonds will never fail you, my father said, because for Jews most other worlds were blocked. And that wouldn't really surprise Hobbes," Jozef added. Tessa understood then. She knew, too, by observing Jozef's comprehension of his reading grow into clarity, that his was a destiny thwarted by circumstance. But in their world, at least, weren't many destinies circumscribed? Long before the invasion by the Germans they had thought about that, but only occasionally, and—in the comfort of their modest but tidy home, alongside other Jewish families living near Oosterpark—never with any urgency.

Tessa had been married to Jozef for sixteen years when one day a new thought came to mind: that in all their years together Jozef, who under different circumstances might have been a scholar, had never asked her if she had yearnings for something else, beyond her present station in life. Did she? The truth was she had no idea, as she had never even asked herself that. Earlier that day she'd gone to the Jewish cemetery to visit the graves of her parents. As she placed a stone on the grave of her father, so many memories of him had surfaced: his favorite brand of tobacco, the shaggy wool scarf he wore around his neck, the very sound of his voice, a resonant baritone. On Shabbos it was her father who chanted the blessings, and it seemed to her that time stopped then, the sound of her father's mellifluous voice and the sound of ancient Hebrew conspiring to transport them all into the timelessness at the very heart of the meaning of Shabbos. Her father had once put it to the family in those very terms. And Tessa remembered.

But when she placed a stone on her mother's grave she couldn't recall as much. She saw her mother in the shadows left by her father, lighting the Shabbos candles but reciting the blessing in only a whisper. She saw her mother at the stove in the kitchen, but could recall only the shape of her back, as if that familiar pose was all they saw of the woman, so often stationed there. Most perplexing of all, her mother's voice no longer sounded inside Tessa's mind, where she scurried the longitudes and latitudes of it in search of any long-lost signals.

That night Tessa began to wonder if she, too, wasn't enough of a person to be remembered. And she began to ask herself new questions, such as what did she want to know about, if she could learn anything? She knew her passion was not the philosophy Jozef was so drawn to, but what was it? She felt the desire, pressing at times, to spend more time by herself so she could find out. And by that she didn't mean being home when the others were away and where there was always another chore to do, but rather alone out there, in the hubbub of the streets, where no task beckoned to her beyond that of being part of it, a rightful worldly presence. A desire came then, simply enough, to walk. And so she did. On a Thursday in March of 1936, after she'd seen the family off, washed the morning dishes and swept the floors, she closed her front door and set forth—but not to the market. For the first time in her married life Tessa was aimless, free.

Which made Amsterdam look different. The day was cloudy, but the streets of her neighborhood appeared more colorful than ever before. Even the bricks of the many apartment buildings she passed seemed striking. She stopped several times to look, as if for the first time, at buildings she'd seen her entire married life. She soon became entranced with the variety of doorways, some painted brightly, others marked by a colorful mishmash of tile work. Walking north, toward the old Jewish neighborhood of her youth, she passed the Portuguese Synagogue and then the Ashkenazi one, the Great Shul as it was known, where her father had gone every so often when she was a child. Back then she knew nothing of what went on inside except that her father returned from the place serene and invariably satiated, and that's how she'd learned that prayer was a kind of food, and that the dimensions of life went beyond the physical. That morning, passing the Great Shul, the blessings that her father had chanted on those long-ago Shabbos evenings came back to her, filling not her ears so much as her lungs. She stopped, breathed, and then continued on, enlivened.

Soon, she found herself at the Amstel River, which she crossed, walking toward the businesses of Rembrandtplein. On this side of the river she was leaving the streets of her youth. But she wasn't anxious, offering friendly glances at whoever she passed. For a good half hour she trekked south again, by the river's edge, finally stopping to throw a small stone into the river, wishing on it first: *May this simple act of walking alone continue.* Then she wished for health for Jozef and her daughters. This was a most ordinary wish, the hope of any wife and mother, but one that she wouldn't tell them, she quickly decided. Her secret made her smile. She could do that, she realized—decide for herself what to share or not—and that choice gave her another surge of energy, even stronger than the one she'd felt earlier from recalling the old prayers.

In the months that followed, as she walked two and even three times a week, she kept other secrets from her family: that once she'd used some of their precious money to buy herself lemon cake and coffee and had sat in a café, unashamed to be seen licking the cake's scrumptious icing from her fingertips. Or that she'd dared to go into an art gallery—a showing of small paintings of the local streets—and the dealer took her to be someone who knew something about serious art. Or perhaps he was just desperate, the current economic depression souring every business. Still, when he spoke to her his questions seemed genuine. "Do you like that?" he had asked, and she'd said, firmly, "No." "That?" "Oh, yes." And she'd even given a reason: the unnatural colors of the sky and road added feeling. She was looking at a painting of a lone woman walking on a country road, and the fact that the road was painted pink and the sky a subtle violet seemed to tell Tessa as much about the woman as about her world. It was as if the woman's presence had colored the world. The art dealer agreed. Another secret: that like a painting, or like people, the Amstel had its moods. That it talked to you if you bothered to listen. That every day as she walked she would stop to throw two stones into it, a kiss and a wish on one stone in honor of Jozef and the girls, for all good things. And a kiss and a wish on the other stone in honor of herself, for days. For days and days of walking.

Six months into her walking she stopped in Oosterpark and spotted a painter, an older gentleman, standing before his easel, smoking as he worked. The day was dull, overcast, all too typical, and yet the painting, she noticed, moving closer, was anything but. "You've captured that end of the pond and those trees and that path as if for eternity," she told the man quietly, hoping not to intrude and yet wanting, desperately, to speak to him. "I paint it to remember," he told her as he swiped a tiny brush across a corner of his canvas. As he spoke, she thought his cigarette might fall from his mouth, but it didn't. "There might come a day when I don't remember," he added. "There might come that very day."

After this encounter she took to inscribing her memories too, not by writing or returning to drawing, but by way of embroidery. In the evenings after dinner she listened to Jozef, as always. They talked, and read some, and talked some more. But she began to stitch, too, onto squares of linen, and that's where she poured her secrets. She embroidered a bend of the river, a scene toward South Amsterdam. She replicated the stones on the walkways she still enjoyed staring at, emphasizing their nuance of color. On another swatch she created two lit candlesticks, a memory, an honoring of her childhood Shabbos evenings. All the while Jozef talked or didn't talk. She listened now to both his words and his silences, each way of being suddenly of genuine and equal interest. But something else occupied her: the need to add types of stitches to those she already knew. She even invented stitches, to better capture the world she was out and about in. With time, her sense of things had changed, required texture, as did her ever-burgeoning central thought: that it's always unmapped, this journey toward oneself. That each person must become a pioneer on that singular trek. One night, looking at Jozef, reading as always, she almost told him that there's not so much a lesson to be learned as a *dimension* to be felt in every new mile of it, a dimension and then another, just like the turns from Wibautstraat to Sarphatistraat to Utrechtsestraat that she'd taken over the last months. The *vastness* . . . That's what she was just beginning to grasp on those solitary sojourns, still a young woman, a strong walker, her skirts swishing, her scalp tingling beneath her hat, her mind racing as she considered her daughters and her husband, her relatives and her friends. But now there was herself, too, to consider. And she sensed a vastness there also, within her. "I know things," she'd wanted on more than one occasion to tell Jozef, immersed in Hobbes, immersed in Grotius, but she didn't really know as much as sense things, and all of it was unverifiable, a world away from the seemingly inarguable logic of philosophy. Her biggest hunch was that her husband wouldn't understand. And that, too, was there in their marriage to be experienced. Loneliness, even when sleeping in bed beside the one you wanted. She walked more blocks, north, west, past the town hall, and then the Queen's Palace, accepting whatever appeared around each corner just as at home in the evenings she accepted entrance into the neighborhoods of each new feeling—impatience, boredom, and then suddenly, as if from an abyss, the most violent surge of erotic passion. She'd flick off the lamps. She'd grasp Jozef's hand. There were dimensions to every new dimension. She thought of a diamond then, cut, polished, held beneath a lit lamp and sparkling with countless reflecting lights and colors. *All of it,* she wished upon kissing the stone she'd throw the next day into the unending Amstel. *That's all I want—all of it.*

She was still taking walks in April of 1940, before the Nazis invaded. And the elderly gentleman who'd painted years earlier in Oosterpark was outside now too, developing another scene. Like before, he smoked incessantly as he worked and didn't seem to mind when passersby stopped to watch him. One day a group of three children gathered around the man, who didn't lose a moment of concentration even when the children began to imitate him, each one standing as if before an easel, arms raised. Nor did he stop when, on another day, a younger man approached, settled himself nearby, and began chatting. On another day it was Tessa herself who spoke. "Won't you have some peanuts?" she said, handing the painter a small bag that she carried. The man ate a few. Then, after a quick nod to Tessa, he returned to his work, where she saw that he, too, was after all of it: the trees, the diverging paths, the pigeons pecking at food, the sun breaking through a cloud cover, and the children who had imitated him just days before, there in the distance, playing at life.

ALL OF IT, AS IT turned out, was pretty good preparation for the time to come. When the worst arrived, the Nazi occupation of 1940, Tessa had long ago opened herself to the consistency of change, which was the Amstel's way, its greatest lesson. For some time already she'd known better than to expect anything like a simple stream of ease from life. Nor did she want that. She was beyond small notions, stirred by what she thought of as her own deeper currents. And now Amsterdam was suffering, was sieged, and now, even after enduring the economic losses of the '30s, they had to make do on even less income and more rationing of food. Well then, she quickly grasped, they would. Now they had to acquiesce to some new rules: no Jews here, no Jews there. So be it. They'd go elsewhere. In the new world all time was an urgent "now," and now she couldn't walk anymore, had to say goodbye to that magnificent and transforming time on the streets, but she could do that because by then the neighborhoods and markets and city streets lived inside her. In this way, no matter the external circumstances, she could always take walks along the roadways of her own being.

Winter of '41 Jozef chose to work for Ollie van der Waal, even though the Asscher company, so much more substantial an enterprise, was still producing well. Humility. Fine. If she could step into it—and she did—she could show Jozef how he could too. "Take the job," she said of Ollie's offer when Jozef almost balked. She knew he enjoyed his stature as head polisher at Asscher, but that was then and then was not now.

A year later they were going to live for a time with Ollie. And so she'd packed and readied the girls. In addition to clothes and necessities she encouraged them to pack a favorite thing. Ruttie chose her beloved charm bracelet. Sophia chose her letters from Aaron Taube. In the course of their time together, he'd written six. What mattered to Tessa were her embroidered squares of the sights of the city.

And now, while they stayed with Ollie, she was teaching the others everything she knew, because all that—about stitching, about something she thought of as being like the Amstel, in flow no matter the weather—was quite possibly going to keep them alive.

Weeks later they were home again, briefly, before they left for good, and it was Friday evening, time to tie Sophia up. Just as Ollie had instructed Jozef. "Tie her up." "Yes," Tessa had said minutes after they'd left Ollie's apartment. "We'll do that. Tie her up." But Jozef couldn't.

Yet she could. Because it was necessary. Because it was the next thing. Because she was a mother and what couldn't a mother do for her child?

But that Friday, as she watched Jozef hold Sophia close, consoling her, whispering in her ear, assuring her that Aaron Taube was fine, Tessa stood back, said nothing. For just those hours she retreated into the old way: deferring to her husband's judgment. And it was during this time that Sophia pulled from him and bolted out the door. And then what were they to do?

Tessa raced outside and called for Sophia, but she'd already rounded a corner and was beyond reach. *How in the world did they let this happen again?* she all but cried as she turned on Jozef, fierce with rage. "*Coward!*" Tessa finally called Jozef, whispering but doing so with fury, and when Jozef, hearing her, fell to his knees she fell beside him.

She was about to speak, to include herself in her condemnation, to take back the word, but Ruttie had come to them and Tessa silenced herself, just as she would in the anguished months ahead. She would be silent, then more silent, until she became—as they fled farther and farther from Amsterdam—almost nonexistent, a mother without her motherhood, a mother who barely spoke to the one daughter who remained.

◊

GROWING UP STEPHANIE HAD FOUND HER GRANDMOTHER TESSA strange: sitting on her couch, embroidering all the time. Every visit to the West Hartford apartment was the same. Stephanie and her mother would arrive, greetings would be shared, and everyone, including Stephanie's grandfather Jozef, would quickly gather around Tessa, who was often too much in the throes of stitching to stop. The craft had a momentum, apparently, that only Tessa, holding a threaded needle, could really feel. The work of embroidery just seemed slow to Stephanie, who, once she'd learned to read, always brought a book with her when visiting her grandparents. Without that, a given visit would feel too long.

But once Stephanie turned nine she began to spend a night each month there, her bed the couch her grandmother used for her stitching, and her grandmother was different then, more attentive. She didn't sew when Stephanie slept over but rather baked, and once she taught Stephanie how to make poppy seed cake, a recipe passed down from Tessa's mother. Learning that, Stephanie stared at her grandmother as if looking for clues to the past. The woman had short gray hair, was stooped in the shoulders, and wore her cardigans—always a cardigan—at least a size too big. She wasn't pretty but neither was she plain. Her face, while carrying a typically serious expression, was not grim. Still, it was impossible to imagine Tessa as young.

Stephanie was twelve when Tessa began to talk to her, only during those sleepovers, about her life in Amsterdam. They would be baking then. Tessa had been adventurous when she was younger, she told Stephanie once while stirring the batter of a butter cake, and by that she meant taking long walks by herself along the Amstel River, which didn't seem that adventurous to Stephanie, who often walked beside Lake Topaqua alone. Tessa was rolling pie dough when she told Stephanie that she used to draw with pencil and ink when she was younger but had dropped that. Later she'd suddenly taken up embroidery, which had stayed with her. On another visit, while making babka, Tessa spoke about Sophia, the other daughter, who also liked to draw. Though Stephanie wanted to hear more about Sophia—the family's ghost, as Stephanie already saw it—she didn't dare ask, fearing to shut down her grandmother as she had her mother whenever she'd asked about the odd Oosterpark chant, "your ugly, lopsided pond." Somehow, Stephanie sensed that it was Sophia who first uttered those words.

It was that year, after learning a series of new recipes, that Stephanie sometimes began to bake on her own, at home, for her mother. Doing so Stephanie couldn't help but notice that what made her grandmother most talkative seemed to be the act of baking, and yet the product of that baking seemed to make her mother the most quiet, the warm sweets instantly silencing her, though she ate them greedily, and always with a cup of freshly brewed coffee. Seeing that her mother seemed to enjoy the desserts, Stephanie kept baking during her teen years, learning recipes at her grandmother's and taking them home to feed some old hunger of her mother's.

Stephanie was fifteen when Tessa became a widow. Some months after Jozef's death Stephanie's mother wanted Tessa to move to Wells, but Tessa was used to her apartment, she explained, and could easily walk from there to a nearby grocery and deli, and to the bank they used, the convenience of which was her best argument against Ruth's gentle pressures to move. Moreover, she couldn't drive, she added. She needed to live close to the places she relied upon.

But even though Tessa refused to move in with them, sometimes Ruth would drive to West Hartford and bring Tessa back to Wells for a weekend. During one such time, in May of 1979—just months before Stephanie would start college and just months before Tessa would rapidly succumb to non-Hodgkin's lymphoma, a different cancer than Jozef's—Tessa knocked on Stephanie's bedroom door. It was a rainy Saturday afternoon. Stephanie thought her grandmother, who seemed tired when they'd picked her up that morning, was napping. But there she was, in the doorway, another frumpy cardigan drooping from her shoulders.

She sat on the edge of Stephanie's bed and held a small jewelry box out to her. Opening it, Stephanie was surprised to see a ring with a small pink diamond at the center.

"Your grandfather polished that diamond. I always liked pink ones. I wished for one. And then he gave it to me. I never asked." Tessa paused, smiling. "He knew me. You see?"

"Your wedding ring?" Stephanie held it up to the light. Soon a nearby wall sparkled with the diamond's refracting, reflecting light.

"Not my wedding ring. My marriage ring. The one he gave me after a long time. The one that means the most, because, well, it wasn't easy, really. Life wasn't easy, and we went through it together. I gave your mother my wedding ring. It's beautiful too. A ring of hope, that's hers, and a ring of experience, that's yours. Both are important."

Her grandmother's words came out smoothly, her accent's inflections, its highs and lows, matching the words' meaning. She'd never spoken so determinedly. "Jozef was a good man," she said next.

"I know."

"But maybe I didn't. Not always." Tessa looked out the bedroom window where rain still fell, a steady patter on the lake's surface.

Stephanie waited for more, but her grandmother didn't speak further of her marriage. But she hoped Stephanie would have a long one.

"If you get married," she said, "You can use this ring. It's got goodness in it. Experience. It stands for real love, not the silly kind. That's what you want, Stephanie."

Stephanie did want real love, though she'd never told anyone. She thought that the absence of real love, as she vaguely defined it, explained her all-too-common loneliness. She was hoping she might meet her real love at college. Quietly, secretly, every day, she hoped for just that.

She hugged her grandmother, who hugged her back. For a time they stayed like that, which was unusual. After they'd let go Tessa asked, "Would you like to learn to embroider?"

Stephanie shook her head. It wasn't her thing, she explained. Too picky. Too slow.

"It is slow," her grandmother said, slowly rising to her feet.

"You can stay," Stephanie said. Before Tessa arrived, Stephanie had been doing homework, reading about the three branches of American government, a separation of powers, a series of checks and balances. Not everyone was honest, after all. The Founding Fathers knew that. She saw her grandmother eye her textbook, dropped on the bed beside them as they'd looked at the ring.

"Just wanted to give you that." Tessa then trudged out of the bedroom. That she was already ailing was something no one yet knew.

Briefly, Stephanie placed the ring on her finger to get the feel of it, of real love, as her grandmother described it. *College,* she thought, *here I come.*

◊

The last evening in January, a Wednesday, Ruth Pearl sat in her wingback chair, her feet resting on the stool covered by her mother's embroidery of Amsterdam, her lap loaded with legal opinions that she'd brought home from work to study. That week she'd been searching beyond the ordinances in Wells that Wilson Keller had looked for before, and she'd chanced upon the theory of estoppel, which could create a legal path, or so she dared to hope, to save her lake view. The argument went as follows: since she'd been living next to the Cousinses for fifteen years, she had every right to expect things between them to stay the same. Her neighbor had ceded to her, implicitly, the right to her view—a cherished sight—by never obstructing it all this time. Under the law, then, Bill Cousins was estopped, or barred, from obstructing her view.

She would try out the argument on Stephanie when they talked next, and if that went well she'd try it out on Wilson Keller and see if he might raise it with Bill Cousins. From the pile of photocopied cases on her lap she picked up another involving estoppel, dealing, as they all seemed to, with landlords and tenants, and not lake views. She couldn't find a case more factually on point. Still, she hoped—crafting the words in her mind, then closing her argument with something that sprang forth from deep within her: "Fifteen years, Bill, we've been neighbors fifteen years." She kicked her feet furiously on the heart of her mother's embroidery. "But you know me," she said, the words surprising her with their ring of familiarity. It was Dr. Cohen, she gradually recalled, speaking to the maître d' of a restaurant on Sarphatistraat where Jews, suddenly, couldn't enter. "Willem, it's me," he'd said just before he'd taken his wife's arm and turned to go.

8

Germany, November 25, 1941, by the Eleventh Decree of the Law on the Citizenship of the Reich: The German nationality of all German Jews living abroad—including the Netherlands—is revoked. All possessions of these people are declared forfeited to the German state. Forfeited funds will be used for the furtherance of all purposes related to the solution of the Jewish question.

THE FIRST SATURDAY IN FEBRUARY Judge Arthur Cantrell sat at his kitchen table, pen in hand, trying once again to organize his thoughts about Willa Fletcher's complaint. He'd yet to do this despite having received the official copy she'd filed with the Judicial Review Council. Upon getting that he'd set up an appointment for that evening, informally over dinner, with Attorney George O'Rourke, recommended to him by Wilson. Should the complaint come to something—and it likely wouldn't, Wilson had insisted—he'd want counsel. Even though Arthur didn't need to respond to the complaint at this early stage he was too anxious to wait and see what the Review Council's initial assessment turned out to be. He'd quickly made the appointment and had risen early to prepare notes. He just had to change his bed sheets, slightly damp, and shower first. After such a long time—he'd hoped he was cured—it had happened again.

But as soon as he put pen to paper he felt agitated, as chased by Willa in the form of her complaint as he used to be by his father. Now, as then, the punishment didn't fit the crime, which he knew wasn't judicial bias or anything else but rather his having hurt Willa with his prolonged silence. But even if he'd broken up with her rather than merely dithered, he didn't deserve what she was doing. He looked up from the table to the window over the kitchen sink. A cloudy morning, the new blue bottles were not glowing but were calming to see nonetheless. Since placing them there he'd in fact found comfort in them. A little bit of the past—glass bottles like his mother's—had turned out to be, in this case, a good thing.

But returning to Willa's words revived that sense of being chased by her in what appeared to be her madness. And that chase, in turn, generated a madness in him, the same righteous anger that he used every day in his work to help guide him toward his judgments. Justice, he knew, was the answer to this familiar form of chaos. Of bullies determined to get their way. Of intentional cruelty. Justice was a form of coherence, a place where up was up and down was down, and everything made sense. Sometimes, while sitting at the conference table at work, he quietly contemplated the very feel of justice. It was cool, impartial, yet as gentle and welcome as a light snow shower. Sensing it just then, he glanced up from the kitchen table. Across the room the bottles had finally captured enough light to delicately glow. The soft blue they emanated seemed the very color of justice.

YET FEELING CHASED ALSO GENERATED fear. And this particular form of dread was such an old thing with him, always just beneath the surface of his life, buried under his judgeship, which he daily covered himself with as if it were costume and mask. He could fool even himself most days that the past was behind him. Yet just that morning, Willa, at five foot two, loomed as large as his six-foot father. The scale of her rage matched his too. And that she aimed, by way of her complaint, to destroy him, was the very goal of each of his father's wild chases. "She wants my life," Arthur declared out loud, the certainty of it startling him.

He rose hastily, unwittingly, propelled by a burst of adrenaline, and as he did he knocked the coffee mug he'd been using off the table. Hitting the floor, the ceramic shattered. Coffee soon spread as far as the stove.

After wiping up, he pulled a broom from his utility closet. Then, returning to the closet for the vacuum, he spotted the unopened box marked, "To Arthur, with love." Impulsively, he grabbed the box rather than the vacuum. It was almost weightless, which seemed strange, something he didn't recall from when he had first stored it there.

Inside were countless whittled butterflies, each one wrapped in tissue paper, which he threw in messy heaps onto the newly swept floor. He found, too, a note from his mother explaining that his father had carved the butterflies. More surprising than even that was how beautiful they were—delicate, painted in tones as rich and improbable as nature's colors. That his father had something to offer was not what Arthur expected to find in the box. That his father was capable of beauty seemed impossible. But the very existence of the carved butterflies proved as much.

Despite the carvings and what they implied about his father's nature, more complex and manifold than Arthur in his aggrieved state wanted to acknowledge, he laid a dozen of the butterflies in a row on the floor. His adrenaline still surged. He grabbed a hammer from the utility closet and raced to the kitchen with his arm raised, the hammer ready. One by one he smashed the carved butterflies, wooden flecks flying as he pounded. When he finished, he retrieved a dozen more, lined them up, and swiftly destroyed them. He did this until all of them were gone.

HIS BREATH SPENT, HIS WRECKAGE strewn everywhere, his newfound destructiveness, including its satisfaction, a surprise, he sat again at his kitchen table. He didn't know himself, he admitted. Not really. Perhaps, he thought, his mind turning again to Willa's complaint, he could have been more stringent about staying clear of any matter, however small, in which Wilson played a role, even when both parties, like Jack and Stacy Byrnes, wanted him there. Or he could have been more careful about not saying a word about any case before him even if the comment—like his to Willa about the Byrneses' anger—had no legal implications. For the first time in his career he doubted his fairness, the very foundation of his work, just enough to see merit in Willa's points. He picked up one of the many broken butterflies. He couldn't believe it and yet it was true.

◊

When is loving like death? It had been a question Ian Lima threw out to the universe, and since he'd asked it the world had been stubbornly silent. Ian's tailbone was still sore from his fall on the ice and perhaps he was getting his answer, he figured, in the lingering pain. *All the time,* it suggested. *Loving is like death pretty much all the time.* Saturday morning, the first weekend in February, he rose early as usual, went for his predawn walk on the ice, and while in the secluded space between the lake's islands lit up, doping, as he did lately, just enough to take the edge off. The rest of the time on the lake was as always, the fantasies unfurling, the wind zipping, the ice groaning. "Hey, pal," he told the ice at one point. A ghoulish sound ricocheted between the islands. "Tell me your woes, I'll tell you mine."

When he left the lake, he went to the Moretti School, where Angelina had called for an unusual Saturday morning rehearsal. She aimed to better prepare Sarah as their performance date in March approached. Angelina was clearly nervous that this performance—the capstone of the spring gala, the school's primary fundraiser—wasn't coming together quickly enough. First there was the problem of Ian's untimely injury. Then there was Sarah, improving but not enough. "Is it something about the love story?" Angelina asked Sarah first thing that morning. Sarah shrugged and said she didn't think so.

Ian snickered. The answer seemed an obvious yes, yet somehow everyone remained confused. He was sitting on the floor, knees up. Jase was standing across the room. When Ian laughed everyone stopped, glanced at him, and he quickly shut up, realizing he was more buzzed than he knew. While Angelina and Sarah conferred further, Jase unfolded a chair and sat, then dropped his head into his hands. He looked bored, tired, and miffed to be there. He looked different from the guy Ian had envisioned so clearly, just a short while ago, while on the lake. That guy had been joyful and energetic. He'd gladly taken a few tokes. Then he'd suggested they walk out from between the islands, brave the open waters. As they did, the wind whipped, the sun rose, and a few lights in the houses lining the shore snapped on. The world was waking up as if, together, he and Jase had orchestrated such a monumental emergence. Someone had called out to Ian at one point, "Everything okay?" A man was outside. He wore an orange hat. A green parka. He looked as tiny in the distance as Ian must have looked to him. The lake was wider when you stood on it like this, in the middle of its most open expanse. Ian nodded until he realized the man would likely not see that. "Okay!" he called, and then he yelled, "Okay, okay, okay!" He didn't love his voice, but he loved how the wind set it sailing.

That time on the lake was fun, a kind of relief. After an experience like that Ian didn't even mind showing up for the extra rehearsal. But clearly Jase did. When Jase finally began to move with Sarah, his arms were uncharacteristically slack. Upon lifting her—something he'd done so easily in days past—he struggled to hold her up. His demeaner was cool and detached, which was confusing since he and Sarah had been partnering well, Sarah finally coming alive with Jase beside her. After each recent rehearsal Ian had come home dejected, barely eating his sandwich, telling his mother he preferred to get to bed rather than watch TV. They were working just that hard, he'd lied when she'd looked at him, alarmed. Under his heavy blankets he'd slept well enough, but when he woke the sinking feeling had become unbearable. He took off then, swiftly, to the lake.

An hour into the rehearsal and Sarah was almost crying. She, too, was confused by Jase's shift, his coolness, his inexplicable clumsiness. "What's with you?" she finally snapped.

Jase, holding her elbow, quickly let go. Angelina kept the music on though the dancers merely stood, their backs to each other. Ian watched, surprised by the hostility. He blinked to be sure he wasn't dreaming. He reached into his heart then, that closet where he'd stored his last millimeter of hope, the kind that was sourced from reality, not dreams. He dared to expand its scope by another millimeter.

ANGELINA STOPPED THE SATURDAY REHEARSAL. She apologized for the bad timing. "You kids need your rest," she added, looking specifically at Jase. He still seemed irked. She then asked Ian, "When we start up again, you ready to resume your part?"

As Ian nodded, he watched the relief in Jase's face travel through his body. He relaxed, uncrossing his arms. He nodded at Ian, almost smiling. Ian reciprocated with a huge grin, which, unthinkingly, he held and held. "Frozen?" Jase finally said. He stepped forward and snapped his fingers in front of Ian's eyes. Ian winced, as if slapped, and shook his head. "Fucking shit," he said without meaning to. "Tell me about it," Jase answered, and to Ian's relief, agreeably enough.

Angelina decided to treat them to lunch. She dropped them off at Mitchell's Dairy and said she'd return in an hour. But inside the restaurant the touchiness of the morning resumed. The three picked at their food. Ian had ordered a BLT but, despite his raging hunger, held himself back, fearing he might overdo it again. Jase had ordered a burger and fries, and though he'd eagerly smeared ketchup on everything, in the end he just pushed the food around his plate. Sarah, who'd ordered a strawberry milkshake—"It's a *meal*," she'd insisted—took only a few sips.

Everything at Mitchell's was decidedly bland: its flat background music, its faded wallpaper borders. The smells were overwhelmingly of frying meat and toasting bread. Even Ian's BLT tasted of burger. Another silent minute passed. Jase finally ate some fries, and perhaps because he caught Ian staring at him, offered him some. He then offered some to Sarah.

Sharing food opened the door to the cage they'd gotten locked in. They finally ate. Soon they found common ground in talking about their neighboring towns, Wells and Portland, both in all ways too small.

"Someone, please, rescue me," Sarah said.

They agreed they'd go to New York or Boston as soon as they could.

"No movie theater, no clothing store," Ian noted about Wells. He described the rundown houses on Main Street. "Ever notice? And at school not a single AP class." He almost laughed at himself, saying that. But they agreed: the school systems sucked. Then this sucked and that sucked, until *sucked*, repeated so often, became too hilarious to say.

The complaining, then, was fun, non-urgent. They could have been talking, simply enough, about the weather outside, a mild snowstorm, not much bother. Ian told a story of his mother's, how when she was young the downtown store owners let little kids paint their storefront windows for Halloween—ghosts, pumpkins, whatever they liked. "That's actually sweet," Sarah said, surprised, then added, "What happened?"

Soon they were outside, in the snow, where they raised their heads, arched their necks, and opened their mouths to catch falling snowflakes, pretending as the flakes landed that they contained wondrous flavors: blueberry, rhubarb, even meatloaf. They whooped at "meatloaf," Ian's contribution. He followed that with "peas and mashed potato," which was just something to say, to keep them standing there, spinning. Remarkably, they laughed like crazy. So he kept the performance going, dreaming up new flavors: Reuben sandwich, Fruit Loops, mac and cheese. With every new one he watched Jase as he'd never seen him before, turning haphazardly, his mouth, gathering snowflakes, open to the sky.

Jase then ran into a field adjacent to Mitchell's Dairy and Ian and Sarah followed. When Sarah threw a snowball Ian's way, Jase did too. Then they chased each other: Ian after Jase, Sarah after them both, the two boys turning on her suddenly, as if planned, Sarah screaming and racing in the opposite direction, all the way to the parking lot, though they'd stopped following her long before she got there.

With Sarah gone, Ian and Jase turned to each other. Ian held a snowball and approached Jase with his throwing arm raised and Jase held his ground as if daring Ian to let loose on him. He looked just like he did whenever Ian managed a card trick: grinning, eyes wide, excited. Ian walked closer, then closer, as if he really did have a trick up his sleeve. But when he reached Jase, he simply stood before him, gradually lowering the arm carrying the snowball, which he let drop. They were face to face. He leaned forward, ready and willing to fall into Jase's arms. He figured he was about five millimeters from Jase's body, the very length of his tiny rope of hope. But then Jase stepped aside, causing Ian to fall to the ground.

In the next moment Jase jumped on Ian, throwing fistfuls of snow into his face, and Ian lay on his back, crying *no! no!* though he adored it: Jase straddling him, laughing.

Apparently exhausted, Jase then fell onto Ian, blanketing his upper body. They looked at each other. Jase moved his chin enough to gently rub Ian's, and Ian returned the gesture. Moved by the affection, Ian, without thinking, wrapped his arms around Jase's frame. For several seconds neither of them moved. Cold bits of snow under Ian's coat collar chilled the back of his neck but he didn't dare turn his head. Jase's breath, falling onto Ian's chin, was warm, moist. Ian liked it as much as he did the weight of Jase's body on his. As their eyes met again Ian reflexively closed his. At the same time, he kissed Jase's lips. For a millisecond—perhaps by instinct but perhaps not—Jase kissed back.

In the next instant Jase was up, his smile replaced with a look of bafflement. "Jesus, Ian!" He leapt back. "You think I'm like *you*?"

Ian shot up. His backside was damp and cold. He touched his still tingling lips. He blinked as snowflakes fell onto his eyelashes, blurring his vision.

Yet even through the snow he could see well enough. Jase, running away from him and toward Sarah, calling out to her, then taking her in his arms. Kissing her, endlessly. At first, limply, Sarah just stood there, let Jase do all the doing. But Ian watched as Sarah slowly came to life, lifted her arms, returned the embrace and no doubt the kiss that Jase so determinedly offered.

Ian collapsed backward. As he lay there, the frozen ground chilling him further, his mouth fell open. Soon he rose and ran forward, though he was blinded by tears. A car backing out in the parking lot honked when Ian slammed into it. "Watch out!" he heard the driver yell. "Son of a bitch!" Ian called back, pounding the car's trunk. He pushed off again, running, slipping every so often. "You think I'm like *you*?" he cried each time he did.

◊

What began with a series of marshmallows—first three, then seven, then half a bag, then the entire next bag, all eaten in one boundless night—had ended for Willa Fletcher some hours ago, on a Saturday early-morning run in the freezing cold, and in the dark, on Middletown roads pocked with black ice. But she'd risk it, she figured, because she had to get out. Out of her head, of course, which was filled with words like *idiot, fool, moron*—words she'd been hurling at herself ever since Mrs. Rizzo had asked her, appropriately, "What are you going to do?" But she needed to get out of her house, too, where she was hitting walls, pacing as she was across the kitchen and back, popping marshmallows as she went. By two a.m. her stomach spasmed with cramps and her entire body trembled from a massive internal sugar storm. Bizarrely, she craved more marshmallows and had gone so far as to jot down the address of the nearest twenty-four-hour grocery. But even more passionately than marshmallows she craved that old shoebox full of letters—*Proof: Of Love*—that she'd thrown out some months ago when her life seemed full of promise, about the time when she'd tasted her very first marshmallow and immediately called Arthur to tell him how good it was. By three a.m. she had willed herself, by slowly tearing apart the Yellow Pages, away from the impulse toward the grocery store. Then, at four, she'd pulled on her running clothes, over which she'd thrown on a down vest. Outside, the air in her lungs stung. Her stomach ached. Her legs felt like lead, as did her feet, to the degree that she could feel them at all. The entirety of Middletown, she figured, passing one darkened house after another, was asleep. But she, alone, was running.

She was alone.

Therefore—is that how the argument went?—she was running.

She reasoned through the predicament as she went on, her body gradually heating up where her vest covered it, but otherwise, at her extremities, gradually freezing. She reasoned, turning the logic over and over, until her body forced her to stop. She doubled over, heaved. When she rose again even her face, though cold to the touch, was covered with sweat. Inside her vest she could feel that she was drenched. She unzipped the vest, letting a flow of cold surround her core. For a moment she stood there, both hot and cold, staring ahead. She didn't know which road she was on, but she was sure, still, that she could retrace her steps home. Even in her distress her mind had never shut off, it just began thinking, talking to her, ever more lucidly. *Alone. Because. Therefore. Run.* She cried then, not with sorrow, but with a need to release the toxins of the night—even through her eyes. She fell into a crouch. She heaved again.

WHEN SHE WOKE AT THE hospital later that Saturday, she couldn't remember how she got there. It was a doctor, a young man with a quiet voice, leaning empathetically over her gurney, who told her she'd gotten a ride home, then called 911, but perhaps, the doctor gently suggested, she should have come straight to the hospital. Who told him that, she had asked, to which the doctor had said, confusingly, "You did." Then she remembered the car that had slowed as it passed her, still crouched and heaving.

The driver, an older man, had taken her home, his radio all the while playing Sinatra, his heater set on high. She remembered, too, that once home she'd immediately collapsed, her breath short, her body a pool of sweat which she blamed on the man, blasting the heat like that. But in all likelihood, she saw in hindsight from her hospital bed, he'd helped save her life. Then she remembered that she'd gotten herself to the phone, fast. A whirring feeling, a little wheel spinning round and round at the core of her chest, had become activated. *Just in case,* she figured. *Call.*

But how did I know? she would wonder in the next weeks, unable to comprehend her luck: the driver who picked her up on the roadside, the inner wisdom she'd not only heard but heeded by crawling to the phone, the EMTs who in fact reached her in time and had shocked her back to life when she'd gone into cardiac arrest almost immediately upon entering the ambulance. It was a heart attack, that whirring that she could feel but that didn't really hurt. The symptoms were different for women, she was told, the degree of pain you felt, for example, or didn't. She'd probably been at the start of the attack, various doctors explained, when she was heaving on the roadside in the night. What the doctors couldn't explain was her survival. Major, they called the attack. "And there you were," that young, quiet doctor said, checking in on her during his Saturday afternoon rounds, shaking his head, his hand on her shoulder, "Willa, all alone, out there in the night, in the cold."

◊

THAT SATURDAY AFTERNOON, BILL COUSINS SET OUT TOWARD THE FROZEN lake. He brought a crate to sit on, an ice pick, and a fishing rod. He sat on the crate and began to pick at the ice, finally breaking through, then picking at it more. He was creating a larger and larger hole, which made no sense insofar as fishing was concerned—the average size of any fish he might catch would be modest. But it felt good to hack away, which became its own reason for being out there. From where he sat, he could see his bungalow on the lake's shore, could see the wall of the room he was adding on, and thought he could see his wife, Ellen, offering his kids tomato soup and grilled cheese sandwiches for lunch, though given how intimately he knew his family's routines he might have been imagining that scene rather than actually viewing it through a distant window. Instead of eating with his family he'd felt compelled to get away, and some minutes back he'd told Ellen that he had a hankering to go fishing.

"Go fish yourself," she'd said. And they'd both smiled just a little.

So here he was, by himself, the hole in the ice growing bigger as he hacked at it, the ice chips flying pell-mell, his gaze less on that than on his home, expanding for his parents as they contracted.

He would have to come to terms with it, he knew, thinking of their mortality, that thing he'd been unwilling to face each time he visited them. He could *do* for them, sure, but to just *be* with them was to see it, to face it. A part of him wanted to go wherever they went, to the ends of the earth and beyond, which is the same part of him that kept him all these years in Wells, right by them, when his brother had gone off to distant Buffalo, New York. Bill didn't even know that his existence was so buoyed by theirs until this winter, when he could sense theirs rounding into a final lap of sorts.

He hacked at the ice for a time and then slowed down, chipping at it, just for something to do. When he finally noticed the size of the hole he laughed. The word *outsized* came to mind. The hole was outsized, a perfect manifestation of his fears.

He turned then to his fishing rod, dropping its line into the lake waters. Almost instantly something bit and pulled on the line, nearly throwing him off his crate. Reeling in the catch he stared, stupefied. Outsized, the trout was. Bigger than big.

"Hey, pal," he told the thing, unhooking it, briefly staring at its face, an open eye glaring back at him. The trout's body was speckled and yellowy in parts. Its mouth was agape. Quickly, Bill dropped it back into the hole from which it emerged. "Didn't mean to bring you out of the depths," he said, surprised to see such a thing surface from a lake he'd always thought of as circumscribed and relatively shallow. But just then the frozen surface surrounding him seemed vast.

"Go on, go on," he said next, encouraging the trout long past the time when he could see it, leaving only a few bubbles, flimsy proof of its surprising, grand existence.

Some minutes later, inside the bungalow again, the kids were watching an old movie on TV and Ellen was grilling the first of the cheese sandwiches he'd imagined she'd already served.

"Come on, let me take you out." He said this to the whole family and the three kids looked at him as wide-eyed as the trout he'd just snared, looked at him as if they didn't believe him. Ellen tried to check his goddamned temperature. "Can't a guy treat his family?"

"Something happen to you out there?" his son Rich asked.

"But it's no one's birthday," one of the twins argued.

The other began to spin around. "Go fish," she sang, as if the phrase were a spell she meant to cast on them. "Go fish."

◊

That Saturday, while Arthur Cantrell finished sweeping the shards that used to be his father's hand-carved butterflies, and while Ian Lima rose in a dizzy haze from the field beside Mitchell's Dairy, his last bit of hope shrunk to nothing at the sight of Jase Moretti embracing Sarah Toms, and while Willa Fletcher lay in her bed in the ICU of the Middlesex County Hospital stunned at the news that she'd nearly died just hours earlier, and while Bill Cousins doggedly convinced his family that his taking them out to lunch did not mean he was batty or sick—while all this was going on Missy Lima sat in a slightly elevated styling chair at the Cutting Edge hair salon on Route 66 in Middletown. Searching the Yellow Pages earlier that day she'd been drawn to the salon's name, the risk it suggested. She decided to take a chance. "I don't know, I just want to look sharp. Feel sharp," she told the hairdresser, a woman at least a decade older than her, with icy blond hair that she clearly dyed. The woman had buzzed down to nothing much of the hair on the left side of her head, an asymmetrical look Missy had never seen in person. She thought it was perhaps too young for the woman—too much cutting, too much edge—and that worried Missy. Had she come to the right place? But a moment later she felt she had when, after telling the hairdresser, "but not as sharp as you," the woman threw her head back, laughed, and said, "I get that all the time." She then asked, "Want some coffee?" Missy nodded, told the woman she took it black then said, "I mean, cream and sugar. That's how I like it." When the drink came, warm and sweet, and the woman said, "Whatever you like," Missy relaxed further. The music playing was jazzy, piano and sax. Taking to it, Missy hummed along. She took a sip of her coffee and then another. Looking into the mirror she asked the woman, "What do you think? Is there hope?"

Two hours later, Roy Kirk affirmed that there was hope aplenty. She'd stopped by unannounced, only the second time she'd ever done that.

"I'm off-schedule."

"You're right on time." He was already leading her to the bedroom. Her coat was still on. "Look," he said, "we might as well take this thing to the next level. Every other Friday morning, like always, and the occasional Saturday?"

He was joking, she knew, but she in fact liked his idea about the next level. It relieved a certain pressure, one she didn't dare let herself feel. In the bedroom he lit a candle. She pulled off her coat, then her shirt. As always, without fuss, they got to it. He walked toward her, then cupped her face in his hands. He kissed her with a passion she didn't expect. Then he fluffed her new hair. "Honestly, Miss, I think changing it up like this is the best thing you've ever done," he said.

THAT SATURDAY, EVEN BEFORE STEPHANIE PEARL HIT I-95 NORTH, SHE'D been singing while she drove. She'd brought along a tape of *Man of La Mancha*, and her crooning had become a soft weeping when the song "The Impossible Dream" hit its peak. She was crossing the Delaware Memorial Bridge then, driving in an emotional and musical fog, swiping at her tears, almost laughing too at the absurdity of it, which included identifying with the role of the prostitute Dulcinea, seen as a noblewoman by the deranged but lovable Don Quixote. The way he *saw* her. That's what brought the tears.

By the time she hit the New Jersey Turnpike she'd turned to another musical, *Hair*, which didn't make her cry. Instead, stirred by the music's energy, she began to accelerate, passing nearly everyone until she spotted a police car in the distance and swiftly slowed. *Let's not get carried away*, she told herself, though she was deeply carried away and had been since her mother called the night before to say she had something on her mind, something she wanted to run past Stephanie, and Stephanie, before she even knew it, had agreed to come right up as if the two lived seven minutes away rather than seven hours. She'd been up to Wells just the week before, though given how the week had dragged on it felt like ages had passed. Every minute of each day since her reconciliation with Rona had failed, and since she'd returned from Wells with a familiar ache at her core and a trunk full of useless baby food, she'd felt numb, then number. In her efforts of late to get going again she'd just hit walls. At work, as best she could tell, she was there, chatting it up with Thea, Aileen, and the rest, but somehow sleepwalking too. Until her mother's call awakened her.

That morning, by the time she'd taken off the sky was already bright and clear. On the car seat beside her lay the oatmeal cookie she'd inadvertently taken as she rushed from Rona's the week before. Seeing it, she'd first thought of it as a friendly sign, much like the day's good weather. But then, recalling her failed visit, she abruptly ate the thing, by now stale, coughing as she swallowed it. Then she snapped on the first of the two musicals, beginning with Don Quixote's declaration that he was indeed who he said he was—grand, mythical, and boldly on a quest—and she told herself as the music flowed, the tears welled, and the miles flew past, to keep going. That surely something in Wells would be there for her, that Lake Topaqua would be, even if her mother, though physically present, was, in her way, absent. For the minutes it took to cross the Delaware Memorial Bridge, Stephanie, by then under the sway of Don Quixote's "The Impossible Dream," convinced herself that she was doing more than driving north and driving south so many weekends like this as if driving away her life, but rather the ping and pong of it was part of some yet to be defined but still meaningful quest. It all had a purpose, surely, which she'd discover soon enough. Crossing the bridge she told herself, out loud—as if she were split in two, a self telling another self how to survive this long and difficult journey: *Sing, dammit, sing.*

Early that afternoon Ruth Pearl spotted a blue jay and for a moment felt lucky. All week she'd been thinking about the legal theory of estoppel—and even planned to present it to Stephanie—but seeing the bird took her thoughts in another direction. Back when they lived in Amsterdam her mother had once embroidered a blue jay, inspired by one she'd chanced upon while taking a walk. Before then she'd never seen one, and she delighted in its brightness. "There, girls," she said once she finished embroidering the likeness, a way to memorialize it. They looked. They nodded. Pleased, their mother then offered a treat: fresh coffee. And it wasn't even Sunday. But the three had happily indulged. When they finished, they went out, to Oosterpark, as they hadn't in a while. This was two years before the Germans arrived, and the possibility that they would ever feel distress in such a familiar place was beyond their imaginations. Remembering, Ruth could see herself skipping eagerly as they entered the park and could feel, as if she'd never lost it, the rightfulness of her presence there. Estoppel, she named that feeling—a word that captured the unfairness of having something so precious and long-held snatched away. That day, once they'd settled on benches in the sun, a woman with a little dog on a leash walked past, the animal yanking the leash as it tried to approach Ruttie. The woman yanked back while calling the dog *Diment*, a familiar Yiddish word. A minute later two older men walked past, reeking of their cigarettes. On the frozen pond in the distance three boys began to skate, the faint sound of their blades scraping at the ice marking their arrival. When Ruttie turned their way, she saw that beyond the pond the woman and her dog named Diment were getting small, then smaller, until stepping beyond the park they instantly vanished from sight.

As abruptly as that, Ruth came to. The day, which had been bright, had become darker. Though it was but two-thirty in the afternoon she felt the familiar melancholy of the coming winter dusk and saw that outside the sky had indeed dimmed with cloud cover. The shifting light moved something inside Ruth, who had become lost to her memories, and it was as much Ruttie as Ruth who rose, went downstairs, put on her coat, gloves, and hat, grabbed her skates, and set out for the dock to lace up. Perhaps she could find her there, Sophia, another vanished soul, on the ice. Perhaps Ruth would be graced by that phenomenon that happened sometimes when she was skating at dusk, when Sophia would all but appear before her in response to the call, *Come to me.*

She tied the last knot on her skate boot. She stood, inhaling deeply despite the chill. Looking out, she saw someone on the ice, in the middle of their circle of lake. And the person indeed resembled Sophia.

With a mad energy—so like Sophia's when she attacked a tree at Oosterpark bearing the sign *Voor Joden verboden*—the figure, a boy, kicked at something. And kicked again.

◊

After Arthur Cantrell had cleaned his kitchen he took off for Wells, to calm himself by rummaging about at Brooks's junk shop before his meeting about Willa's complaint that evening. Driving into town he could still feel the high of smashing the wooden butterflies. He felt, too, that new, anxious self-doubt. But nearing the turn to the junk shop, he kept driving. He puttered along Lake Road, staring at the lake to his right and the houses, modest and cottage-like, on the left. A light snowfall had begun, and flakes sprinkled the road, which made his driving so slowly, below the speed limit, reasonable. But when a car behind got on his tail, an annoying proximity surely meant to move him along, Arthur pulled over.

He parked by a part of the lake he didn't know. Before him lay a small sphere of water alongside the larger mass of the lake's main body. Two islands sat near the middle of the larger sphere, but this part of the lake was clear, open. He settled himself on a boulder that abutted the lake's shore. He knew he should go home, work more on his notes for his meeting that night. He just didn't want to do that quite yet. Here, he had a lake to look at, to study even. Every inch of it seemed worthy of his attention—the part at his feet, where the ice began, and the part farther out, where the ice was rippled, and that part in the distance, not too far off, where someone was now running, a boy it seemed. He was running and falling, then rising and running, then yelling *son of a bitch,* Arthur thought he heard, then disappearing, vanishing right through the ice. Though it couldn't be, the ice was solid, thick, so there had to be a hole there, a fisherman's hole, Arthur gathered as he set out, running, calling to the boy, "*Hold on—*"

But by then there was no more boy.

Rather, he only saw a woman, rushing from the opposite direction toward the spot where the boy had fallen through. The woman appeared to be skating, and as Arthur stumbled forward, nearing the spot, calling again and again "*Hold on—*" the woman approaching seemed to hear his calls as directed at her, as if she were the one in need of rescue, rushing right at him as she was.

PART THREE

9

Netherlands, January 7, 1942, by Directive of the Advisor for Social Questions, from the Office of the Special German Commissioner for Amsterdam: The Jewish Council must supply 1,402 Jewish unemployed for transport to labor camps in Drenthe from Amsterdam Central Station on January 10 at 10:00 a.m.

IN THE END, DESPITE JOZEF Jacobsen's promise to Ollie van der Waal, Jozef couldn't tie up his daughter Sophia. She wasn't an animal, he'd reasoned that day, their last Friday in Amsterdam, before she'd ventured once again out their front door on the eve of the Sabbath. She was simply a girl, grieving, madly so. Instead of tying her up Jozef resolved that last Friday to hold her in his arms. He would take extra care that day of days, beyond all the care he'd taken in the days preceding, to console her. She would feel her father's boundless love and she would not need to leave her family as she had those other Fridays to "prepare for Shabbos" with a walk that was surely, more and more, as the policemen's presence foretold, a death walk. As for Sophia's self-absorption, the way she put them all at risk by willingly putting herself at risk, Jozef forgave her weeks ago.

For grief was just that encompassing, a world to itself. Sophia was spinning on a planet only she inhabited. In time, though, she would come back to them and live once again in their shared universe. Jozef knew that as surely as he knew his name. In time she wouldn't require this wild expression of despair. Time, he had whispered into Sophia's ear as he held her close that morning and later again that afternoon. Time, Sophia, would soften it—it just would. And she was young, he said. So very, very young. So there was lots of time. Lots of time for the slow work of softening.

She listened. She rested her head on his chest. Once she nodded. She seemed calmed by his words and embrace. That's what he was here on earth for, he sensed as he held her, to be the father of this girl and of Ruttie, even younger, who stood back, taking in so very quietly her sister's temporary flight from rationality. There was a time when he'd thought of himself, simply enough, as the man Tessa loved, and becoming her husband was a wild leap toward becoming the person he was meant to be. For so long that was enough; that was everything. But then the daughters arrived, and he'd leapt forward again, and again, his purpose for being enlarged by their being.

His daughters awed him. That was the truth of it. Their very existence gave his life its deepest meaning, a fact that he came back to year after year, decade after decade, in his attempts to reconcile with the choices he made that Friday.

He had consoled Sophia that day, held her, and, in the end, hadn't tied her up. Which was exactly why she had had the freedom to slip out the door when his grip relaxed, when he wasn't looking—this time not announcing her departure.

When she came back to them, already dead, lying in the arms of a German policeman who clearly knew to whose home she belonged—probably one of those who had previously called forth "Spinning Girl, Spinning Girl"—Jozef grabbed Sophia and held her just as he had earlier. Her body was hard, as if frozen. Bruises marked her neck. From her torso hung her leggings and underwear, ripped to near shreds.

"What have you done to her?" Jozef asked. He was on his knees, holding her. He must have fallen. He heard wailing in the background, seemingly many streets away. But it was Tessa's cries, he knew, and when he looked, he saw that she stood in the kitchen doorway, unable to step closer.

A policeman standing behind the one who had delivered Sophia suddenly appeared at the open front door. Whether these two men had merely found Sophia or had participated in her demise was impossible to know. They were both serious, official, detached. "She shouldn't have been in Oosterpark," the second one said, as if that explained the murder of Jozef's firstborn, simple enough. "You know the laws. She did too."

* * *

THE NEXT AFTERNOON, WHEN OLLIE came to them—an unexpected last visit—he didn't rebuke Jozef for letting Sophia slip out the door yet again. Ollie sat for a time in the living room and heaved as he cried. Then he washed away drops of blood in the doorway so they wouldn't see them when they passed through later that night as they left to begin their impossible journey. That they would leave in darkness didn't matter. Ollie washed the entranceway as if the sun was shining right there and all was visible in the brightness of day. Then he fed them, forcing them to eat: bread, cheese, water, the last of an apple cake. He gave instructions and more food. He paid the smugglers he'd hired only half their wage, he explained, to better ensure that they'd show up, if only to get the rest. People were like that, he muttered. Anything, anything, for coins. He went to the girls' bedroom to see the body. He consoled Tessa, who had joined her dead daughter on the bed, curling herself around her girl. Tessa, shaking, finally washed her. Then she wrapped Sophia's body in a sheet. Ollie would make sure Sophia had a proper burial. He had promised Tessa that, and now he was promising Jozef. Not to worry about it, he told them. Then he apologized for saying something so absurd. "Not to worry about at least *that*," he corrected.

"I couldn't tie her up," Jozef told Ollie as he was leaving. Ollie had been with them for just over four hours. It had taken Tessa almost the whole time to come downstairs and begin to hide the additional diamonds that Ollie had brought—the reason for the last-minute visit. Her sewing needle quivered as she sewed the gems into their clothes. While she sewed, no one spoke. Ruth—for she would never think of herself as Ruttie again—lay near her, on the living room couch, her face in a pillow, her body convulsing as she silently wept.

"Of course you couldn't," Ollie answered, his gentle tone the antithesis of the stern one he'd used two nights before when he'd insisted Jozef tie up Sophia. Ollie held Jozef's arm. "I mean, I'm not sure I could have done it either," he said.

◊

What most concerned the boy, drenched and shivering, sitting at Ruth Pearl's kitchen table, was that no one should tell his mother what just happened. The bathtub was filling with hot water. Judge Arthur Cantrell had dragged and then carried the boy to Ruth's bungalow, and once inside she had stood back as the judge pulled off the boy's clothes and wrapped him firmly in the two blankets Ruth had given him.

"We've met," Ruth told the judge when, the tub still filling, they settled at the kitchen table. She mentioned Wilson Keller, which caused the judge's face to wince, a look that confused her given their friendship.

"I have an engagement tonight. Someone Wilson knows. Almost forgot," the judge said. He turned then and explained to the boy for the third time that it was his—the judge's—responsibility to call the boy's mother. That she simply had to know about the accident, as the boy had described the event to them. He'd been crossing the lake and had fallen in. The judge said, as he had before, "You're a minor. I'd be remiss if I didn't tell your mother." At that the boy hung his head, his protestations silenced. When the judge handed him a paper and pen the boy wrote down his mother's name and phone number. He pushed the paper the judge's way. The judge tucked the note into a pocket of his parka. He hadn't taken the jacket off. "Good boy," he said. "She'll be here soon."

The judge's appointment was important, he explained minutes later, getting ready to leave. The boy's mother still didn't know—she wasn't there when he'd just called, but the judge promised to keep trying her. The boy was now in the bath. The sky outside was nearly dark. Had the event happened just a little later in the day neither Ruth nor the judge would have been able to see him. "In the nick of time," she said out loud, glancing at the closed bathroom door. She and the judge stood just outside it. The boy had asked for privacy while he bathed, though she didn't think that was a good idea. She didn't believe him, insisting it was an accident. The judge said, "If anything looks questionable, call an ambulance." But how could she see? She had wanted to ask but feared questioning such an esteemed man, the judge. He asked if she would be okay. She nodded. He then left. That's when she knocked on the bathroom door, began checking on the boy by talking and asking him questions. No, was one of his answers. No, he wouldn't try that twice.

She knew then. But she'd known already. Known as soon as she'd seen him kicking at the ice, reminding her of Sophia. The judge must not have seen that.

The judge then returned. "Sorry," he told her. "What was I thinking?" He asked for the phone, canceled his meeting, and called the boy's mother again, to no avail. A half hour later Ruth, the judge, and the boy were at the kitchen table, the boy drinking black coffee and Ruth and the judge cups of tea. The boy no longer shivered. He was wearing a robe she'd lent him, a thick one. He felt okay, he assured them. Just tired, maybe. As she watched him sip his drink, then hold his cup with both hands, something clicked, a memory. She knew this boy. But when she told him that, he simply glanced her way, his eyes confused. "Missy's son. Right? Missy Lima?" The boy nodded. "I knew your mom when she was your age. Missy Mulligan. My daughter's best friend." At that the boy looked at her more steadily, so she went on. "Yes, Missy and Stephanie," she said. "They thought they'd be friends for the rest of their lives. But that's how it is to be young," she said. "You think nothing changes. You have no idea what's to come." She didn't mean to frighten him but worried she had when he quickly turned away. The judge patted his arm as if to calm him.

An hour passed, during which time she brought him a cup of hot chocolate, which he said he'd like, and some toast with butter. She and the judge ate too. "Lima," she said at one point and the boy said, as if she'd asked a question, "Portuguese." "Ah, I've been there," she said next, quietly. "When I was about your age. In Lisbon." The sky had darkened so much they could no longer see the lake. She recalled how alone she'd felt in Lisbon despite her parents being with her, but just then the boy cried a little and she'd rushed to get him tissues. The judge held his shoulder, then got up to call Missy again. Finally, Missy arrived, rushed in, grabbed Ian, and held him close. "Oh my God," she repeated, weeping, while Ian, his face pressed against her, still said nothing. After some moments Missy said, "Those damn ice fisherman.

What a terrible accident." With that Ian looked at Ruth, catching her eye, beseeching her. She said nothing to correct Missy.

"How can I thank you, Mrs. Pearl?" Missy asked Ruth before she left. But Ruth just shook her head. Then Missy thanked the judge. When all three had gone, Ruth drained the water from the tub, sitting on the tub's ledge the whole time, watching the water spiral downward until there was nothing left to watch. After that she returned to the kitchen.

They'd been gone for less than a half hour when Stephanie arrived. "I'm here!" she called, stepping inside. "Such a lot of traffic. Two terrible backups or I'd have been here much sooner. Long, long trip. Still, I made it. A quick visit, that's all. Mamma. Mamma? You here?"

Ruth tried to call out. But no words came. Stephanie finally found her, at the kitchen table, in the dark. Ruth patted the chair beside her where Ian had sat, and Stephanie settled herself, obediently. She was about to speak when Ruth silenced her by holding a finger to her daughter's lips.

"What happened?" Stephanie asked minutes later, her voice a whisper. "Mamma?"

But for the rest of that evening and well into the next day, when Stephanie departed, Ruth simply couldn't talk.

THE FOLLOWING SATURDAY HER DOORBELL rang. It was just past eleven in the morning. She was still in her bathrobe, the one that Ian had worn after his hot bath. She had washed it the next morning, though the boy hadn't dirtied it. Rather, he had infused it with his spirit, his blend of youthfulness and desperation. She wore the robe every night that week, and even after the washing she felt something coming alive within her that was connected to him. An awareness emerged. Just like Ian, she too had been a desperate teenager once, alone in her pain. And obviously that was what Sophia was. All these years, Ruth realized, she'd been angry at Sophia, for giving up, for throwing her life away. But now, wearing the robe that Ian had worn after his suicide attempt, she could feel a new thing, which was not her own pain but that of Sophia's, the engulfing depth of the loss that made her sister so crazed. Inside Sophia's mind, Ruth grasped, thoughts were like windblown snowflakes, an icy flurry of helplessness and incoherence. Nothing made sense. Not even the meaning of her existence, which she so readily gave up. For so long Ruth had wanted to say to Sophia, *stupid, stupid, stupid.* But now Ruth wished only to reach back in time, to lift Sophia from the cold waters of despair just as she'd managed, with the judge's help, to lift Ian.

Thus, when the doorbell rang on Saturday morning, her eyes were bright with seeing and wet with tears. Under any circumstance the sound of her doorbell would have surprised her; people didn't ordinarily stop by. Stephanie—the only visitor in as long as she could remember—just walked in. But that morning the ringing more than startled her—it shocked her senses. She slapped a hand to her heart. She stood in her kitchen as if frozen. The thick, white robe that encased her body was like a cocoon, and all morning she'd been deep inside it, shifting, transforming. Solitude and silence fit her as never before.

She stood for a while then, calming her breath, taking in the steadying sight of Lake Topaqua to do so, before heading upstairs to the front door. No one was there. But a bunch of flowers lay at her feet, a half dozen red roses. They were wrapped in brown paper and bound by a yellow ribbon. She bent to get them and upon rising saw the boy, Ian, walking away.

"Thank you," she called, holding them up, and he turned. He crossed his arms over his chest. His parka was navy blue and puffy, which made him look so much larger than the week before. He stood for a while and she waited, despite the chill of the morning air. Finally, he nodded, waved, and turned to go.

"I rather like roses," she thought to tell him but didn't, as the words came too slowly. By the time they surfaced the boy had gone.

THE NEXT TUESDAY EVENING, CLOSE to seven, Ian returned. Though the doorbell again startled her, and she responded slowly, this time he was still there, in the doorway, a slight figure wearing a big navy parka. He offered her another bouquet of roses, which she looked at for a time and then nodded. "Come in," she finally said, and he followed her through the living room and down the stairs of the bungalow to the kitchen. She had been home from work for over an hour but hadn't eaten yet. Instead, once she'd changed out of her work clothes and into the robe, she'd simply sat in the wingback chair, her bare feet on the ottoman covered by her mother's old embroidery. She knew that time passed, that night was settling into full-blown darkness. But Ian's arrival put her in motion, and once downstairs she promptly began stirring chocolate powder into warming milk. She sat with Ian while he sipped his drink, taking his time. He stared more at the tabletop than the lake, and never at her. Their mutual need for silence seemed like an agreement, one they'd easily reached. But then she asked a question. Had he told his mother the truth yet? He shrugged, shaking his head.

"If you don't, I may have to tell the judge. You're a minor. He'd have to tell her."

"It'd kill her," Ian said, seemingly sure of it.

"Might kill you not to tell her."

Ian looked at her, and then at the tabletop. "I fell for somebody," he said. "Fell in love."

"Is that what it was?" She rose to make herself tea. Several minutes passed and when she returned to the table Ian had his parka on. "Going? I was ready to hear about it, your love story."

"What love story? There was only love one way."

He sat again but didn't remove the parka. She waited. But he said no more. A half hour later when she asked him if he'd like more cocoa and maybe some toast this time, and perhaps chicken noodle soup, he finally spoke again. "Yes," he said, pulling off the jacket. "I really would."

While the soup warmed, she turned the radio on, a bit of Mendelssohn playing.

He listened, his head raised. "We danced to this once," he said. He stayed that way, listening, while she waited for him to say more. When he didn't, she turned the music a notch louder.

HE CAME BY AGAIN ON Friday but this time he didn't bring roses. He had told his mother it wasn't an accident. He reported the news as soon as Ruth opened the door. She hadn't yet changed out of her work clothes, wasn't wearing the robe. She was just herself, tired from the week. But she awakened, reached out to him as he reached out to her.

"It pretty much killed her," he said, leaning into her, sobbing.

She held him until he finally quieted. Whether that was a few minutes or a good half hour she didn't know. She thought about that later, after Ian had left, once she had settled in the dark on her bed, the robe thrown over her body like a blanket, her bones tingling with a new sensation, a little warmth. She had held him, and he had held on to her like he might a lifeboat in a stormy sea. He had clung with everything within him, not unlike the way he'd managed to reach for and grasp the edges of the ice surrounding the fisherman's hole he'd thrown himself in, a survival instinct, even stronger than the impulsive leap he'd just made, an instinctual act that made it possible for her and the judge to grab him and pull. Lying on her bed she reached out, as if she too could cling to someone, and she felt the comfort of it, of sobbing sloppily, shamelessly, into another's chest. But she was alone. So when the tears finally came, from so deep within her, sorrow rising from her very bones, she turned to the robe, clutching it, pulling it close, throwing her face onto its absorbent fabric, heaving into it what seemed like a lifetime of buried sorrow. After, she lay on her bed listening once again to silence, which this time arose from that internal place she'd just emptied, a stillness even more profound than she had experienced while wearing the robe all week.

Earlier that night, what she'd said to Ian was, "You did the right thing." He'd just stepped back from her and she had turned, motioning him to follow her to the kitchen. "Wasn't easy," she continued, sensing him trailing her, "but you did it. You're brave. You did the right thing."

WHEN JUDGE ARTHUR CANTRELL HAD FINALLY REACHED MISSY LIMA THE night of Ian's accident her voice startled him. On the one hand she seemed eager to see who was on the line, her *Hello?* sounding as a hopeful question. And yet the greeting carried vulnerability too, a wavering, as if she didn't trust the world to bring her the good news she wanted. Hearing that tentativeness had stopped him. He understood the uncertainty, had lived that way his whole life. "There was an accident," he'd said then quickly added, "but your boy is just fine. Just fine."

He figured he would call back to check on both her and Ian the next day, or maybe the day after that, but the days became consumed with the advice his new counsel had given him when they finally met, to prepare a draft response to Willa's complaint, just in case it survived an initial investigation. It likely wouldn't but "You never know," he'd said, which was the very creed of Arthur's life. So he'd gotten to it, later that night, early the next morning, and during any idle moments he had in the days that followed at work. At night he would pull out his legal pad, look over his words, cross them out and then rewrite the same ones. *Mutually agreed upon settlement. Success. Mediation. No rulings. Basketball court. Friendly game with colleagues. No talk of law. No talk, ever, of cases.* He felt compelled to add, though he knew this was for himself only: *I'd hit a familiar wall with Ms. Fletcher, gone as far as I could go.*

The next Saturday, a week after the episode with Ian, Arthur once again drove out to Wells. He stood for a long time at the lake's edge, just where he'd stopped the week before. Out on the ice he spotted what looked like a crate, covering the hole that Ian had dropped into. Arthur wondered if Ruth Pearl had put the crate there but then thought it might have been the fisherman who'd generated the hole, or anyone out there for that matter. Beyond the covered hole was the dock that Ruth Pearl had pointed them toward and above that was her little house. After grabbing the boy by his arms, then his armpits, and pulling him onto the ice, he had then put the boy's arm around his shoulder and dragged him toward the dock. Ruth Pearl had helped, slipping the boy's other arm over her shoulders. Once at the dock he had carried the boy up the path that connected the dock to the house. Drenched and fully clothed, the kid was impossibly heavy, but Arthur had somehow gone right up. Inside, he had tugged off the boy's shoes, then his pants, then his soaking jacket. Ruth Pearl was still outside pulling off her skates. In those moments when it was just him and the boy he'd said something to him, something like, "It's okay. You're all right," something gentle. The boy had looked at him, nodded. Then Arthur had wrapped the boy in a blanket and made sure it was tight around his frame. He was a string bean of a boy, but solid. Once or twice Arthur had vigorously rubbed Ian's back as if that were the best way to generate some quick heat. Ruth Pearl was inside by then. She had the tub filling and the tea kettle wailing. He could hear her rushing about, searching for more blankets.

Recalling the events of a week ago, he pulled the note from his coat pocket with the kid's phone number. *Missy Lima,* the boy had written above the number. Arthur put the paper back in his pocket. He's fine, just fine, he'd reassured her, a woman who seemed to be perched on only the edge of happiness and therefore could so easily get pushed off.

THAT NIGHT ARTHUR AGAIN PLAYED one-on-one at the YMCA basketball court. But this time he did something different: he rammed himself into Wilson's side and Wilson fell. Arthur grabbed the ball, dribbled fast, made the shot, and only then thought of helping Wilson up. "What are you doing?" Wilson asked, clearly surprised by Arthur's aggression. Teenage boys played hoop at the other end of the court. Their calls echoed. Their bodies moved this way then that, like fish darting in rough waters. They were dancers, really. Their sneakers squeaked as they stopped, pivoted. Arthur had no idea what he was doing. He sat on the floor. Wilson sat beside him. "Look," Arthur said, nodding toward the boys. Soon enough his breathing evened. Soon enough he wanted only to be where he was, there, on the floor of the basketball court where he could watch the beautiful kids play.

THE NEXT WEEK WAS A long one. On Wednesday—days before Ian would tell his mother the truth about his suicide attempt—Arthur ran into Ruth Pearl on the sidewalk of Middletown's Main Street, heading to work. He asked her if she knew anything more about the boy. She told him he'd been by twice. "He was sad that day," she said. "He told me he loved someone who didn't love him back."

"The pain of rejection is its own force," Arthur acknowledged, Willa's complaint filed in his briefcase proof of it. So that explained why the boy hadn't seen the hole, Arthur thought to himself, heading onward. He'd been distracted, sad.

The following Saturday morning, when Arthur returned to the lake, he could see them standing on the dock across the way, Ruth Pearl and the boy. He thought of walking across the ice to them, but he wasn't confident anymore about the ice holding and drove instead. Once at Ruth's house, he made his way onto her deck and down to the dock. If they were surprised to see him, they didn't show it. They each held a hot drink. When they said nothing, he felt foolish to have happened by like this. What Ruth and the boy had between them, he sensed, was just that: between them. He waited a moment, then another. Finally, instead of hello, he said an awkward, "We meet again." Then he added, "Sorry to intrude. But it's not often in life that you pull someone out of the water." Saying this he recalled, as he had many times since that day, the way his sister and mother had repeatedly fled his father. Not once had Arthur been able to help them.

When he noticed the boy again, he was pointing at the crate covering the hole he'd slipped though. "X marks the spot," Arthur told him, stepping closer, enough to take in a whiff of chocolate, which seemed to emanate not from the cup the boy held but from the boy himself. Ian nodded. He glanced at Arthur before he pulled his arm back, held the cup with both hands and, a little off balance, tipped toward Arthur who raised his arm in case the boy needed his help again.

YES, HE HAD TOLD HIS mother, Ian reported to Arthur some minutes later, just after he told Arthur the truth—that he had deliberately jumped in the lake. Ruth Pearl already knew, and he had told his mother the other night. "It wasn't pretty," he said. They were inside then, at Ruth's kitchen table, drinking coffee. Ian, too, opted for coffee this time. Ian said, "She drove me here today. She needs to know where I'm going and if I got there. She's created a bunch of rules." He glanced lakeward, then back at Arthur. "They're posted on the fridge. Rule one: I'm never to be alone. Never. She's going out today to buy us each a cell phone."

Listening, alarmed, Arthur felt for the boy, who wasn't merely sad that day but rather despairing. And Arthur felt for the mother, trying to regain control in an unpredictable world. He'd always done the same thing and still did with his cautious habits, even though the wild card of his life, his father, was long dead. He took that in too. Soon, the three started a game of rummy. Ian shuffled the cards then dealt them fast, like a pro. "Practice," he said to Arthur, surprised by Ian's skill. During the game no one spoke much, but something had shifted with Ian's truth being shared. The quiet was friendly. After a time, Arthur stood to go, glancing lakeward as he did. The view was partially obstructed, something he'd not seen before, and when he remarked, "What's that?" Ruth Pearl sighed heavily. Her neighbor had begun some construction just as winter was setting in, she explained. "But to see this lake," she said, her voice quivering, "is everything."

"You might want to see how it's impacting her property," Arthur told Bill Cousins minutes later, pointing toward the construction and then at Ruth's house. "Go take a look," Arthur suggested when Bill seemed surprised.

On the drive home, Arthur—forever the litigant before the real judge, his father—reviewed the facts and they weren't all bad. He had believed a lying boy, hadn't suspected a thing. Then again, he hadn't even probed to be sure. But by all appearances—and this was what mattered—Ian was doing okay. Arthur could tell from the way Ian, looking at both him and Ruth Pearl all morning, was clearly engaged with them. It was now two weeks since Ian's suicide attempt and the impulse, he insisted, was gone. He had visited Ruth Pearl, apparently, three times before this and in their quiet way they were becoming friends, Arthur could see. The kid had cleared the dishes from the table and then asked her what else he could do. He wasn't ready to leave, he said, when Arthur was, but rather felt like hanging out there, and it touched Arthur to see how Ruth Pearl stood back, as if making room for Ian. Since the events of two Saturdays ago Arthur hadn't noticed much about Ruth Pearl, but suddenly—and this was just before he went next door to inquire about the wall blocking her view—he did.

◊

A WEEK AFTER RETURNING FROM WELLS AND STEPHANIE PEARL KNEW that she wasn't going back anytime soon. All that last trip, despite her mother having asked her to come, she'd confronted only a wall of silence. In fact, her mother had barely spoken the whole weekend except to say that something surprising had happened out on the ice. Something incredible. Was everything okay? Stephanie had asked over and over, and each time her mother had nodded but said no more. In the days since, during phone calls, her mother had talked a touch more, and then more, about Ian Lima, Missy's son. That Saturday he had fallen in the lake, her mother told Stephanie, and she and the judge—"Judge Cantrell"—had pulled him out. The judge happened to be in Wells. Stephanie asked her mother why the boy was out on the lake. "I'm sure he had his reasons," her mother said.

Stephanie felt as if she, too, was out on the lake, metaphorically so, an internal chill she couldn't shake having settled into her bones ever since she'd left Wells. At work she procrastinated in her tasks, found reasons to leave and step outside, and even yawned, rudely, unable not to, at several meetings. To her surprise—because she was unfocused these last months—Thea was now the most successful fundraiser, outpacing even Stephanie, recruited all those years ago specifically for her fundraising skills. "I've taught you too well," she told Thea Friday morning as they happened into the office kitchen at the same time. Though Stephanie's tone was joking, she in fact meant the words; she'd never intended to render herself irrelevant at GTW. Thea stirred her coffee thoughtfully. "Can't thank you enough," she finally said.

Even before that moment Stephanie knew she had to get going, less at work than on the bigger task of building back her life post-Freddy, and now, she knew, post-Rona too, and even post-her mother. Whatever she was looking for in that last relationship—and she wasn't even sure how to put it—she wasn't going to find it.

Later that Friday, her phone quiet, no emails to return, she got the first inkling of what she might do next, something just for herself: she was *done, done, done* with doing good. She left the office early then, determined to play hooky, and took in a movie at a small arts theater at Dupont Circle. One of only three people there, she felt good about having abandoned work, which in her entire adult life she'd never done for a whole afternoon. The movie was Argentine, about a mother with Alzheimer's who, despite some confusion, manages to lovingly engage in a renewal-of-vows ceremony her son has arranged for his aging parents. Stephanie grew teary at the unexpected sweetness of that. After the movie let out, she wandered into an Italian restaurant on Connecticut Avenue, took a seat at a table by a window, which she gazed out from as she nibbled antipasti and drank wine. Outside, people rushed to the Metro station, eager to get home.

"Celebrating?" her waiter asked. He was handsome, Italian, sexy.

"Here's to my awful goodness," she told him, raising her third glass of wine. Her words, she knew, sounded stupid, flat. She couldn't even smile back at him. "I mean, my lovely badness," she added, and quickly drank more.

On Wednesday of the next week, she again left GTW early to continue to shed what she now saw as her one-dimensional goodness, all those efforts, especially through her work, to right the wrongs of the world, to make it a place that would never have done what it had to her mother. She could see that now. How tethered she was. How bound.

The heaviness.

She could see that too, how right Freddy had been.

After an aimless walk, she went back to the Italian restaurant of the week before. This time she did smile at the sexy waiter, who smiled back, she was glad to see. She ate heaps of antipasti. She drank nearly a bottle of wine. Finally done, she was glad for her full belly, her loopy mind, and the way, after the meal, the waiter lingered at the door as he held it open for her, telling her, leaning her way, "Come back soon, right? Always a place for you here."

She wandered again at lunch the next day—Connecticut Avenue, to K Street, to 13th, to F—landing at last at the National Portrait Gallery where she strolled the wide halls taking in the faces of American history: Benjamin Franklin, Frederick Douglass, John Adams, Pocahontas, Alexander Hamilton, Harriet Tubman, Chief Joseph, Dolley Madison, the whole group of them carrying deep expressions of worry—much like her own—except for Abraham Lincoln who, surprisingly, was depicted looking the happiest of all, serene and smiling. Only a day later, leaving work early again, she went down to the National Mall, and once there she strolled toward the Washington Monument, stood for a time squinting up at it, then strolled back, breathing deeply, enjoying the cool air. Mid-February, the skating rink at the sculpture garden was still open and on a whim she rented skates. Only a few others were on the ice, unlike the time over Thanksgiving when the crowd had made her attempt to skate there with her mother distressing. This time, though alone, she felt the ease she'd hoped for then. She was glad, too, to be at a rink where she and Rona had never gone, where she wasn't haunted by Rona's absence. The sun just beginning to set, the group on the ice thinning more, and soon she shed her all-too-reliable loneliness as if it were an old coat, the flimsy protection of which she no longer needed. She stopped briefly, confounded by her new lightness. A moment later she pushed off, glided to the rink's center, and gathered herself into a move, simple enough, that her mother had always called "the impossible spin."

The next day, Saturday, Stephanie headed to the Mall again for a rare weekend visit there. But its long stretch made for good walking, its simple beauty never grew old, and it invariably drew a mix of runners and families and even some solitaries like herself, which gave her just enough human fellowship to burn off the edge of loneliness that had crept back into her consciousness overnight. From there she went to a bakery on F Street, then decided to head to the women's art museum, the place of Thea's new internship program. The museum's special exhibition was on appliqué, pieces of fabric sewn onto more fabric, some incorporating needlework, depicting a range of images, both familiar and abstract. Stephanie found herself drawn to landscapes—mountains, fields, and roads—and to colorful, playful depictions of fruit in baskets and on plates. Her grandmother's embroidery of an Amsterdam street scene came to mind, and another of a tea set. She stepped close at times to observe the various fabrics patched together or the links of stitches, and she stepped back at times to better see the whole of a work. After a while she sat on a bench in the middle of the exhibition hall and looked at the work from there. A quietness filled her. She stayed for a long time, looking, not thinking—that quietness, like a river, a live, flowing thing.

ON SUNDAY SHE WALKED THE streets around Dupont Circle, past a Japanese tea shop and the Phillips Collection, then went farther north into the neighborhoods of Kalorama and Woodley Park. As it had the day before, the sadness she set out with yielded in time to a quiet calm. She chalked that up to the sights on her walk, colorful townhouses and huge trees for the most part. That there was so much nature in D.C. was one of its secrets, she concluded, passing yet another oak or maple, marveling at its height, maturity, vastness. Later, at the Bishop's Garden at the Cathedral, the near total privacy she enjoyed there was peaceful, enchantingly so. She was lost to it, relishing it, only to be shocked when an elaborate, lengthy, and inordinately loud peal of ringing bells, marking the end of church services, cut through the serenity, suddenly dominating. She hadn't realized church was in service and she laughed to be caught like that, in a whirlwind, in an echoing wilderness of sound. For a good while she let the clamor swirl around her. The next day, walking to work down Connecticut Avenue and eventually crossing the bridge from Woodley Park to Kalorama, she found that the bridge's incredible height was likewise thrilling—she felt herself airborne, soaring over Rock Creek Park, so very far below.

Minutes later she was forced to stop at the corner of Connecticut and Florida Avenues for an oncoming presidential motorcade, police manning every nearby intersection the first hint of it, no cars or people crossing anywhere, the major route hushed by the imposed inactivity. Soon came the long train of police on motorcycles and then the lineup of police cars and limousines, headlights on, windows dark. She and the others with her on the street corner waited, chatting amiably to pass the time. When an elderly woman walked past and mistakenly stepped into the road, her hearing too weak to notice the grand hush, it was Stephanie who got to her before a policeman did. She gently turned the woman around, speaking into her ear, "Can't cross yet. We have to wait." The woman understood then. "He's coming?" she asked, and Stephanie nodded. Ohers asked similar questions. "He's in that one?" "Maybe." "Did you see?" A presidential motorcade still a wonder, Stephanie forgot all the upset about the election and the mess that followed. This was now, here, home, D.C., a place, like any place, with its particular forms of awe and pleasure.

But just a year later—after the attacks of September 11—that awe and pleasure would vanish. Immediately after the attacks a military presence would fill downtown D.C., armed soldiers at every intersection. And soon an anthrax scare—poisonous white powder sent through the mail—would turn Connecticut Avenue into a thoroughfare of wailing ambulances, anything powdery and white, even sugar, terrorizing people. Most nights Stephanie could barely sleep. Within weeks, the war in Afghanistan against al-Qaeda began, and just months later, in January 2002, came news of al-Qaeda's kidnapping then beheading of American journalist Daniel Pearl, stationed in Pakistan for *The Wall Street Journal*. Of all the bad news since September 11—and this now included a shoe bomber and the first talk of weapons of mass destruction in Iraq—it was the story of Daniel Pearl that hit Stephanie most personally. She read all she could about the man whose name and age she shared, and whose last words described the reason he was murdered—"My father is Jewish, my mother is Jewish, I am Jewish"—words that equally described her and hauntingly described why her aunt Sophia had been murdered sixty years earlier. After Daniel Pearl's murder, Stephanie taped his photo to her refrigerator. She thought of him then every time she ate—which was something, at least, that she could do.

BUT ON THE DAY OF the presidential motorcade all that was still to come, and later that day, after work, Stephanie took a figure drawing class, which led to another class each of the next two evenings. With the return of drawing, the city, which she'd lately been so full of, simply dropped away. She was thinking only of bodies, their lines, curves, and angles. On Tuesday she bought a new sketch pad, pencils, many erasers. On Wednesday she drew Thea eating her lunch—bent over the table, her back a long curve. Then she sketched Casey, beside her mother in a highchair purchased as a GTW business expense. The whole crew had cheered upon deciding such a purchase was only right, a way to support Thea when she occasionally brought Casey in. "Want to hold her?" Thea had asked as soon as Stephanie saw the girl, but Stephanie, who typically reached for Casey, shook her head. "You hold her. I'll draw," she said, and when she'd completed the sketch—the baby's chubbiness connoted in circles upon circles—she was eager to start another. "I'm just getting the hang of it," she told Thea.

That evening, home for the night for the first time in days, she realized she'd somehow done it, had got going, gained momentum. At least, one moment had led to the next. Playing hooky and going to see an afternoon movie had led to frequenting a museum, which led to a long walk, which led to another, which led to the city feeling fresh again—or maybe it was Stephanie herself, drawing again, improving her skills—and the next weekend she signed up for another class, this one on the basics of embroidery. Had she come full circle? The thought occurred to her as she threaded yet another needle and began, midweek, to practice feather stitching. She'd already learned backstitch, running stitch, straight stitch, and the French knot. Feather stitching came fast, as had the others. *What you know in your hands* was a phrase that came to mind as she stitched, speaking to the connection she felt, as she moved the needle, to things she didn't know in her mind—like her grandmother Tessa's memories, or like the woman herself, who'd died three years after her grandfather Jozef had, when Stephanie was eighteen. Stephanie had visited her grandparents so many times and seen pieces of her grandmother's work in both West Hartford and her mother's home in Wells, but only upon taking up embroidery herself did Stephanie grasp what little genuine attention she'd ever paid to it. She had simply thought of embroidery as her grandmother's quirky habit, something slow and tedious. She'd declined the offer to learn it from someone she now realized was as true an artist as the women who had made the exquisite appliqués she'd seen at the women's museum. Nor had Stephanie prodded her grandparents about their past, which seemed as private a matter as her mother's, as closed off, as taboo. She knew of a box in her mother's closet full of her grandmother's needlework, always on linen panels, a box Stephanie suddenly wanted to open and study. *The encyclopedia of my life* was another phrase Stephanie latched on to, as if hearing her grandmother describe the multitudes in the box. *Fun mayn lebn.* Of my life. Even her grandmother's occasional Yiddish became accessible, a frequency coming through to Stephanie more readily than even her own biological clock, which lately had quieted its chronic clanging. For the first time Stephanie wondered if all that noise was less about a baby than a yearning for deeper human connection. She sensed that was so. She phoned her mother. Could she mail the box?

"Come," her mother said.

"Really? You want me?"

"Of course, Stephie. What are you waiting for? Come."

STEPHANIE WENT. ARRIVING MIDDAY ON Saturday, she was surprised to find Ian Lima there, in her mother's kitchen. Ian and her mother were playing checkers at the table. But when had her mother ever done that? Stephanie wondered. A deck of cards lay on the table too, along with an apple pie, half eaten. "Ian brought me this," her mother said looking his way, almost coyly.

While the two played on, Stephanie indulged in a large slice of pie. She was still eating it when Ian, upon winning, rose and tipped himself into a celebratory handstand. He stayed upside down for some time.

"Boys are fun," her mother, watching Ian, whispered to Stephanie.

"Girls, too," Stephanie said. She was sorry to hear herself sound defensive, even childish, but her mother didn't seem to notice.

Her mother and Ian played several more games that took up the bulk of the afternoon. Stephanie watched for a time but then drifted to her old bedroom where she tried resting, stared at the ceiling, stared at the lake, and impatiently rested more.

Later, after Ian left—retrieved by Missy, who waved from her car while Stephanie and her mother stood at the door—Ruth explained more fully what had happened. "He got hurt in love. Went a little crazy. But now he's coming along." Even after the car drove off her mother lingered in the open doorway. "Crazy and young in love. Like Romeo and Juliet." Her mother paused. "Like Sophia," she then said.

The sister's name stopped Stephanie. She waited for more, but nothing came. "Come, Mamma," Stephanie finally said. Her body was shivering by then. "Let's close the door. Winter's not done."

STEPHANIE ROSE EARLY THE NEXT morning and without waking her mother headed off for a walk around Lake Topaqua. The morning was cold, cloudy, quiet. Most people in Wells would be at church, she knew, or getting ready for it. The Cathedral bells of the weekend before came to mind, her obliviousness to the religiosity of Sundays catching her by surprise. Here in Wells Sundays were much like her last in D.C., filled with a particular hush until the church bells in the distance began to ring. As she walked she remembered countless Sundays like that and recalled, too, the quiet of those afternoons, as it wasn't customary then for businesses to open on Sundays. As a schoolgirl she'd felt even more the outsider on Sundays, not attending church, being Jewish when no one else was. But on Route 66, heading closer to town, the signs of changing times hit her; she passed an open drugstore and a McDonald's, brand new to town. A half hour later, on Lake Road, she passed the Topaqua Grill, its lights on, its parking lot partially filled, its staff, she figured, getting ready to serve lunch later that day. Maybe she'd treat her mother to lunch, she thought.

But when she arrived back at the bungalow a meal was already in process: Ian Lima had come for brunch. He scrambled eggs at the stove while her mother sat at the kitchen table, wearing a white bathrobe and slippers, her hair surprisingly loose. "I have company," she said, as Stephanie sat herself at the table, too. "Can't quite shake him," her mother added, loud enough for Ian to hear.

"It's better here," he said, looking their way.

Her mother nodded. "Missy says it's okay. I called her." She sipped her coffee. "So long as she knows where you are, she said."

"She knows." Ian brought two plates of eggs to the table, one for each of them. Then he got another for himself.

As they ate, Stephanie glanced at her mother, who looked content. Ian, too, seemed happy enough. *So this is how it is now,* Stephanie thought, and she wasn't hungry anymore, taking that in. For a time the three ate—Stephanie only nibbling—without talking.

But then Ian said, "I'm going to go back to the dance studio." He'd finished his food.

"Will she be there?" Her mother looked concerned.

"Probably, but she's not the problem." He looked at his empty plate. "His name is Jase," he said, still looking down. "Jase Moretti. He'll be there. I'm almost sure of it."

Her mother stared into her coffee. Then she looked at Ian, who was glancing outside this time, at the lake. "You're full of surprises," her mother said, quietly, "but not such big ones. Not to me. Tell your mother yet?"

Ian looked at Ruth now, as did Stephanie, who was startled by the intimacy between the two of them. They didn't even seem to realize she was there. "Not yet," Ian said.

"Ah," was her mother's remark, a soft, sympathetic sound, entirely new to Stephanie. "Well then, all in due time," she said, the calmness of the comment, and its implicit compassion, startling Stephanie even more.

ABOUT AN HOUR LATER IAN was ready for the dance studio, and Stephanie—wanting to leave the bungalow, which felt particularly cramped—offered to drive him there. "Why are you rehearsing on a Sunday?" she asked as they headed downtown.

"We've got a performance soon. We're trying to catch me up." Ian explained that he had fallen and had to sit it out for quite some time.

From his cell phone he called Missy, and Stephanie heard her ask, "You sure?"

"Pretty sure."

"Call me," Stephanie overheard.

"Yup." Ian snapped his phone closed and crammed it in his parka pocket. "I kind of hate this thing," he told Stephanie, who was thinking just then about all that Ian hadn't told Missy in that brief conversation, the obviously careful choreography of what he said to whom about his life. By then they were at the dance studio. She watched as Ian took off, disappearing quickly into the building.

Driving home, she pulled into the parking lot of the Topaqua Grill, thinking Missy might be inside working. *And why is your son all but living in my home?* she wanted to ask Missy straightaway. Not that she didn't like Ian or feel for him. But did he have to be there all the time? Then she caught herself, jealous again, and of a kid in need, no less. She'd just say hello, she figured next. After all, what she wanted, really, was someone to talk to.

Indeed, Missy was there, but outside in her car, and once Stephanie spotted her, a familiar redhead sitting with her head lowered onto the steering wheel, it was obvious that Missy didn't want company just then. But when Missy looked up again for some minutes, Stephanie decided to chance it with her. She knocked lightly on the car window, which startled Missy in just the way Stephanie hoped to avoid.

"Sorry!" she said when Missy opened the window.

"Scared the shit out of me, Steph."

"Just wanted to say hello." She paused. "Hello."

"Hey."

"May I get in?"

Missy nodded. The air was chillier in Missy's car than in Stephanie's. She wished she had gloves and a hat, but she hadn't brought them, assuming a quick trip.

"Was just thinking of you." Stephanie rubbed her hands together. "I dropped Ian off, just so you know."

"I know, I know. I called him."

"Working on a Sunday?" It was at least something to say.

"Catching up on shifts. Missed a bunch of days."

Missy's voice cracked. She'd obviously been crying in the minutes before. Stephanie searched her pocketbook for a tissue, which, once found, Missy grabbed.

"Do you know about Ian?" Missy asked.

Stephanie didn't know what to say. If she were talking about Ian's sexuality—and it was possible she was—then it was his business to tell her, she decided. "No, don't know anything."

"Your mother didn't say?"

"No. You know her. She barely says anything."

Missy nodded. "Well, the impulse is gone, apparently. He won't try that again, he says. But should I believe him? Should I leave him alone?"

Missy looked at Stephanie as if she knew a damn thing about mothering. Stephanie fiddled with the strap of her pocketbook. Their talking, the subject of which still confused her, had quickly fogged up the car windows.

"Walk a bit?" Stephanie pointed to a small field that abutted the parking lot, the snow on it, an inch from the night before, still pristine except for a set of deer hoofprints running diagonally across it into some nearby woods.

Almost obediently, Missy followed Stephanie to the field. For lack of anything better to do Stephanie threw a snowball at the closest tree. She missed it.

Missy followed suit, aiming for the same tree. When her throw also fell short, she tried again. "What are we doing?" she finally asked. Each had thrown four times, never hitting the nearby tree.

Stephanie shrugged. "Didn't we used to be good throws?"

"Can't remember," Missy said. "Except I think we used to be good at a lot of things."

Missy's tone seemed especially defeated. "Want coffee?" she asked, tiredly. On the way back to the Grill they stopped at Stephanie's car so she could get gloves from her trunk. That's when Missy told her about the suicide attempt. She whispered the news.

"Didn't know," Stephanie said, stunned, unable to square this with the morning's other news. "My mother never said." She wasn't sure what to say next.

"Worst thing is that while my kid was jumping to his death, I was getting my hair styled. Thinking about my looks! And then I thought I looked so good that I went to see Roy. Roy Kirk. Remember him? We have an arrangement. Every other Friday morning. Except when I get my hair done. Then it's an instant fuck, no appointment needed. And the whole reason I even thought about a new look was seeing *you*," Missy said next, almost accusingly.

"Me?" Stephanie, opening her trunk, couldn't imagine what Missy meant, nor did she recall Roy Kirk.

But Missy interrupted her thoughts. She pointed at the many jars of baby food, still in Stephanie's trunk. Stephanie had meant to give them to Thea, or to throw them out, but had forgotten. "Steph, are you—what—pregnant?"

Deeply embarrassed, Stephanie shook her head, then searched frantically for her gloves, which she couldn't readily find. While she looked, she told Missy that the baby food was for a friend's kid. "Always good to help a friend's kid," Stephanie said as she closed the trunk, empty-handed, and turned to Missy. The remark had devastated her. Missy stared across the road at the lake, her surprise of a moment ago gone, her face grim, her eyes welling. "Oh, Miss," Stephanie began. "I'm so sorry. I don't know what I'd do if my kid did that. *If* I had kids, of course." She mumbled the last part.

"You soldier on," Missy said. After a minute she teared up more. "I don't know what went wrong. We were doing good. For years, good. And he's still a *minor*." With that Missy sobbed and Stephanie grabbed her arm, pulling her back to the field where they'd thrown snowballs, beside the deer hoofprints. It seemed a good place to let it out, if that's what was happening. Missy weeping, sniffling, and all. Stephanie, out of courtesy, turning away and staring at the deer trail that disappeared into the forest behind the nearby tree, the easy target neither could reach.

LATER, SHE TOLD HER MOTHER about the visit.

"Couldn't have been easy, raising him alone," her mother said, as she had once before.

"No, it wasn't. Missy said as much."

"Did she?"

Stephanie waited for more conversation, but her mother had fallen into a familiar silence. Stephanie broke it with an idea, a hopeful one. "Can I make you something special for supper?"

Her mother shook her head.

"How about a cake then? A cake! We always love cake."

But her mother shook her head again. "Cooking so much lately for Ian, it's made me full." She looked out the window, stretching her neck to see over the new, partial wall. Stephanie couldn't tell if it still bothered her. "That's just it," her mother said after another long pause. "Ian's an eater."

Then she added, confusingly, "Romeo and Juliet. Worst story ever."

Later, Stephanie would realize that her mother was still talking about Ian, a teen, in love, driven to suicide. But after hearing the comment, Stephanie had left, gone to her room, where she lay on top of her bed and, without knowing it, drifted away in her mind. By the time she came to, her consciousness returned to her body, her mother's words finally grasped, she was surprised to find it was already midnight.

FOR SO MANY YEARS AFTER LEAVING AMSTERDAM TESSA JACOBSEN couldn't see Sophia's face. Each time she remembered her daughter, another face appeared instead—the face of a girl Sophia's age whom they'd met in Lisbon, there without any family, stranded. Tessa had met her only once, as she and Ruttie sat on a small beach near a pier with two columns and steps—the Quay of the Columns—beside the

Tagus River. This was early morning, late June of 1942, and Jozef had already gone off on the daily business of trying to gather the necessary papers: the visas, ship passage, everything, before it was too late. And yet it probably already was too late. In Lisbon, Tessa knew, they were all but hiding in plain sight. Though they'd arrived legally, the Portuguese police, Jozef said, were not to be mistaken for friends. He therefore urged his family to lay low, stay inside, in the single room they'd let from a local shoemaker, but the sun was so bright, the day so glorious, their souls so weary, that Tessa had grabbed Ruttie's hand just minutes after Jozef left and outside they went, just as they'd done most mornings since their arrival two weeks back.

On the little beach beside the pier the air was alive with breezes that were so pleasant Tessa experienced them not as air currents but, like their daily lunch from the American Jewish Joint Distribution Committee—"The Joint"—as free food.

"This is good, Ruttie," Tessa said, still holding the girl's hand even though they were no longer walking. "Good, yes?"

Her daughter whispered, "Ruth. *Ruth*." After a pause, she said, "Can we stay here?"

The sun glistened on the surface of the Tagus. Tessa remained silent as she watched several sailboats quietly pass. Since the start of March they'd been attempting to make their way to Lisbon, and miraculously—despite the terror of border crossings, and the half day of panic when a guide temporarily failed to show in Paris, and the seemingly endless delay in southern France as they worked to obtain the next round of papers—they had finally managed it. They had stayed for a time in Lyon and then, more briefly, they'd gone to Perpignan.

"But we're on our way to a place even better," Tessa finally said.

"Home?"

"A new home. Even better." In fact, Tessa didn't know where they were going. They had visas for Curaçao, a Dutch island, but Jozef was set on America.

Hearing about the new home, however vaguely put, Ruttie—for Tessa couldn't think of her daughter with her more formal name—nodded, a merely dutiful gesture, Tessa knew.

She released Ruttie's hand and lay down, feeling the nurturing warmth of the sand on her back. In her desperation for just that she thought of filling her pockets with sand, keeping its sustenance close. Ruttie remained standing, not speaking, looking at the river. Some gulls flew close, then rose high in the air. Tessa was following their flight, gazing skyward, when she heard someone walking nearby. She tensed. Bolted upright. Pulled Ruttie close. Furiously hushed her, though she wasn't speaking—had barely spoken, in fact, in the months it took to get there, except to ask lately for her beloved friend, Henny, whose family she knew had planned to flee to Lisbon too. For the moment, at least, Ruttie had supplanted her wild despondency over losing Sophia with the even wilder hope of finding Henny. It dawned on Tessa to dig a hole in the sand—quickly—for Ruttie to hide in.

But the stranger, who looked to be the same age as Sophia and whose face would become the face of Tessa's daughter for years to come—the self-protective reflex of a mother too broken to see her daughter's actual face—was just a girl walking by, carrying only her worn shoes in her hands. Just yards away, the girl turned suddenly, then lifted her hand, tentatively waving it. For a moment, she smiled too, which caused her high cheekbones to rise, a lovely enough feature though she wasn't a great beauty. She had brown hair worn in two braids. Her skirt was subtly checkered, possibly made from a tablecloth, a common look on café tables. Had she stolen the fabric? The thought crossed Tessa's mind just as Ruttie shyly waved back and said, in Dutch, a timid hello.

The girl drew closer, sat a few feet from them, her back to the Tagus. Speaking German, she answered the greeting. They soon understood that she was alone and had lost her family. She was a Jew, then, most likely. "Spain," she said, pointing north, confirming Tessa's sense. "They can't get out." The girl shrugged. Tessa assumed she spoke of the internment camps, which, with the help of Dutch authorities in Lyon, Tessa and her family had avoided.

They didn't speak more but the girl stayed there, sitting with them for the next half hour. All three lay on their backs for a time until they sat up, as if called suddenly to follow the flight of gulls. As they did the girl gathered sand in her hands and dropped it, gathered it back, spilled it out again. Finally, she rose, said goodbye. The high cheekbones, the brown braids, and a chipped front tooth that Tessa noticed as the girl quickly smiled, parting ways with them: this was the face that would replace Sophia's, the face of a lonely girl who never told them her name, a name about which Tessa and Ruttie forgot to even ask. *Lost,* Tessa began to call her when she saw her in her mind, always with the same wistful smile, always cupping and dropping sand, always saying in German a polite goodbye.

But then, so many years later, the face of Sophia returned, a sight as unbearable as it was longed for. Tessa and Jozef were new to West Hartford then. With Felix Pearl's help, they had a home that no one would take away, and Jozef had a steady and good job, the work he was trained in, polishing diamonds. Tessa, invariably, had needle and thread in her hands and a lifetime of memories to stitch into being. On this linen square, a bit of the Amstel River. On another, the Great Shul. The willow trees of Oosterpark. The family's kitchen table, her mother's dishes set for dinner. Two little girls sitting on a couch, reading. She stitched that: one wearing a yellow dress, the other in red, slices of cake on the table before them, waiting for each girl. While she stitched the girls were there, children once again, politely waiting for her permission to eat their cake. She could hear the pages of their books turning. She could sense their relaxed joy. She was thinking of something funny to tell them—perhaps how the egg she put into the cake batter had cracked right in her hand before she even knew it—always eager to see them laugh. At night in West Hartford, her needles resting, Tessa cried for the lost world, so tangible through her work, but come morning, dry-eyed, she carried on undeterred, compelled to bring the beloved scene to completion. She still had her memories; they had stolen everything, *everything,* but not that, she said with each stitch. It was after she'd finished that scene that the image of Sophia's face—her long hair, her bright eyes—began to come to Tessa, but only in a recurring nightmare. The dream culminated with the sound of Sophia's neck being cracked by the policeman who'd brought her to them, dead in his arms. But maybe the sound was the guffaw of the young man's laugh. Or maybe both. A broken body, cracking, and a laugh. Or a crack *then* a laugh. In the end, her two interpretations blurred—and what did it matter anyway, she realized with each breathless waking, the violence of the attack or the perverse joy of violence. No doubt each worked to kill Sophia in exactly the same way. Tessa, through her dreams, knew it was so.

At last the nightmare faded, and she could see Sophia free of the violence that had killed her. This was the eighteenth year in America, and the first of the new life in West Hartford, where she and Jozef remained—awake, asleep, what did it matter?—living their unimaginably altered lives, days full of simple tasks, rising, eating, Jozef going to and coming from work, Tessa stitching and stitching, the embroidered scenes piling up. Each Friday the two of them lit candles, for the Sabbath and for Sophia and Ollie, their grief both embodied and assuaged by the ritual, and their guilt too—his for not holding on, hers for not speaking up. All these years and they weren't done with it, not really. They looked at each other most days like strangers. That they were in this American life together was clear—Jozef would go to work and make money to pay bills, and Tessa would cook meals and mend his clothes—but they no longer sat together at night as they used to, talking. He no longer read the philosophy books that were once his passion. Instead, he listened to the radio or watched TV, sometimes chuckling along with a sitcom's canned laughter, a response he couldn't help, she sensed, like a hiccup. "I'm tired," he often told her those times when she bothered to ask how he was doing. "Quite tired." From the other end of their living room couch she would nod as if she'd heard him, but in her mind and in her work she was in another year, and thousands of miles away, remembering. He was tired. In her way, through her stitching, she was tireless.

One day in the summer of 1960 Tessa got a phone call. A man from the local museum, the Wadsworth Atheneum, an acquaintance of Felix Pearl, wanted to see her embroidered scenes. She allowed him to stop by and sat at the kitchen table folding and refolding a paper napkin while the man—bearded, solemn—looked and looked and occasionally asked her a question. With her permission he then took several of her panels, and some months later Tessa, Jozef, Ruth, and Felix celebrated with a dinner out before heading to the museum for the opening night of the exhibit the man had curated. Something like life was happening again, Tessa thought that night, wandering through the museum, seeing her work as if for the first time, detached from her. She knew she'd made those now-framed scenes, felt the intimacy of each moment they depicted, and yet they seemed miraculous too, as if someone else—a little wiser and more clear-eyed than she was—had conjured them forth.

Soon after that Ruth gave birth to her child, Stephanie, and a larger shift took hold of Tessa. She might have died that very night that Sophia had. Right there in the doorway to her kitchen where she was stopped by the sight of lifeless Sophia, deposited in Jozef's arms. That would have been the easy thing. But with Stephanie's birth there was finally meaning to Tessa's unbearable survival. Now, for the first time in decades, she was truly awake. Truly *willing* to be awake. On her first visit to see the grandchild she took the infant in her arms. "Stephanie," she said, "you're going to be somebody. Yes, you are."

10

Netherlands, March 25, 1942, by Order of the Commander of German Security Police: Jews cannot marry non-Jews.

IN THE AFTERMATH OF LEARNING from Ian what he'd really meant to do at the lake, Missy waited for him to tell her more. But all he said about what they now called "the event" was that he didn't want to talk about why he'd done what he'd done. Not with Missy, not with a therapist, and not even with his friend Maddie, who'd called several times to check in on him—he stayed home from school. She'd even stopped by once, but Ian didn't want to see her. "He needs time," Missy told herself as much as Maddie. She then resumed the impossible waiting.

To bear it, she took her supper, as usual, to the couch and switched on the TV, blindly watching until bedtime. Briefly, she let her spotless house go, but Ian, who didn't join her on the couch, and who ate his sandwich alone in the kitchen, finally picked up a broom, then a floor mop, then the necessary sponges and cleansers for the tub and toilet. Ian, she knew, was also spending time at Mrs. Pearl's house, which perilously abutted the lake that had almost swallowed him. She could lock him up in his room, she figured, to be sure he was okay, but instead she bought a cell phone, checking in on him as constantly as she used to wipe her kitchen counters.

On the evenings when he visited Mrs. Pearl, Missy began to eat his sandwich, too. Soon the button on her pants didn't close so easily. One evening, three weeks since he'd told her it wasn't an accident, she caught a glimpse of herself in the hallway mirror. More than the touch of plumpness in her face it was the cool look in her eyes that shocked her so. She blinked at the image. Then she trashed Ian's uneaten sandwich before flopping back down before the TV. Later, when

Ian returned from Mrs. Pearl's, he sat with her a few minutes before leaving for his room. "Everything okay?" she asked as he rose. His response was a surprise goodnight kiss on her cheek.

The next night Ian surprised her further by talking, at last, about his despair. He'd already told Mrs. Pearl.

"Of course," Missy replied, though she was surprised to hear it. She knew he visited but had imagined something like their old, easy ritual with *Jeopardy!* happening there too. She never imagined that he and Mrs. Pearl spoke of matters of the heart.

He then explained that he thought the whole thing was out of his system—"the impulse," as he put it, which at the time he simply couldn't resist. But it seemed very distant now, like a dream, he claimed, and he was done, too, with the feelings that caused all that. He'd been in love, but he wasn't anymore. "I'm not in love," he said, "because I wasn't loved back."

"Sometimes that's the way it happens. Not your fault. Not the other one's fault either. Just how it works sometimes." Her nervous words came fast. Briefly, she wondered what Mrs. Pearl had said. "You're perfect," she offered next. "But even perfect people sometimes aren't loved back. Doesn't mean you're not perfect."

As she spoke, she turned from the TV to Ian. He looked taller and older than when she'd last noticed, but he shook his head when she asked next if he'd grown over the last few weeks. It was Thursday night, and he was home from rehearsal and had already showered. He smelled faintly of Ivory soap. All seemed well enough—especially now that she knew what had happened and that he believed he was past it—when Ian said one more thing. He looked away from her. He paused. "Just so you know," he finally began, "it was Jase Moretti who didn't love me back. I faced it. I did." He then looked at her, surprising her with his directness. "I jumped into the water one way and came out another way. Came out clear. And it's not been as weird as I'd have thought to go back to dancing."

In fact, Jase had been particularly kind, Missy thought she heard, the shock of Ian's words making them almost impossible to take in. What she seemed to hear next was, "Jase likes girls. Though he's not into anyone right now. Not even Sarah. So that's it. He was mean that day at Mitchell's Dairy, really mean, but he wasn't trying to be mean."

"What does that mean?" Missy asked, the last of Ian's words registering clearly. She snapped off the TV. "How can you be mean but not be trying to be mean?"

"I get it," Ian said, tiredly. "I think it happens all the time."

Missy was stunned. She closed her eyes, opened them, closed them again. After some minutes of silence Ian said, his voice less sure, "Could you tell? Does everyone know?"

"I never knew, no."

"Am I okay then?" He looked away. "Okay by you? I mean, would you hate to be like me?"

She pulled him close. Despite being caught off guard, she knew the answer. "Like I said before, you're perfect. I'd be lucky, just lucky, to be so wonderful as you."

"Anything changed?" Now he was tearing up but trying not to.

"Nothing's changed." She held him a moment longer. Something, of course, had changed, but she'd think about that later.

They sat again in silence. Ian wiped his eyes, finally rose, and went to the kitchen. There, he called to her, "I stopped smoking weed. It was making me stupid."

"Oh," she replied. She didn't know about that, either. She saw it then, the depth of her blindness.

She joined Ian at the kitchen sink. After he rinsed her plate, he said, "Does it run in the family? Suicide?"

She shook her head.

"But could it run on Dad's side?"

He was past the impulse, he explained, but if it was part of something inherited then maybe it would return. Maybe he couldn't stop that. He mentioned Sarah Toms's fear that she'd inherit her mother's MS. "Is suicide like that?"

The question took her breath away. "No," she finally said. "You're not doomed."

She rerinsed her dinner plate, senselessly. Then she cupped his chin in her palm. If anyone had ever told her that parenting could result in a conversation like the one they were having that evening, she'd never have believed it. "In a hundred years you'll still be alive," she said. "Promise."

IN THE DAYS THAT FOLLOWED she made phone calls, hoping to track down her ex, Frank. In fact, she didn't know the answer to Ian's question. Did suicide run in his family? She tried to reach Frank for personal reasons too. Not since the early years of parenting alone had she felt so overwhelmed.

She tried Frank's mother first, but over several days never got an answer. After significant research—she went to the town library for the first time in years to use their computer—she found numbers for a former colleague of Frank's from the Pratt & Whitney plant, and finally for Frank's younger brother, whom she was loath to call, some old embarrassment at having been left by Frank still pulling her all these years later into the solitary confinement of shame. The brother, Jeff, was Frank's only sibling. She was relieved when the number she had no longer worked.

But on Wednesday of that next week, while shopping at Ebbitt's Grocery in Wells, she ran into a former coworker from Mitchell's Dairy, Brenda McGarry, who'd been particularly supportive of Missy when Frank left her. After a hearty round of hellos, Brenda told Missy that Frank's mother had dementia. Brenda's sister was one of the home health care workers who had her case, she said.

Later that day Missy phoned her ex-mother-in-law, Margie Lima, again. She now knew to give the woman time enough to answer. Margie picked up after seventeen rings. "I love you," Missy said to her, right away, the very sound of Margie's voice recalling her kindness. Her mother-in-law had sometimes babysat Ian and had brought them many a home-cooked meal. Occasionally she'd stopped by, unannounced, to walk Ian to the lake while Missy gladly rested. Missy had always valued her mother-in-law—herself a single parent—but had cut her off, defensively, when Frank abandoned them. In the confusing aftermath Margie had said something particularly harsh, that perhaps Missy didn't know how to please her husband, and

Missy couldn't get past that, even when it occurred to her that Margie might just be voicing her own insecurities over why her husband, ten years before, had left her. Looking back, Missy could see that neither of them could handle with grace what was happening then. Of course they couldn't. "I was mean," Missy told Margie after identifying herself to the woman. "I was mean, but I didn't mean to be."

"Well, honey, that's okay," Margie said, though she clearly didn't know who she was speaking to, or about what.

Missy changed subjects quickly. "Are you okay? Need anything?"

"Sweet as applesauce," Margie said, confusing Missy. Then, "Cindy, you here tomorrow?"

"Can't. Not tomorrow. But I'll call you."

"Sweet as applesauce," Margie said again.

Missy called the next day and then the next. The following week when she called on Monday evening a woman answered, identifying herself as Donna. Another nurse, Missy assumed.

"Can I speak to Margie? Is she up?"

"She died five days ago," Donna said. "Funeral, very small, was today."

Missy, shocked, quickly calculated that she'd last talked to Margie five days earlier. She must have died later that afternoon or evening. It was all too much to take in. She paused, asked Donna to repeat what she'd said. Missy then asked, "Is there family there? Is Frank *there*?"

"Hell no, Frank's not here. We told him, but he was a no-show. My husband, Jeff, is here. That's Margie's other son. The *good* one."

In the following days the confusing news that Frank, who clearly was reachable, hadn't even shown up for his mother's funeral hit Missy at odd moments: when she was making coffee in the morning, as she prepared the sandwich board at the Topaqua Grill, seemingly every time she started her car. The idea that had seized her the night of Ian's talk a few weeks back, that she could reach out to Frank for help after all this time, now seemed beyond stupid. He might be someone who could be reached, but he was as forever gone to Missy as his deceased mother.

She was the parent. The only parent.

And it was time, clearly, to be a better one. In the back of a dresser drawer, she found the notes she once kept for Attorney D'Orrino, just in case. *Oh my God,* she thought, almost reeling as she looked them over, *it's happening again.*

BEING A BETTER PARENT MEANT getting serious. The first thing she did was to cut things off for good with Roy Kirk, whom she was selfishly fucking, she reminded herself again and again, just when Ian was drowning.

"But your earrings are still here, those weird feathers," Roy said when she phoned.

"Keep them."

"But your special pillows are here. A pile of them. All down. I got them for you."

"Throw them out."

"But we've been at this for, well, a long time, Miss."

"Time's up."

"But we've got something here. We're just starting to get that, right?"

"Wrong."

"Aren't you going to give me a reason?"

"Friends with benefits don't have to give reasons."

"Friends with benefits are still friends. More than friends. Miss," he said after a moment, his voice quieter, the news obviously sinking in, "what's wrong with happiness?"

"Everything, Roy. Everything's wrong with happiness. That's just it," she said.

Being a better parent meant reinstating order, starting with scrubbing the kitchen sink and then reorganizing the contents of each kitchen cupboard. Then she washed the kitchen floor, then each floor throughout the apartment. After work the next few days, room by room, she dusted, swept, and vacuumed. "I've got it," she said to Ian on Wednesday evening when he tried to help her clean the bathroom. "Go have a nice sit." Then she smiled at him to make the suggestion, which came out like an order, sound more loving, less about her gnawing fear than about caring for him. That was another thing she'd have to sort through and straighten out. Her needs. His needs. His came first. "How about a nice sit?" she sweetly said.

Being a better parent meant telling Ian the truth about his father. First, she told him about his grandmother's death, four days after the funeral, on a Friday evening. They were at the dinner table rather than in front of the TV, which was decidedly off, another better-parenting rule. "I didn't know about it until after," she said.

"Is Dad here?" Ian looked hopeful, his eyes opened wide. The look suggested he'd just been thinking about the man, perhaps was always thinking of him, and Missy's heart broke to see that.

"I can't explain it," she said. "But no. He's not here."

Later, she checked on Ian as he got into bed. Even after learning of his suicide attempt, in the interest of privacy, she hadn't done that. She hadn't literally put him to bed in years. But that night, as she walked into his room, she noticed how he followed her every motion. *As if his life depends on it,* she thought, knowing it did—of course it did—and then she took a deep breath.

She adjusted his blankets, then switched off the light. Then she flicked it on again. She said, "Whatever the hell your father is doing, it was never about you. Got that?"

Ian nodded.

"Totally got that?"

He nodded again.

She stared at him, finally smiling a bit. He didn't smile back but he was alert, listening. She kissed his forehead. "Catch you in the morning," she said and turned the light back out.

She was relieved by his next words. "Catch you then," he said.

BEING A BETTER PARENT MEANT making Ian a proper breakfast and dinner. Breakfast was oatmeal or eggs, but dinner confounded her. She didn't have a single recipe book. They'd eaten Topaqua Grill sandwiches for years, and before then it was simple stuff, mac and cheese from a box, bland chicken. She went to the library, which didn't carry cookbooks either, the librarian explained. But four days later, the librarian phoned Missy. "Got one in, just for you," she said excitedly.

The book, *Mastering the Art of French Cooking,* was massive. "Enough here for a lifetime," the librarian said, handing it over proudly. Once home, Missy leafed through the pages. A whole chapter was devoted to definitions, the first ones straightforward enough (*baste, beat, blend*) but soon the terms became daunting (*deglaze, degrease*). Another chapter, the entire thing, focused on sauces, sometimes whole families of them: The Hollandaise Family, The Mayonnaise Family, Missy read to her amazement. She was startled further by the family members: Sauce Riviera, Sauce Rémoulade, Mayonnaise Collée. Within minutes she felt dumb, just as she had when taking her first dance class years ago, the classical music as new as Angelina's use of French—plié, port de bras. The cookbook contained illustrations too, with titles like "How to Use a Knife," "How to Mince, Slice, Quarter, and Flute Mushrooms,"—*flute?* Missy exclaimed—and "How to Line a Dessert Mold with Ladyfingers." When she read, "How to Bake a Stuffed, Boned Duck in a Pastry Crust," she'd had enough. The book's authors were Julia Child, whom she had heard of, and Louisette Bertholle and Simone Beck, whom she had not. "You're out of your minds," she told the threesome. "You ladies are nuts."

She took her frustrations outside, barreling down Barton Hill and then standing stupidly for a minute at the roundabout downtown. Across the street, above the gift shop, the Moretti School was closed, its lights off, yet she could easily envision the open studio, its barres and mirrored walls. A memory arose of what had drawn her there in the first place, the flyer she'd chanced upon at Bob's Surplus. *Musical movement,* it read. *Simple steps.*

It had felt simple then. Take a class, have a job. But she knew that this time the thing she was about to do wouldn't be simple. Flute a mushroom, if that's what it took. Talk more to Ian. Rise to the occasion. Keep notes just in case. Make friends with those three crazy ladies. Be a beginner again.

◊

On the first day of cardiac rehab, almost a month after Willa's heart attack, she and four others were hooked up to wearable heart monitors—slipping them into cotton tie-dyed pockets that hung from straps around their necks and connecting the wires on the monitors to electrodes they'd then stuck onto their chests with sticky pads. The group was then told to walk around an inside track for several minutes, a warm-up for the more rigorous exercise to come. So out they went from the walled-off cardiac rehab gym into the larger public gym, open to community membership, that abutted the hospital. Within the circle of the indoor track were a variety of exercise machines for gym members. Or for normal people, as Willa perceived them, the kind who could work out without being monitored for fatal collapse. The kind who weren't set out like cattle, bodies paraded before the world, branded by their glaring tie-dyed pockets and wires, all of which she'd so much rather have stayed hidden as they marked her as vulnerable and weak. Which was just how she felt. Cardiac rehab, she decided just then, her third lap of the track almost complete, her blood pressure surely rising from the humiliation of it all, was cruel.

After their warm-up, they returned to the smaller cardiac rehab gym to begin aerobic exercise on the machines there. The relative privacy of the separate gym was welcome, but as Willa began walking on a treadmill, building to a mere 1.5 miles per hour, well below her old pace, she tired so quickly that she began to tear up in fear. Was it happening again? "Help!" she called, with far more speed and urgency than she had the night of the attack. The rehab director rushed over.

He asked if she felt any pain. As she shook her head, she could see how familiar he was with the post-heart-attack panic that had seized her and lingered, even with him there, holding her hand. "You're okay," he said, checking her blood pressure and pulse. He adjusted his glasses. "Can you handle a little more?"

She released his hand, which she'd in fact been clutching. Realizing this, she apologized, but he only grinned. His name was Carl, she read on his identification card. Then she remembered that he'd introduced himself earlier; she'd just been too anxious to pay attention. She slowed to 1.2 miles per hour. Carl nodded. "I'm here," he said, "and we've got you covered." He pointed to her heart monitor. She took a step, and then another.

AT HER SECOND CARDIAC REHAB session she nodded when she saw Carl, but he was busy and didn't look up just then. Still, she was relieved just to see him. She was all hooked up, her wearable monitor on, her tie-dyed pocket slipped around her neck, her electrodes stuck in place, and despite still feeling more visible and vulnerable than desired she enjoyed the easy pace of their warm-up around the track. It dawned on her as she followed behind two men that she was the sole woman in their cardiac rehab cohort. Two other men walked behind her. "Did it hurt?" she asked one of them as they entered their rehab gym. She took a treadmill, and the man took the one beside hers.

"Like an elephant was having a picnic lunch on my chest."

"An elephant?"

"Maybe two."

"That's odd. I felt something, but nothing like that," she said. "I didn't even know if I should call for help."

"Me either," said the man, which confused Willa.

"Do elephants often dine on your chest?"

"Hey, life is rough. I figured it was just that, something rough. Momentarily rough."

"Ah," Willa said. "But you did call. Obviously. You called for help."

"Wife called."

"Ah, wife." Willa moved the speed of the treadmill from 1.5 miles an hour to 1.9.

"Who called for you?" the man asked.

"No one," said Willa. "I was alone."

"Hey, that's not good. Thank God you got to the phone."

"I crawled." Willa, though tearing up, still moved her speed from 1.9 miles per hour to 2.1.

"How's it going?" Carl asked, suddenly there, tissue in hand.

The man beside Willa told Carl that she'd been alone when it happened.

"That was then," Carl told Willa, patting her back and then taking her blood pressure. She started up again, returning to 2.1 miles per hour, then bumping up, bravely she thought, to 2.3.

"Not alone anymore," Carl said. He pointed to the other four exercising in the room. "Willa, these are your friends."

She glanced at the men either walking or pedaling. Everyone did so in earnest, their faces serious as if such simple, slow movement took massive concentration. Everyone, she realized, feeling a spread of compassion for her cohorts—and even for herself—was just so scared.

WAS IT HAPPENING AGAIN? THIS was a Thursday evening, following two more rounds of rehab, the first on Monday, the second on Wednesday. After popping a tablet of nitroglycerin, which made her temporarily woozy but otherwise didn't have any impact, she went to the ER. The whirring sensation in her chest was back.

When she returned to cardiac rehab the following Monday—she'd missed Friday's session as she'd spent most of the night before at the ER—Carl already knew about her scare. "You checked out fine," he told her, just as she'd been told that night. She was hooking up her electrodes, her T-shirt unselfconsciously raised to do so. Her body, after so many probes and needle sticks and sticky electrodes, seemed hardly her own anymore.

Since the last time a woman had joined their group, and during warm-up Willa paced behind the woman, curious to watch her as if she were a new breed of human: the woman-heart-attack kind.

"Did it hurt?" she asked the woman once they were back in their rehab gym.

"Some," the woman said. "But not my heart. Just my jaw, for two weeks. I thought the dentist had messed up. I never made the connection: jaw, heart. But it's common, apparently. Did yours hurt?"

Willa shook her head. A "massive" attack, but it didn't hurt. "No," she said, simply enough. Her pace was a comfortable 2.5 miles per hour, which she bumped up to 2.8. "But everything was hurting. In my life, I mean. Everything." Endorphins were kicking in and she laughed, absurdly, at what she'd just said. The woman, walking at a cautious 1.8 miles per hour, looked as serious doing so as Willa and the others had last week. When the woman turned and nodded—an act of polite sociability more than of understanding—Willa stopped talking. It was enough to walk beside her, this frightened woman, by all appearances about ten years older than Willa.

"I'm Sylvia," the woman said at last. "And I think right now I'm a survivor."

WILLA WENT TO THE ER again that night, some soreness beneath her left breast having flared just before bedtime. She'd waited to see if it were momentary pain, took a nitro, waited some more, then decided she couldn't take any chances. When she apologized to the ER doctor for coming back so soon, probably for nothing again, he confirmed that she'd been sensible. "What are you going to do?" he said. "Stay home and take that gamble?" And so the routine began again: the enzymes tested, the chest X-rayed, the talk about insurance, the physical exam, the lying there in those ice-cold ER rooms, the asking for blankets, and then, underneath them, the waiting.

THREE WEEKS INTO CARDIAC REHAB, after a full week without more trips to the ER, Willa and Sylvia had coffee following their workout at a small café just beside the check-in counter for gym members. "Should we?" Willa asked Sylvia. Willa felt she had a friend in the woman, though all they had were a few sessions of cardiac rehab in common. But they'd taken to walking with each other during warm-up and they gravitated to side-by-side treadmills after that. By then Willa knew the basics of Sylvia's life: she had taught high school social studies until she retired last year; she was divorced, with two sons, both out of college and working, one married, one not. Sylvia, too, had been alone when it happened.

Sylvia's cardiologist approved of coffee, she reported, so they went for it, gleefully, as if the drink were as indulgent as a banana split. Since her hospitalization Willa had been avoiding coffee, and the familiar taste now soothed her, bringing her that much closer to the feel and texture of the life she'd almost lost.

"I wasn't exercising enough," Sylvia said, "but with rehab I feel just a little bit fit." Willa nodded. She'd over-exercised before all this—Jazzercise and running and running, she explained, but had come out of the attack all jitters, wobbles, and weakness. "I feel solid again. I feel *here*."

She and Sylvia didn't speak more but sipped their coffee congenially enough. Beyond the café, gym members drifted in and out. Through a nearby speaker innocuous music played, piano and guitar. Just as Willa was noticing the sound a sunray fell on her and she inched over, placing herself in the center of its warmth. "Such a cold winter, you know?"

Sylvia nodded. Another sunray broke through, and she scurried toward it.

"Simple stuff, huh?" Willa asked, pointing at the coffee and the sun.

"Simple and good." Sylvia closed her eyes briefly, and in the sunlight she looked radiant. Willa followed suit, closed her eyes, and felt as if she, too, glowed.

"See you next time?" Sylvia finally said. She reached for her jacket and pocketbook. For a moment she fussed to find something and finally did. "Almost forgot. For you," she said, handing Willa a small bottle. "To take off the stick."

The adhesive pads for the electrodes left marks on their bodies that soap and water just didn't remove. By this time the sticky remains nearly covered their front torsos.

"Who knew?" Willa said, holding the bottle of adhesive remover to the sunlight. The liquid formula, a small miracle, was orange and ran thin.

IT WAS JUST TWO DAYS later, in the morning, Willa's body cleaned to perfection, when a note arrived from Arthur Cantrell. The envelope, blue, bore the Hallmark brand on its back side. Above it she saw the return address, gasped, and clutched her chest. Was it happening again? Since it was Wednesday, she dashed off to rehab, where the heart monitors were and where she'd be observed, pronto.

Once there, she got herself hooked up and began on the indoor track. Sylvia had yet to arrive, and Willa walked alone this time. But doing so, going around like that, calmed her. She didn't feel self-conscious anymore about her monitor and wires. Rather, parading before a row of gym members on elliptical machines she felt a surge of something new, a little pride that she was, as Sylvia had put it, a survivor.

Inside the rehab gym she hit the treadmill, quickly accelerating to 3.2 miles per hour. A few minutes later she accelerated more, to 3.4. Carl walked over, took her blood pressure and pulse, then nodded before he left. The man beside her was going just a touch faster. She had noticed him before, younger than the other men. He wore headphones and whatever he listened to absorbed him. Willa didn't mind the lack of sociability. She was absorbed too, in walking and watching, the endorphins once again kicking in, her mood rising, the familiar face of Carl monitoring them, Sylvia, arrived at last, waving as she headed out to warm up around the track, the man in the far corner on a cycling machine—a person she knew by then as Steve, survivor of three attacks—stopping and rising to chat with Carl. And she noticed, too, her own tie-dyed pocket containing her monitor gently bouncing off her chest, releasing and returning, lifting and falling, a rhythm steady, clear, strong.

She arrived home feeling relaxed. Mrs. Rizzo stopped by and brought her a tub of freshly made minestrone soup. "For you, for you," the woman said, with so much warmth that Willa hugged her for the first time, promising that as soon as she felt up to it—and it would be "soon, very soon"—she would read to Mrs. Rizzo again. After Mrs. Rizzo left, Willa drank some water and settled at her kitchen table, flicking off her Nikes, opening the morning paper. She was working from home these days, only a few hours at a stretch, and she would get to all that later. For now, there was time, and it was clear she was in it, moving through it, living, as people did, their everyday timebound existence, and that seemed like plenty to do. She wanted, strangely, for nothing.

In the distance, on the coffee table in her living room, sat the unopened note from Arthur Cantrell. Willa spotted it but it didn't bother her as it had before rehab. Nothing about Arthur Cantrell bothered her, she realized, even recalling the way he had kissed her that evening at the Y's basketball court, greeting her as if nothing had changed when something clearly had. But the kiss was just his nervousness, probably equal to hers. She'd known this and yet with the force of her anger had convinced herself of something else. For a moment her thoughts returned there, to what seemed a lifetime ago, to what was in fact a lifetime ago when she took her momentary cardiac arrest into account. Then. Now. Now was better.

WHAT ARTHUR'S NOTE SAID WAS, *Willa, This envelope came with a genuine card, which I can no longer find. You deserve the card, something more than my bad penmanship on a legal pad. But I write (despite everything) to wish you well. I know what illness can do to you. Had rheumatic fever as a kid, pretty serious, a full year to recover. I suspect you'll see good days soon. To your speedy recovery, Arthur.*

She read the note two days later, after returning home from cardiac rehab and putting in a few hours of legal work. The envelope said Hallmark, but it contained only a scrap of lined paper. Three days later she wrote back, via email, *Thank you.* That was enough, she thought. But then she added, *I'm coming along. I'm lucky, really. What you wrote is true: What illness can do to you is something. I'm not sure I grasp its meaning yet. The note on the legal pad—don't we always have them handy?—was better than a Hallmark card, more authentic. My friend Sylvia, who I met at cardiac rehab, calls herself a survivor and I'm moving toward that myself. I feel it's so.*

A few days later Arthur returned her email: *Willa, That luck, which you talk about, is perhaps more available to us than we even know. I think about that sometimes when I'm in the dungeon with it. In the dungeon of feeling unlucky. Or alone. When I think there's no other way, but there is. I helped save the life of a teenage boy some weeks back. He fell through the ice of a lake in Wells. I'm guessing he might be thinking about these matters too. I hope your recovery continues to go well. Arthur.*

Two days later she replied, *Here's my luck: As the heart attack set in, a man drove past and gave me a ride home. He would have taken me to the hospital if I had asked, but I had no idea I was so close to the edge. Then I knew to call 911, just in case, even though what I felt didn't really hurt. Then the paramedics arrived, and then, lickety-split, my life was saved. So, yes, I think there's more luck around than we even know. Which is strange to consider. I'm sorry about the boy. Whatever drove you to go to Wells was a good thing for him, lucky indeed.*

She was hoping he would write back soon. But four days later he still hadn't replied. She was almost there, in the dungeon with it again, no key to free herself in sight, wondering which of the words she'd written were wrong or off putting, when she caught herself on a familiar path of self-blame, overthinking, holding on too tight. Road to nowhere—she knew enough to call that. So she hopped off, stopped hoping. Soon afterward she got a response. It was the last Wednesday in March. *Willa, Because I wore a brown sock today and a black sock I thought that the world was going to crash on me for getting my socks wrong. My socks! But then a case before me, quite complex, easily settled. Then I read something of interest, that playwright Arthur Miller, lecturing at the Kennedy Center last night—with Justice O'Connor in the audience—criticized the Court's intervention in the election, and my eyes opened a bit. All in all, the day was fine. But the socks were not a match. And that made me wonder, as you have, what do I think about when I think of luck? I think I've gotten all that quite wrong, made it all too simple. However it happened, I'm glad I was there for the boy. His name is Ian.*

MONDAY OF THE SECOND WEEK IN MARCH AND IAN WAS UP EARLY, dressing for school. He would finally return, his first day back since "the freeze," as he'd come to call what he did at the lake. But feeling anxious, he sought out the photo of his father, there in the old Fruit Loops box in his closet. Though his need for comfort was typical of other times he'd visited the man in the photo, his conversation with his father went differently than before. "Where are you?" he asked him. Then, "What in the world kept you from your own mother's funeral?" Ian stared at the photo calmly, as if time itself would evoke the answers he sought. He still felt no anger toward the man, only a familiar, mild confusion. "Do you love me?" he finally asked his father, then added, with words that were nearly rote, "Because I've always—"

But he stopped before he finished the line. A new thought had come to him, that loving was like death when you're not loved back. He'd learned that lesson all winter from his experience—so hugely dumb—with Jase Moretti. And now he'd got that lesson down. He returned the photo to the box, which he then took to the kitchen trash. "Alex," he said as he threw it in, "what is unrequited love?" He could have bet millions on it, so sure was he of his answer.

THOUGH MADDIE HAD CALLED DURING his time at home, he hadn't phoned her back. The only person he wanted to see in the immediate aftermath of the freeze, besides his mother, was Mrs. Pearl, who didn't ask questions but got the truth out of him anyway. Without her pushing, he'd wanted to tell her things. Then more things.

But Maddie, when he finally saw her, was all questions. "Where you been?" she asked when he sat beside her in their morning study hall.

"Home."

"Sick?"

He nodded.

"With what?"

He shrugged.

"You sure had something. I talked to your mother once or twice. She never said what was wrong, just that you needed time."

He nodded again.

"I'll help you catch up," she then offered. He'd been receiving homework assignments but still needed help. He nodded, turning her way. That's when he noticed her many changes. She'd intensified the blue dye in her hair, switched her nail color to a blinding chartreuse, circled her eyes in thick, black lines, and pierced her nose, twice. Two gold loops ran through her right nostril.

"What happened?" Ian asked.

"Nothing. It's just nail polish. It'll rub off. And the hair will grow back. And the dye will wash out. And even this comes off." She pulled at the nose rings, frightening Ian, but they didn't pierce through her skin after all. They slipped off. "It's not real," Maddie said. "But my parents don't know that. No one's talking about Choate anymore. They think I've gone off the deep end."

Ian was quiet for a time. The deep end was no place to be, he almost said. "You're scaring me," he finally offered.

"Scaring myself," Maddie muttered. More clearly, she said, "Missed you."

"Missed you, too," Ian said.

AFTER SCHOOL, MADDIE DROVE HIM to her house. Angelina Moretti, out of necessity, had pushed back the spring performance a full month, which eased their rehearsal schedule. He had the afternoon free. He called his mother at the Topaqua Grill to tell her his plans. She was okay with them so long as he was home for dinner. "Making bouillabaisse tonight," she said.

He and Maddie went to the upstairs pottery studio. Maddie shaped a small bowl while Ian relaxed in the womb of the dry bathtub. But Maddie grew impatient with her awkward work, squished it back to formlessness, and they cleaned up and moved on sooner than usual. Once downstairs, they drifted to Maddie's father's study, where they scoured the bookshelves. Ian found the same book he'd looked at before, about the baseball rivalry between DiMaggio and Williams, and he pulled it out again, taking it to the leather reading chair while Maddie still searched the shelves. But she couldn't settle on anything. Finally, hands empty, she joined Ian in the reading chair, wide enough for them both.

For a time she just sat there, oddly book-free, but soon she placed her head on his shoulder, and in response he moved an arm around her. It was good, he felt, their being together again. All he could see of her most recent, strategic changes were her chartreuse nails. He said, quietly, "You love school. You love learning. It's your number one thing. It's who you are. For someone like you, how bad could a better school be?"

"Now it's *you* who wants me to go?" She raised her head.

"No. But you should be yourself. That's all. People should be themselves." He knew that better than ever now.

She was quiet for a while. He finally continued, "Wells shouldn't hold you back. You're better than that. You're not really from Wells, anyway, you're from Middle Haddam." He'd never explained how different he found the two places, but she understood his point. She nodded.

"What about you? Is it holding you back?"

"I'm not a reader like you," he said.

They sat for time, Ian's arm still around her, Maddie leaning his way. As daylight ebbed, the room became darker, more shadowed.

Maddie soon turned to him, her neck arched. Before he knew it, she'd kissed him, several times.

He was about to push her away—though gently, not like Jase's repulsed push. He was about to finally tell her about himself, as he'd done with Mrs. Pearl and then his mother. To his surprise, neither had been put off. He knew now that he didn't have to be so afraid. But Maddie's assumption that he was straight offered him an immediate, breathtaking, seductive sense of comfort. Until he felt it, more sharply than her kisses, he didn't even know he craved that.

You think I'm like you?

He still shivered from those words.

Maddie's racoon eyes were shut, waiting for another kiss. He'd tell her later, he figured, still luxuriating in that comfort. He'd tell her the next day or the next. Or maybe never, since she was soon likely to go off to some other school. Yes, he continued thinking, maybe never, as he might find that he liked this too, though he didn't just then. That he could so easily rationalize using her was something he'd take in later, when just before she left for Choate the next fall they promised to write each other daily, the lies upon lies of his feelings for her by then a messy heap. He would finally spill the truth to her in an early letter. *But did you ever love me?* she responded, as they began the fight his parents never had.

For now, he watched as she wriggled closer. He thought about it all for a few seconds more. The comfort, the lies, the new lies he'd have to tell, covering the old ones. He took her face in his hands. He kissed her back.

◊

THOUGH IT WAS JOZEF JACOBSEN'S FRIEND OLLIE VAN DER WAAL WHO had introduced Jozef to the philosophy of Spinoza, it was a Jewish refugee from Belgium, a midcareer professor of philosophy from Ghent University, who taught him to love Spinoza's noble thinking. Jozef met the professor in Lisbon. The professor rented a room from the Portuguese shoemaker and his wife who had let the room beside it to Jozef and his family. Payment to the shoemaker was close to nothing, but for the Portuguese couple, they learned, the small change was a windfall. A stream of refugees had let the shoemaker's rooms for the last several years. Sometimes the shoemaker heard a rumor that tickets for boat passage were available from a certain so-and-so at the such-and-such café, or at a particular shipping agency, and he would pass that news on, more by gesture than by words. He was a quiet man with whom, due to a language barrier, Jozef and the professor, Ernst Fein, could barely communicate, but they knew to take any tips from him seriously, as he'd helped several of his previous boarders find the boat tickets that were almost impossible to come by. "Shoes talk," the man once said, modestly enough, his German a near-garble. This was early in the morning when only the men—all three—were up, sipping coffee. The idea that shoes talk meant nothing to Jozef but, like Ernst Fein, he nodded in agreement.

By then, late June of 1942, Ernst Fein already had shipping passage, four tickets, for himself, his wife, his daughter, and her husband, tickets he had managed to purchase back in Belgium. But the boat tickets were for some months hence and he thus needed to extend his Portuguese transit visa monthly, all the while convincing the local authorities that he was leaving soon. And he still needed to obtain American visas, which due to American immigration laws was impossible at this time without his family being physically there with him. Four tickets, and to America no less—a miracle—but he and his wife had been separated at the Spanish border. There, without all the necessary papers, or maybe because she looked afraid, his wife, who had been interviewed separately from him, had been detained—no doubt interned. Meanwhile, Ernst had had the luck to encounter a tired and gullible border patrol officer who, after learning of Ernst's appointment at the prestigious Catholic University of Leuven—one of many false identifications he had carried with him—assumed he was therefore Catholic, instantly softened his tone, and subsequently believed Ernst when he explained that he was traveling to Lisbon to catch a boat to America where he would teach philosophy there, at Princeton University. He showed the officer, a man close to his age, the passage tickets along with a forged letter of appointment from Princeton, something he had written himself, mistakenly locating the school in Boston, Massachusetts. Telling all this to Jozef, Ernst laughed at that part of it, but he was otherwise grim. That morning he wore the same suit and tie that he'd worn every day, his only clothes it seemed. He was identical in height to Jozef, a tall man, thin, with wispy gray hair that needed trimming. They were disheveled, both men, and their worn clothes mildly stank. They agreed they would take a day off soon to finally air their outer garments. Cleanliness could bring good luck when it came to persuading the consuls.

They talked like this, in a quiet Dutch murmuring, in the early mornings as they walked from the cramped shoemaker's apartment toward the business center of Lisbon, where they often spent time in one queue or another, attempting to procure the needed papers and stamps that would allow them to escape Europe at last. Ernst spent additional time writing letters to his wife, whom he'd not heard from in two months. He had no idea of his wife's current address but still he wrote, saving the letters to give to her when she arrived in Lisbon.

His daughter and her husband were to have followed him and his wife, and had likewise not arrived in Lisbon. Even trying to communicate with them, he felt, was pointless. His plan had been a naïve one. Perhaps he had inadvertently sent his daughter and son-in-law, married just that year, off on a journey from which they would never return. And that might very well be so for his wife, whom he had met when they were but children. *How could he forgive himself?* he once asked Jozef. That day was a typical one in Lisbon, glaring with sunlight, offensively bright. Following Ernst's questioning, Jozef looked up, blinked, then quickly shaded his eyes.

But when they didn't talk of visas they spoke about the philosopher Spinoza, including the circumstances that brought his family to Amsterdam. As Ernst explained to Jozef, Spinoza was born to a father who had once, as a boy, fled Portugal, following centuries of persecution of Jews by way of the Catholic church's Inquisitions in Spain and Portugal. In Spain, Ernst continued, there had been the burning at the stake of all so-called heretics, which often meant conversos, converted Jews. Against Jews—non-converted—a rash of pogroms: the Jewish quarter of Seville, after rioting, burnt to ashes, an estimated four thousand Jews dead in one day, survivors converting or leaving. Similar rioting in Castile, Aragon, and Catalonia. In Barcelona, for example, mobs assaulted the Jewish Quarter, killing some three hundred Jews, an event followed by forced conversions. And there were anti-Jewish laws: Jews forbidden from being tax collectors, holding public office, or engaging in commerce; Jewish physicians forbidden from treating non-Jews; Jewish men—to mark them as Jews—required to wear their hair and beards long; Jews forbidden from carrying arms. And forced confessions of identity that led to more conversos burnt at the stake. By 1492, the Spanish Inquisition in full force, the General Edict on the Expulsion of the Jews signed into law, and the remaining Jews in Spain either converted or fled, some to Portugal. But there, too, the crime of being suspected of being a Jew was punishable by death. Wear clean clothes on Saturday, the Jewish sabbath? Risk death. Spread a clean tablecloth on Friday, before the start of the Sabbath? Risk death. After explaining all this, Ernst then said, "So it's a little ironic that here we are again, Jews, running back to a place we once ran from."

Jozef's Jewish side had Eastern European roots, so Jozef saw himself as a bit distinct from the Sephardic Jews of Amsterdam, Jews like Spinoza's father. But that difference no longer held. "We've come full circle," Jozef said slowly, absorbing the professor's lesson.

Ernst Fein nodded Jozef's way. He then spoke kindly, as if Jozef really were his student. "Exactly that," he said.

HOW NAÏVE OLLIE HAD BEEN those months back, Jozef began to see—pushing them out the door of their home, out of Amsterdam, out of the Netherlands. He'd done that even though the immediate reason for fleeing—Sophia's recklessness that endangered them all—ceased to exist upon her murder. "It's still not safe," Ollie had said. "Jozef, don't you see the writing on the wall?"

Ollie's arrangements—with smugglers who would help them cross into Belgium and France, taking them as far as Paris, and who would hopefully find someone to get them past the demarcation line into unoccupied southern France, along with Belgian and French currency and several more diamonds—had in fact landed them in Lyon, where they sought assistance from a Dutch businessman there whom Ollie had heard of and had sworn would help them the rest of the way. Ollie may have been right about some things—in Amsterdam there was indeed writing on the wall, even more signs of their doomed Jewish fate, and there was indeed a helpful Dutch businessman in Lyon, along with a sympathetic Dutch consul. But what Ollie couldn't have known was that he was sending the family off to another kind of ruin—being trapped in southern France, where internment at any moment was possible and where obtaining the necessary papers to leave France and travel through Spain into Portugal was like facing a precipitous mountain impossible to climb. A French exit visa depended upon a Spanish transit visa, which depended upon a Portuguese transit visa, which depended upon an entrance visa to a country abroad toward which one could set sail from Lisbon. Indeed, Portuguese rules required that Jewish refugees show proof that they would be leaving soon. Many had come and gone without every bit of official this and that, but with time movement from country to country had become more physically dangerous and administratively daunting. "Go to America," Ollie had said, as if Jozef could simply choose to do so. That last night in Amsterdam, Ollie had a letter for Jozef from distant relatives of Ollie's in America, people in Queens, New York, who would sponsor Jozef and his family upon their arrival, and Ollie had thought that note, along with a simple trip to Lisbon using Ollie's contacts that got them only as far as France, made such a passage foolproof. Idiotic, was what Jozef thought of it all from the vantage point of Lyon, where the more he learned about the challenges ahead the more helpless he felt.

To add to the complications of the visas, Dutch consuls no longer officially existed in Vichy, France, and to obtain transit visas it took activating a network of downgraded Dutch officials (the former consuls), working for the downgraded Office Néerlandais, which took the place of the Dutch consulates after they were dissolved under German pressure. And only the Swedish consulate general in Vichy, overseeing the downgraded Dutch officials, could authorize the issuance of passports stamped with the visas. It was the Dutch businessman in Lyon who explained all this to Jozef, who nearly fainted hearing it. They were in the man's home, in his study. He had the windows closed, though the day, even at dusk, was warm. Jozef was sweating, both from the room's stuffiness and from fear. "But there's a good man here, whom we still call Consul. Consul Jacquet. He can get you legal housing and rationing tickets. Now come upstairs. Lie down. I've scared you," the man finally said.

Only years later would Jozef come to see the scope of it all, including how slim the chances were that he, Tessa, and Ruttie would have survived if they'd stayed in Amsterdam. According to most figures that Jozef would eventually see, some 75 percent of the Jews in the Netherlands perished, many of them at Auschwitz. Jozef's queries to the Red Cross ultimately revealed that this figure, the highest Jewish death rate in Western Europe, included Aaron Taube, his mother, and his father. Yet Jozef, Tessa, and Ruttie had lived. He told Tessa once that he couldn't understand their strange luck. "Luck? Did we have *luck*?" she replied in a rare burst of anger. But he did see their part in the larger tragedy that way, and forgiveness for Ollie's eager push out the door, for oversimplifying what had been complex and terrifying beyond measure, came even before Jozef—along with the world—had gathered an awareness of the magnitude of what had happened. It came when, thanks to Ernst Fein, they sailed on the *Serpa Pinto*—not to Curaçao but to America. On the ship, Jozef always recalled, he felt he could finally take a full breath. This, though Ruttie retched the whole time they were at sea and wailed for days that they had abandoned her friend Henny. Their Amsterdam neighbors also had intentions, of which Ruttie knew, to flee to Lisbon, and she asked her parents every day when she would see Henny again. When? It was the only subject she spoke to them about. Jozef assumed that the other subject, the sister also left behind, was well beyond speech. Though Ruttie had remained in a dry-eyed stupor in the months since they'd left Amsterdam, after only a few hours on the *Serpa Pinto* she broke down, her tears and cries unstoppable. "But we can't leave, Papa. Henny's coming," she pleaded, even on day four, a clear day, the water glistening and stretching in every direction as far as the eye could see.

In Lyon, resting in an upstairs bedroom of the Dutch businessman's home, Jozef had the first experience of what would become a recurring nightmare during those months in France, waiting while the paperwork wound its way through the labyrinth of bureaucracy: that each transit visa was a brick, and that the bricks were multiplying, surrounding him, ultimately imprisoning him, Tessa, Ruttie, and gradually a mass of people whom Jozef didn't even know. And it was overcrowded finally—hot, stinky, no windows, no air, there inside the four walls made of impenetrable stone visas.

SOME WEEKS AFTER JOZEF'S ARRIVAL in Lisbon, he and Ernst Fein sat on a bench near the shore of the Tagus River. From a pocket Ernst pulled out a pipe and a small bag of tobacco. He lit up. The smell reminded Jozef of Ollie's pipe, and Jozef breathed it in as determinedly as if he, too, were smoking. Ernst was carefully rationing his tobacco, he explained, and this smoke would be but a weekly treat. Today seemed like a good day. After a minute Ernst offered the pipe to Jozef, who shook his head. It was enough to be near the smoke, the smell. "Reminds me of home," he told Ernst.

They then returned to the subject of Spinoza, whose philosophy, according to Ernst, plucked God from the heavens and put God here, into everything on earth. "In Spinoza's thinking," Ernst explained, "God is no longer a transcendent creator. God is no longer a being at all. For Spinoza, God and nature were the same thing. But by 'nature' he didn't mean simply this." Ernst pointed at the Tagus, which looked to Jozef more like a sea than a river. The many large-scale shipping vessels it contained didn't even fill it. Ernst continued, "God or nature is more like a mathematical principle, undeniable, existing for no other reason than existence itself, and the very source of everything else that exists. According to Spinoza, God didn't create the world. Rather, God *is* the world, insofar as God is the single, underlying substance of the world from which everything derives. You, me, the Tagus here, the wind, we're all modes of this underlying substance, which is God or nature. In 1656 they excommunicated him, the Jews of Amsterdam, in all likelihood because even then, as a young man, he'd expressed such a heretical notion. But the idea wasn't heretical just to Judaism but to all religions ruled by God. And that's important to consider. According to Spinoza, if God is synonymous with physical reality and nothing else, then God must be the same regardless of a given religion. Spinoza removed the rationale for the competition between religions. Do you see?"

Ernst paused for a hit of his pipe. He then continued, "In a world like Spinoza's there would be no cause for the Inquisitions. We'd all be the same relative to God. Spinoza envisioned a world in which God, no longer a kind of being, could not possibly favor one group or another, and in which it would be impossible for a group to claim God's favor. Spinoza was a rationalist, and under his vision his father would never have had to flee from Portugal to Amsterdam because it would have been impossible, nonsensical, *irrational* here in Portugal for the Catholics to dominate the Jews."

Jozef saw the Tagus go on and on and continued to be struck by its reach. "So he was a good son, a man who loved his father, who knew his pain?"

"Yes, that pain, and the pain of his ancestry subjected to the Inquisitions. That's what I think. Somehow his philosophy, pushing beyond the latest thinking of Descartes, nevertheless looped back and spoke to a tragic Jewish history. I think he felt it. But that's just a guess. In his time terrible wars raged between Christian factions, no doubt concerning him too. Spinoza's is a cold philosophy insofar as it's written dispassionately, one logical step after the next, as if he were composing mathematical proofs. But he meant his logic to be convincing, as undeniable as a perfectly solved equation. He wanted the world to follow his logic and to change. He very well knew the consequences if it didn't. The underside of Spinoza's cool argument, you see, is a warm heart."

Jozef turned from the Tagus to Ernst. He almost reached for the pipe, as if an inhalation of its powers would bring better understanding. "You think Hitler would have stopped this business with the Jews if only he'd read Spinoza?" he finally asked.

"Hitler's argument with the Jews, and with anyone else he's after, isn't about religion but about ethnic purification, about race. Spinoza surely would have found that kind of human difference to be of no consequence, either. But no, reading Spinoza, even if Hitler understood him, wouldn't have stopped all this. Something else drives that man."

"And it isn't reason. It isn't logic."

Ernst smiled, sadly. "Exactly that," he said.

THOUGH ERNST CLAIMED TO BE rationing his tobacco, in the days that followed Jozef found him smoking constantly. He looked drained and he smoked as if to fill an ever-growing internal void. He barely ate. He was awake well before Jozef and even before the shoemaker rose to brew their morning coffee. He often walked those solitary hours in the early morning. Then he'd come back, sip coffee, and head out again, but not toward the offices in central Lisbon. He went this way and that, toward the river and away, an incoherence of direction suddenly seizing him. He'd lost his aim, his purpose, his sense that his family would arrive in Lisbon. At night he wrote frantic letters to his wife and daughter, as if they were still at home in Ghent, as if he could still reach them.

Jozef and his family had been four weeks in Lisbon when Jozef rose one morning to find an envelope slipped under his door. "My friend, for you," a note inside the envelope read. And there were Ernst Fein's boat tickets to America, on the *Serpa Pinto*, a passage that would depart some months hence. In the other room Ernst lay dead yet unbloodied. He had to have swallowed poison, Jozef tried to explain to the woeful shoemaker by mimicking slipping lethal pills down his throat.

A month earlier, Jozef and his family had left France, traveling from Perpignan by then, with stamped visas for the island of Curaçao in the Dutch Indies, which had no appeal except that it wasn't Europe. But now, with Ernst's tickets, and with help from a Jewish relief worker with the American Jewish Joint Distribution Committee in transferring the tickets to his name, Jozef sought American visas. He still had the letter from Ollie's distant relatives in Queens. And he had diamonds, proof to the consul, he hoped, that in America he wouldn't be a public burden. He had Tessa's wedding ring to show off his polisher's skills. He could even tailor a bit, too. In America he'd go right to work, he'd say convincingly.

But once there, the official who interviewed him, an assistant to the consul, was most interested in whether Jozef had people back home, in the Netherlands. Was there family there?

But of course. There was his brother, who had disappointed his father by not taking up diamond polishing, and who lived with a wife and child. And there was Tessa's aunt, still alive, walking now with a cane. His own parents were long gone, but his father had a brother, and that man had children and grandchildren, and though they didn't visit much they were indeed family. And there were the men of his chess club, close as family. And there were his fellow diamond workers at the Asscher factory, whom he missed to that day. They had been family, too, before all this. And then there was Ollie van der Waal, who had risked so much for Jozef, who was not family by blood but family by something deeper than that, by something that perhaps only Spinoza's logic could properly define. The question was simple enough: Did Jozef have family back there? *But what* is *family?* he wanted to ask in response. Where between people do you draw the line?

He'd been prepped for the question, though, by the relief worker. The immigration laws in America had tightened. American officials considered it a risk to bring in Jewish refugees with relatives in the German-occupied lands. Such people just might be German spies.

Which seemed preposterous and cruel. "Isn't that the same as saying no Jews allowed?" Jozef asked the man from the Joint. He pronounced the phrase he'd come to see all over Amsterdam: *Voor Joden verboden.*

At the consul's office, he said, "No. No family there. It's just me, my wife, and my daughter, here in Lisbon. They're waiting outside. Should I get them? We had another daughter, but she died, was . . ." He let his voice drop as he contorted his face in pain. He was using Sophia's death for his own advantage, to gain sympathy, and that night and for many to come he'd vomit, sickened by his own cunning. But at the time the look and the silence helped. The official nodded, seemed to know what was implied.

The man's next words were ones Jozef would have liked to tell Ernst Fein. "This will take a while. But it's not completely impossible. What I mean is, you're in Lisbon. It's simply not the place to abandon hope."

11

Netherlands, May 3, 1942, by Decree No. 13, Article 1: All Jews appearing in public must wear a Jewish star.

LATE MARCH OF 2001, SATURDAY evening, Arthur was playing trombone at the kitchen table—"If I Loved You"—the song he'd played only a thousand times before. The melody stirred an old longing, but the yearning was vague, directed at no one in particular. Even though he and Willa had recently corresponded a bit, he still feared her, though upon hearing of her heart attack he'd felt compelled to reach out. If he knew one thing about Willa's life it was that she was as alone as he was. Arthur played on, the song rote, the object of his longings unknown, yet the desire palpable and raw. *If.*

A year later he'd be playing that song again but finally for someone. This would be the conductor of the Middlesex County Community Orchestra, which Arthur had decided to join after Wilson Keller's wife, a clarinetist, urged him to. He was dining with the Kellers, alone. He'd recently dined with Willa Fletcher, after a year of no contact, her ethics complaint having been withdrawn. The dinner had been her idea and treat ("Let's face it, I owe you one," she'd said), and she seemed different than before, more relaxed. Whether they'd meet again or not didn't concern her. Unexpectedly, despite his initial wariness, he had fun. And then, dining at the Kellers, Rita Keller said of the orchestra that it, too, was fun. "I think you need that," she added. He did need fun, had needed that for a long time, and so after work one rainy Tuesday he went to the high school where the community orchestra rehearsed, auditioned, broke the conductor's heart with this most unusual musical choice, or so he claimed, and suddenly Arthur was no longer an isolated trombonist. His first rehearsal, he walked in just as the group was starting to tune up, and Rita Keller cried out, "Welcome, Judge!" She stood then, out of delight, but the other players must have thought it a legal formality. They rose too. So there Arthur was, facing a standing orchestra. He tugged at the scarf he'd yet to remove from his neck. "You may be seated," he said at last, shrugging. The group members laughed, settled back down, resumed their tuning. The sounds were all over the place and then, quite swiftly, they came together, a unitary hum. "Hello," said the tubist to his left. Arthur nodded. He would need better glasses for this, he realized, squinting at the sheet of music before him. "Nice to meet you," he whispered back just as the conductor raised his baton and cued the strings, then the winds, then the tubist, and then him.

BUT A YEAR BEFORE, ON that Saturday night in late March of 2001, after he'd played his trombone for a time, then packed it up, then sat for a spell at the kitchen table, the tune still in his mind, the age-old yearning still alive in his heart, the image of butterflies came to mind. Earlier that day he'd read that double markings on a so-called "butterfly ballot" in a Florida county had cost Gore the presidency. The ballot, designed to help the elderly, had in fact "discombobulated them." Many in that county were Jewish, too, and eager to have voted for Lieberman, Gore's Jewish running mate, for vice president.

Perhaps the news brought the butterflies to mind. He wasn't sure, but having already associated butterflies with his father's carvings and tirades, he felt agitated at the very thought of them, and he took off for one of those walks he typically reserved for the morning. As he trekked, his thoughts—once again on *Bush v. Gore*—fluttered about, like butterflies, not settling down.

Until they did. Something had ended with that decision, he suddenly sensed—an arm of democracy had gone limp, and on a matter at the crux of democracy, no less. Arthur agreed with the 554 law professors who'd put that ad in *The New York Times* stating that the decision was political, had achieved voter suppression rather than expression. And he agreed with Arthur Miller, the playwright, who'd said everyone in government was now an actor—Bush acting as though elected, the Supreme Court acting like the Supreme Court, and Al Gore acting as though overjoyed in defeat. *But why on earth would we put ourselves that much closer to the edge?* he wondered. He felt a shiver, as if it wasn't merely a matter of justice but of something deeper, a matter of safety, he realized, sensing his own fear as if his father were chasing him again, as if he were back in a world ruled by an erratic, cruel dictator. But then he shook himself out of it. He was overreacting, imposing his past on the entire nation's future. His self-absorption surprised him. Moreover, *Bush v. Gore,* surely an anomaly, wouldn't bring the country down, he knew. And yet something had ended . . . He knew that too but couldn't name what that something was.

He arrived home more agitated than when he'd left.

And he remained that way each day of the following week; this was so even after he heard from the Judicial Review Council that Willa Fletcher had acknowledged "confusion in the wake of personal loss" and had withdrawn her complaint. The news was good, a deep relief, but the next Saturday he woke as unsettled as before. And it made him nervous to hear again from Willa. *I'm up to 3.9 miles per hour on the treadmill,* she wrote to him. *I can honestly call myself a survivor now.* She then explained that she'd earned a certificate of success for completing cardiac rehab. She'd graduated. *I'm going to miss rehab,* she wrote. Then, finally, what he was looking for, a word about the complaint: *I was not in my right mind. The heart attack, strangest of all, has brought me to my senses. I'm truly sorry.* He replied, the last words of their unexpected correspondence, *I'm sorry, too.*

For years since his mother had died Arthur had driven monthly to visit her grave at the Catholic cemetery in New Haven. That meant also seeing his father's grave, half of the stone his parents shared, but he always made a point to ignore that half. He had already decided not to go that morning—the thought of seeing even his father's name causing him angst—but after reading to the end of Willa's note he felt different, finally more composed, a little back to his senses, as she'd put it, and he set out, stopping to buy daffodils along the way.

At the grave he laid the daffodils in front of his mother's side of the shared stone. He stood before his mother's side, too, and reported to her the news that came to mind. After a time, he added, "You did the best you could. I know that." In case she missed his meaning he gestured toward his father's side.

With that he turned to go. The morning, which had been sunny, was now cloudy. He was glad to be beating the rain that would no doubt soon arrive. He started his car and was about to leave when Willa's words came to him, *I can honestly call myself a survivor now.* He'd in fact thought of the words several times on his way to the cemetery, but they'd left his mind while he visited the grave. But recalling them again, he turned off the engine. He returned to the shared stone of his parents. He positioned himself at its center and stood silently, simply looking at it for some minutes until he felt moved to lift a single daffodil from his mother's bouquet and place it over on his father's side.

ARTHUR DROVE TO WELLS THE next morning curious to see if Ian was once again at the lakeside bungalow. The ice of winter had melted some weeks back, and driving on Lake Road it seemed impossible that what had happened there just two months ago had in fact occurred. But the seasons moved life along whether you were ready or not. He had brought Ruth Pearl a gift of tea and shortbread. He and she could have tea and a chat even if Ian wasn't there, he'd figured.

But Ian was there, and the three played rummy again. As they did, Ian ate nearly half the shortbread cookies, then apologized. "They're very good," he said, offering a half smile.

"I should be feeding you something more sustaining," Ruth said, but gently, obviously glad to see Ian enjoying himself.

"Want to play some hoops?" Arthur suddenly asked. Something about the kid was delightful, and the question sprung from that sense.

Ian was just as surprised. "Me?"

"Better you than me," Ruth Pearl quipped, which made them laugh.

"My mother, you know, doesn't play basketball," Ian explained after he'd phoned her to tell her where he was off to. "But other than that, she's perfect."

* * *

A MINUTE LATER ARTHUR AND Ian were driving to the Y in Middletown when Arthur, unused to having a passenger beside him, and glad for it, said, "Lucky."

"Talking to me?" Ian glanced Arthur's way.

"We were lucky that day. That's what I meant."

"Oh, that." Ian went silent for the next ten minutes until they hit the bridge over the Connecticut River. Arthur grew worried about bringing it all up again. But once they'd crossed the bridge Ian perked up. "Crazy lucky," he finally said.

The words relieved Arthur. "Growing up I had trouble with my father. Might have been good to talk about it then. So, you know, if you ever want to talk about whatever it was—"

"Did he run away?" Ian was upright, interested.

"Ran *toward*. He was a presence, not an absence. I hated him. I did. But I finally realized that's no way to live your life, hating someone who couldn't do better than he did."

Arthur, surprised, hadn't even said that to himself yet. In fact, he didn't know what had made his father so mad, but sensed its likely connection—like his own woes—to the ongoing, imperfect familial story the man had been born into.

Ian grew quiet again. On the court, he scrambled all over, shooting and shooting. Clearly, he didn't know the rules of the game. But he still made baskets most of the time.

They were driving back to Wells when Arthur told him, "You're a good shot."

Ian's pensive answer surprised Arthur. "I guess," he said. Then he added, coolly, almost as if Arthur had accused him of something, "I'm a lot of things."

They were closing in on Ian's home when Ian added, as if he'd been talking to Arthur the whole while, "I don't hate him. But I don't love him, either. I stopped loving him because what was the point? He never loved me back."

"Not saying you got to love him. Just don't hate him. Can waste your whole life, that hate," Arthur said, surprising himself again.

* * *

JUST AS ARTHUR WAS DROPPING Ian off, Ian said of Ruth Pearl, "She thinks the world is ending with that renovation going up. I wish I could help her like she's helped me."

It was Ian's words that got Arthur thinking, leading him back to Ruth Pearl's bungalow, where he didn't visit again but stood close enough to her property to take in her lake view. He walked over to the property next door and looked from there too, taking in the bungalow, the new construction, a second wall up now, and the steepness of the bank leading to the lake. He went back and forth and then, grabbing a legal pad from his back seat, he sketched what he saw. On Monday, even before he went to work, he drove into Wells to examine the building permit Bill Cousins would have had to apply for. A town clerk gave him a copy, which gave him the measurements he sought. On Tuesday, during his lunch break, he went back to Wells, this time to Brooks's junk shop, where he bought a ragged children's game that contained plastic miniature men, animals, and some trees. Back home, in his garage, he started constructing the model he had in mind, turning the gameboard upside down. Reinforced by some plywood beneath it, the old board made for a solid foundation.

◊

SINCE ARRIVING BACK THOROUGHLY DISHEARTENED FROM HER TRIP TO Wells, Stephanie had been plagued with headaches, as bad as her mother's used to be. Almost daily she needed aspirin, and several times at work, another headache exploding, she'd had to close her door, lie on the floor, and try to nap it off. She was tired too, the headaches keeping her up at night, and she lacked energy for the boundless walks of the month before. The momentum, as she'd called it, was gone. When she did walk, always with aspirin tucked into a pocket, just in case, she merely plodded.

Sometimes she only made it several blocks from her apartment to the bookstore up the street, where she'd grab a book—it didn't matter which—and sit for nearly an hour in one of the store's many reading chairs, spacing out. Once she went as far as Chevy Chase Circle, farther north, to shop at a women's boutique—artsy clothes, the kind she especially liked—but upon arriving she turned instead toward the nearest CVS, where she bought more aspirin, extra strength. This was a Saturday, a sunny midafternoon in early March. She took two pills then trudged back home, went to bed, and hoped against hope she would feel better if not that day then the next.

At work she pretended to care about GTW's mission, about her colleagues, pretended, in fact, to be working when all she really did was push papers from pile to pile on her desk. Sometimes she locked her office door, needing yet another quick nap. Other times she locked it because she preferred her solitude. She knew the others were talking about her, had heard Aileen, for example, say to Thea, "Give Stephanie time, she'll come back." After that she locked her door for the entire afternoon, hearing Aileen's words as permission, of sorts, to isolate.

Wednesday, the third week in March, Thea knocked on her door. She had a present for Stephanie, which was odd as Thea had stopped with the anxious gifts some time ago. But the gift was simple enough, a few chocolates, and sitting across from each other at Stephanie's desk they each took a piece.

"Sometimes it's the little things, yes?" Thea said, offering another candy. "I have an idea," she said next, then proposed a second internship at the very bookstore Stephanie had been frequenting of late, taking her endless sits. Learning to order books, and to consider the store's customers—who reads what—could be both enjoyable and educational, Thea argued, pointing to a chocolate. But Stephanie didn't need a bribe to take another of Thea's ideas seriously.

"You've got my blessing," Stephanie said, which was as much as she'd said to Thea in weeks.

"How's it going?" Thea then asked, concerned. She stood, getting ready to leave. Stephanie didn't know what to say. She had no idea how she was, the headaches obfuscating the rest of her life. She was tired and in pain. She wanted Thea out of her office already. "You've got my *blessing*," she repeated, this time firmly, even angrily. Thea, eyes wide, rushed from the room.

The next day Stephanie left the office at midday. She didn't aim to walk as much as to escape, as everyone kept stopping by that day to ask her how she was. She'd only gone as far as 20th Street, still close to GTW, when she abruptly stopped. Across the intersection she spotted Feddy, emerging from a coffee shop, holding a woman's hand. The light changed, the walk signal flashed, but Stephanie didn't move. Freddy and the woman each held to-go coffee cups in their free hands. They were talking, their heads turned toward each other. Stephanie could barely see the woman's face, but she saw Freddy's clearly. He was focused on something the woman was saying, grinning, nodding. Then he kissed the forehead of the person Stephanie knew was his wife.

Back at work she closed her door, locked it yet again, and sat at her desk, silent, frozen, for the next hour. By the time she rose, unlocked her door, and took off for home, a small crowd had gathered outside her door. "You okay?" she heard again and again. She rushed out, saying nothing. The next day she felt like a fool for the scene she'd made. She offered apologies up and down the hallway. "Saw Freddy," she said, which seemed to settle the matter quickly. So she said it again the next day when she needed a handy reason to leave the office kitchen. She'd joined several others, Aileen delightedly making room for Stephanie beside her, when a creeping claustrophobia had Stephanie fleeing.

That night she called Missy. Knowing that Missy, too, was in pain, Stephanie felt a renewed kinship with her old friend. Missy still blamed herself for not knowing Ian's feelings toward Jase. "How could I have missed it? Where have I been?" she asked Stephanie, who listened to another round of self-recrimination before telling Missy that she'd said the same thing about Freddy once.

Then she told her about losing Rona. "Let's be comrades," Stephanie suggested after that. "Comrades in—" She almost said *failure* but stopped herself, the word inapplicable and harsh for Missy's situation though just right for hers. "Bewilderment," she said instead. "Comrades in Bewilderment."

"Here's to us, then," Missy said.

* * *

IT WAS LATE MARCH, THE weather warming, the headaches finally ebbing, when Stephanie took some initiative at last, reaching out to her former colleagues at her old workplace, One Earth, consoling them when Bush refused to sign the Kyoto Protocol, aimed at reducing the greenhouse effect. As bad as she felt about the refusal to sign on, she felt good about sending the notes. She had just dropped them off at the post office and then dashed into Whole Foods when she ran into Rona Adler. Stephanie was as surprised to see Rona shopping there, in the District, as she was by Rona's obvious pregnancy.

"Wow," Stephanie said to Rona even before saying hello.

"I know," Rona answered. "We're going for it again. We thought, more life. That's what we can do." She paused and then asked Stephanie, "How's your mother?"

"Fine. Busy. Busier than usual," she said, though she hadn't called her of late. But with all her caring for Ian Lima it had to be true. Staring at Rona's baby bump she wondered where Rona's enormous frustration with mothering had gone. "And yours?"

"She's happy about this." Rona pointed at her belly. "More life. It makes sense." A phone in Rona's purse began ringing, and she whipped it out. She told Daniel to speak louder. She asked him if he preferred fish or chicken. Then she asked about rice or noodles, then about rye or wheat. Stephanie, waiting, finally waved goodbye. But Rona, still on the phone, hand on her belly, eyes to the floor, didn't see.

That night, feeling her nascent hope quickly unravelling, Stephanie called Missy again. "Hey, Comrade."

"Hey," Missy glumly said.

BUT THE NEXT TIME SHE called, the first week of April, Missy's voice was different, excited. Roy Kirk had come by, she explained, and he wouldn't take no for an answer.

"And what was the question?"

"Us. Him and me. He thought we should make it official. Be a couple. No commitment, just no hiding, no secrets. The best part was when he fell to his knees, just like he was proposing, and said, 'I'm not going to take no for an answer.' I fell to my knees too, from shock!"

Missy happened to be cooking when he came by, cassoulet and crème brûlée. "It was romantic, with the French food and all. And handy that I had it all prepared, for Ian, but he wanted to stay at your mother's that night for supper."

Of course, Stephanie said to herself.

"I don't know how to put it into words," Missy said more seriously, "what I feel about your mother. I just can't thank her enough. I always liked her, I did. But I never really saw it before, just how caring she is, Stephanie. How deeply, deeply caring."

When they hung up, Stephanie was the one to fall, not to her knees but backward on her bed. It wasn't as if she and Missy had gotten all that close again, but knowing she'd just lost her "comrade," Stephanie missed her as if she were all that she had.

She reached for the phone. She longed for her mother. But she wouldn't do it, she'd told herself since returning from Wells. She wouldn't reach out to her again. However caring her mother was toward Ian it didn't translate to her. It never had.

She quickly changed clothes and dashed out to the skating rink in Wheaton. There, alone, she pushed herself around and around.

Around and around, senselessly, because unlike all the people who managed to go forward in their lives—Thea and Freddy and Rona and Ian and Missy and even her mother—she couldn't think of anything better to do.

IN THE NEXT DAYS THE headaches were back, worse than before. Trying to cope with the pain, she locked her office door for the entire day on Friday. On Saturday, even though the headache had lifted, she spent the day in bed. On Sunday morning she opened her medicine cabinet. She gathered all the pills she could find—aspirins, cold medicine tablets, and some long-ago prescriptions for conditions she couldn't recall. She'd already pulled down her shades and covered her mirrors. As she lay on her bed, the pills spread around her, she sensed how long it had been there—her anguish. Lurking, but only at the edges of her consciousness. She'd never allowed herself to see it, feel it. After all, what, exactly, had happened to *her*?

But then another thought, more desperate, broke through, *This will show her. It will.*

She took one pill and then the next but stopped when yet another thought came to mind—slipped right in, as if from some foreign source, a visitation. Grace, she would come to call that thought in hindsight. *Open the box,* the new voice said. *Open the box.*

SO SHE DID JUST THAT: finally opened the box containing her grandmother's embroidery that her mother had given her just as she was leaving Wells. That her mother had remembered to give it to her, and that Stephanie had forgotten she'd even come for it, had surprised them both. "Here." "Thanks." "Bye." "Goodbye." That's how things had gone then. But now, the box opened, the pills pushed aside, she pulled out the first of the linen panels. There, in a scene, she saw what had to be her mother and Sophia and two pieces of cake set on a table. On the next panel she saw a park with a pond. On yet another she saw the doorway to a synagogue, its Star of David making that clear. In the next minutes she laid linen squares on her kitchen table, then placed more along the seat of her living room couch, then put others on a coffee table. To accommodate the squares strewn about on nearly all her surfaces she ate for the next week sitting on the step stool by the kitchen stove. She watched TV while lounging on the floor rather than the couch. In the evenings, after dinner, she often sat at the dining table silently looking at the embroidered scenes, focusing on depictions of her mother as a little girl. They had no photos from that time. But now she could see that her mother, at least in Tessa's eyes, was a happy little girl, a normal little girl. She was called Ruttie then, Stephanie knew, and over the next days she began to talk to Ruttie. To say hello to her each morning and each evening when she returned from work. To ask her how her day was. "Ruttie, do you like your book?" "Ruttie, do you want some tea?" "Ruttie, did you play in the park today?" "Ruttie, what did Sophia say that was so funny?" She asked that last question because whenever the two sisters appeared together in one of Tessa's scenes Ruttie tilted, as if she couldn't help it, Sophia's way.

That's when Stephanie decided to take a trip to Amsterdam, fast, before the pills called to her again. It just might save her, she sensed, to try and get to know her, this very normal girl named Ruttie, and to imagine the place she came from before everything changed.

◊

Did her husband still know her? That's what Tessa Jacobsen wondered, two nights before Jozef's death, as she sat on the bed beside him. It was June 1976, and they were in West Hartford, in their apartment. She held his hand in hers, felt wisps of bone, skin thin as an onion's. She fed him, as the daytime nurse had instructed, chips of ice. She chattered on, though about what she couldn't recall later when she took to her own bed, provisional, a pillow and blankets thrown on the living room couch. All that week, as she and Jozef's time together clearly shrank from years to months to days, when he spoke it was only of Ollie van der Waal. Of Ollie, and not of her, his wife of fifty-six years. Was she even there? Did he see her?

Just that day, Jozef had wanted to know where Ollie was. Then, hours later, as Tessa attempted to feed him a few teaspoons of warmed broth, he'd wondered if Ollie was hungry. Give him the soup, Jozef had urged, his voice peeved. "Him, not me." Later still, as she rose to leave the bedroom for a night of tossing on the couch, Jozef opened his eyes briefly. Had they repaid Ollie in full, Jozef implored with a clarity he hadn't managed in weeks. *"In full?"*

"Paid," Tessa said, referring not to cash but to decades of lighting candles for Ollie. What else could they do? In America they'd become just the littlest bit religious since learning of Ollie's death. From then on, they remembered Sophia and Ollie each Sabbath, which didn't change that on other days they were remembered too. Indeed, year after year, at most any time of day, Tessa would suddenly sense that she heard Sophia calling to her and she'd turn, expectantly, only to find that no one, of course, was there.

Certainly, Jozef knew Tessa. How impossible to imagine otherwise. But the next night, Friday evening, the candles lit, Tessa wondered anew. Though barely speaking, Jozef had nevertheless managed that day to ask twice for Ollie, and he'd pointed ahead as he did as if he saw him, over there. But where? What was Jozef seeing? Out the window the streets of West Hartford had quieted, the business day done. Jozef's near-death breathing—a scratchy, labored sound—was louder than any traffic. Tessa moved away from that sound and sat by the open window, let the spring breezes come to her. Ruth would be arriving soon from Wells, she had said just an hour ago.

Jozef was periodically pointing ahead, but Tessa, as she attended him, was looking behind, gathering the years, compressing them into meaning, one year folding on top of the next. *Our life*, she wanted to say to him, and to have those simple words encapsulate all the layers, all the years.

But when she rose and whispered into his ear her summation came out as "Sophia."

Their daughter's name nudged him awake. A moment later he was speaking, his voice just audible. "You know how seasick you got on that ship to America?"

"Not sick every day," Tessa said. "But you were a comfort to me. I remember." She took his hand. She held it to her heart.

"Poor Sophia got far sicker than you," Jozef continued.

Tessa didn't respond. She gradually placed Jozef's hand back by his side. She sighed.

This is dying, she thought. This mess.

She made herself a cup of tea, drank it by herself, folded some laundry, tidied the kitchen, and then, an hour later, resumed her watch of him. She once again sat beside the bed. While she was gone Jozef's wheezing had started up, even louder.

But then he quieted. With shut eyes, he lay in silence. She checked his pulse, still there.

Minutes later, turning to her, eyes open, he smiled.

"Oh," she said, unprepared for that, a smile as big as any, and all for her.

He was now just love, or so the pureness of the smile suggested. "Sophia," she said again, because a vision of her firstborn's face had just risen in her mind, like a gift, and she received it, sensing its soft and sudden presence as a transmission from Jozef's spirit to hers.

The smile and then the daughter.

But this *is dying,* she thought. As Jozef became more soul than body his generosity, a grandness, took Tessa's breath away.

FOR TOO LONG—*WASTED YEARS*, she thought later that night—she and Jozef were planets orbiting different suns. A measureless distance lay between them no matter that her couch and his easy chair were but inches apart. They weren't angry so much as spiritually destitute. The lucky survivors. Yet something beyond flesh and blood had nevertheless been crushed.

But with Stephanie's birth Tessa revived, wanted to eat more, walk more, bake more, stitch more, visit her granddaughter.

She wanted, too, to resume an old conversation with that distant moon there, chuckling mechanically to some prerecorded laughter spewing from the TV. Just three months after Stephanie's birth, Tessa said to Jozef, "Talk to me."

"Remember?" she asked the man now dying beside her. "Remember that day?"

Jozef lay sleeping, breathing loudly, but all those years ago he had turned her way. He was nearly bald even then, and the skin on his face was slack with age. For almost her entire life she'd seen him daily, but she gasped, only then taking in how time had aged him. He pulled off his glasses and rubbed his forehead. They were in their living room. "What do you want me to say?" he asked.

"Just talk. Like you used to."

When he laughed for a second—nothing fake about it—she did too. For a moment it seemed embarrassing to seek even a modicum of the intimacy they'd abandoned so many years ago. Or, at least, she'd abandoned it. She didn't really know what he felt toward her but thought she could see, from the way he looked at his feet, that he was uncomfortable too. But then he leaned back in his chair. He closed his eyes as if to sleep but instead began telling her about the quiet lunches he often took in a park called Meeting House Corner, at the intersection of North Main and Farmington Avenue, close to the jewelry shop. He told her about the birds he studied there. He had a bird book, he said. He kept it on his desk at work. *The Audubon Field Guide*. Abridged edition. He never took lunch without it. He was still learning about America, he explained, this time by way of the birds. He began to list the most common in the park: robins, jays, crows, sparrows. He could even name some that lived in Hawaii only: black-footed albatross, Hawaiian goose.

She liked Jozef's voice. She always had, she suddenly recalled. And she liked this new subject: America, by way of its birds. She'd been slumped on the couch, but as Jozef spoke she gradually straightened. Soon, and as before—when they were young—she leaned his way, listened.

They began talking again, quietly, nightly. About nothing that made them anxious. Sometimes they turned to music: Mozart or Schubert. Sometimes they simply sat, holding hands, in silence. In time she took to visiting him once weekly for lunch at Meeting House Corner, where they would sit by a circle of open grass. The noise from traffic at the busy intersection of Main and Farmington was loud, but they paid no attention to it. Their sandwiches eaten, he would ask her to pick a state and then would open the field guide. *North Dakota*: gray jay, Clark's nutcracker, black-billed magpie. *Florida*: great blue heron, osprey.

With each bird came a picture to study.

"I like the way you draw better than Audubon," Jozef said once, turning to her before he left again for work. This was in May 1963. She'd needed only a light sweater for warmth. The birds of West Hartford—jays, crows, robins, finches—were abundant and singing.

She kissed his cheek. She walked away from the park, then turned and waved. She was going just the few blocks back to their apartment, passing a neighborhood pharmacy farther up Farmington Avenue, when she stopped. Though she stared into the store's window she didn't see the greeting cards and prettily boxed candies there on display. Instead she saw herself, reflected back, a person with rounded shoulders and flyaway gray hair, a woman who couldn't help but smile shyly as if she didn't know who she stared at, just then a glad soul, purse in her hands, glinting ring on her finger, the diamond he polished for her, a little late, four years after their marriage, but none of that mattered then, for they were young and in love and had all the time in the world.

NOW, JOZEF STILL WASTING AWAY at a pace she couldn't slow, she lay on the couch, a room away from him. From there she not only considered their unexpected late-blooming friendship but could almost taste its astonishing sweetness. She rose, checked on Jozef, then returned to her bed on the couch. But, for fear that he would die without her near him, she barely slept. Ruth hadn't come that night after all, as she'd developed a bad headache. Tessa was, in all ways that mattered, alone.

He was alive the next morning. She fed him more broth. Wet a towel and wiped his brow. Sometime in the night he'd peed and with some careful maneuvering and strength she didn't know she still had she changed his bottoms, a diaper. *Now this,* she remarked to herself in a voice she hadn't heard in the longest time. Something within her, a still-dormant layer of her being, was rumbling, breaking open.

She was emboldened again, stepping out of her Amsterdam home, ready for wherever the walking would take her.

Now she was holding his hand, rubbing it. Now she was climbing in the bed.

"Jozef," she whispered, snuggling close.

He moved his lips as if to speak but no sound emerged.

"Ollie is here," she said, answering his unasked question.

He wasn't going to say anything back to her. Even pressed up against him as she now was, he no longer seemed to see or feel her.

Their ending, then, would be as imperfect as their life.

Imperfect and yet, at moments, perfect. She was still a young girl, squeamish at the sight of a frog's eggs.

She told him that.

He was kind to cover them up. She told him that too.

"We're a good team," she said.

And this, a thought: *Jozef, Jozef, there was never any wrong to forgive.*

"It's okay," Tessa told him minutes later when he began to wheeze. She held him close. He seemed to be choking. "Go to Ollie," she said despite her clinging. Momentarily she let go, raising an arm and pointing, just as Jozef had earlier, a gesture that took all her strength.

THE THIRD WEDNESDAY IN APRIL OF 2001, AS RUTH PEARL DRESSED FOR Ian's dance recital—which had been postponed from its earlier date to accommodate his recovery—she pulled from the back corner of her jewelry case her mother's wedding ring, inherited upon Tessa's death, and polished so long ago by her father. The ring fit perfectly. She wore it on her left hand as if she really were married, and something about the occasion that night, her sympathetic jitters for Ian, her sense of connection to him and the others she would go with, made wearing such a ring seem right. She listed the clan—herself, Ian, Missy, Roy Kirk, Judge Cantrell, and Ian's friend Maddie. She glanced at her mother's ring again. It wasn't a ring of marriage anymore but of family, or maybe of hope. It had remained, as such hard stones do, intact. She glanced at it and a wistful feeling came over her. She wished she could stand before her mother, declaring herself a survivor, and of so many things: Sophia's death, their horrible displacement, her loss of Tessa's emotional presence, and her loss of Felix. "I'm a survivor, Mamma. And so are you," she longed to say.

Ian, she knew, could not take such a strong stand as that. Not yet.

He was still vulnerable, still waking with a wobbly core. "It's like I've been crying in my sleep," he'd said earlier that day, trying to describe the feeling. On top of that, he didn't feel prepared for the performance that evening. His recovery from his falls—on the ice, into the ice—weren't as easy as pie, he'd said. Earlier that day he'd even thrown up his breakfast. But Ruth knew he wanted to dance, despite his fears. And wasn't that the important thing? Wanting was a sign of life.

She felt it too. She wanted the company of the people she'd see that night. She wanted Stephanie there too, but she was away, traveling, hopefully on a relaxing trip. She wanted the next day when Ian would likely pop over to say hello. It was easy to want all days, she realized, when you didn't feel afraid. And ever since the meeting she'd had the morning before at Judge Cantrell's office she'd not had an anxious moment.

The judge had set up the meeting. She'd arrived first and was about to finally ask about the estoppel reasoning when her attention was drawn, instead, to the astonishing model the judge had made of Bill Cousins's bungalow and hers, his with the addition built. The judge had somehow replicated the slope of the bank their homes sat on. He'd dotted the landscape with toy trees. The lake was there too, painted onto a board beneath it all, a winter lake, silvery, like ice. He'd even carved from wood a small woman. "That's you," he said, and he handed her the tiny figurine. "Didn't know I could do that," he said, his voice pleased.

"But I always thought I was tall. Taller than that." She marveled at his work.

"Well, no," Arthur said. "No. You're not."

He took the figurine and placed it in front of the miniature bungalow that was her home. "Perceptions, perceptions," she said, still awed at the scene.

Bill Cousins arrived then, and the three sat at the conference table with the model as a centerpiece. The judge pointed out that the new room would block some of Ruth's view, but not too much of it. Ten percent, maybe fifteen percent blocked, tops.

"That's what I told her from the beginning," Bill said. "I tried the best I could not to block anything, but the shape of the land and all . . ."

Ruth said nothing. It was just like the judge had described, an addition that blocked some, but not all, of her lake view. While she took that in Bill talked about his parents, his father's recent stroke, his mother's frightful suppers. The extra room was for them. He then said, "Why didn't you talk to me? We've been neighbors for fifteen years. Mrs. Pearl, I didn't know you were upset."

Ruth struggled for the words to explain why she was so sure he wouldn't have listened. "But—" she said finally, her voice quickly dropping off.

"Look, I didn't mean to upset you," Bill said. As he paused to think he reached out to touch the model, tapping the roof of his bungalow, then hers. After a minute he began again. "This isn't the only way. I could do something else. I could swap homes, even, with Missy Lima. She could live next door and I could move my family back to Barton Hill. There's room enough in that big house. Or you could take my house and I could take yours. A different swap. I could build the room onto your place without blocking anything from you. See?" He pointed at the model. "Your call," he told her. "I'll do whatever you want."

The judge sat quietly. Bill was quiet after that too, his words surprising even him.

"Good," Ruth whispered after some minutes. Her tone was somber. That Bill Cousins would do whatever she asked was beyond her comprehension. "You're good," she said more clearly.

Bill looked into his lap.

"No rush," he finally told Ruth, who simply sat there, stunned.

She was still thinking about her choices later that evening during the dance performance. But then the curtain finally went up. Ian and Sarah Toms stood centerstage, a single spotlight focused on their motionless bodies. The first notes of music soon began. Debussy. Ruth sat up. Her thoughts vanished. The children—for that's how they seemed, as if too young for all that was coming—turned toward each other, the first move of what would become the struggle to know each other embodied in their dance.

◊

That day, in Oosterpark, drawn there yet again, Stephanie sketched the scene as she sat: the pond, several empty benches, and a weeping willow tree nearby. Soon it was Stephanie weeping—finally, as she'd not done the entire time she'd been in Amsterdam, though feelings were building within her, rising slowly, and here they were now, the unstoppable tears, while she repeated, "But Mamma, it's not ugly at all. It's a beautiful, beautiful pond."

◊

It was a month after the dance performance when Ruth told Stephanie for the first time about her past. Early one evening Ruth felt faint. She worried she was having a stroke like Bill Cousins's father had. But she was just dehydrated. When she got home from the hospital, early afternoon the next day, she and Stephanie—back from her travels—sat outside, sipping tea. Early May, buds on the trees were out, ready to burst, and the few leaves already opened were stiff and bright in their fresh existence. She took that in, then noticed the birds, their various calls. Her own kind of strict scrutiny—discerning attention—is what she gave to the sounds, just as she'd done that winter to snowflakes. When she went inside, she turned back to glance at the lake again. Through her kitchen windows she saw the walls, now two of them, partially obstructing her lake view, but because of the model the judge had built, and the options Bill Cousins had offered, she realized she didn't mind the sight of them anymore. She now saw that the renovation didn't obstruct the view as much as change it, complicate it. The lake was still there, as always. She acknowledged that too.

After dinner Stephanie told her the remarkable news that her recent travels were to Amsterdam. "I had to know," she said, simply enough. But most of the places she described—including the Anne Frank House and the Auschwitz Memorial—were creations of the aftermath. They told a story, yes, but not Ruth's story. "It was so very cold," Ruth then began, "one of the coldest winters we ever knew." The two stayed up past midnight until Stephanie took Ruth's arm and said, more tenderly than Ruth had ever heard Stephanie speak—a tone she would come to hear often when Stephanie, disillusioned with D.C., finally moved back to Wells—"Mamma, let me help you to bed."

The morning was sunny but cool. Upon Ruth waking, Stephanie went to her to report a dream. "Mamma, it was of you," she said, seemingly relieved by that though in the dream Ruth was once again barred from entering Oosterpark. Yet because Stephanie was still half asleep, Ruth sent her, gently, back to bed. A thought then arose, one that circled the edge of all she'd said the previous evening to Stephanie: that it was chance to be here, or anywhere, at any particular time in history. That chance forces shape so much of your fate. Indeed, she might have been quite a skater if she just could have chosen her path.

Now Stephanie slept. And from the quiet next door Ruth assumed that the Cousins family—who were good neighbors, who would stay just where they were—did too. On the dock, wrapped in a light blanket, she sat in a folding chair she had dragged down. She had coffee to sip. This early in spring she missed a certain smell, the one at summer's end when the lake, warmed and full of algae, would blow a musty but beloved scent all through town. But this was good too, she noted, this lighter scent, the aroma of things to come, of beginnings. The sky was bright, and she squinted looking out, the lake's surface sparkly as a diamond. Past the cove were waters that hit a shore she couldn't see from there, and that's where she gazed, to a distant place. A breeze kicked up, some tiny waves on the lake began rolling forth, and for just a moment, before the others woke, she felt she had the whole world all to herself.

AUTHOR'S NOTE

The anti-Jewish laws noted in the headers for each chapter of this novel have been culled from Dr. Jacob Presser's seminal *Ashes in the Wind: The Destruction of Dutch Jewry* (original Dutch title: *Ondergang*), and confirmed in various timelines of anti-Jewish laws and actions in the Netherlands during the German occupation of the 1940s. Subsequent studies of this time, after Presser's, may show slight differences in dates relative to these laws, or slight differences in how a given law is described. I have held close to Presser's descriptions of these laws, with some modest adjustments based on other studies. Bob Moore's *Victims & Survivors: The Nazi Persecution of the Jews in the Netherlands 1940–1945* was also very helpful in this endeavor. The civil laws noted (with two exceptions) were ordered by members of the *Reichskommissariat Niederlande*, the Reich Commissariat for the Occupied Dutch Territories. I have adopted Presser's identifications of these people and included them, when noted, by titles. All worked under Arthur Seyss-Inquart, Reich Commissioner, the leader of the occupying Nazi regime, who, in turn, reported to the highest levels of Nazi German leadership.

While I was not able to confirm that a sign reading *Voor Joden verboden* appeared at the entrance to Oosterpark, given how pervasive such signs were throughout Amsterdam, and given that parks were among the locations specifically prohibited to Jews, Dutch researchers with whom I consulted thought it could be assumed that a sign was posted there. I have therefore included this sign, which would be true to the times, though, to the best of my knowledge, not specifically verifiable.

ACKNOWLEDGMENTS

I'm grateful to so many who helped me with this novel.

Profound thanks to my thoughtful and wise editor, Sarah Stein, and to the skilled team at Harper, including Jackie Quaranto, Kim Hubbard, Betsy Kennedy, and Tanya Fox. And many, many thanks to my agent, Duvall Osteen, for her enthusiasm, guidance, and steadfast support.

Great thanks as well to Marnix Koolhaas, expert on Dutch skating history and more in the Netherlands, who generously reviewed the historical material set in the Netherlands and helped me with countless questions along the way, and who brought me to the Apollohal sports arena when we first met in Amsterdam. In my travels to Amsterdam I had the very good fortune to also meet Joke Wever, Christopher Beck, Peter Drucker, and Jenn Ben-Yakov, and I'm grateful for their deep understanding, sometimes based on personal experience, of the Dutch-Jewish experience of the Holocaust and post-Holocaust. Nina Siegal generously met with me too and offered wise and practical insights. Dutch historian Sierk Plantinga answered my question on inter-European transit during the Nazi era with great care. Librarians and researchers at the Jewish Museum in Amsterdam and the NIOD Institute for War, Holocaust, and Genocide Studies readily answered research questions as well.

Residencies at MacDowell and Yaddo served me immeasurably in moving this novel forward.

Hollins University offered valuable research funds, and librarians Rebecca Seipp and Maryke Barber helped me locate research sources and, in Maryke's case, even helped with translating Dutch.

I'm thankful to several scholars who weighed in, kindly, on my wide-ranging questions. Rebecca Newberger Goldstein, author of the profound and wonderful book *Betraying Spinoza*, reviewed my pages on Spinoza, and her moving writing about Spinoza's philosophy and the problem of Jewish persecution inspired discussion of that in this novel. Distinguished Professor Emeritus Alan Kraut shared his expertise in reading my pages involving escape from the Reich and emigration to the US, and in responding to questions on these matters. Before his recent death, Professor Emeritus Ronald Weber, author of *The Lisbon Route*, commented on pages in this novel involving Lisbon and inter-European transit during the war years.

Professor Mark Brodin generously reviewed several of my passages involving *Bush v. Gore*. Jennifer Sutherland, marvelous poet and attorney, was so helpful to me on matters of law as well. Attorneys Michael Peck and Bob Poliner and, especially, retired Judge Susan Peck offered further insights into legal matters relevant to this story.

Professor Saskia Coenen Snyder offered insightful comments on my pages involving Dutch-Jewish history and the diamond trade. Dr. Jan Burzlaff offered valuable historical guidance as well. Sharon Tash, with her background in Holocaust studies, was likewise helpful in this regard. Marianne Tatom, with whom I've enjoyed Yiddish classes, answered my questions about Yiddish.

Marty Lopez offered support and guidance at important moments during this writing process, as did Melita Schaum and Jean Eglinton.

In addition to my heartfelt gratitude to those already mentioned, I thank my family members for their ongoing support: my ever-helpful sister, Rachel, my generous brother, Michael, and sister-in-law, Debbie (whose mother survived Auschwitz and whose father escaped Vienna), and our dear mother, who at ninety-two is still taking painting classes, writing essays, and baking lokshen kugel. A former potter, my mother advised me on portions of this novel involving pottery making and on details about Wesleyan Potters, where she potted for many years. Our father's memory is indeed a blessing and I'm grateful for his love and support, which sustains beyond his death.

Most of all, I offer boundless thanks to my two trusted readers, both so generous and patient. Thank you to Barbara Wiechmann, intrepid traveler into the text, dearest old friend, brilliant reader, loving guardian of the characters, who offered so much insight on my draft pages and who tirelessly stuck with me.

And then there is Edward P. Jones, who saw the very first draft, mess and all, and didn't run away. And he stayed with it over time. I thank him for the wisdom, generosity, and brilliance of his comments, for his time and care, for the respect he consistently shows me in believing I can leap as high as he thinks I can, and for his long and beloved friendship, one of my life's greatest gifts.

ABOUT THE AUTHOR

Elizabeth Poliner is the author of the novel *As Close to Us as Breathing*, which won the Janet Heidinger Kafka Prize in fiction and was a finalist for the Library of Virginia's People's Choice Award in fiction and the Ribalow Prize. She has also published a poetry collection, *What You Know in Your Hands*, and a novel-in-stories, *Mutual Life & Casualty*. Her stories have been published in *The Kenyon Review*, *TriQuarterly*, *Michigan Quarterly Review*, *Story*, and *Colorado Review*, among others. She lives in Virginia.